KINGS AND CRIMINALS

Eni,

Enjoy the book!

Mungo

MUNGO MAGENNIS

Special thanks to:
Katie McCoach - Editor
David Provolo - Cover Design

"Never doubt that a small group of thoughtful, committed citizens can change the world; indeed, it's the only thing that ever has."

Margaret Mead

PROLOGUE

Set in fifty acres of private land twenty miles south of Edinburgh, Castle Craig looked more like a stately home than a place recovering addicts spent their days in treatment sessions and group therapy. The Scottish hills undulate behind the estate, gifting its visitors to views of rolling mist early in the morning and fabulous sunsets to the west as the evenings arrive.

In the hallway on the first floor, one of the centre's specialist nurses comforted a clearly distressed father.

'This is a major trauma for anyone to go through, especially someone so young. A loss of this kind can stay with a patient for years, sometimes forever.'

The nurse kept her voice low in an attempt not to disturb the young man who sat no more than ten feet away at the desk inside the room that would be his home for the duration of his stay.

'What's the process now then?' the father asked without taking his eyes off his son.

'Well, we'll do some initial tests that will be collated with the assessment that he's had already. Once we have that and the doctor has analysed the findings we'll prescribe a course of treatment. Typically, we aim to do that within the patient's first day with us here at Castle Craig.'

'So what kind of treatment will he have? Can you fix him?'

'Sir, let's not use terms like "fix". They don't tend to sit very well with patients and give a more black and white picture than what is really happening.'

'I'm sorry, I don't mean to. This is all new to me.' He raised a hand to his forehead, rubbing it hard enough to wrinkle the skin underneath it, whilst shielding his eyes from the girl. 'I just want my son back. I feel this is all somehow my fault.'

'This is no one's fault, sir. Trust me. What happened to your son is very natural after an event like the one he experienced. We tend to find alcoholism and Post Traumatic Stress Disorder go hand in hand. Typically, around fifty percent of PTSD sufferers that we see are self-medicating with alcohol. He has a lot of positives on his side, though. He's young, for one. And from what we know, drinking has only been a problem since the event, so you've caught it early. I've seen successful cases come through here who were in a much worse position than your son, in terms of alcohol, at least. Castle Craig has an incredible success rate with over seventy percent of our patients achieving long-term abstinence, and over ninety percent living with reduced alcohol and drug use.'

There was a reason that the father had chosen this particular centre for his son's treatment. Not only had it come with outstanding recommendations, but it also offered an element of privacy and seclusion. A perfect atmosphere to drown out the events of the last few months. This facility seemed like the best opportunity this father had to make sure his son was taken care of and given the highest chance of recovery. It was hard for him to comprehend what his son must be going through as he watched him stare lifelessly out of the window. He couldn't bear to look and turned his whole body away. 'Nurse, I'm sorry, you'll have to forgive me, what did you say your name was?'

'Blair, sir. Are you okay?' She didn't wait for his response. 'He's going to be fine, you know. We'll make sure of it. It's understandable what he's going through, it's completely normal. I can see that this is an uncomfortable environment for you. I'm assuming you've not had to deal with something like this before?'

'Thank you, Blair.' He didn't respond to her question but held out his hand which she accepted with a firm grip.

'Blair, will you personally be in charge of my son's care?'

'Excuse me, sir? I don't fully understand. I'll be part of the team that looks after him while he's here, if that's what you mean?'

'What I'm asking is whether you are able to take full responsibility for a patient? He's young, much younger than anyone else here that I've seen today. I just want him to be alright. You seem like you're not too far apart in age so maybe he'll talk to you about what happened. Every time I try, I just get a brick wall.'

'I'm sorry to hear that, sir. I'll do what I can. I don't mind spending some extra time with him in the mornings and evenings if that would help?'

'That would be fantastic, are you sure you don't mind?'

'It would be an honour, sir.'

'Okay, then it's a deal.' He once again held out his hand. There was an energy about this girl that he liked. She had personality and spirit, whilst remaining impeccably professional at all times. Her kind face showed an empathy and understanding for what he was going through.

He wondered where the other young men were at this moment in time. They had all asked whether they could accompany their fallen brother to help him settle in and adjust to his new surroundings. Each and every request had been denied. It was easier for his father to take the blame whenever he was asked why they wouldn't be able to see their friend. In truth, the new patient had categorically requested that no one be allowed to see him the way he currently was. At this moment, he was glad that he didn't have to hide his emotions from an audience. Looking in through his son's open door, he saw the young man, motionless at the small desk, facing out towards the sprawling lawns and giant oaks that surrounded the grand building. If he had been able to see the boy head on, the visible tears that ran down the contorted face would undoubtedly have unleashed a torrent down his own.

Cambridge, England

Looking around the famous Cambridge Union Society debate hall as he confidently launched into the final verse of his much-rehearsed monologue, the speaker spotted a familiar face grinning at him in the audience. Although comforted by the presence of his brother as they started the next stage of this journey, to avoid breaking into a smile himself, he immediately shifted his focus back down to his notes and proceeded.

'What I mean is that the omniscient God portrayed by organised religion does not have to think about decisions, they are instant, he knows the right thing and how to do it. Those are some of the symptoms of omniscience. If even one millisecond passed between God coming into existence and his decision to create the heavenly bodies and all the creatures that have roamed upon them, this would bring us to question his wisdom. So, it springs to mind that the instant God was created, the universe must also have been created. God has no purpose if there is no universe, so no time can have elapsed between God and the universe existing. If God has no purpose without the universe, then it is not us who need him, it is he who needs us. We should not be slaves to God, God is a slave to humankind. We are his purpose; he is not ours.' He left that thought to hang with the audience.

'Ladies and gentlemen, thank you for your time, it's been my pleasure. One last thing before I go, I'd just like to say thanks to St John's College for participating in the first of the term's series of debates. It's been an interesting and lively discussion. I look forward to many more.'

Stepping down from the podium as the audience clapped, he breathed a sigh of relief, once again finding the face in the back row of the crowd before holding up his open hand to indicate that he needed five minutes to speak with his fellow debaters and some of the college masters in the audience.

Once outside the hall, he found his friend reading a notice board listing the Michaelmas term events. A tap on the shoulder caught the reader off-guard and he spun towards the source of the intrusion. His startled expression was immediately replaced by a wide smile accompanied by open arms. 'Hey! You looked good up there, brother. Sorry I was a bit late.'

'No problem. Thanks for coming, it's good to see you. What time did you get here?'

'Just after four, got completely lost.'

'I'm just glad you made it. It's been a manic few days since I got down here. Must be the same for you up at Oxford.'

Even though they had WhatsApped and spoken every day on the phone since they left home, there was a strong sense of relief knowing that he was here and would be staying at least for the night. He wrapped his arm around the visitor's shoulder and led him away. 'Let's walk and talk. It's this way to the river.'

The pair made their way down the narrow lane past some shops on their left before reaching the entrance to St John's college on their right. The guest marvelled at the sight of the fabulous fifteenth and sixteenth century buildings stood all around them. 'Not a bad place to spend the next few years, hey?'

'You're right there. I bet Oxford can't be that different?'

'I haven't seen that much of it yet, but on first impressions this has it beaten, hands down.'

'I'll have to repay the favour and come visit you next, you can show me around once you know a bit more about the place. Let's go down here, I checked it out on the map and think it goes somewhere quiet. Not really sure if we're allowed though, so play it cool.' He winked and smiled.

The Cambridge student set off through the small open gate and followed the path towards the river. Two lawns flanked the paved route as they entered the square First Court of the college before passing through a narrow tunnel into Second Court where they turned left. After one more passageway they came to a small bridge over the River Cam which led them into the vast and sprawling, deserted lawns of St John's meadow and a path leading along the river's edge.

'Have you spoken to his parents?' the visitor asked.

'Yeah, both of them. They're pretty upset. If anything, I think his dad is finding it harder. It was an emotional chat we had. He gave me the same line about him not thinking it was a good idea to go and see him in that place.'

'What do you mean? You don't believe it?'

'Not one bit. That's not coming from his dad. His dad would want us there to support him. No, I think our friend is too proud for us to see him like this. Apparently, he was pretty strange when he went down to Cornwall. His mum said when she picked him up he couldn't stop crying. Every night he would wake up screaming, sweating. It sounds terrible.'

The pair rounded the corner of the river bank, watching the calm water passing by below.

'I checked the place out.' He bent down to pick up a pebble from the path, tossing it from hand to hand. 'It looks nice, I think he'll like it there. Well, as much as you can under the circumstances, obviously.'

'How long do you think he'll have to stay there?'

'I really have no idea. Could be a month, could be five. I looked into the treatment for PTSD and, to be honest, it sounds fucking grim.'

'Shit, really? What is it?'

'There's something called 'trauma-focused cognitive behavioural therapy'. They basically make you think back to what happened and go over it again and again in detail. I guess the theory is that until you face it and learn to accept it, you won't get better. The alcohol was just the tip of the iceberg. He was drinking to avoid confronting what's going on inside his head. But you can't escape forever.'

The Wirral, England

Not many teachers' offices could claim to have a view as glorious as this one. An expanse of freshly cut grass, now sprinkled with crimson and tangerine leaves no longer bound to their mothers, sparkled in the dew of the morning. The low sun rising in the east cast magnificent shadows across the spaces and buildings that created this secluded world.

These first few weeks of term had been anything but normal. Unbeknown to most of the staff and pupils at the school, that summer had been the setting for a terrible event. Even for those who had heard news of the tragedy, the information remained sketchy.

As he stood and gazed through the glass at the clock tower on the far boundary of the grounds, he took another deep draw on the cigarette resting in his left hand. He blew the smoke out of the partially open window before tapping the spent tobacco into the ashtray sitting on the window sill. On any other day at nine o'clock in the morning, the school would be teeming with life, laughter and energy. Saturday mornings were, however, quite the opposite. As it was too early in the year for even the worst students to be issued Saturday detention, these were rare moments of peace and calm. No screaming, no shouting, no balls visible in mid-air as the masses chased them around concrete playgrounds.

Tranquillity.

Or so he thought.

An unexpected figure from the grass below walked towards the building, shattering the bliss. His heart rate soared, and panic bound through every fibre in his body. He was sure that the advancing male had already seen him through his ground floor window. It was time. He'd known this moment would come and this had to be dealt with at some point. Now was as good a time as any. Watching the stern face of the approaching young man, he extinguished his cigarette with as much composure as he could muster before fully opening the small, high window further to allow the smell of the to-bacco to escape. His office door was behind him to his left and as he lost sight of his quarry, he knew it would be only moments before the sound of flesh and bone knocking on his thick white door would fill the space. He waited, rooted to the spot, imagining the conversa-tion that was about to take place, as one so often does before a confrontation.

The door shook with the force of the battering, summoning him to open. He took one last deep breath before straightening up and moving towards the source. As he clicked the lock, the door imploded towards him.

'What are you doing here?' the smoker demanded as he stepped aside to make room for the intruder. 'I thought it would be clear from the lack of contact that we shouldn't be seen together.' He checked the hallway outside to see if anyone else may have seen the boy arrive before closing and locking the door behind them.

The teacher strode round behind his desk, extending an arm indicating where his guest should sit as he lowered himself into his worn, leather chair. As much as his own fear weighed on his conscience, he could see that the emotions of the newcomer were of a different breed altogether. He couldn't help but feel guilty.

The boy hesitated. 'I needed to talk to you, to someone.'

1

February 2016

Max hated this part. Twenty-five sets of eyes, twenty-six if you included the teacher's, stared at him expectantly, waiting on what he was about to say.

The work leading up to this point, he had loved. Researching terror plots that had taken place since the start of the twenty-first century was fascinating. It was lucky that his AS History coursework happened to be on a subject he was happy to spend hours researching on his iPad or his laptop, in school or at home.

Looking down at the pages trembling in his hand, he opened his mouth to speak. The words wouldn't come out. Lodged somewhere between his lungs and his voice box, he willed them to flow, unsuccessfully. He could feel the beads of sweat starting to form on his temples, not yet big enough to run down his face, but it wouldn't be long. Looking across to Mrs. Logan perched on the side of her desk at the front of the room, he knew she could sense his pain by the concern he saw on her face.

'Max,' she said softly, 'you look a bit hot, why don't you take your jacket off?'

Still holding the papers inside his moist grip, he started to pull at his left lapel with one hand before stopping suddenly, realising that his shirt was probably see through by now. After all, he'd been stressed for the last twenty minutes as he waited for his turn.

'I won't actually, Miss.'

She looked confused at first and he thought he might have to explain but she suddenly relented, saving his embarrassment. The blazer stayed put.

Why can't I do this? The paper is written, it's good, really good. All you have to do is read it out loud. Simple.

But it wasn't simple for Max. The night before, he'd tossed and turned, dreading this moment. In small groups, he was fine. On the rugby pitch he would shout with the rest of them. What was it about this particular situation that filled him with so much fear and anguish? He wasn't alone, of course. Many boys had difficulty with public speaking at this age. But it irked Max that he struggled with it so much.

'When we look at the terrorist events of the past sixteen years, both in the UK and overseas, there are a few that stand out in my mind.'

The words finally started to flow from his lips. The tone was flat, the speed fast, and the delivery left much to be desired. But the words were out there, able to be heard. His heart pounded at well over 100 beats per minute and his hands shook considerably. *Just relax.*

It felt like it was no use, but as he continued through the sentences staring back at him from the paper, he did start to focus more on the words and less on the trauma his conscious mind was currently experiencing.

For the last two months, he'd watched videos and read about the July 7, 2005 London bombings and the stories of the four suicide bombers who had targeted three London Underground carriages and one bus.

'Another four more bombers attempted to target London's transport again only weeks later, this time unsuccessfully. Almost exactly two years later, two bombs capable of inflicting serious injury and loss of life were discovered in cars, once more in England's capital city. The next day, a Jeep Cherokee, laden with petrol and propane gas canisters crashed into the main entrance at Scotland's Glasgow airport. The car had burst into flames and the two terrorists inside jumped out of the 4x4 before attacking people outside and inside the airport.'

A brief smile crossed his face as he thought about a quote from a newspaper about the airport worker who "kicked the terrorist in the groin" whilst he was in flames.

'In 2013, two men ran over and then attacked Drummer Lee Rigby, a Fusilier, outside his Army Barracks in Woolwich. He was unarmed when they then tried to behead him.'

All these events had occurred during Max's young life, but as a five-year-old when the first of them took place, he had only vague memories of people around him talking about them. He had better recollection of the more recent ones but, up until now, still failed to comprehend the impact they had on the country. Living in the North West of England and away from the drama, it was easy to feel like these were events that happened in faraway cities, to far away people. The more research he did, the more he came to realise that anyone and anywhere could be a target.

After covering all the attacks in the UK since the start of the century, he shifted his focus onto the event that had most fascinated him and dominated his research. New York, September 11th, 2001. It was the most horrific terrorist attack of modern times, still mourned on the anniversary every year by millions across the USA and the rest of the world. Three thousand people died as the two main towers of the World Trade Centre collapsed following the impacts of two commercial jets on the morning of the attack.

'There were actually four attacks that took place on

the 11th of September. Two in New York on the World Trade Centre, one on the Pentagon in Virginia, and a fourth plane was heading for Washington DC, but the hijackers were overpowered by the people aboard the plane and it crashed before reaching its target.'

As he read through the material he'd prepared, his mind flashed to the far more exciting unofficial accounts of the day. Although he'd excluded any 'conspiracy' type information from his report, this was the stuff he really wished he could talk about. There was a wealth of information online and a community demanding answers about what really happened that day. Questions about how and why the buildings collapsed the way they did. Questions about the ability of the hijackers to pilot the planes with the accuracy they did. Theories about the lack of military response while the event was happening. Statements from US Senators detailing clear instructions from the US President to find links with countries not yet suspected of being involved. He found the whole debate thrilling.

What had really ignited Max's curiosity about 9/11 were the illusive groups whose names popped up every once in a while. These weren't terror cells, not in the traditional sense at least. These were groups far less visible than explosions, planes and bombs, and supposedly used vast wealth and knowledge to acquire power.

The House of Rothschild is commonly thought to be the richest family in the world. By establishing international banking during the 1700s, the family grew in wealth and other interests. Mining, transport, loans, government bonds. Supposedly, nations called upon the family for help in financing their wars, all the way back to Napoleon. They were said to be 'the brokers and counsellors of the kings of Europe and of the republican chiefs of America'. Influence was in their blood.

Similarly, the House of Morgan, mostly known today for J.P. Morgan, made vast fortunes in banking in the United States before going on to finance some of America's biggest companies, General Electric and US Steel among them. When World War I broke out, Morgan handed out war loans in excess of one billion dollars to America and Europe in 1915, equivalent to twenty-three billion dollars in modern currency. It was reported that the US government was influenced in its decision to enter World War I in order to protect Morgan's overseas loans that may otherwise be threatened by foreign governments. Today, we see their imprint on the skylines of the world's major cities, their names in giant letters across the tops of office buildings seen for miles around. These were just two examples of families that had gone on to build dynasties and powerhouses, taking over industries and making themselves invaluable to those in power.

Next came the secret groups. Of these there were many, known for different reasons, but a couple of names came up time and time again. Bilderberg, known as a private annual conference, is attended by up to two hundred of the world's most prominent leaders and businessmen. The event is off limits to the press and public, leaving what happens there a mystery to those unfortunate enough to be omitted from the guest list. Armed guards patrol every entrance to the event site, sometimes arresting those journalists wanting to know exactly what the politicians and businessmen and women are discussing behind the heavily protected doors and fences.

Further back in time, Max found the Illuminati. Fascinating stories of a secret organisation that started in Bavaria in the late 1700s with the purpose of challenging superstition, monarchies, and religious influence in politics. After initially modelling themselves on the three degrees of Freemasonry, the group easily recruited Masons looking for the next level in a secret fraternity. Before long, the group had members in positions of power across Bavaria and Munich and eventually the group's success led to its demise. Careless talk amongst the brethren unmasked the group and the revelation forced the hand of the Prince-Elector of Bavaria, Charles Theodore. He quickly abolished the

Illuminati by an official order forbidding all secret societies in his province. The story didn't end there, however. Some believe this was just the start of the movement and over the years the legend of this mystical group grew in popularity with speculation and tales of secrecy. A network of underground bunkers to protect the world's most valuable inhabitants should the end of times draw near; weapons capable of replicating natural disasters; involvement with South America's drug cartels; suppressed cures for diseases that were wiping out huge swathes of countries' populations. The internet was awash with theories about the fate of the fraternity and its members.

It was easy to understand how readers could be drawn into these tales of mystery and excitement. Even though the quality of the material presenting evidence or asking provocative questions varied hugely, he could not deny that some of the issues raised were all too visible in the world today. Wealth distribution had never been more unequal. Fifty percent of the Earth's wealth was controlled by one percent of the population. Giant corporations made billions of dollars while the streets of the world's cities were lined with homelessness. The US spent six times more on defence than it did on education and that same money, while paying to send young men and women into the most dangerous situations imaginable, also contributed to the bottom line of huge private companies who directly benefited from the conflict. It was all too easy to trace a path between those making the decisions and those reaping the rewards. It was hard to argue that the people controlling the wealth wouldn't have tremendous influence over those who relied on that same wealth for their existence.

Now, whether the stories were true or mythical was irrelevant. It was the concept that gripped Max. He read that individuals had managed to create wealth, power and influence capable of guiding world events, defining the pages of history books and deciding who would win the bloodiest and longest wars our species has witnessed. Regardless of the vehicle, the idea that it was possible to corrupt the normal ebb and flow of financial and political systems that had developed over centuries was an alarming one. Each family or group's varied histories had enabled speculators to draw conclusions about their secretive natures or their ability to dictate how countries and continents operated. The motives were never altruistic and when simplified always centred around two main themes: hoarding wealth and creating power to hoard wealth.

Max abhorred that these groups were driving change in the world but for all the wrong reasons, even sending innocent lives to fight wars that only served their agendas. Lives like his brother. Lost to one of these wars. And for what? To occupy a country, to kill civilians for over a decade, only to finally withdraw and accept defeat. He paused, thinking of that day when his brother's helicopter took the impact from a rocket-propelled grenade, imagining the faces of the men and women inside who must have known instantly that it was their time as the chopper began to lose control and descend over the Afghan landscape. There was an intense anger he'd fought to hide every day since hearing the news. Looking around the faces of his peers in the room, a thought occurred to him.

If it was possible to create powerful secret groups in the pursuit of perceived evil, then it was also possible to create a group whose sole purpose was the opposite. A group that made decisions, not for self-benefit, but for the benefit of those who weren't in power. A group that would prevent wars rather than start them. *You could spend huge sums of money helping people rather than lining the pockets of salivating vultures.* He tried to imagine how a group like that would operate and what positions they would hold to be able to make those decisions.

'Max, is everything...'

His thought process was cut short as a prompt from Mrs Logan made him aware that he'd actually stopped speaking.

Oh shit, how long have I been silent for? 'Right, sorry Miss.' He snapped back to life, 'Over the last five years, there has been a significant rise in the number of kidnappings…' He continued through his paper, now not even thinking about how the words were spilling out. His only thought was finding out whether his idea was possible. As soon as he was able to retake his seat, he grabbed his laptop and opened it on the table in front of him.

Where do I start?

He didn't have a political or financial dynasty behind him to catapult himself into the upper echelons of the powerful elite. It was going to have to be the hard way. There were so many questions rushing through his head. How would one start to influence? How many people would it take to create influence? How many people would have to know that they were involved? For now, it would be easier to identify positions of power he saw having influence in his country. The government, the courts, the military, the police. Even while spinning this grand idea through his mind he was cautious to maintain some degree of realism; global domination was maybe slightly outside the reach of a sixteen-year-old boy. He'd settle for control of the UK first and make a decision about expansion later.

He imagined himself aged forty, head of a secret

group whose members had taken up positions of power. Where would he be standing? The Prime Minister's office in Downing Street? No, politics didn't interest him. It seemed too much like swimming in treacle, while the treacle is being purposefully difficult. He wanted something with a bit more danger. Having grown up on the books of Andy McNab, he was fascinated by the history of the Special Air Service. Their missions took them into situations that require extreme fitness, of body and mind; calmness under pressure; aggression when it was necessary, and an unwavering belief in one's ability to complete the task at hand.

He thought back to the tales about the clandestine world of the secret services he'd been introduced to by his brother. War time treachery defined by double agents like Kim Philby and the Cambridge Spies. MI6 agents caught sending information to the Soviet Union, defecting after being exposed. Obviously, he knew the imaginary exploits of MI6's most famous employee, the illustrious James Bond. While it was clear that the life of an Intelligence Officer had been glamorised for Fleming's audience, from his other research he learned that the skills one must be in possession of to be a successful spy were the very same skills a group like the one he envisioned would need in order to live amongst others in plain sight whilst executing their plan. Information gathering, building networks of confidants and sources, counter-surveillance, influencing others. It was the perfect avenue for him to pursue. He was sold immediately. Now he had to find out how.

The rest of the day flew by in a haze of ideas bouncing around his head. Every time a new thought leapt to mind, he was careful to capture it, not wanting any of them to be lost in the whirlwind of creativity. By the time he arrived home, he was almost frantic with excitement, jumping off the school bus and running up the driveway to the house. Throwing his bag to the floor, he ran to his desk and sat down to compose himself.

Think logically. One thing at a time...

Of course, this was not a path that he could tread alone and there were other seats at the table he would have to fill if he was going to create something bigger than himself. A solitary person could only have so much influence, he reasoned. The whole premise depended on more than one mind collaborating to bridge the different sectors of power in order to allow the decision-making process to be effective across the board.

It was no use for a Prime Minister to put a law in place without having support in the judicial system; just as it would be futile having the military at your command, ready to take the necessary action but no mandate from parliament to do so. All the most-confidential intelligence in the world was only useful if you had the power to act upon it.

It occurred to him that each person would need a higher perception of their role and why they were so critically important. Trying to picture how each of the different strands would link together and the paths they would take, his head was filled with the image of a loom, the weaver tirelessly pushing and pulling away, sweat dripping as the shuttle moved back and forward. It was the perfect metaphor. You feed in raw product from different angles in its individual strands before manipulating and overlaying them time and again until they were indistinguishable and inseparable from each other. The final product was a rich and colourful, well-planned and immaculately executed cloth worth so much more than the sum of its parts. The result a tightly woven, seamless material, bound together by the precision and vision of its creator. He would need substantial amounts of both if any of this grand plan was to be possible.

It was time to find the other threads to weave his tapestry.

2

S itting in the long, open-plan studio above his parents' garage, Max rubbed his shoulder as he waited. An hour earlier, he'd been dropped off by his friend's mum after another gruelling Saturday morning rugby match and a one-point win against the school's local rivals. The satisfying result was the only pleasure he'd taken from the time out in the freezing cold and the driving rain. That same rain had started to ease only as the final whistle blew and that same rain now lightly tapped on the glass of the sloping Velux windows directly above his head.

Stiff and bruised, he sat at his laptop and opened his plan. There was a table of four columns and ten rows. From left to right the headings read: *Name; Position; Why; In?*

So far, under the first heading was just one name; his own. Below '*position*' read the words *Chief of Secret Intelligence Service*, followed by *NA* in the *why* column and a capital *IN* under the column indicating whether the person was in or out. In the rows beneath his ambitious title were the names of other positions that would be essential in building a powerful network capable of influencing major decisions in the country. The next on the list was the most important of all in his mind: *Prime Minister.*

It had been only two days since the idea had sprung into his head, but he'd already thought carefully about each of the roles, the importance they would have, and crucially, who he knew that he'd ask to fill them. Although the school had no shortage of talent in many different fields, Max was looking for people who stood out for their ability to lead and influence others. This would be crucial for anyone that he asked to join him.

Three hours earlier he'd sat in the cold, smelly changing rooms of his school's sports ground, surrounded by the noise and energy of sixty boys. Usually, he'd be talking with his team mates, laughing, joking. Today was different. He was quiet, thoughtful, looking at the people around him in a completely different light. In the throng that occupied the small space allocated for their team, there was one other who was calm, almost serene.

Was this the first time that Max had noticed Sebastian's pre-game ritual? Was he normally too busy talking with the others to spot the unique calmness of the boy? He watched from the other side of the room, ignorant to everything else that was going on around him.

Sebastian looked focused, pensive. To any other

onlooker, it might appear that he was a bit of a loner. This couldn't be further from the truth. Max knew what he was doing. As he watched Sebastian staring straight ahead, he could see the small wrist movements paired with tiny tilts of his head, mimicking passing the ball. He was visualising the game, walking through their set moves, estimating who would be where and when, ready to take the ball and smash it through the opposition line.

As the scrum half, the man responsible for collecting the ball from a ruck or maul, he was involved in nearly every offensive play, directing the forwards where to go next or looking for quick plays that incorporated the back line. The position demanded a range of skills and the best scrum halves were adept at them all.

Speed and agility were key in obtaining the ball and getting oneself into the right position to set up the next play. Vision was critical in identifying where to send the ball next and his ability to spot weaknesses in the other team's line-up was better than most. He had what they called 'rugby brain' and Max had watched jealously over the years as Sebastian had been honoured at every level he'd ever played at.

It was the combination of all these skills that made him a great rugby player. However, Max knew that it was his emotional intelligence that made him a great leader. His teammates had respect for him both on and off the field. When he spoke, every player listened.

He had no time for personal glory, only that of the team. Coaches saw this in him from an early age and had developed him further, pushing him to develop all of the skills needed on and off the pitch. Max saw in him a selfless boy who would let someone else take the credit for scoring a try rather than risk holding onto the ball only to be tackled or have it stolen from him. A true team player, willing to sacrifice himself for the greater good.

As Sebastian had made the final loop in his left bootlace, he'd looked up and caught Max's staring eyes. His face instantly transformed into a smile as his fist clenched and shook in the universal sign for power. He stood, winked at his friend and silently gestured with a flick of his head for the pair to head out to the field. Max grinned in return and rose to his feet, stamping his boots on the hard floor one after the other to allow them to find their perfect fit before following his teammate out of the room.

Max had known even before he'd seen Sebastian's behaviour that morning that his would be the next name on the list. This morning had solidified just how essential he would be to his plan.

He typed the name in the cell beneath his own on

his plan. Sebastian Dean, Prime Minister. It had a ring to it.

Just as he clicked *Save*, he heard the gravel outside turning under the wheels of a heavy car driven far too quickly around the driveway that circled the house. As the noise grew louder, he closed the laptop before turning to stand on the soft beige couch cushions, pulling the grey handle at the top of one of the sloped windows. It turned on its hinge, allowing a cold blast of air into the space.

The driver applied the brakes hard and the car skidded over the gravel, wheels clamped in position, until coming to a halt just inches from the sandstone cornering that separated the gravel track from the sprawling grass lawn. Out jumped a showered, fresh looking Sebastian, now in jeans and a striped shirt. A bruised cheek and temple were the only indication that two hours earlier he had been lying unconscious on the middle of a rugby field covered in mud whilst seven other boys wrestled and punched each other around him.

The door to the driver's side opened shortly after his and a brown, leather boot landed on the gravel. Max always loved seeing Sebastian's mum. She glided out of the car and stood for a moment, running her hands through her long blonde hair to straighten it out. Turning, she caught his face peeking out of the open window and she smiled and waved. She was younger than his own mum, by a good few years, and she looked amazing. She always dressed like she was ready to take the dogs on a long walk or go for a hack.

As Sebastian strode towards the side door to the garage, his mum shouted a goodbye after him. He waved his arm without looking back. She made eye contact with Max again before rolling her eyes up towards the sky, still showing her perfect smile. Back into the 4x4 she hopped, shutting the door and rolling down the window to give a final wave before the wheels span as she reversed and turned simultaneously, slamming on the brakes again to create yet another skid and set of tracks in the gravel that Max knew he would have to kick back into place later. Finally, the car set off back towards the front of the house and the noise faded.

By the time the car was completely out of earshot, Sebastian was climbing the final step of the three-sided staircase that led up from the front door to the studio above the garage. Max turned to him, complimenting his new look. 'That's quite a shiner, you're going to get some attention from the girls tonight! You'll have to be a bit faster to get out of the way next time.'

'Did you see the size of that guy?!' Sebastian protested, 'There's no way he's our age, he looked at least forty. Not even Dave has a beard like that! And he clearly smashed me in the face with his elbow on purpose.'

'You're just a sore loser, I would have taken him.'

'Whatever, I'd like to see you try!'

'I did. How do you think his nose got messed up?' Max was quick to claim the glory.

'I thought that happened in the collision.' Sebastian was puzzled.

'Nope. While you were having a little snooze on your face, we sorted him out. We all saw him do it on purpose, as did the ref might I add, and we barrelled in. I got a lucky swing that landed on him before I had to duck out of the way of a million flying fists. I think he got the message.'

He winked across at Sebastian and they both laughed as the injured party prodded the bruised graze up the left-hand side of his face. It was clear from the wince that it was delicate, but he'd tried his best not to show it.

Max liked that about him. He was tough. He didn't show fear and he would never let anyone see that he was hurt. When he had come around on the rugby pitch, the coach tried to take him off, but he insisted he was fine. He was a little dazed but five minutes later he was hitting harder than he had before his muddy siesta. One lesson they had always been taught was that if you hit someone hard enough, they'll think twice before crossing you again. And it worked. The next opportunity he had, he slammed into his attacker with all the force he could, ensuring his ribs felt the full impact of the tackle. The culprit had shied away from him for the rest of the game.

The rain had stopped and the sky had even started to clear showing signs of the sun beyond the clouds though the grass was still wet from the morning's weather. The two of them headed outside—they both always leaned more toward the outdoors. As they padded around the green expanse, leaving footprints in the fine moisture, Max turned to his friend.

'Have you thought about what you want to be when you're older? Your career, I mean.'

Max watched his friend's face as he initially started to reply but stopped himself, taking a few moments.

'Do you know what? I really can't decide what I want to do. There are so many options that I can't pick. Obviously, mum would like me to follow her footsteps and go into medicine. I'm sure dad would like me to follow his as well, but I don't really fancy being offshore on an oil rig for months at a time. Must admit, something about medicine doesn't do it for me either. Every time I think about the future, I get a sort of paralysis.'

This was music to Max's ears and exactly the sort of answer he'd hoped for when rehearsing this conversation over the last couple of days. He knew that it would be much more difficult to change someone's mind, to alter an existing plan, than to help them formulate it from scratch.

He took the opportunity to delicately introduce the topic of the 9/11 events he'd talked about it his presentation days earlier. He knew that the events had had a significant impact on Sebastian's family. His uncle had worked for an asset management organisation stationed in the north tower. He had been away on business at the time but his wife, a secretary at the company had lost her life along with the 3,000 others. Her remains were never found but DNA samples taken from Ground Zero confirmed that she was among the dead. The funeral had been covered by all the major news outlets, thousands of people lining the procession route, throwing flowers onto the roof of the hearse as it passed. His uncle had been devastated by the loss of his wife and, finding it hard to be in the same city that had claimed her life, moved back to England to be closer to his family. After the tragedy, he'd turned to alcohol, along with many of the survivors and their families, as his way of coping with the loss and as a result had moved in with his sister, Sebastian's aunt.

'It was awful, I still can't believe they did it, the fuckers. I hope one day we find and kill everyone that was involved.'

'Well they shot Bin Laden already, didn't they?' Max responded. He didn't really believe that Bin Laden was responsible for the attacks, but one thing at a time.

'Even so, it can't just have been him. He didn't fly any planes that day, did he?' Sebastian asked rhetorically. 'Have you heard about what happened at the Olympics in Germany years ago?'

'No, but tell me.' Max was keen to hear.

'There was an attack on the Israeli Olympic team where they were taken hostage and killed.'

'Holy shit. All of them?'

'No, not all of them but I think maybe about fifteen.'

'Fuck. Did they catch the guys who did it?'

'That's the best part of the story. The Israelis meticulously tracked them across the globe and killed off anyone who was involved, one by one. It took them twenty years, apparently.'

'How did they kill them?'

'Lots of different ways, all pretty brutal, you should check it out. They made sure that it was a sign that they were not to be fucked with. Few of them were killed with bombs, like under a desk or a bed, and then someone would ring the phone and ask for them, as soon as they knew it was him they'd just blow up the house or flat. Few of them gunned down in the street, lots of bullets. Well anyway, that's what I hope happens with these guys.' Sebastian's hands now twisted as he spoke, and he furrowed his brow. 'Everyone who helped plan it or do it. I hope we go in under the cover of darkness and grab them. We'll keep them alive but make them suffer, a lot. They need to pay for what they did.'

'Man, you okay? How's your uncle doing?'

'Not good, he doesn't really do anything anymore. He just sits in my aunt's house or the garden, drinking, staring into space or watching TV. I feel awkward whenever we go around there. It's a bit nicer when it's the tele because at least it's not as uncomfortable as sitting there in silence. Mum and her sis are good with him. Sometimes I see them talking for hours on end about Gill, smiling and laughing.'

'I'm always smiling when your mum's around!' Max laughed. He sensed the need for a lighter moment.

'Fuck off!' came Sebastian's reply as he pushed him, just nearly hard enough to knock him over. Once Max regained his composure, he fixed his friend's gaze with his and innocently asked, 'Sebastian, if you could make sure that it never happened again, would you?'

'What do you mean? Of course I would. Who wouldn't? Why would anyone let something terrible like that happen?'

'Have you seen any of the theories about what

happened on the day? About what really happened over there?'

'You mean conspiracy theories?' Sebastian was dismissive.

'Well, some call them conspiracy theories, some people call them facts. There's loads of stuff about it online. Did you know that the military were conducting drills for that exact scenario on the same day that it happened?'

'I hadn't heard that.'

'Yeah, I looked into it.' Max continued, 'George Bush is on record only days later saying that an attack of that kind was "unimaginable". How, when their own air force was practising that exact situation, could he come out and say that it was unimaginable? There was so much confusion as to whether the reports were part of the drill or not that no fighter jets were even scrambled to intercept any other aircraft. They were there, literally ready to deal with the exact attack that was happening, but they were still powerless to do anything about it. I don't buy it. And that's just the start.'

'Is that true?'

'Look it up, there's loads of information about it. And lots more interesting stuff too. Have you ever heard of the Illuminati? Or the Masons? Or Bilderberg? Groups of people who get together to influence or control. There are loads of them. I keep reading about them and it's fascinating.

'A person or family makes lots of money and they create these dynasties that spread around the world. They invest and set up other companies that become hugely successful, making vast amounts of wealth that seem to get bigger and bigger. This is where it gets really interesting. Some of these groups have been around for hundreds of years and there are links to all kinds of politicians and world leaders.

'Whether they're giving them financial support or their companies are supplying weapons and goods to support wars or takeovers of other nations, it all leads back to benefit the group. They end up with friends in high places and the ability to influence conversations, policies, even wars.'

'You can't be serious.' Sebastian frowned. 'How would that ever go unnoticed? Surely it would be common knowledge that the politicians were being controlled by these people?'

'I thought the exact same thing. I couldn't believe it at first but the more I looked into it, the more convinced I became. It's not just in the US either. We assume our government is free to decide on what they want to do but when you look at the amount of money that the government receives from different groups, all trying to push an agenda that suits their company or policies, it's hard to think that it's in exchange for nothing. It's called "lobbying" and it's basically the western equivalent of what we label "bribery" when it happens somewhere else. Something that we convince ourselves happens on foreign shores, far away from here. Something that our government criticises and pretends has no place in civilised countries. Ours is just a more "civilised" way of doing it. In plain sight, under the masquerade of "business".'

Max gazed ahead into the distance. 'It makes me sick to think that what we call democracy is actually just a club. A club of old boys, all lining each other's pockets by doing deals that benefit each other. You scratch mine, I'll scratch yours, yada yada.' Max noticed Sebastian in his peripheral vison, staring at him. Max blinked purposefully, turning to meet his friend's eyes. 'I don't want to live in a world, knowing that decisions are not being taken for the actual good of the country but for the good of those who are meant to be helping others, who have the power to help others. Do you?'

'Hell no.'

'I'm going to change it. And I want you to help, Sebastian.'

He let the words hang for a minute and analysed

his friend's face as the cogs turned. Bewilderment was the term for what he saw. Confusion, followed by incredulity were portrayed by a furrowed brow and then a short laugh and a smile. Max could tell that his friend thought he was being ridiculous.

'How on earth would we ever be able to do that?! Do you know how crazy that sounds, Max?'

'Only a little crazy, if you ask me. Think about it. How do people get to positions of power? Okay, maybe a few have done it on their own, but I bet you most of them have had some help. What if we created our own group and all helped each other to get where we need to be? I've been thinking about it a lot, and trust me, I know it sounds ambitious.'

'That's one word for it, at least.'

'Just hear me out. Power is just the ability to control, whether it's to control people or events. What gives you that power is something different. I can only see three things that enable power. Money, status, and knowledge. The first gives you the second. But there are other ways to have status, and that's dictated by your position, by what you do. Whether it's the CEO of a bank, or leader of a trade union, or the owner of a football team. All these people have status and power. Obviously, we don't have bank vaults overflowing with gold and diamonds that we can put to use, but we've got something just as valuable. Our potential. Potential to achieve status and to acquire knowledge. And those are two very powerful things indeed.'

Sebastian's brows furrowed again, but this time Max could tell it was in thought.

Max quickly kept on, afraid to lose Seb's intrigue 'What I'm proposing is that we do everything necessary to acquire status, to acquire power. Think of the most prominent jobs in the country. Not just us, we'll need others, of course, but we'd each take one job and set our sights on that. Every decision we make will be with that job in mind. Everything we do will be in order to get to that one position. It obviously has to be something that would fit with our personalities and likes, or it would never work and we'd never keep the motivation to get there, but we'll all help each other and make sure that we all get to where we need to be. We can do lots of research and find out what we need to do to get the right jobs and all that.'

He paused. What was Sebastian thinking? He'd expected resistance and was ready to deal with any questions that came his way. Unfortunately, silence was all he received at that moment.

'I know it sounds crazy but the more you think about it, just ask yourself why it's crazy. We're young, smart, we've got families who will support us, even admire our ambition. We go to a good school, get good grades. There's absolutely no reason why we couldn't do what I'm saying. You just have to look at the logical steps we would need to take to make it happen.'

'Which job would you have?'

Max snapped his head back in surprise.

'That's easy, I'll be God.' The pair laughed.

'Well, I have to hand it to you. You do think big, Max. Do you really believe you could do it?'

'Believe *we* could do it, you mean.' He leaned forward. 'You and me. We'll need a few more good people, obviously, but we know where to find some of them, don't we now?'

Sebastian raised his eyebrows, and then after a beat, shrugged. 'Where would we even start?'

'I have a few ideas.'

3

One week later, back in the room in which they had first discussed the idea, they found themselves once more. This time not in sunshine but quilted by the darkness that lay over the house and surrounding fields, enclosing them in the space, removing the outside world altogether. Unlike other Friday nights that started in this room, this time they had a purpose.

After the initial conversation in which Max had introduced Sebastian to the concept, the pair had retreated to their own worlds. Max to analyse his performance, Sebastian to try to comprehend what was being asked of him by his closest friend. It was easy for Max to power forward. The concept had been burning in his mind for almost two weeks now. Sebastian, however, had needed a little more time to accept the possibility.

His homework, in the loosest sense of the word, was not of the conventional sort, and watching streams of videos and documentaries was favourable to most other kinds of toil. Max had sent him away to do his own research into what he had been told. He wanted Sebastian to develop his own opinion, with a bit of careful guidance from his new teacher, of course.

Suggested films and documentaries were on the list, 9/11 the main theme throughout. Once he'd completed those, it was onto those names that Max had etched into his mind, Rothschild & Morgan, Bilderberg, the Masons, and the Illuminati. Max was curious to see what his friend would find. Where would his mind take him once he had learned of these well-known power players on the world stage? Max had set Sebastian the task under the guise of needing to split the workload, of breaking it down into manageable chunks. It was not for his own benefit, however. Max had watched everything he could find, read every available result at the end of his keystrokes. He'd barely slept since the notion had blossomed in his mind, unfurling its petals in layers that, like any flower, craves light and sustenance.

Whilst Sebastian was doing all this, Max continued his research into the types of people who formed these circles and their journeys through life. How did they end up in those positions and what had they had to do to get there? Every day he would sit in class, racing to complete the work so that he could divert his thoughts to his new goal. Each lunchtime he would wait for Sebastian outside of class and they would disappear out of the school gates towards Sebastian's house to share what they were learning, feeding off each other's prodigious ability to learn and retain information.

Within days, it was clear to Max that Sebastian was hooked. Every time they spoke, Sebastian would regale Max with more information about the theories and videos he'd found. It sounded like he'd done nothing else but watch and re-watch hours of footage, reportedly showing bombs detonating inside the twin towers and comparison reports with other skyscrapers that had burned for far longer periods of time than the New York landmarks without collapsing.

They talked about the footage of World Trade Centre 7, apparently undamaged by the initial impacts, falling perfectly to the ground. Demolition experts who had not before seen the footage and were unaware of the building's significance gave bewildered testimony that no building would ever collapse in such a way under natural circumstances. He'd read how World Trade Centres 3, 4, 5 and 6, all positioned closer to the giant structures that had collapsed right on top of them, while heavily damaged, had remained standing, needing to be manually brought down later by engineers.

Max was relieved and excited that someone else

found the evidence and events as compelling as he did. It was clear that there was now officially a group. Even if it was only two of them so far.

'I'm sure of it. Someone definitely knows more than the US government's story, it's some kind of cover up. I thought you were a bit mad at first, I'll be honest with you, mate.'

Max stayed silent as he listened to the new recruit pouring out facts and information, barely pausing for breath.

'Whether it was the government or some darker group operating, I don't know. But that's what excites me even more. The fact that there could be a group of people out there who has *more* power than the US government. I'm in. Let's jump down the rabbit hole.'

Max opened his mouth to speak but was unable to get a word out before more came his way. He didn't mind a bit. He smiled.

'I think we need to start looking at the jobs we want to do,' Sebastian continued. 'And the jobs we need others to do.'

'That's my man, Sebastian! You're right, and I'm already a few steps ahead of you there. I thought we'd play a little game. I'll list out the jobs I think we need, and you say which one you think each one of us suits best.' Max watched as Sebastian nodded his approval.

'But before we do that, I think we need to create some rules for the group.'

'Yes, yes, we'll get to all that, but I want to know what job you want, first.' Sebastian pushed.

'Okay, in a minute.' Max held up his hand. 'We have to at least start with one rule now.'

'I'm listening, go on,' Sebastian blurted out impatiently.

'Secrecy. This has to be key. Nothing we talk about here can ever be discussed anywhere else. I'm serious. In everything I've read, the biggest threat is other people. Other people knowing what is happening or what is going on. People always get caught because someone knows too much, says something stupid. What we're planning on doing here will last for years. And we need to protect that.'

'My, my, my, look at you, getting all serious,' Sebastian teased.

'Don't you agree?'

'I do. I've just never seen you look so serious before. It suits you. You just need some glasses and you'd look right at home in the House of Commons.'

Max raised an eyebrow, puzzled. Had he even mentioned the role of Prime Minister to Sebastian?

Max smiled, he appreciated that Sebastian didn't automatically try to claim the top position for himself.

He had sort of assumed when he started this every person he brought in would compete for what they saw as the most visible, most powerful role. He wasn't surprised at Sebastian's response, though. His everlasting selflessness was one of his most admirable features. Of course, standing aside and letting someone else through a doorway first is not the way to become the Prime Minister. He'd deal with that later.

'I'm being serious because this is serious. If we want to do this properly and bring other people in on board, bring them here, then we have to know the rules right from the start. Everyone does, and everyone will have to follow them. Always.'

'I like it, this is good. Complete secrecy, no excuses, we're agreed.' Sebastian held out his hand.

'No words spoken in this room whilst doing "business" will leave it. Punishable by death!' Max's eyes widened with intensity before narrowing as he started to laugh. Sebastian chuckled. Max went on, 'Great, well there it is, our first rule. Our most important rule. The first rule of fight club is, you do not talk about fight club.'

The pair laughed once more. They'd watched the film countless times together.

Max was eager to switch the focus to roles. Until now, he'd been careful only to implant the seed. It was already enough of a leap of faith to convince Sebastian that groups like this existed, never mind persuade him that the only way to achieve such a task was by assigning him one of the most coveted jobs in the world. He saw the coming discussion as his next challenge. How would he persuade Sebastian, as humble as he was, that he was the right man for the job?

'Seb, here's what I have so far. There are some obvious ones and then some not-so-obvious. To start, we have the top spot. Prime Minister. This is the most obvious one we would want. The most powerful person in the country. Tricky though, very tricky. I know nothing about politics and I'm not interested about finding out a great deal to be perfectly honest with you. I can just see them lying every time they open their mouths. All you ever hear is "how great we are and what we do for you" and all they're really thinking is "how great we are and what can we say to get your vote". I'd find it amazingly refreshing, for once, for someone to just come out and say what they really fucking think. No scripts, no lines, just what they think.'

'You mean like Trump?' Sebastian joked.

'Don't get me started on that fucking criminal. We'd need someone honest and sincere, and trustworthy that people will like. I don't have the first idea of how someone would become Prime Minister, but we'll do some research.'

Sebastian nodded. 'I'm happy to go and research that, if you like?'

'I was hoping you'd say that.'

He looked at Max, confused. 'It's no problem, we need to split the work up, don't we?'

'I mean I was hoping that you would go and research that particular one for a reason.' He paused without blinking, his eyes focused on Sebastian's.

'Seb, that's your role. It has to be, you're perfect for it.'

'Max, surely that's yours? Isn't that what all this is about? Really, I mean. Isn't this your way of reaching the top with a group of people to help you get there?'

Max took a second to consider his answer, or at least give the impression that he was, for he knew the words that were to come.

'Yes, and no. When I think about reaching the top, I'm not thinking about the individual jobs. Yes, the PM is the one that everyone sees as having the most power. And yes, it may be the one with the codes to the nukes, which is basically the most power anyone really has, right? But we're not going to be individuals. We're going to be one unit. Each and every person has to be right for the part they play. I'm not right for that, and I know it. But I know that you are. And you're the only person I would trust in that position.

'There's a reason I came to you first with this whole thing. We're going to be the leaders, the core. We're going to have to steer this thing at every point. This is just an idea right now but what we're talking about is going to be the hardest thing that you and I, and anyone we bring in, will ever do. There will be disagreements on the way and we'll have to deal with that when we come to it. But you and I will have to be rock solid. I don't know anyone on this planet as well as I know you, and I trust you with my life. I need to know that the person sitting in that seat is the one person who I trust as much as I do myself.'

He tried to guess what Sebastian was thinking as his gaze sank to the floor. He'd never said anything like this to him before.

'Max, I'm not sure I'm the right…'

'You are. Trust me. I can see you don't believe it, but you are. I see you every day, interacting with people. You've got a gift. People respond to you, they love you. The fact that you can't see it is the reason they love you. You have no agenda; you just get on with being you. You're going to do great things, my friend. And I'm going to help make it happen. Listen, you don't have to commit now. If you really can't bear the thought, then we'll find another one for you. Just give it a bit of time and I think you'll come around. I hope you do anyway.'

There was a drawn-out silence in the room.

Max broke the lull. 'Phew, that was intense. Enough of the soppy shit.'

'Max, it's not that I don't think I could do it.' Sebastian was smiling now. 'I just assumed that you would be claiming that one for yourself. You know how you love the attention and all that.'

'Nope, that's you. You have to be the PM. You're a natural leader. People listen to you whether it's in class or on the rugby pitch. And you're persuasive. Even with that face you've still managed to con girls into kissing you – my rebounds, obviously.' *Besides, I can't even stand in front of a class.*

'Ha! Once I told them you were gay it was easy after that.'

'See! You've mastered manipulating the truth already. Oh, but there's something else I thought about.'

Sebastian raised his eyebrows.

'To be really successful, we're going to have to keep our noses clean. You know what the media is like, they find anything and use it against people to ruin careers or make them out to be bad people. It's important that no one ever does anything bad enough that it stops them or us from reaching our assigned positions. I'm telling you this because it would affect you more than most. You can't be the PM if you've been caught up in some major scandal, the papers would have a field day and could completely kill all your chances of ever getting there.'

'I think you're more likely to be in a scandal than I am. But you are right. Next time I'm asked if I want to be part of drugs running venture or human trafficking, I'll just have to say, "not this time guys, the boss won't be too happy with me."'

Max narrowed his eyes. 'Ha ha, very droll. I think I've made my point.' He leaned his elbows on his knees. 'Alright, mine next. It's not all about you, you know, Sebastian.'

'Okay, what do you have in mind for yourself?'

'Any guesses?' Max prodded.

'As I thought you were going to say PM for you, I'm a little on the back foot. I'm thinking something like Army?'

'Close, but it's not the one. This is one of my favourites. Bond, James Bond.'

'A spy? I hadn't thought of that.'

'That's why I'm the mastermind! And you're thinking way too small. Not a spy, but a spy king. Head of the Intelligence services. These guys know everything, they have to. Remember when you told me about the Olympics and the Israelis? Well the guys that spent the next twenty years killing off all the terrorists were highly trained Israeli spies. I looked into it. They worked for their version of MI6, Mossad, and they were brutal. Completely and utterly brutal. There's so much happening that we have no idea about. Terror threats, other countries spying on us, us spying on them. The amount of information gathered by these guys must be vast, and it would go a long way to help a group like ours. I think this is as important as the PM. If knowledge is power, these guys are the shit.'

'And you're sure this is what you want to do? Remember, this is going to be for your whole life.' Sebastian challenged Max.

'Yeah, I'm sure. I think I was born for this.' Max's response was confident and without hesitation. 'Next up, we would need the military,' he continued. 'It's our country's muscle when it comes to other nations. It's how we defend ourselves should it ever come to that. It's how we start a war should we ever need to.'

'Now hold on, mate.' Sebastian was visibly perplexed. 'You said we were doing this for good, why would we ever need to *start* a war? The whole point is to end these stupid things, stop people dying unnecessarily, to help people.'

'I know, and you're right. We wouldn't ever start a war like the ones happening now. No oil wars, no wars just to make our friends who build submarines and cruise missiles wealthy. I just mean that if ever there was a situation in which we needed to, we could. But let's not get bogged down with that. That's not the main reason we need the military. Most of all it's so we can play with all the guns and stuff as our guy will be in charge.'

'You and guns, you're a bit obsessed really, aren't you?'

'They are cool as fuck. Why do you think I joined the Army Cadets? You Air Cadets don't do anything but watch planes all day.'

'One day I'll be able to fly one of them. I'd take you and your rifle out without even breaking a sweat.'

'I guess I'll just have to be sure to keep you onside then, won't I?'

'Especially when I live in 10 Downing Street and go on holiday with the Queen,' Sebastian joked.

'I'm not sure that's exactly what happens but I'm sure you could arrange it. Anyway, next, I thought we'd need to cover law, someone in the legal system. The legal system holds massive power over the country. It basically defines everything that people can and can't do, including politicians and spies. I haven't done much research into this one yet, but it's next on the list.'

'Okay, let's think about it logically,' Sebastian said. 'Who's the most powerful person in the legal system?

If the government makes the laws, who enforces them? It has to be the courts, right? A judge is the one who decides whether people are innocent or guilty.'

'Actually, I'm not sure that's right. Don't juries decide who's innocent or guilty and then the judge decides what the punishment is?'

'Ah, you're right. I'm sure I've seen a tape of a panel of judges deciding as well, though,' Sebastian mused.

'Now that you mention it, that rings a bell too. I think that's a different type of court, though.'

Max made a note on a pad in front of him to start looking into the different parts of the legal system and where the power really lay. 'I'll take this one and do some research. Dad's got loads of buddies who are lawyers, maybe I can talk to one of them.'

'How are you going to ask loads of questions without him wondering why?'

'I don't know. I'll say I'm doing a school project or something. No, actually...' Another brainwave hit Max. 'What if I said I was going to do an article in the school paper? That way we have an excuse to ask all the questions we want and nobody will wonder why. Shit, why didn't I think of this earlier? If I was on the school paper, I could interview lots of different people, ask questions about their lives and how they got to where they are. I write an article about their job and everyone's happy. No one wonders why I'm asking questions and we get all the info we need.'

'I like it. And I must say, it's pretty genius. Whoever thought you actually had a brain capable of focusing on one thing for long enough to come up with so many good ideas?' Sebastian grinned a cheeky smile and accompanied it with a wink. He had just started to laugh when a small, square cushion flew across coffee table in the middle of the room and hit him in the face, knocking his head backwards.

As he recoiled from the blow, he was greeted by Max's beaming smile. 'You're a cheeky bugger sometimes, Sebastian!'

The cushion once more took to the air, this time in the opposite direction. Max quickly ducked to the right, letting the cushion fly over his left shoulder before making contact with the drum kit directly behind the sofa he was sitting on. The object flew straight into a stand holding a large cymbal. It teetered on its wide base, before the momentum and gravity took over. Sound exploded as it contacted first with the cherry red coloured tom-tom before hitting the bass drum and sliding down its side, coming to a rest on the floor.

As the first sounds of chaos had erupted from behind him, Max had turned to witness the descent.

Upon returning his gaze to the culprit, he saw a boy that was expecting some abuse. Sebastian's face was scrunched into a look that was immediately apologetic, his hands clenched in fists in front of his mouth as if it were about to bite them off.

Instead, Max laughed, jumped up and walked around the couch to pick up the fallen piece and examine the damage. Not a mark could be seen, either on the kit or cymbal. He righted the stand before flicking the cymbal and letting it ring. He walked back around the couch as Sebastian apologised profusely.

'Don't worry about it, mate, no harm done. But, on that note, and excuse the pun, I think we have some more digging to do before we meet up again. I'll go away and look at where laws come from and who decides who goes to jail. Why don't you start doing some research into Prime Ministers?'

'Okay, so where do I start?'

'That's a good question, and that's what we need to find out. I guess just start with David Cameron and try to find out as much about his life as possible.'

'Yeah good, I think we'll need to go further than that though,' Sebastian added.

'What do you mean?'

'We should look at all of the Prime Ministers from the last century. They must all have things in common, universities, school types, clubs, you know, all that kind of stuff.'

'Brilliant, see, you're already showing why it should be you,' Max teased and gave a wry smile.

'Yeah, piss off. You're in trouble when I'm in charge of the country.' He rose from his seat, puffed out his chest to form a mock power pose and pointed down at Max with his finger of authority. Max pretended to cower away. They both laughed.

'You're forgetting who I'm going to be. I'll be the one really in charge,' Max corrected him.

'How do you figure that?'

'I told you, spies know everything. Everything about the government, everything about the politicians. Everything. I'll have access to information that not even Cameron knows. That's where the real power is.'

'Yeah, sure. What about the thing with the paper? Should we both join?'

'What do you think? Probably one of us is enough,' Max mused. 'I'll go and speak to Alistair on Monday and see if I can join and start writing the articles.'

'Actually, yeah. I'll let you deal with Alistair, he's a weirdo. I try and avoid him when I can.'

'He's not so bad. I was in the same class as him in prep school, so I know him pretty well. He'll be fine with me.'

'Rather you than me, anyway. Right, well if all that's out of the way, should we get going?' Sebastian rose from his seat. 'We don't want to be late for the film.'

'Which one did we decide on again?' As Max spoke, he grabbed the notepad from the table and slid it under the sofa, away from prying eyes.

'I can't remember, the girls chose it. Something soppy and romantic, no doubt. Are we going to have to watch another display from you and Harriet this evening?'

Max sensed a pang of jealousy in Sebastian's tone. It was no secret that they had both been keen on Harriet when the two boys met her at a friend's party. That night, Sebastian had struggled to speak to her, while Max had immediately asked the host to introduce him. They had spoken for what felt like hours. It turned out that they had a lot in common: skiing, parents who were doctors, a love of dogs, the list went on. It had only taken a matter of weeks for her and Max to become completely entwined.

Whilst knowing that Sebastian had wanted to ask her out had no bearings on Max's feelings for Harriet, his competitive nature had chalked it up as a win. And he loved to win, especially when it came to competing with his best friend.

'I'm afraid you might, buddy. What can I say? She can't keep her hands off me.' Max gave Sebastian a teasing wink.

4

From the library's first floor balcony, Max could see just about every part of the sprawling school grounds. To his right lay the steeple and clock of the prep school chapel, indicating the east boundary. To his left was the glass conservatory reserved only for those who had the honour to be called sixth formers. Directly in front, now covered in a thick layer of fluffy snow, was the vast grass lawn that served as a cricket pitch and athletics ground, complete with long, triple, and high jump areas.

He'd been quite sure where he would find Alistair at this time in the morning. What he hadn't accounted for was the disruption caused by the snow that had fallen over the previous night. Lucky enough to be given a lift to school by his dad on the way to an early meeting, he'd avoided the walk to the school bus but had paid for it with an earlier arrival time than usual. Even at his normal arrival time of 08:05 the school would be deserted but he often caught a glimpse of Alistair opening up the school library, where the newspaper office was housed. He'd often wondered what motivated Alistair to get up to so early in the morning. Today he would find out.

Having found the main door locked, Max climbed the fire escape leading to the balcony so he could look out across the fresh white carpet sitting on top of the lawn and low buildings that made the giant square campus. Enjoying the cold morning, wrapped in his parka, scarf and hat, he was slightly nervous as his mind ran through what he would say to Alistair. The silence was broken by the soft tapping on the window behind him. He spun to see a confused face staring at him through the glass. Alistair's raised eyebrow and open hands prompted Max's key-turn gesture in return.

With a click of the lock and heavy heave from the boy on the inside, the door reluctantly shimmied open.

'Max, what are you doing out there? You know we're not allowed on the balcony.'

'Good morning to you too, Alistair. It's fine, there's no one around. I just wanted to check out the view. Maybe even throw a few snowballs at the teachers if they catch me.'

Max made his way through the floor to ceiling door before turning to heave it shut. It was clear that this wasn't an item on the maintenance men's priority list by the sheer effort it took him to move the door into a position that suited the slightly rusting twist lock.

'I was actually looking for you, anyway. When I saw you weren't here yet, I thought I'd just hang around.'

Although the two of them had known each other for many years, theirs was a relationship that extended no further than the school gates, not since the days of prep school, at least, when they would see each other at the birthday parties of boys in the class.

'How are you?' Max asked casually.

'Not bad, thanks. What do you need?'

This was something he did remember about Alistair, his directness. He didn't sound rude, just like he was a busy young man who didn't have time for the luxury of idle chit-chat. And from what Max heard, he was a very busy young man. He was assistant to the librarian, not because of his love of reading but because of the access it provided him. The school paper was housed in a side-office that was previously unused, except for the storage of an indiscriminate collection of props and stage backdrops, painted and repainted for the variety of plays and performances held in the grand school hall throughout the school year.

The story was that Alistair had single-handedly persuaded first the librarian, then the Deputy School

Head to allow him to petition the Head Master with his idea to revive the School Newspaper. Of course, strictly speaking it wasn't his idea. He owed part of his current acclaim to his father, Sir James Lovell, the publishing magnate.

Max tried not to focus on the lack of manners being shown and adopted a slightly impish demeanour.

'I'm well. Thanks for asking,' he responded to the absent question, a dry smile on his face. He didn't pause when Alistair realised his mistake and tried to speak. 'I'm wondering if you can do an old boy a favour?'

'That would depend on the favour, old boy.' The last two words from Alistair were laden with sarcasm.

Max found this amusing and jumped straight to the point.

'I need to be on the school paper.'

'We're fully covered at the moment, Max. Maybe next year.' He turned to walk away towards a cart full of books.

'You won't have to do anything.' Max followed him. 'I just need to be part of it. I'm getting hassle from my folks to do some extra-curricular ahead of our final year next year and this is something I want to do. I want to do interviews with famous people and their success stories. Surely that will look great in the school paper?'

'Okay. Can you write?' Alistair asked as he picked up books one at a time, placing them onto the shelves in their rightful place.

Max chuckled, 'Of course I can write, everyone here can.'

'I don't mean "*can you physically write*", idiot. I mean can you write properly, and for a newspaper?'

'Well I know my way around a phrase and I know I'm good at asking questions. As they're going to be interviews, I figured they'll pretty much write themselves.'

Max smiled at his tormentor, sensing his lack of amusement and a desire to protect his precious publication.

'I'm not sure it's really the kind of stuff we're looking for in a school paper. We try to focus on relevant issues and what's going on in the school. How would this be relevant to anyone here?'

Max wasn't sure if it was the idea or him that Alistair was objecting to. If it was the first, then he could talk him round. The second was harder to deal with. But not impossible. He continued to push. 'It'll be inspirational. We see successful and famous people all the time on social media, or TV or movies or whatever, but no one ever really knows what they had to do to get there. I think by showing people, it will maybe open their eyes to new possibilities, you know?' He wasn't sure if he was pitching this right as he watched Alistair's disinterested face. 'And the routes they can take to get there. Not everyone round here knows what they're going to do with their life, like you.'

'What makes you think you know what I want to do with my life?' Alistair challenged as he placed a book on human anatomy back on its shelf.

'Well, I just assumed...'

'You assumed wrong then, didn't you?' Alistair barked before taking a breath. 'Alright, wise-guy, it's an interesting idea, you can give it a go. I'm not guaranteeing that your interview will be published but let's see what you can do. Who did you have in mind for your first interview?'

'David Cameron.' Max was matter-of-fact.

'What! How the fuck do you expect to get an interview with *him*?'

Max now had his undivided attention. 'Well, that's the other favour. I was hoping you might be able to help me there.'

'Ah, now it's two favours you need? Don't you think if I had the chance to interview David Cameron I would have done it myself?'

'Have you tried?'

'Yeah,' his response was instant, and clearly a lie.

'No, you haven't, Alistair.'

'Well, he's not going to just do an interview with some school kid. He'd be far too busy for that.'

'But you haven't tried, so how do you know?'

'Okay, I haven't tried. But only because it's a crazy idea.'

Max was getting used to that phrase but wasn't put off. 'I even have a way to sell it as something different. I want to call it, '*David: Inspiration for the next generation*'. I want to do a biographical interview with him and look at the decisions he made in his life to get him to where he is now. You know, inspire the next generation to become interested in politics.'

'It's not bad.'

'I'd like to try. You never know. I'll do the work, you don't have to anything,' he paused, 'unless you want to?' He raised one eyebrow and tilted his head subtly.

Alistair hesitated and Max watched him closely. He could see a thought process taking place in Alistair's inquisitive brain and slowly Max knew he had won.

Alistair didn't talk in school about what his dad did as he thought people would treat him differently knowing who his father was. But in an institution like this nothing was secret. Sir James Lovell himself had founded the school newspaper during his time there. At age fifteen, he'd met with the School Head and negotiated a trip to London with another member of the paper to attend the State Funeral of Winston Churchill and cover it for the school paper. From there, he went on to start what would become one of the largest publishing houses in the world, acquiring company after company around the world in his bid to spread his brand of honesty in publishing. By the age of thirty-five, his meteoric rise had earned him the honour of being named Time's Man of the Year, and an article called "James Lovell: the new empire on which the sun never sets".

Max knew very well who Alistair's father was and that if he hoped to speak with the Prime Minister, someone like James Lovell was the best chance he would get.

Alistair turned away and started walking round the landing towards the newspaper office. 'I may be able to help, I'm not promising anything though.' He didn't look back.

'Help how?' Max shouted after him.

'Leave me to it. I'll come and find you later if I manage to sort anything.'

Max wasn't sure what had just happened. He had thought Alistair would point-blank refuse but it seemed he'd incensed something within the young man. He didn't know what Alistair was about to do but he hoped it was to make a call to someone important.

5

Max and Sebastian looked down out of the first-floor window at the party going on below them. This was the civilised hour before debauchery began. Revellers were still arriving, either dropped off by their parents or walking from the nearest bus stop. The sagging shoulders of those walking betrayed the weight of their cargo in plastic bags. One or more had managed to convince the lucky individual that happened to be serving in the off-license that night that they were genuinely of age to legally buy alcohol. Of course, there were also those who relied not so heavily on alcohol for a good time, but on the more medicinal options available. Ironically, these were much easier to procure.

Max and Sebastian would normally have shouted welcomes to the newcomers but, on this occasion, they wanted some time to discuss progress. It was only earlier that morning that Max had met with Alistair in the library. He'd still heard nothing of the interview.

'Do you think he called his dad?' Sebastian asked.

'I hope so. Imagine if he was able to make it happen.'

'I doubt it, who even is his dad anyway? I've heard of him but don't know what he does.'

'My mum was at a dinner party at his mum's house a while ago. She said the walls were full of photos of their family with all kinds of famous people, politicians, film stars and authors, all types. He owns one of the biggest publishing houses in the world. Lives all over the place since he divorced Alistair's mum. I heard he has a superyacht worth £100 mill and he keeps it in Monaco. That's where Alistair spends all his holidays.'

'£100 mill? Fuck off! He must be absolutely loaded! How did I not know this? I've spent the last five years in school with a kagillionnaire and didn't have a clue.' Sebastian was shaking his head.

'You're obviously just not in the know, pal. I text him after I saw him and invited him here tonight. He never normally comes to these, although he does randomly know loads of the girls from the girls' school.'

'Did he text you back?'

'Yeah, said he might come by. I asked if he had any news but got silence after that.'

'Well it's obvious, right? He couldn't have managed it already, could he?'

'I don't know, but I'm starting to like him. What do you think about him as the next recruit?'

Regardless of the openly hostile conversation that had taken place in the library, Max liked Alistair's bluntness. He thought it might help to keep the group grounded. Or its two existing members anyway.

'Well, if we're looking for power and influence, it sounds like he fits like a glove.' Sebastian agreed. 'Let's see if he shows up tonight and then you can talk to him and I'll see what he's like. How do we tell him after that? Do you think he'll be interested?'

'I hope so. And yeah, there was something in his eye today when I talked about meeting the Prime Minister. I think he was pissed off that he'd never thought about doing it himself. There's a rebel in him, he loves a challenge.'

'Fine, just be sure that he wants in before you tell him completely about the idea. Not a soul outside can know of the group.' Sebastian mocked Max's speech about secrecy.

'Of course. Let's see if he turns up and has any news and we can decide from there.'

'Okay, good. Are we done?' Sebastian asked. He peeked out the window. 'Perfect timing, there's Emily and Charlotte.'

The two girls laughing intensely as they sauntered

up the driveway went to Oxton girls', which was twinned with Oxton Boys' School that Max and Sebastian attended.

With a mischievous smile, Sebastian beckoned his friend. 'Let's go have some fun.'

They had both been to this house enough times to know where the bulk of the party would be. As they slid open the heavy oak bedroom doors to step into the large open gallery, the beat hit them. Don't Let Me Down by the Chainsmokers flowed through the open double conservatory doors at the back of the house. They descended the stairs and walked through the hallway covered in family photos and animal art, out through the conservatory doors and climbed the stairs to the pool, all the time the music growing louder and louder, now mixed with laughter, shouting, and splashing. They arrived to the usual scene: lines of shots on the long wooden table sitting between the water and the pool house.

Sarah's parties were legendary. Her parents' house was amazing and perfectly set up for these kinds of events. There was a heated pool, a pool house, a tennis court, a massive trampoline and, best of all, alcohol. One of their family businesses was a wholesale booze importer and distributor. One third of their three car garage was at any one time full to the gunwales with wine, champagne and spirits. Luckily for John and Carolyn, Sarah's parents, teenagers of this age hadn't acquired the taste for champagne or wine yet, but the spirits did have a habit of disappearing every time they were away on holiday. This time it was their supply of Sambuca that had been pilfered by the gang and now lay flaming in a line surrounded by fresh, excited young faces.

And so, the evening continued. The bass intensified along with the shouts and laughter. Beer and sambuca lifted the guests' spirits and everyone was enjoying a good time. Groups had started to spread across the house; locked bedroom doors guarded ever increasing nakedness and nervous deeds done for the first or second time. There was one locked door behind which was not nakedness but a proposal of a different kind.

Max had found Alistair on the tennis court with three girls. They were playing drinking tennis. If you messed up a shot, you drank, and by the looks of it the group had missed a fair number of shots. Alistair looked pretty handy with a racquet and was by far the least hindered by alcohol, impressing the girls with his skills. He laughed and joked with his partner, Helena, a tall, elegant girl of Greek descent. Her long dark curls bounced off her shoulders as she played a range of badly timed air shots. Every time, both she and Alistair would explode with laughter. Max felt bad interrupting but he needed only fifteen minutes of his time so he stepped into the middle of court and shouted to the players.

'Ladies, I can't tell whether you are terribly drunk, or just terrible at tennis. Alistair here is putting you all to shame, although I have enjoyed your choice of outfits.'

The girls had previously been in the pool and were still wearing just bikinis. He was met with exactly the reaction you would expect from a drunken bunch – shouts and jeers. One of them ran over to punch him in the arm while Alistair's partner hit her mark with the ball for the first time that night. As the ball bounced off Max's shoulder he raised his hands in surrender while laughing and grabbed the nearest girl to him, partly to ask forgiveness for his flirtation but mostly as a human shield from the stick that was now coming his way.

'I need to borrow Alistair for a minute,' he announced loudly. 'Don't worry, Helena, he'll be back to find you shortly.'

Helena smiled at Alistair whilst he rolled his eyes at Max, shaking his head at his new friend's attempt to embarrass him. He turned to the ladies, still smiling, and shouted over the music, 'Excuse him. I'll be back soon to continue the lesson.'

With that, he walked towards the narrow gate that

led off the court. Max joined him at the opening and as soon as they were out of sight. Alistair punched him in the arm.

'Cheers for that, buddy.' Alistair was in a good mood despite the violence.

'Well I needed to get your attention somehow. So, what news do you have for me?'

After collecting more drinks from the table by the pool, they headed to the same room in which Max and Sebastian had held their earlier conversation. The music outside swelled to epic proportions and could now be heard no matter where you were in the house.

'Well, my first reaction when you asked earlier was spot on,' Alistair started. 'It's a ludicrous idea. I spoke with a couple of people at my dad's company and they laughed when I first asked them about it.'

'Shit.' Max was dejected. 'Fair enough, I knew it was a long shot. So, it's not going to happen?'

'I didn't say that. You're going to have to stop assuming things, Max. After they stopped laughing and I was allowed to explain the concept, you know, your "inspiration for a generation" bit I saw a glimmer of hope. It appears that old Cameron is in need of some good PR. They thought that Westminster might go for it. They said we'd have to wait until next week before she can make any calls as it's Friday.'

'Who's "she"?' Max probed.

'Oh, sorry, thought I mentioned that. Dickla. She's—'

Max interrupted him. 'Dickla? What kind of name is that?'

'I know, that always used to crack me up too. She's Chief Editor at one of my dad's magazines. The name's South African. She's great, and really hot too. Anyway, once I'd explained your idea she sounded quite intrigued. She's going to let me know next week if there's anything she can do. She did have a couple of suggestions, although I have a feeling they were more like demands.'

'Go on.'

'Well, depending on how well it goes, they'd like to cover it too. Maybe publish it in one of their publications.'

'Hmmm,' Max nodded slowly, 'there may be a slight problem with that.'

'I'm not sure they'll help us if we say no to their first condition!'

'Well, I need to tell you something. And ask you something, actually. But it has to be between you and me. You can't tell anyone else, and I mean *anyone*.'

'Okay.' Alistair replied with a hint of curiosity and wariness in his tone.

Without hesitation, Max changed the subject and launched into a set of carefully planned out questions.

'How often do you see your dad?'

Max had known after the first time he and Alistair had spoken that he would be having this conversation with him at some point. And he knew he absolutely needed to convince him. If he couldn't, he risked the whole plan before it was even out of the gate. He had run though this moment numerous times, his whole afternoon in school disappearing whilst he stared out of windows thinking about how to lure Alistair in.

The thought had occurred to use Alistair's father as an example of the power someone could achieve alone, and stress how much more power was up for stake if you had similar people spread across various areas of industry and government. He had toyed with the idea of trying to manipulate Alistair by challenging him to be as good as his father, as powerful. He knew this would be risky, though. If Alistair saw through the tactic, he would not be left with a favourable impression of Max. He decided the best way was to engage Alistair and use his own desires for the future as the backbone for his reason to be part of the group.

'Maybe a few times a year. He's away a lot so I don't see him here that much. It's mostly when we go and spend time with him on holiday.'

'Do you ever ask him about his work?'

'Yeah, I talk about it a lot with him actually. It's really interesting. He has some amazing stories. Whenever we go out for dinner, he amazes the whole table with tales about who he's met, or had drunken nights with, the places he's been. Some of the situations he was in when he was younger are crazy.'

'Really, like what?'

Before he answered, Alistair walked over to window and opened it as wide as it would go, repeating the same with the rest of the windows in the room. He took a seat on the long dresser facing out of the main long window and pulled a small green case from his pocket. Flipping the lid expertly, he pulled out what appeared to Max to be a rolled cigarette.

'I didn't know you smoked, Alistair.'

'Oh, I don't. Not fags, anyway. It's a joint. Don't tell me you've never smoked hash, Max?'

'No, I haven't actually. I'm kind of surprised that you have.'

'There you go assuming again. There's a lot you don't know about me, Max. I don't do it a lot but once in a while it's quite relaxing. It's all over the place in Jamaica. A Rasta taught me how to roll when I was there last year.'

He pulled a shiny brass Zippo lighter from his

pocket and flicked it into life, igniting the end of the joint with the bright orange flame, pulling the thick smoke into his lungs before blowing it out towards the window. The sweet, floral scent hit Max's nose immediately, making him recoil.

'Wow, that stinks.'

'Why do you think I opened the windows?' Alistair smiled. 'Do you want to try some?'

'What will it do to me?' Max asked, cautiously.

'Nothing bad. It just gives you a buzz, makes you a little lightheaded. Try some if you want. I'm not forcing you.'

In the spirit of trying to bond with a potential new group member, he leant forward and took the joint from Alistair's hand.

'Okay, but if I freak out I'm going to blame you.'

Alistair laughed. 'If you do, I've got you.'

That was the type of mentality Max wanted in a member. He gingerly raised it to his lips and mimicked what he'd seen Alistair do only moments ago. As soon as it hit his lungs, he exploded into a coughing fit. Alistair, who had been watching carefully, laughed hard.

'Don't worry, that happened to me the first time as well. Try again but this time, don't inhale so hard. Just do a bit.'

After the first coughing fit subsided, Max raised

the joint to his mouth once more and this time sucked a small amount into his lungs, once again coughing but not quite as hard. With eyes red from the involuntary reaction, he handed the spliff back. Suppressing the urge to cough again, he tried to get back on track.

He coughed again, once more. 'You were about to tell me about your dad's crazy tales.'

'Oh yeah.' Alistair continued, 'He told me about this time he was out in the States trying to set up one of his magazines over there. They were having a hard time and they didn't have much money then, so they rented an old car and were staying in dodgy motels. They hit one town on their trip from New York over to LA. They'd always heard of the famous route 66 so they drove out to Chicago where it started and followed it across the US. They stopped in a really redneck town one night and checked into a cheap looking place. There was a girl who ran the desk and dad's partner took a shine to her. They were both young and, from what I hear, quite a hit with the ladies, especially over there. She'd probably never heard an English accent. Anyway, so Dick stayed at the reception desk talking to the girl whilst dad went and found the room. After about ten minutes dad said he started to hear noises outside his room so went to the window.' Alistair started to laugh as he continued the story.

'When he looked out the window he could see their car, parked about twenty feet away, bouncing from side to side, groans coming from inside. Anyway, dad was used to Dick's shenanigans so went back to whatever he was doing. About five minutes later he heard a gunshot outside so raced to the window again to see Dick being dragged out of the car by his feet.'

By now, Alistair could barely tell the story because he was laughing so hard. The joint had obviously started to kick in because Max was starting to giggle as well.

'It took two of them to drag him kicking and screaming out of the car, his trousers were around his ankles and the girl was standing shouting at the men, trying to cover herself up. She started hitting one of them and in the commotion, Dick tried to get up and run away, but because of his trousers, he just kept falling over. Dad said watching his friend, terrified, trying to get away from these guys was the funniest thing he's ever seen. It turned out the girl had switched shifts with her twin sister that night and her sister's boyfriend had called round and assumed it was his girlfriend in the car. It was lucky they hadn't shot him before they realised it was a mistake. In the end, the rednecks ended up buying them all dinner at the steakhouse next door to apologise.'

'That's hilarious, in hindsight. I'm not so sure it

would have been that fun at the time. So, is that why you're on the paper? Because of your dad?'

'Yeah, it is. He'd like me to follow in his footsteps and take over the company one day.' Alistair exhaled smoke and rolled his eyes.

'You don't seem so sure?'

'I would love to run the company. It's amazing you know, when you see their headquarters in London. It's great. He's like a king to the guys who work for him.'

'And you want to be part of it?'

'Yes and no. I've been toying with the idea of doing Medicine.'

'Really?'

Max saw an opportunity here. Being the son of doctors, he had a unique insight into their lives and how hard they worked but he wasn't going to push too hard over this first conversation.

'What attracts you to medicine?'

'I like the idea of helping people. You know, saving lives and making a difference.'

'You don't feel like your dad makes a difference?'

'Yeah, I guess, but in a different way. They publish books which people enjoy, their papers and magazines help to educate people, so yeah, they do. But they don't get to experience the joy, or relief, or thanks of the people they help.'

Max watched as Alistair took a big draw, coughing slightly as he exhaled. His response had been exactly what Max was hoping for. Though his mind was starting to become a little foggy, he tried to concentrate.

'What if I told you there was another way you could help people? And many, many more than you could ever in a lifetime as a doctor.'

'I'm listening.' Alistair seemed less combative than he had been at the start of their conversation.

'To steal from one of the greats,' Max continued, '"I have a dream". And it's a big one. I can't say too much about it here, but I'd like you to come over to my house tomorrow if you're about. Not for long, I'll tell you all about it. I need to ask two things of you now, though.'

Alistair looked at him through narrowed, inquisitive eyes. At Max's last statement, he simply nodded.

'Firstly, you can't mention it to anyone. Obviously, you can say you're coming to mine if anyone asks but don't tell them why.'

'I don't bloody know why I'm coming yet, do I?'

'Good point, but don't mention what we talked about here tonight. It will all become clear tomorrow.'

'Sounds very mysterious. And what was the second thing?'

'How well do you know Sebastian?'

'Not that well, really. We've had a couple of classes together but he's more in with your lot, isn't he? Never really spoken to him apart from in school.'

'Yeah, he only came in first year. I'm trying to introduce him to a few new people. He'll be there tomorrow so we can all chat then. The second thing I need from you is an open mind. I need to fully explain before you make any decisions. Will you allow me that?'

'Of course, I can't wait to hear all about it. It's all very cryptic.'

'Good, I'll text you the address.'

'I know where it is, Max. My mum points it out every time we drive past it.'

'Right then, let's go find that little filly, I wouldn't want to spoil your night.'

'She is something. I do have a girlfriend though. How about you, do you have your eye on anyone?'

'Oh yes. I have something special waiting for me later.'

With this, they opened the doors and re-joined the party.

6

By 12:30am, the party was still in full-flow, but Max's interest was starting to wane. In his mind he was somewhere else, and very shortly the rest of his body would follow him there. Anyone watching him would see his face illuminated by the white light coming from the screen of his iPhone as he stared at it endlessly. What a viewer would not see was the content of the conversation being bounced from phone through the cell mast half a mile away which relayed the signal through the air to another cell mast approximately six kilometres away in Oxton village and into the receiver of the Samsung sat in Harriet's soft hands. By this point Max and Harriet had been seeing each other for a few months and took every opportunity they could to be with each other.

Harriet: 'I can't wait to see you. xxx'

Max: 'Well you should hurry up and get home then! x'

Harriet: 'I won't be long, I'm just waiting for a taxi. xxx'

Max: 'Okay. I'll set off shortly, it will only take me ten minutes to walk to yours. I've been thinking about you all night. x'

Harriet: 'Really? :) what have you been thinking about? xxx'

Max: 'I'll show you when you get here. x'

Harriet: 'Tell me now! xxx'

Max: 'I can't wait to kiss your lips and hold your hips, before slowly sliding them round to your bum, feeling you in my hands. x'

Harriet: 'Max!!!!!'

Max: 'Sorry, I've had a bit to drink at the party :) What are you wearing? x'

Harriet: 'A dress, why? xxx'

Max: 'Which one? x'

Harriet: 'My bright blue one, why? xxx'

Max: 'I'm looking forward to taking it off! x'

Harriet: 'Max, you're being naughty. Who says I'll let you?!?xxx'

Max: 'Okay, I'll be good. Promise :) How far away are you? X'

Harriet: '2 minutes away. xxx'

Max: 'Thank god! I can't wait any longer. x'

Max stood and waited at the top of the set of five stone stairs leading up to the front door from the driveway of the big house surrounded by woods. He'd been here many times and knew the house and the grounds well. On this occasion, Harriet's mum had taken her sister away on a spa weekend for her birthday. Unlike last week, there would be no surprises tonight.

Waiting excitedly, he finally saw headlights and the steep paved driveway and front of the house was illuminated in the bright white light. Max stood at the top of the stairs, grinning. If he hadn't been for the blinding light he would have seen her giddy face smiling back at him. She hurriedly paid the taxi driver, already having the cash waiting in her hand. Harriet turned toward the stairs and as she walked she bowed her head as she raised her shoulders. She swung her bag in front of her. Max loved the way she acted shy every time they first saw each other. She started to climb the stairs one at a time before jumping up the last few, flinging her bag to the floor. They wrapped their arms around each other and kissed deeply, their hands running all over each other's bodies. Suddenly, Harriet stopped kissing and pulled away, a naughty look in her eye. She turned her body around, still keeping eye contact, and bent over to pick up her bag, revealing just how short her dress was. Max reached out a hand to touch her but she teasingly jumped out of reach and ran towards the front door, laughing. Max shook his head with amusement before chasing her, poking her as he caught up with her.

He wrapped his arms around her stomach and kissed the back of her neck, pulling her towards him as she rummaged through her bag to find her keys. She moaned as she finally pulled them out of her bag and pushed one into the lock on the third attempt. He could feel tremors running through her legs which made it all the more difficult. The door sprang open and once again she flung her bag to the floor, now turning to meet his lips. He pushed her backward, never letting his lips leave hers and, in this fashion, they climbed the stairs together, clumsily. As they reached her room, she put one hand to his chest and stepped away from him. He wasn't sure what to expect next. He was surprised, and slightly disappointed when she reached down and slowly started to pull up her dress. Before she had it above her waist he stopped her.

'I was looking forward to doing that.'

He softly took hold of her hand, opening it, allowing the thin material to slip from her grasp and return to its starting position so that he could have the honour of de-robing her.

After what felt like hours of teasing and playing, they both lay satisfied on the bed, the light from the moon casting a radiant glow throughout the room. Harriet slowly slid to the edge of the mattress, lifting herself from the comfort to move towards the bathroom. Max watched her walk, naked on her tiptoes, her hips shuffling from side to side. As she reached the door, she paused, allowing him the pleasure of one last look before she disappeared behind the door frame.

A minute later, she came back out of the bathroom to find him deep in thought, now lying on his back gazing out of the window.

'What's on your mind?' she asked as she lit a tall white candle on the window sill.

'I'm just thinking about something that happened tonight. Have you ever met Alistair Lovell?'

'Yeah, I know him a little. Mum knows his mum quite well. We used to see a lot of him when we were kids but haven't really spoken to him for a while. Why?'

'I've had an idea. And I want him to be part of it. I had a chat with him tonight about it.'

'What do you mean by "an idea"?' she asked as she climbed down onto the bed, cuddling up next to him, resting her head on his chest.

'You'll think it's stupid.' He felt a little embarrassed to tell her, wondering what she would think.

'Why would I think that?'

'Well, it's a bit grand, to say the least.' He wondered how much he could tell her given that he'd been the one to swear Sebastian to secrecy. He convinced himself it was okay to just give her the outline of the plan.

'Oh, come on, you know I like that you're "grand".' She reached down with her left hand and rested her palm on his crotch as she giggled. He smiled, appreciatively.

When talking with Sebastian and Alistair about the idea he always felt like he was selling it, to both them, and himself. With Harriet, he wanted her to fall in love with his ambition.

'I want to take over the world.'

He let the words hang and observed a slightly confused look cross her face as she twisted her head so that she could see his.

'Plain and simple, I want to be part of a group that takes over the world. And not to destroy it but to make it better. Have you ever heard anything about space travel and humans going to Mars?' His speech was excited.

'Well, of course I've heard of it, but I don't really know anything about it.'

He leant up on his side so he could look at her as he was talking. 'Okay. So, I watched a documentary which talked about how big plans, you know projects that cost billions of dollars, like space travel or solving global warming, have to be completed within ten years, or they probably won't happen.'

'Alright, but why?'

'It said that massive projects that cost that much

and take that much time, if the timeline is too long, there's a chance that political changes and pressure will cause the project to be shelved, possibly even after millions have been spent on it. One example is going to Mars. There's a guy in the States who's obsessed with sending humans there, but he knows that we have to use existing technology and go straight there rather than build new technology and do the journey in stages. The problem is that he can't get any of NASA to sign off on the trip because the people who have to review and approve it all know that if his project goes ahead, it will make their projects useless. For example, they want a plan that incorporates their multi-billion-dollar lunar base as a launch pad for the Mars mission. They know that if he comes up with a way to go straight there that they won't get to build their moon base.'

'Okay, so your plan is to go to Mars?' Harriet asked with a genuine look of confusion.

'No. Well not right now anyway. Maybe one day that could be part of the plan, I guess. I mean that it's an example of why something that should be done, like exploring our solar system, isn't being done because of political and financial issues getting in the way. How many other issues are there that aren't being dealt with because of red tape and politics? Take global warming, do we really think that by telling people to recycle and use energy efficient light bulbs that we'll stop what's happening? Of course not, it will take a much bigger effort than that. It needs governments and big companies to work together to reduce our emissions globally. Have you ever noticed that no one ever talks about the Earth's population and reducing it even though it's undeniably linked with global warming?'

'Why would controlling the population help?'

'If there are seven billion people on the planet today and we emit say ten billion tonnes of CO_2 into the atmosphere every year, if that population rises to fourteen billion then we'd expect our emissions to be twenty billion tonnes per year.'

'But can you really tell people not to have children?'

'Why not? The Chinese did it. I just think it's interesting that it's an obvious solution, but I've never even heard about it being discussed as a possible option. You would think that someone somewhere would be at least looking at it. I think the problem is that everyone is so concerned with saving the Earth for their kids that they don't realise that their children will become one additional source contributing to the issue. The point I'm making is that, even though that is one way to solve the problem, or at least stop it from getting worse, not a single politician on the planet has the courage to say it because they know that people would react badly. I'm not saying that it's the right answer, I'm simply saying that it's an option that is not being considered because it would be political suicide to have it out there.

'That is the fundamental problem, politics is popularity. Not intelligence, or success, or really making a change. It's merely the most palatable solution rather than the right one. They're so obsessed with their own careers and success that they'll only put ideas forward that they think people will like or will get them voted into power. They avoid anything that could impact them negatively.

'Anyway, I digress. What I want to do is form a group of people who will act in the best interest of the country and the world and make sure that things get better instead of worse.'

'Okay, but how will the group have the ability to change things like that?'

Max's excitement was taking over and the deal he made with himself was quickly starting to unravel, forgotten in his desire to speak his mind. 'That's where it gets good. Each person will be assigned a role or a job. And then they'll have to do anything it takes to get there.'

'Like what?'

He saw the cynicism in her eyes.

'No,' he exclaimed and laughed at the same time. 'Nothing bad. I told you. The whole idea is to make things better. All the others will help each other out and make sure that every person gets to where they need to be. Once we're there, we'll be able to actually do things that can make real changes happen, without all the bureaucracy getting in the way.'

'I'm not sure I understand. What would the roles be and how would they help you to do that?'

'It's a pretty ambitious plan, I'm aware of that so don't laugh. But these are the types of people who you would need.'

He started with the big gun, knowing it would provoke a reaction from Harriet.

'Prime Minister.'

Just as he had with Sebastian, he paused, awaiting a reaction. He looked at her carefully as he did. And then he saw it. Her eyes widened and as she smiled she lowered her head. A moment of confusion washed over her face as she tried to assess whether he was joking. She was now staring into his eyes, but he didn't flinch. She silently tried to extract information from him by changing her expression from confusion to pleading, eventually reaching out for his hand and breaking the silence.

'How in the world do you think you could become Prime Minister, Max?'

'I thought you'd never ask. This isn't something that I just thought up five minutes ago. How many people our age out there are seriously talking about becoming the Prime Minister of the United Kingdom? Not many, maybe a few. But how many of them are part of a group of people all supporting each other, all working towards the same goal to ensure it succeeds? How many of them are working with like-minded people to make sure that nothing stops each and every one of them getting to where they need to be?'

'Well when you put it that way, I see your point. But how? It's easy to have an idea like that but imagine how many things could happen that could stop it.'

'You're right. And that's why the group would be there. We all work together, do the research, make the plans, and if anything happens we have all our collective minds all working to solve whatever it is. Obviously, we can't guarantee that we will all be successful but those of us who can make it to those positions will help the others.'

'So, what are you going to do that will get you to Downing Street?'

'Me? Oh no, I'm not going to be Prime Minister. I have a much more interesting job in mind.'

She laughed with derision. 'What could be more interesting than being Prime Minister?'

'Being a spy master. I'm going to be head of the security services. A real-life James Bond.'

'You know it's not really like that, all guns and chases.'

'How would you know?!' he teased. 'Have you never heard of the Cambridge five? That all sounded pretty exciting to me!'

He proceeded to tell her the stories he'd read about Kim Philby and how he evaded being discovered whilst working for the Russians, all the while actually working undercover as part of the Secret Intelligence Service, his rise through the ranks and his eventual defection.

He had spent the last few weeks reading everything he could about MI5 and MI6 and the characters that had flowed through their doors. His fascination had continued to grow as he learned more old tales from when the intelligence services were fledgling groups, the Home Section and the Foreign Section, combatting the threat of Germany's expanding military. He found the bravery of these men and women to be remarkable, it seemed there was nothing they weren't prepared to do in the service of their country. Many had died at the hands of foreign spies, never to be seen again by their families, some generic story fed back to their parents, very little recognition conveyed at all. The nature of the organisations meant that details about operations had to be kept secret.

He followed the progression through the first world war and onto the second, the new challenges faced by a new style of war. Technology had changed dramatically in the twenty-one years between the end of the first and the start of the second, and the agencies were the tip of the spear, intercepting transmissions and working day and night to decrypt them in the rooms of the Government Code and Cypher School at Bletchley Park. From here he would move to the rising threat of Communism and the stalemate that was the Cold War. Years of suspicion on both sides, years of double agents and double crossing, betrayal and murder. It was captivating.

The modern threat, he knew, was very different. This brought him full circle to his new-found purpose in life. SIS would be out there right now, tracking ISIS and Al Qaeda targets around the world, trying their hardest to make sure that nothing like the events of September 11, 2001, would ever happen in Britain.

'It sounds fascinating. And ludicrous. Do you know how many things have to happen in someone's life to get them all the way to Downing Street? How do you know so much about all this anyway?'

Max sat on the edge of the bed as he let adventures flow from his mouth and brain. The naked Harriet lay spread prostrate on the bed, challenging every statement he made, forcing him to defend his position on each of his arguments.

After what felt like hours of back and forth, debating and discussing ideas, she rose and walked to the bathroom once more, returning with two glasses of water. He watched as she came back into the room, crossing the beams of white light that illuminated first her face and then her body as she moved through them. Max sat silent as she approached, taking in every inch of her. She set the glasses down on the bedside table before moving round the bed to stand in front of him. His mind was now far from the plan and as she stood between his legs looking down at him, he gently ran his fingers up the side of her thighs, instantly feeling her tremor. The pair fell back on the bed once again, kissing and letting passion of their debate take hold of them.

7

Although it was hard to leave Harriet alone, cocooned in her white, Egyptian cotton sheets, one of the joys of being up so early on a Saturday was feeling like the rest of world had somehow vanished into thin air overnight. Free from noise and chaos.

Rather than call a taxi, Max decided to walk home in the fresh spring air, taking a detour towards the Heswall shoreline so that he could revel in the sun's early rays, undisturbed in his thoughts. As he trotted along the sand exposed by the low tide, his mind ran over the previous night, replaying every minute of his time in Harriet's bedroom, a discernible smile painted on his face.

Reaching home, he walked over the gravel leading up to the front door of his parents' house and switched his mind to the day ahead. Alistair and Sebastian had not spent any real time together outside of school and this was something that Max would need to remedy if they were to become as close as he would need them to. The first step was today's meeting. The first of many, he hoped. It was important not only to ensure that Sebastian and Alistair hit it off, but also that Alistair bought into the idea. If their meeting in the library yesterday had been anything to go by, he knew Alistair had an inquisitive mind and was open to a challenge. What he didn't know was whether his mind could be changed from the path on which it was already set. The desire to help, which is apparent in all medical staff, is one that is innate and would not easily be broken. Only through convincing the aspiring doctor that Max was offering the opportunity to make more of an impact on peoples' lives would there be any hope of diverting his course.

In preparation, he listed any potential objections and questions that Alistair might raise, and for each he rehearsed his response. As well as the research into the roles and careers that he and Sebastian had identified, Max thought it would also be useful to upskill himself in negotiating tactics. After his first conversations about his grand scheme, it had become quickly apparent that not everyone would share the same confidence in his vision. Maybe rightly so. However, this only gave him more drive to learn how to overcome these hurdles.

He thought back to his conversation with Harriet only hours earlier. He'd made a point that was undisputable. How many people out there at this stage of their lives were putting the wheels in motion to elevate someone to the most powerful position in the country? They had the opportunity to plan every detail down to the letter. She'd pushed him, challenged him and questioned him. He found it thrilling to debate with her. Her intellect allowed her to call him out on any bullshit and he'd found himself tied in knots trying to defend a position to which she had taken the opposing side. She'd filled him with self-doubt at the same time as inspiring a stubbornness in him that made him want to succeed even more.

The next step was using the same stubbornness to convince Alistair and help him to open his mind to the possibilities.

Having invited Alistair to come slightly earlier than Sebastian, he would use their time alone to warm him up and give him the basics. Sebastian would be the back-up, helping to show how much thought they'd put in so far.

The challenges in bringing anyone new on board were numerous but the first was helping move someone forward from the initial disbelief in the grandeur of what was being attempted. So easy was it to hear the words 'Prime Minister' or 'Head of Intelligence' and allow an instant wall to be erected in the mind. Max had some experience in this approach and with the very same person only twenty-four hours earlier. Only the last time the most powerful man in the country had been spoken about it was in a different context. That time they wanted to talk with him, this time they wanted to be him.

What made this easier was that Alistair was going to be asked to fulfil a role that he was familiar with and one that he'd been exposed to for many years. It would be a natural progression for son to follow father, to want the same success, money and power. He was more than capable of becoming the successor to one of the largest publishing houses in the world. Focus on that reality now would only ensure that he would be more prepared and more successful. He could use the time to harvest every scrap of knowledge and experience from his father, learn from his mistakes and how to avoid them. His network, which he had been establishing over the course of his life without knowing it, would penetrate circles that few even know exist. The more Max thought about it, the more it made sense.

He spent the morning playing his drums, his headphones blocking the outside world and allowing his imagination to run amok. From Foo Fighters and

Alabama Shakes, to Muse and Metallica, he had created playlists of his favourite music and knew every beat
perfectly. His kit was his proudest possession and he
had spent years adding to it, changing it, adjusting it.
It was his workshop. Today was especially stunning and
the orange light beamed through the Velux skylight directly onto him and his noisy entourage. By the time
he was finished, the sweat ran down his naked torso
and he was in need of a shower.

Washed and dressed, he made his way back to the
studio space and waited for his companions. The familiar crunch outside signalled the arrival of the first
and he leapt to his feet to admire whichever new sports
car Alistair's mum would be driving. He was not disappointed. The unmistakeable grill of the black Aston
Martin Vanquish appeared around the curved driveway and stopped. Max realised Alistair had not been to
his hideaway, so he ran down the stairs and the hundred yards to where the car had come to rest. Alistair
had wandered to the front door and pushed the small
round white bell button set in a round plate of steel.
Max's mother had just opened it and greeted the young
man, already expecting his arrival. Looking out over
his shoulder she spotted the car and, placing her arm
around Alistair made her way to invite his mother in for
tea. Max rolled his eyes and smiled before motioning

to Alistair to leave the mothers to their refreshments.

As Alistair climbed the stairs to the open space, he immediately locked onto the drum kit, as did everyone who had climbed the steps for the first time before him. Max knew the look and experience told him that the attention of his guest would not be fully his until their curiosity was satisfied. Sticks in hand, Alistair started to bang randomly, eventually forming some semblance of a beat. Five minutes later, not making much progress, he retired from the leather drum stool and joined Max on the couches.

'So, come on, what's this all about?' Alistair started.

'Straight to the point! Well then. Where to start?'

'At the beginning, maybe?' The sarcasm poured out, accompanied by a subtle smile.

'Do you remember the assignment I had to give in history class? The one about terrorism?'

'Yeah, just about.'

'Nice to know you were paying attention. Well do you remember what I said about the 9/11 attacks in New York?'

'Yeah, I remember you talking about them.'

'Have you ever seen the footage of it happening?'

'Yeah, of course. There's documentaries about it every year around the time it happened.'

'Do you think it was terrorists?' Max asked.

'Of course, who else would it have been?'

'I heard a theory, read about it rather. The theory suggests that it wasn't terrorists but some kind of inside job by the Americans. Did you know there was another building that collapsed?'

'You mean the second tower?'

'No, not the second tower. I mean there was a third building that collapsed that day. One that shouldn't have. It was seen collapsing seven hours after the second tower fell, exactly as if it had been demolished by professionals.'

'No way. Seriously? Why have I not heard about it?'

'Exactly. It wasn't massively talked about, but it happened. Clear as day, there's a video showing the whole thing collapsing in on its own footprint, straight down. It doesn't lurch or topple, the whole thing just sinks into the ground.'

'I need to see this…'

'I'll show you that, and more.' Max grabbed his iPad from the table and opened Google Chrome. He typed as he showed Alistair various videos and articles that supported what he was telling him.

'So, what are you saying? The Americans did it?'

'I'm not saying they did it. What I am saying though is that the story is not as it seems. We have been lied to. I don't know whether they did it or they allowed it to happen so that they could start a war. I don't think we'll ever truly know. I really wish we did.'

'Okay, so this what you wanted to talk about? A conspiracy theory?'

'Not quite. I wanted to start you thinking about what is possible.'

It was clear from the tone of voice and the look on the face of his guest that a fair amount of scepticism would need to be overcome.

'Just imagine *if* a group of people inside the US government had engineered that situation, *were* able to engineer that situation. What kind of people do you think they would have to be?'

'Masterminds. Geniuses. Psychopaths. Traitors.'

As he talked he stared straight ahead, thinking. Max could see that he was at least trying to comprehend whether something like that was possible. The fact that he had not instantly dismissed it was a win, for now.

'Agreed,' Max continued, 'it's hard to fathom how someone could do it. Why someone would do it is an entirely different question. But I do know one thing, that it had to be as small a group as possible. One capable of carrying it out but small enough to be able to control. Imagine a world where decisions that affect so many are made by just a select few. Do you believe that's possible?'

'Of course. It's called politics.'

'Ha, I like how you think, Alistair.'

'Is that what you want to do? Go into politics?' The derision in his voice was pronounced.

'Yes. Not me personally, but you're on the right track. What I want to do is create one of those groups. I want—'

Alistair interrupted him, 'What? So you can start wars and kill people?' There was anger in his voice as he shook his head.

'No, absolutely not, Alistair. Completely the opposite, in fact. Imagine a world where we could stop all these things from happening. One where the lies and games of the politicians wouldn't dictate how the world was run. We'd have the chance to change things, I mean really change things. For the better. I don't want to kill people, I want to stop things like 9/11 happening to justify invading countries to benefit the people who make money out of war.'

Alistair had calmed down and his demeanour now took the form of distrust over anger.

'Let me finish explaining and then you'll see what I mean.' Max continued his practiced persuasion before coming up for air and waited for any objections. So far, the words that tumbled from his lips seemed to be resonating with his audience. He continued.

'So far, we are three, that's if you decide to join us, of course. Three of the smartest people I know.'

At this point, Alistair smiled. 'That's pretty arrogant of you to think you're one of the smartest people you know.'

It caught Max off guard. His ability to read people had failed him.

'And how do three people make a difference like what you're talking about?' Alistair pushed.

'We won't be three for long. We need more. And we would need to be strong and have perseverance. Of course, it won't be easy and there will be lots that can go wrong along the way. That's why we need each other. Here's what I see as the plan. We'll all be assigned a role and then dedicate our lives to fulfilling it. And when I say, "dedicate our lives", that's exactly what I mean. I'm talking about something that will literally last for as long as we need to achieve what we set out to. I'm not talking about the next five years. I'm talking about the next forty-five, our whole careers, our whole lives, if necessary. We'll support each other and make sure that everyone of us is successful in what we need to do. But there is a catch. No one can ever know. I mean no one. Not our parents, not our friends, not Facebook or Instagram. No one. Only through complete secrecy would we really be able to connect all the dots and really have an impact.'

'But why? Why do you actually want to?'

'Like I said, imagine having the ability to really change the world. Imagine looking back on your life and saying that we ended poverty, stopped a war, or solved climate change. Imagine saying that we made interstellar travel possible. All these things are possible. If only you can cut out all the bullshit, the stupid disagreements about petty issues and petty politics. Think about how much time and money is wasted in this world on things that do nothing but better the lives of...'

Max stopped himself. He had been about to say, "better the lives of the rich and powerful" but thought better of it. He didn't want it to appear as if this was a witch hunt of the super wealthy like Alistair's father. '...the lives of the people in power. When people go against each other it causes friction. Friction is a waste of energy. I read a quote by a guy called Saul Alinsky that sums it up perfectly. "Only in the frictionless vacuum of a non-existent abstract world can movement or change occur without that abrasive friction of conflict." I want to create that world. My aim is to remove that friction. To allow things to move more smoothly. Faster. More efficient.'

'And what would my role be?'

'I think you know that already. You wouldn't be

one of the smartest people I know if you didn't.' A wry smile accompanied the comment. 'What I had in mind is something that I'm sure your father has been hoping since the day you were born. If you chose to join us, I'd hope that you follow in your father's footsteps and take over the business to become even more successful and powerful than he is.'

'And if I don't want that life?'

'Well, of course, if that's not something you want then that's fine and that would be the end of our conversation. You can leave now and we'll never talk of it again. I'd also ask you not to mention to anyone that we've had this chat.'

Alistair didn't move. Max added this to his mental checklist as another win.

'However, when we talked yesterday about helping people, this is a way you can do that. You can help far more people doing this than you could being a doctor. It would mean the chance to help thousands, maybe even millions. You can help to get rid of corruption, cover the stories that need to be covered, expose the real crimes that take place all over the world, not by petty criminals in the street, but the ones committed by the leaders who are supposed to be above all that.'

'And you think a secret group is the way to do that?'

'I think that a secret group is the *only* way to do

that. The group that we'll build will be to serve people rather than to be served, like politicians today.'

'And what will your role be? Prime Minister, I suppose?'

'No, I told you, I don't want to be in politics. I'm aiming for Head of the Intelligence Services.'

Max guessed that by now he was able to be a bit more forthcoming with the grand titles and ideas without causing more shock.

'That's something I truly believe in. A way to save lives, here in England and out there in the world. And with the help of you and the others we can achieve that, together.'

Alistair clasped his hands and rested his chin on his two outstretched index fingers. Silence. It felt like minutes before he spoke but Max could wait. And did.

'I won't lie to you, Max. What you are saying sounds batshit crazy.'

'I can understand that.'

'But I don't think you're completely wrong. We don't really make big changes any more. And I do see politicians as self-serving, afraid to say what they really want because of fear of how it will be interpreted. It would be nice to live in a world where it felt like things only got better. We do have the ability, and the money, to do things like end poverty but it just feels like no one is doing it. And it makes me wonder why.'

Max struggled to control his emotions. He felt the adrenaline surge through him as it looked like he had now managed to convince another member to join him.

'But I do still think it's all far-fetched. How in the world would we even start?'

'Well, the challenge will be bigger for the rest of us. Your role is ready-made for you. All you have to do is follow the natural path that someone in your position might have anyway. The rest of us have some serious work to do, but we'll need your help there as well. And in fact, you've already started.'

'How do you mean?'

'The interview you're helping to set up. It's really some research. The first part of the plan is to find out as much as possible about the people who we are going to become. In this case, the Prime Minister. The newspaper will be our reason to interview him. And to interview a whole host of others that we need to find out more about.'

'You sneaky bugger. I knew you were up to something, but I had no idea it was anything like this.'

'Well, now you know. Will you still help me?'

'That depends.'

'On what?'

'Two things: Who else would be in the group. And how serious you are.'

Max leant forward to stare into Alistair's eyes. If there was any way he could now lose Alistair, it would be in this moment. He had to choose his words carefully.

'I'm deadly serious.' He paused for effect. 'I've been thinking about this for a while now. And I've had all the same doubts you're having. But when it comes down to it, now that the idea has hatched, I can't get rid of it. Every day it just grows and grows. The more I think about it, the more I can see what's possible. I know we're capable of it. And as for who is in, you know of two and very soon you'll know the third. Sebastian is on his way here now. He was the first one that I asked.'

'Why him?'

'Because he'll be brilliant at it. And I can trust him, as can you. I know you two don't know each other very well but you will. He's going to be the PM.'

'You think he could really do it?'

'I do. I know he can. And he could do it without our help. But he won't have to.'

8

Racing through middle-England's green pastures at over 120 miles an hour, the Virgin Pendolino train tilts into the corners like a bobsleigh weaving its way down the ice track at the Olympic Games. The six degrees of tilt allows the train to maintain high speeds through the corners whilst reducing the outward force on the passengers. Some on board barely realise that it's happening, whilst others not only notice it but find it rather strange, in some cases even nauseating. To look out of one of the five-by-three-foot windows to the outward side as the train leans gives the viewer a scene more commonly experienced from a circling plane. The view of the flat earth is lost and replaced with only sky.

Sebastian and Alistair had both made this journey before, either with the school or with their families so they knew what to expect. It didn't, however, stop them from looking out of the window every time it happened, still fascinated with the technology.

Alistair ate a breakfast his mother had prepared him. An argument had taken place little over an hour earlier about the practicality of him carrying the wicker basket she had used to arrange the contents and as a compromise they had decanted the food into his brown leather satchel. They rushed out of the house with just enough time to collect Sebastian on the way to Liverpool Lime Street station.

A week earlier, once the interview had been arranged, Max had volunteered to stay back at school whilst Alistair and Sebastian made the trip to London. It made sense. Sebastian was the chosen PM and this was his first step on his path to that height. Alistair was the editor of the newspaper and it had been decided that he would write the article. He'd also arranged the interview and knew the people who would be helping them. Alistair had asked why they couldn't all go but Max resisted, saying he needed to concentrate on recruiting their next member.

As they made the journey that morning, predictably, traffic was not in their favour and they only narrowly avoided missing the train. They'd been dropped at the Liverpool-side exit of the Queensway tunnel connecting the Wirral to Liverpool, and ran, bags flailing behind them like capes, up the cobbled street alongside the World Museum and the Central Library they'd visited many times on school excursions. Upon reaching the station, they had a frantic dash to the departures board and, after locating their train, shot to the platform and jumped on the first carriage with only a minute to spare. Unfortunately, a long walk to the opposite end of the eleven-carriage train was necessary to find the first-class seats that had been purchased for them by Alistair's father's Personal Assistant. Now, safely in their seats and sharing Alistair's food, they poured over the printed list of questions they would ask the Prime Minister.

Arriving into Euston station, through the ever-increasing urbanisation that is London, the greenery disappears into the distance and the steady growth of brick and concrete from earth once ploughed rises up and removes any pretence that you are anywhere but a densely populated city. Whether planned precisely or just by sheer coincidence, the researcher from Apollo Publishing waited directly outside their carriage to collect them as they left the train. Holding a Costa Coffee in one hand and a cigarette in the other, she dropped the fag to the floor and stubbed it out under the pointed toe of a shiny black stiletto as she saw them coming.

The instant they'd stepped off the train, Sebastian had been struck by her. Elegantly dressed in black, from head to toe, she looked more like a barrister than a researcher. Her slender frame was outlined by the Reiss overcoat she wore, and wore well. Her clutch gave away another peek into her sartorial inclination and both the boys had mothers interested enough in handbags to know that she was carrying a Louis Vuitton item.

'Morning boys,' she greeted with warmth and charm, 'how was the trip?'

'Morning. Just fine, thank you, Annabel,' Alistair said. 'Bit of an early morning dash but we made it. Have you been waiting long?'

'Not too long. Ten minutes, maybe,' she replied as she kissed him once on each cheek. 'We have some time this morning so we're in no rush. Firstly, have you eaten? I'm starving so I thought we could grab some breakfast.'

'I could go for breakfast,' Sebastian jumped in at the first opportunity. 'Happy to meet you. I'm Sebastian, how do you do?' The young man outstretched a hand expecting hers in return, only for it to crash straight into her stomach as she approached him to greet him the same way she had Alistair. The collision left Sebastian flustered.

'Oh, I'm so sorry. I thought... well,' were the words that spluttered from his mouth. Internally, he berated himself. *Smooth, Sebastian. Real smooth.*

'My, my. Aren't you formal? We don't shake hands

in media, darling.' Annabel smiled and laughed, apparently completely unflustered by his clumsiness.

As the trio walked up the ramp from platform 1 into the main station concourse, the boys flanking Annabel allowing her to lead the way, Sebastian studied her trying to figure out her story. He'd already established that she was dressed like a woman who earned at least five times what she must as a researcher and had come to the conclusion that she must be from a wealthy family. Too young to be independently wealthy from her current job, she either hadn't gone to university or was maybe on a gap year and had a contact who had given her an opportunity with a major publishing house.

She led them out of Euston's main station doors and down the steps to a blacked-out people carrier parked outside the Royal George pub.

As they travelled south through London's busy streets, Sebastian wanted to find out more about her but was aware not to sound overly keen. After a few failed attempts to convince his mouth to do what his mind wanted, he'd eventually found the courage.

She hadn't mentioned her family, but he'd learned that she was on a year out before starting her course in journalism at Leeds University. Clearly a very social creature, she fit perfectly in the world that Sebastian imagined to be publishing.

She changed the topic of conversation back to the day ahead. 'Okay, so a few agenda items. We'll grab breakfast and then we're meeting the photographer at the Ritz at twelve. The interview isn't until this afternoon, so we have time for some photos and prep beforehand. Obviously, we'll have some with the Prime Minister too, but we want some of you two for our story.'

'I'm sorry, your story?' Sebastian enquired.

'Well, of course. There's no such thing as a free lunch. *Your* story is now *our* story. If you're interesting enough, that is.'

A smile and a wink floated across the car in Sebastian's direction and hung in mid-air. The blushing boy couldn't help but look away, shifting his focus out of the window as he talked in an attempt to hide his crimson cheeks. His blushing had not gone unnoticed, at least from Alistair. He saw the discomfort and smiled.

'Well, even if that was the case, which it won't be, I'm sure the PM will more than make up for it. But I'm confident we'll get something good for you.' Sebastian tried his hardest to be assertive and funny. He attempted his own wink in retaliation but the awkward gesture was lost on Annabel who was now scrolling through emails on her BlackBerry.

'Right boys,' she exclaimed, 'firstly breakfast. I'm heading to Pret to grab some food or I'll starve to death. Alistair, your father's secretary emailed me and said he will meet us at the Ritz before we head off for Number 10.'

'My father? Really? I thought he was in Hong Kong.' Alistair's head quickly snapped round to face Annabel.

'Apparently not. He's flying in this morning to wish his boy luck. Do you think he'll join us at Number 10? He must know the PM?'

'He's met him a few times, I think. It's my turn now, though. He'll have to let me have this one. He can read about me in the paper for once!' Alistair replied, a hint of annoyance in his voice.

The car pulled up outside the maroon shop hoarding and Annabel pulled a credit card from her bag, took Alistair's order of a latte and Sebastian's for water before disappearing into the throng of people on the pavement.

'Taken a little shine to Annabel, have we?' Alistair grinned at his companion.

'Of course, she's amazing. A little old for me though.' Sebastian thought it would be useless to deny it.

'Nonsense, she's only a couple of years older than us. And with where you're going, I don't think age will matter. You should tell her that you're going to be the PM one day,' Alistair teased.

'Shut up. Let's see how the interview goes first.'

They hadn't noticed the driver's smiling eyes, visible in the reflection of the rear-view mirror. In a second, the look was gone as the eyes flicked to the sliding door opening on the pavement-side of the car. Annabel re-entered the opposite door from which she had left, meaning that she had to squeeze past the boys to re-take her seat opposite them. As she did so, she used Sebastian's knee for balance with the one free hand she had, prompting him to look up and meet her eyes that were momentarily fixed on his. To him, there seemed a pause before she continued to her seat, and a look that ignited a flame within him. She handed out the refreshments and took a sip of her own. The shriek of 'Onwards driver!' accompanied by an outstretched arm was her sign to pull away and into the traffic.

The next leg of the journey took no more than twenty minutes, during which time Annabel took a number of calls and stared at her phone when she wasn't talking on it. The young men stared out of the windows, chatting, picking passers-by out of the crowd and commenting on their appearance and trying to guess what they all did for a living. As they drove past Green Park on their right, the round bulbs making up the sign of the Ritz came into view. The driver turned into Arlington Street towards the side door of the hotel.

As the trio gathered their things, the door sprang open thanks to the helping hand of the driver. One by one, they descended the single step to the ground and proceeded into the lobby with Annabel on point, the boys once again flanking her.

They arrived in the round hotel lobby and Annabel approached the concierge desk. Clearly, she'd been in the building before. A smart gentleman rose to his feet as he saw them enter, revealing his crisp dark jacket with four stripes on each forearm, neatly fitted over a grey waistcoat, white shirt and a blue and gold tie. It reminded Sebastian of a Navy officer's uniform.

She gave her name and those of the two young men stood waiting nervously five feet behind her. Something she said made the receptionist look up from what he was typing on his keyboard, stare at Annabel for a moment before peering round to look at the boys. Sebastian guessed that the Lovell name must have been mentioned, maybe even with the formal prefix, 'Sir'. It gave Sebastian a little kick of adrenaline just to be associated with it.

Annabel took three shiny black cards from the concierge's outstretched palm before turning to him and Alistair, motioning down the hallway known as the Long Gallery. One of the concierges stepped out from behind the desk and guided the group in silence down the warmly lit hallway adorned with marble pillars holding arrays of flowers every five feet. They craned their necks to take in the opulence that surrounded them. Just a little further and they hit The Grand Hall that led into the Queen Elizabeth Room.

As they entered, two giant chandeliers hanging from the ceiling instantly grabbed Sebastian's attention whilst a photographer sat cross-legged on a gold and white armchair at the far end of the room, illuminated by the light infiltrating the floor to ceiling windows that gave the occupants a view into the Royal Green Park that sits behind Buckingham Palace.

He closed the magazine that he'd been idling flicking through as he became aware of their entrance, placing it down on the short, glass-topped table next to him. His assistant was making some final adjustments to the lighting equipment near the windows and when Annabel burst into the room, it was clear that she knew the pair well by the kissing and chatting that took place immediately as they spoke of a shoot they had been at a few days earlier and a night that had followed.

Sebastian got the impression she was very well connected within the company, even though she could only have been there for a short while. Alistair and Sebastian looked at each other, standing politely, smiling at first before growing bored with the gossip. Sebastian raised his hand to his mouth and made the most out-wardly-obvious triple cough he could manage, extending the last of the sounds before letting it fade out.

Luca, the photographer, stopped talking instantly, almost with a slight jump, and turned to the source of the sound, craning his neck in the funniest manner as he spun 180 degrees. Annabel recognised it was Sebastian who had interrupted. She stared at him, eyes slightly narrowed, waiting for his eyes to meet hers.

He said nothing, only tilted his head and raised his eyebrows to indicate what he thought of her lack of manners and introductions.

The photographer stepped forward to introduce himself. Sebastian, in turn, advanced to accept his handshake and Luca moved towards Alistair to extend the same greeting.

'Mr Lovell, I assume?' Luca guessed correctly.

'Yes. But please call me Alistair.'

Sebastian interrupted. 'So, Luca, what were you thinking? Me reclining on the couch over here?'

He moved to a chaise long in corner of the room and adopted a Monroe-style pose, one hand running through his hair, elbow aloft, 'Or something more serious?' He sat up and jabbed his clenched fist, thumb over first knuckle towards the photographer, mimicking a politician.

The photographer chuckled, tipped his head forward to peer over his Tom Ford sunglasses at the impressionist in front before dryly replying in his thick northern Italian accent, 'I didn't realise we had a comedian amongst us.'

'Why thank you, I do my best.' Sebastian now turned his attention to Annabel, 'So what's the plan?'

'Well, it's midday now so we're right on track. Alistair's father will be here in twenty minutes or so—'

Alistair stood up from the seat he had perched on. 'Shall we have some photos now then?'

'Would you not like to wait for Mr Lovell?' she asked.

'Well, we'll have some with him as well but it would be nice for Sebastian to have some of the limelight for now.'

It felt to Sebastian that Alistair was eager to have some of the limelight as well before the well-known and powerful figure that was his father strolled into the hotel and into the suite in which they sat and stole the show.

'Luca, shall we?' Alistair pressed.

Luca looked over at Annabel, clearly unsure. Her response was a shrug of the shoulders and a soft closing of her eyes. Luca took this as all the permission he needed and sprang into life.

'Right, Sophie, a little make-up, if you will.'

Sophie, his assistant moved towards them carrying a small black case, filled with lots of clear glass pots with different coloured lids. A blusher brush appeared and she swilled it round one of the pots before reaching out to Sebastian's face. He recoiled.

'Is this really necessary? I'm pretty much an oil painting already.'

'Oh, come on, Sebastian. It's only a bit of make-up, you scared you'll turn into a girl?' Annabel teased.

'Okay, well make-up is one thing but I draw the line at a mani-pedi.'

'I think we'll just stay with the make-up for now, no one wants to go near your smelly feet, young man,' Luca chimed in.

Annabel smirked at Luca's cattiness.

Looking down towards his shoes, Sebastian conceded. 'Well it does feel like it's been a long day already, so maybe for the best.'

Once the make-up had been applied to Sebastian, Alistair was next. He positioned his face like a seasoned professional and allowed Sophie to work her magic. She then raised the brush at Annabel to test whether she wanted a touch up. Annabel shook her head.

'Then I think we're all done.' Sophie turned back to her make-up case. 'Luca, over to you. Where do you want them?'

Luca was lining up various pieces of photographic equipment on a dresser that stood against one of the ornately decorated blue and white walls.

'We'll start with just the two boys. Sorry, young men,' he corrected himself. A wry grin followed. 'Let's have you over here.'

What proceeded was a plethora of positions: both boys sitting, both standing, one sitting and one standing, the pair looking out of the windows, the pair standing next to the windows, one sitting in a chair, both sitting in chairs flanking the windows, looking over their notes for the interview, shaking hands, shoulder to shoulder, the list went on.

Just when Sebastian thought they had exhausted all possible options, there came a firm knock at the closed door. Without waiting for a response, a gloved hand pushed the door inwards revealing the same escort that had led the first party here. He announced the arrival of Sir Lovell before backing out of the room.

In strode a vision of confidence and power. Standing tall in a finely cut navy Saville Row suit, complete with polished brogues and matching tie and pocket square, Sir James Lovell was now in residence. He moved to the centre of the room swiftly but in no rush, stopping in front of his son. Alistair reached out a hand, but Lovell Senior batted it away, pulling his son in close for a strong hug.

'Alistair, how are you, my boy?' Sir James asked.

'Good thanks, dad. How are you?'

'All the better for seeing you.' He smiled warmly. 'Introduce me to your friend.'

Sebastian stepped forward and, like Alistair, offered his hand, Lovell once more batting it away and bringing the boy in for a much warmer greeting. This time not quite as intensely as for his son but it made an impression nonetheless.

'So, you're Sebastian. Why have I not heard your name until recently?'

Sebastian was unsure how to answer, stumbling over his words initially, looking to Alistair for help.

'Well, we've… we've only really recently become friends…'

'Ah, I see. Well you've been missing out then. Welcome.'

Annabel was next to receive the greeting. Sebastian watched as the pair embraced warmly.

'Stunning as always, my dear,' James complimented her. 'Just like your mother. How is she?'

The penny dropped in Sebastian's head. This is how the world works, he thought. It's not what you know, it's who you know.

'She's well. She sends her regards.' Annabel smiled.

'Good, very glad to hear it. Send her mine in return, would you?'

'Of course, Mr Lovell.'

'What have I told you? Please, it's James.'

'Sorry, of course, James.'

'Right, I see you've already started with the pictures. How are they looking, you two?' He now brought the photographers into the conversation.

'Very good, Mr Lovell,' Luca was the first to reply. 'We have two naturals…'

Lovell looked sternly at the Italian, who needed no explanation of what the look implied and instantly corrected himself, 'James.'

After a final introduction with Sophie, Luca suggested a number of photos for the three males but James resisted.

'I think just one for the family album will do fine, Luca. Otherwise, I'd rather capture these three,' he said, pointing to Annabel and the two boys. 'We don't need my old face spoiling the memories.'

9

t's a strange feeling the first time you fire a weapon. Nerves and fear, excitement and trepidation course through your entire body as you slowly lie down, front first, in the prone position. Only a few moments ago you stood in line, alongside your friends, and merely observed as your hand shot into the air when a request for demonstration volunteers came from the loud man in front. A hard-faced range instructor stands over you now, pulling your elbow this way, adjusting your knee that way, unceremoniously moulding your body into the correct position. A modified SA80, the weapon of choice for the British Army, dictates the line of your torso, the butt searching for the nook in the top of your shoulder, the hand grip sliding back and forward in your left palm as you search for the perfect angle that allows your elbow at least some level of comfort on the gravel trap you're lying in. Downrange, a target resembling the upper half of a man stands one hundred meters away, courteously waiting perfectly still for you to make your move.

Removing your right hand from the pistol grip, you pick up the pre-loaded magazine lying to your right. The scratched black, curved metal box feels heavier than when you've handled it before. That's because this time it contains twenty live rounds of 7.62 NATO ammunition, designed to exit the weapon's muzzle at 940 metres per second, nearly three times the speed of sound and it's only at this moment that the gravity of the situation sets in: wherever the steel barrel happens to be pointing at the moment you squeeze the trigger is going to be visited by hot metal, at a very high speed. You've heard the war stories about injuries from being shot, and every fibre in your body concentrates on ensuring it, and you, keep pointing towards the sand bank behind the target. Today will not be the day that Max Mercer is featured on the news for killing a fellow cadet.

The magazine slides into the opening and you hear the signature click of metal on metal as the clip locks into place. Now it starts to get really exciting. Keeping the butt wedged into your shoulder, you lift your hand once more from the pistol grip, taking hold of the cocking handle, a piece of black metal that runs along a guide rail from just above the grip to the opening the spent cartridge is ejected from. You know from your weapons lessons that when you pull sharply back on this and release it forward, one of the live rounds will be pushed from the top of the magazine into the chamber, and you're officially a killing machine. Two small movements stand between you and the metal in your hands becoming a living, breathing dragon. You can't help but think back to the chilling words of Dr Oppenheimer after The Manhattan Project successfully tested its first atomic bomb: *"Now I am become death, destroyer of worlds."*

Your left eye closes slowly and you line up the sights of the rifle towards the cardboard enemy facing you.

'In your own time, five rounds at the target in front!' comes the shout from behind.

The ability to be heard over live gunfire is not one that everyone possesses, but it's a key part of the job description for an Army Range Instructor. They somehow manage to achieve a new level of man-made sound, creating a wave that echoes off the surrounding structures, replaying the initial bark until it fades away. However, in this moment, filled with adrenaline, fear, excitement, and the sound of blood rushing through your ears, your brain barely hears the words, but rather only recognises that now is the time to move the last piece of the jigsaw. A small round button, located above your right index finger, slides through to the opposite side of the rifle housing as you apply the pressure. You feel for the trigger and move it to the point of resistance, there's a pause as you start to squeeze.

There it is.

A jolt of force pushes the weapon into you, much softer than you imagined. A cloud of sand emerges from behind the target. The smell of cordite hits your nose, and then silence. It's a true moment of feeling unstoppable.

After repeating the cycle for five rounds and making the weapon safe by unloading it and checking there was no ammunition left in the chamber, Max climbed to his feet and dusted off the remnants of gravel and twigs now stuck to the front of his cadet uniform. As he spun around, the Range Instructor asked for volunteers to be in the first group of riflemen. At the front, eagerly waiting for his chance, Max saw a lean, rosy-cheeked recruit called Nicholas. His skinny frame, however, was an unfair indication of his true stature. Max had played rugby alongside him for the school team and had watched many times as the opposition had wrongly taken his size as an indication of the fight within him. Equally feisty as a cadet, Nicholas was one of Max's most competitive rivals when it came to the assault course, fitness tests, boot shining, or just about anything that could be taken as a competition.

When compiling his list of roles and names, Max didn't even have to think about who he would approach for the role of Chief of the Defence Staff. As soon as he'd identified that there would be a military role involved, an instant connection was made to Nicholas. Having already expressed an interest in the Army or Marines as a career, Max hoped Nicholas may be the easiest sell of the lot.

The day on which Max's two new comrades had disappeared to London on their fact-finding trip with the PM, was the same as the Army Field Trip to the Altcar Training Camp just north of Liverpool. This would be a good chance to groom Nicholas ahead of the main conversation.

After each of the discussions he'd had with Sebastian and Alistair, Max had looked back and assessed his performance. What had he phrased well? What had he been saying when they'd raised an objection? He needed to be clearer up front about his motivation. The two boys, as well as Harriet, had given him the impression that one would be hard pressed to find someone who genuinely believed that a person would want to gain power and wealth for the good of other people. Their instant cynicism captured exactly the point he was trying to make. Even though they may argue with the evidence he presented them with about 9/11 or the 'money trail' as he'd come to call it, it was still clear that even for these adolescents there was an in-built distrust of politicians, power and money. As worrying and saddening a realisation as this was, it could only possibly help his cause. After all, it was much harder to get someone to fight against what they thought was right.

As he now mentally ran through the approaching conversation with Nick, he looked back at how he had approached the others, not the words this time, but the locations, the situations. As more people joined he wanted to be careful about ensuring that he had enough time with each of the newcomers to make it apparent that this was his brain child and he was in charge. There would be a fine balance between wanting the new members to feel like their input was asked for and valued and ensuring that he retained his position as the leader of the group.

Conscious that there would be an ever-enduring threat to his leadership from those who wanted to change or modify the plan, Max would need to rely on his closest cohort, Sebastian, to help alert him to any murmurings or displeasure amongst the group. Of course, with the type of people he was recruiting—ambitious, intelligent, driven—that risk would always be there, especially as they all grew older and wiser, but he would cross those bridges when they came.

For now, the only bridge he had to worry about was the messy display of logs and rope standing between him and the other side of the river.

Their obstacle was a ten-foot gap between the bank on which they stood and the crumbling remnants of an old faded, brick bridge, protruding from the opposite side of the river. Their challenge, timed, was to build a temporary structure capable of transporting the team of four and their kit across. The punishment for failure was simple: a plunge six feet into the water below, which, at this time of year, or generally any time of year in England, was not the most pleasant experience. It was a basic reminder that this race would not be won with speed alone. Without attention paid to the design and craftsmanship, the team wouldn't finish at all.

He and Nick had been selected as leaders of two of the teams and as they finished selecting their teammates, they looked at each other through narrowed eyes. Nick raised two fingers to point at his own eyes before pointing them at Max's. Max repaid the favour, bringing his thumb up to the right-hand side of his neck and dragging it across the jugular and windpipe.

Nick's team was first out of the five groups to tackle the challenge and they started well. Nick was efficient at giving instructions and seemed to know exactly what he wanted the team to do. Being given the honour of first pick when selecting his team, he had a capable bunch to help him build the perfect bridge. Max was now slightly worried that he would be beaten, however, Nick's team had one distinct disadvantage: they were first to go. Max now had the chance to watch all the other groups, spot their mistakes and devise a strategy to avoid them. As he watched the current team in action, Max talked to his team, pointing out any mistakes and discussing areas where they could make improvements. He wanted them to have a plan ready to spring into action. After what felt like an hour of watching the first team struggle with the ropes and logs, a whistle blew, and it was time to test the assembly.

The crew lifted it from the ground and raised it into the vertical position at the edge of the bank. The method they had chosen was to plant the nearside of their contraption in the ground, anchor it behind a boy's foot at either side, with the other boys using their strength to lower it down using ropes attached to the top. Max knew this was a bad idea.

As the vertical structure started to move, the weight of the bridge was easy enough to manage using the weight of the two cadets whose feet were not being used as doorstops. However, as the angle between the ground and wooden fence posts narrowed, it became harder and harder to control and the young men struggled to keep their grip on the ropes. With the assembly swaying out of control, Nick gave the command to drop it in the hope of it landing in place safely. As he shouted the words, his opposite number who was helping to secure the bottom of the wooden structure leapt out of the way for fear of being hit by the falling beams. The bridge impacted heavily with the far side of the river bank and bounced dramatically, the shockwave from the impact reverberating through the wooden post and onto Nicholas's foot.

The cheers of success from his team drowned out Nick's cries of pain as he hopped away from the bridge, tenderly trying to test putting weight on his left foot, before succumbing and falling to the wet ground, bum first. The Commanding Officer wandered over and questioned the boy in his well-known tone of sarcasm and derision.

'What's up, Archer, have you got a splinter in your vagina?'

A shriek of laughter came from the other boys. They were used to his amusing inability to comply with political correctness and took great delight from it. He barked most of his commands in a mix of a lisp and splutter. The commonly told tale was that he had lost half of his tongue in the Falklands war whilst taking a beach. More elaborate versions included capture and torture at the hands of rebels and militia men in locations like Oman and Somalia.

'No sir, I'll be okay,' Nick replied, a smile on his face. 'It's just a knock. How's the bridge?'

'It was looking good until you numskulls managed to drop it. It's looking a bit ropey now, though.'

'Ha, nice one, sir!' one of the cadets chuckled.

The CO obviously had not intended the pun, and it took him a few moments before he got it.

'Alright, alright, pipe down, Davies. You'll have your time to shine soon enough. Lads, time to test your creation.'

He helped Nick to his feet.

'You okay, son?'

'Yeah, yeah. I'll walk it off, sir.'

It was clear the discomfort was considerable, but he limped over to his team and the nearest point of the bridge. He told the group that he'd go first to test it and slowly crouched down and eased his sore foot onto the bound posts trying to put as much weight as possible onto the structure. So far, it was stable and solid. Bringing his good foot up to meet the bad he again eased forward venturing past the point where the bank ended and the water began. Still crouching low, he inched forward feeling the far side of the wooden poles starting to sink into the grass and mud that topped the brickwork at the far side of the gap. Left after right, after left, he made his way across the gap before finally reaching the other side, taking a knee as he got onto the solid old bridge. With arms raised into the air, he shouted back, 'I think we've done it boys, we're good to go!'

One by one, the rest of the team stepped onto the makeshift bridge and nervously made their way across. As the last of them, Davies, stepped over the gap, one of the blue nylon ropes holding the contraption together snapped, instantly allowing the tightly bound posts to come apart. Davies, now flailing for balance, attempted to dart across to safety, making it no more than another foot before falling to his right and back first into the water below.

A cheer rang from the waiting crowd as they rushed towards the bank to see if he was okay, whooping and laughing. Davies resurfaced only moments after he entered, none the worse for the fall but the cold water had clearly given him a shock and he scrambled towards his team who had descended to the bank to offer assistance. It took all three of them to pull the soaking cadet from the water. Even after they hauled him onto dry land, he was still gasping for breath from the cold but managed to find some humour in the situation and instantly jumped on Nick who crumpled with the additional weight on his bad leg. The pair fell to the ground, Davies ensuring that he made his captain as wet as possible. What Davies didn't realise was that he would now have to go back into the water to collect the fence posts and rope for the next group to use.

With the equipment now back on dry land, the following group stepped up for their attempt at the crossing. After starting well, their bridge looked sturdy and sound. However, they had not learnt from the previous group's lowering technique and the bridge, along with the boys, slid down the river bank and into the water. The team, upset about losing valuable time, now started blaming each other and shouting. It was a few minutes before the captain was able to get them back under control and focused on the task of hauling the bridge back up the steep bank. They lost nearly ten minutes to the mistake which would most likely put them out of the running.

The next team were a marked improvement and, even though their captain was indecisive and slow, they managed to build a bridge that looked like it would hold as well as choosing a different method of connecting the bridge with the other side. Instead of hoisting the bridge to the vertical position and lowering it like a drawbridge, they opted to keep it level with the ground and ease it towards its destination with two boys holding ropes tied to the far end to stop it dropping down. They hoped that a slower, more controlled effort was the right way to go. The manoeuvre started out well but as the weight of the wooden structure peeped out over the bank, the two boys holding the ropes quickly realised that the weight at the far end was soon becoming too great for them to support. They started to struggle and within seconds, before they had a chance to effectively communicate with their leader, they were being pulled down the bank. Both let go of the ropes and the collection of wood, now soaking from the repeated water excursions, once more found its way into the muddy stream below. The team tried a few more configurations of rope holding and bridge pushing before the CO intervened.

'You lot are about as much use as a cock-flavoured lolly pop. Faulkner, are you intending on getting across this today?'

'It's impossible, sir, we've tried everything.'

'Okay lad, pull it back up and take it apart. Let's see if at least one group of you dummies can get us all across. Mercer, you're up. Come on, son. Let's see what you can do.'

Without a word, Max and his team stepped forward. Their observation and planning meant that very little communication was needed, and each knew exactly what he was supposed to do. He had no clue whether his idea would work but he was excited to see. The team sprang into action, lining up fence posts and efficiently lassoing them together tightly. They had gone for a sleek design, only using two thirds of the amount of rope and posts on their bridge as the other groups. Max could hear the other teams start to murmur about it not being big enough or strong enough, but he ignored the chatter. He had purposefully told them to use as little rope as possible on the bridge itself. He started gathering up all the other bits of rope he could find and began tying them together with the reef knots he had learnt from sailing trips, laying the ropes down on the ground from the bank towards their bridge.

'Longer ropes ain't gonna make it any lighter, lad,' the CO remarked.

'I think they just might,' Max replied, not looking up from the task at hand.

Once the three others had finished tightening the ropes around the posts, they grabbed the three unused posts and lay them perpendicular to the river bank. Max attached the lengthened ropes to the bank-side of the bridge. The four boys lifted the bridge onto the three logs laying on the ground. It was now clear that they aimed to use the extra posts as rollers. Max had noticed that the end of the bridge not being supported by the ropes dug in to the ground whenever the previous team had tried to push it out over the gap. The rollers would allow the bridge to slide outwards more easily, but he wasn't finished there. They moved the bridge slightly forward, more murmurs from the crowd who fully expected the contraption to still end up in the river, now just much faster than the previous one.

On his command, Max and his teammate took hold of the lengthened ropes and attached thick sections of loose branches to the ends, drawing more confusion from the group surrounding them. In unison, they threw them up and over a thick limb jutting from a tree near the river bank that leaned out over the water. Catching the sections of branch, the pair now pulled on their ends of rope, demonstrating the simple pulley system they had created to take the weight of the far end of the bridge. The pair exchanged a glance and a nod before they started to pull on the ropes to test the system. It proved a little too effective and as the boys both leant their bodyweight onto the twine, the bridge tilted dramatically upward before they managed to correct the balance.

'That's not allowed, sir. We weren't allowed to do that!' came complaints from behind.

The CO laughed and then snapped, 'I said nothing

about using the trees. You should have used your brain a bit harder!'

With the far side of the bridge now being supported by two of the team, the remaining two were able to easily push the bridge across the rollers. The rope-holders only needed to slowly let some of the rope out to allow the bridge enough slack to move. Within a couple of minutes of starting their attempt at securing the bridge, it touched down on the opposite side of the gap.

They exchanged smug glances as they safely made their way, one-by-one, across the gap to the far side. The captain went last and was greeted by cheering, jumping and high fives. Max turned around to face the boys at the far side of the gap and there was Nick, clearly disappointed by his own team's performance. He lowered his head in defeat and clapped his hands together softly a couple of times to acknowledge the victor.

'Well done, Max.' The CO patted him on the shoulder. 'Good job, very resourceful to use the trees. We might make an engineer out of you yet, lad.'

Max modestly acknowledged the praise and walked off to pass it on to his team. After sharing the good news, he sloped off to speak with Nicholas who was helping to collect up all the items that had been used during the exercise.

'Unlucky, mate. I thought you had nailed it down pretty early there.'

'No, no. You guys won fair and square, that was clever with the tree. I should have thought of that.'

'Thanks, I think we had a bit of luck going last and seeing how hard it was to get the bloody thing over there. I'm pretty glad we didn't get wet though, don't fancy the look of the river, especially how cold Davies looked after coming out. He got you good.'

'Yeah, he did, the little bastard. I was nice and warm until then.'

Max noticed his limp and asked about his ankle.

'I'm sure it will be fine, just a bang, nothing a good afternoon of running around shooting stuff won't fix!'

'Glad to hear. Listen Nick, I want to talk to you about something. Come and find me at lunch and we'll go for a walk,' before correcting himself, 'well, a sit down in your state, maybe.'

Nick looked confused. 'Sure, okay. A talk about what?'

'Oh, nothing exciting. I'll catch you in a bit.'

Max left Nicholas wondering what the mysterious request was about and jogged off to his team who were laughing and talking, clearly happy with their win.

'Amazing job, lads. They never stood a chance.'

10

Annabel, Sebastian, Alistair and James were led into the Cabinet Room at the end of a forty-five-minute tour around Number 10 Downing Street. Few rooms in the world hold more gravitas than the one in which the group now found themselves.

Alistair was trailing behind Sebastian when the young man in front stopped dead, frozen to the spot at the sight of this iconic space.

'What's wrong, Seb?' he whispered as he nearly crashed into the back of him.

He saw Sebastian's eyes wander around the room. 'Nothing. I mean... well, I've just seen this room so many times on websites and in books over the last couple of months. I never thought I'd actually be here. I've seen a really famous portrait of Winston Churchill, sitting right there'—he pointed into the centre of the room— 'smoking one of his Maduro cigars.'

Maduro cigars? How the fuck does he know what

kind of cigars Winston Churchill used to smoke? It hit him how much research Sebastian must have actually done before this meeting.

Ever since Max had come to him in the library, he'd felt like all this was a fantasy that would fade away once he and Sebastian came to their senses and realised that it was impossible. He'd initially doubted whether Sebastian was even the right choice for their so far fictitious and fabricated roles. Now, however, he couldn't doubt that Sebastian was at least taking this meeting seriously.

Maybe I was wrong about him. He watched Sebastian cautiously venture across the threshold, eyes aloft, studying the plaster entablature that bound the cream walls to the white ceiling.

Sebastian's foot caught on something and he stumbled forward, one foot, two feet, before catching himself on the back of two polished, leather-clad, wooden chairs. The force of his fall shifted the furniture forward into a long table, the sound of the impact attracting the attention of his fellow guests who suddenly looked as sheepish as if they themselves had caused the commotion.

On second thought, maybe I wasn't. Alistair chuckled to himself, as he watched Sebastian flush red with embarrassment, looking down, searching for the offending article. It appeared he'd tripped over the base of a Corinthian column.

Alistair moved towards Sebastian to see if he was okay. Annabel joined them at the foot of the pillar, touching Sebastian lightly on the shoulder.

'Pretty impressive, hey? Did you ever imagine you'd be standing in here?' she asked quietly.

Sebastian's eyes followed the line of the column from the base to the ceiling and he rested a hand on the cold, immovable object. Without turning, he whispered back, 'Have you ever asked yourself, "if you could have the key to one room, any one room, in the world, what would it be?"'

'I can't say I've ever thought about it,' she mused.

'I have.' Sebastian nodded. 'I used to think it would be the Oval Office, or the Vatican Vaults—'

'Or maybe the Victoria Secret's changing rooms,' Alistair interrupted.

Out of the corner of his eye he could see Annabel smile and roll her eyes at him.

Sebastian continued as if he had not even heard the comment, or at least didn't acknowledge it. 'But I think I've changed my mind. Think of all the conversations that have taken place in this room, all the decisions that have been made, good and bad. It's pretty humbling. Did you know—'

He was cut off before he had a chance to impart his knowledge on the pair as the Prime Minister strode into the room.

'And what do you think you're doing in here?' David Cameron's voice was commanding.

In an instant, Annabel's hand recoiled from Sebastian's shoulder, Sebastian's hand in turn recoiled from the pillar, all three of them spinning round to see the smiling man now walking through the doorway behind him.

The only people now not as rigid and upright as meerkats were the PM himself and Alistair's father who, before the PM's entry, had been perusing the books on display in the two mahogany book cases flanking the door to the Private Secretary's office.

'Prime Minister,' Sir James greeted. 'It's a pleasure to see you. How are you?'

'I'm well thank you, Mr Lovell. Usual games with the opposition but you know all about that.'

'I always like to stick firmly to the middle, sir. Not that you would know about *that*.' The pair chuckled as James introduced the rest of the group, 'I'd like you to meet Annabel, Sebastian, and my son, Alistair.'

The PM warmly shook each of their hands. Alistair thought back to Max's challenge, "Have you tried? No, you haven't, Alistair." He'd just shaken hands with the

PM and all it had taken was one phone call. Imagine what else he was capable of.

James continued, 'I must admit that I can't stay for the main event, but I couldn't miss the chance for the tour. I hope these three behave themselves and don't go too Dimbleby on you.'

'I'm sure we'll be fine. I can't imagine these rising stars are going to be too troublesome.'

'Well rather you than me, David. I hear Sebastian is fairly sharp when he wants to be. You three, don't let this man get away without revealing some state secrets, we could use a few eye-openers for tomorrow's headlines.'

He walked over to Annabel and gently rested his hands on the tops of her arms, she leaned in and kissed once on each cheek.

'Annabel, thanks for your help, you're a star. We must all have dinner next time these young men venture to London. Alistair, appreciate every minute you spend in this building and with this man. He has a lot to teach every one of us. And Sebastian,' he moved over towards him, 'give him all you got.' He accompanied this with a firm handshake and a wink.

Turning, he approached Cameron. 'Prime Minister, a pleasure, as always. I hope to see you again soon. Keep up the good work.' And with that he strode out of the Cabinet Room into the ante room.

'Right, before we start, have you been offered drinks? I could do with some tea.' The PM turned to an older gentleman waiting by the door and asked for the refreshments.

'Certainly, sir. What can I get for the rest of you?'

'Tea is good for me,' Annabel said.

'And me,' Alistair agreed.

'Just water for me, thanks,' Sebastian said.

'Thank you, Nigel. Okay, let's sit.' The PM gestured to one side of the table as he moved to the opposite side and strode across the ornate gold and green carpet.

Alistair followed as Sebastian confidently led them along the row of chairs. Sebastian stopped suddenly behind a chair close to the centre of the row, apparently knowing exactly which chair the PM would choose, even before the PM himself had stopped walking.

Wondering how Sebastian knew where the PM would land, Alistair noticed that the Prime Minister's chair was the only one in the room with arms. Had Sebastian known that already? Was this yet more homework he'd done? Alistair couldn't help but be impressed. He himself had not even spotted the different style of chair until now.

Mr Cameron stopped behind the predicted chair and rested his hands on the back of it. Sebastian stayed in position directly opposite, whilst Annabel filed in to his right and Alistair took up position on Sebastian's left, leaving an empty space in an attempt to remove himself from the direct conversation that was about to take place. This had not been discussed prior to the meeting but when he saw Sebastian look first at the empty chair and then to Alistair, he received a soft nod and an unspoken acknowledgement and 'thanks' passed between the pair.

'Prime Minister, would—'

'Please, Annabel, call me David.'

She paused, 'Er, yes, sir. I mean, David.' She was struggling for words now and her companions found it rather amusing. 'Sorry, I'll start again. David…' she emphasised heavily, 'Would you mind if I record the interview?' she asked as she pulled her phone from her bag along with a small microphone and stand which she placed directly in between Sebastian and the PM.

This had already been agreed with the Press Office weeks ago, so it was less of a request and more her way of letting him know that she was about to start recording.

'Of course, please.' He indicated with a soft bow of his head. 'Why don't we just wait for the drinks, however, then we'll not be disturbed or mess up the recording.'

'Ah yes.' Annabel agreed.

As if by magic, Nigel returned to the room carrying

an oval silver tray, complete with china tea pot, three matching china cups and saucers, and a crystal beaker containing Sebastian's ice water. He set the tray down on the small, square, green-topped side-table abutting the main conference table, and delicately poured the tea into the cups before carefully placing them in front of Annabel, Alistair and the PM. He returned and placed the final receptacle onto the brown leather coaster in front of Sebastian before collecting the silver tray and leaving the room closing the door behind him.

Annabel motioned to her phone on the table, received a nod of approval from David and clicked it into life.

All eyes were now on Sebastian.

Alistair, unsure how the next phase would unfold, became worried after a few seconds of silence that Sebastian had frozen with nerves.

Seb cleared his throat and sprang into life. 'Prime Minister, David, thank you for agreeing to meet with me today. I'd like to use this opportunity to gain an insight into the man behind the title and the path that led you to this building, this room and to that particular seat.'

Alistair was shocked at the confidence now pouring from his friend as he spoke. His tone was steady and calm, his gaze direct. He managed his cadence well and the words flowed sincerely from his mouth.

'It's humbling to be in a place that has defined so much of the history of not only the United Kingdom but so much of the world. It's an honour and a privilege to sit where so many of our great politicians have, whether in times of joy or turmoil. My aim with this article is to inspire the next generation of leaders to take an interest in politics and world affairs, and to give you an opportunity to connect with an audience that you may not have the chance to engage with very regularly.'

Alistair had no idea that this little opening speech was coming, and from the look on Annabel's face, neither did she. She stared wide-eyed at Sebastian.

'The first question I'd like to ask before we look at your early years in politics is about the room we're sitting in, the Cabinet Room, for the benefit of our readers and listeners. I mentioned its significance, but is there one specific event or decision that these walls have witnessed that stands above the rest for you, personally?'

'Well that's a good question, Sebastian.' Cameron paused. 'I think choosing one event would be quite hard. For me, this building, and this room in particular, symbolises what our government is meant to be. Strong, supportive, unfaltering, unwavering, constant.

'Personally, I have one memory of this room that stands out and conveys all those things. Unfortunately, it was long before my time and I'm not sure why this one particular image sticks in my mind but it's a picture of the great Winston Churchill.'

Alistair glanced to his right and saw the faintest hint of a smile being suppressed on Sebastian's face.

'Here is a man,' David continued, 'in the first year of his primacy, at war with Germany, unknowing of what horror the next five years would bring. Yet there he sits, almost serenely, peacefully, alone at this table, smoking a cigar and reading papers.

'I've been lucky enough to be Prime Minster for six years and I've sat at this same table, with the UK once again at war, but let me tell you, not once have I felt the sense of calm that seemed to reside in that man. He was either fearless or an amazing actor. Regardless, he was a great man. I often come in here late at night if there is a decision that weighs heavily on my mind, away from the noise and the staff and try and put myself into the mind of Churchill. I find that it allows me to focus.'

'I think I know the picture you mean, Prime Minister,' Sebastian agreed. 'It's one I've seen many times while doing my research for this interview and, I have to say, there is something captivating about the shot.

I like to imagine that the picture captures him in a moment of peace, smoking a last cigar, before leaving through the famous number ten door on his way to parliament to give the "beaches" speech.'

'Now that is an interesting image. The thought had not occurred to me.'

'It's unlikely, I know,' Sebastian continued, 'but they can't have been too far apart.'

'Sorry, the "beaches" speech?' Annabel interrupted.

Alistair saw Sebastian look to the PM, clearly unsure as to who should respond.

Cameron nodded to the young man who, without hesitation, gave Annabel a concise description of the famous speech Churchill gave to the House of Commons shortly after taking the reins as Prime Minister. The most famous part of the speech, heard time and time again the world over, is only a small extract of the entire address he gave to the House of Commons that day, comprising 3,767 words but will be remembered forever as a key moment of British resolve and solidarity. Sebastian recounted it line for line:

"We shall go on to the end, we shall fight in France, we shall fight on the seas and oceans, we shall fight with growing confidence and growing strength in the air, we shall defend our island, whatever the cost may be, we shall fight on the beaches, we shall fight on the landing grounds,

we shall fight in the fields and in the streets, we shall fight in the hills; we shall never surrender..."

Annabel looked impressed, as did the PM.

'You've clearly done your research, young man. If I were to guess, I would say that he was also your favourite Prime Minister.'

'Present company excepted, of course.' Sebastian smiled and bowed his head to his host.

'Of course.' David smiled back.

'He's an easy character to like, and dislike, depending on your point of view,' Sebastian conceded. 'He'll always be associated with one of the most harrowing times in British and world history and will be remembered as the great strategist that helped overcome the Nazis. I think he was an inspiration to many at a time when our country faced unbelievable hardship and tragedy. At least, before he was unceremoniously kicked out of office as soon as the war in Europe was over. That is one thing I struggle to understand. The man who had carried a nation through hell, only to be forgotten about as soon as it looked like the sunshine was breaking through the clouds.'

'I agree,' said David. 'Although, we mustn't forget that the country hadn't elected a leader for over ten years due to the war, so people may have felt the need for change. But I do agree that he will be remembered as one of the greats.'

'Do you ever wonder how you'll be remembered?' Alistair ventured to ask.

Responding to a hint of negativity in the question, Annabel jumped in before David could respond, 'Sorry to cut in. I'm just conscious of the time, Prime Minister,' she apologised. 'It's just that we have a set list of questions to cover, maybe we could come back to that one if we have time at the end?'

'Of course, Annabel. So easy to get distracted when talking about the history of our little island.'

Alistair cut a look at Annabel. He had a feeling the answer may have given some insight into the PM's perception of his current popularity in the run up to one of the most significant referenda in history that would decide the UK's future in Europe, or out of it. She clearly felt this was no place to challenge the PM or bring the ongoing issue into discussion.

Sebastian ignored the glances being exchanged across him. He picked up the stapled papers in front of him and began with the prepared list of questions.

'So, Prime Minister, let's take it back to the start and talk about your school life...'

11

After excitedly meeting at the usual spot between their two schools, Harriet and Max had climbed aboard the school bus shared by their schools. Harriet and Max sat not on the back row, but three rows forward, as was their place at this age according to school bus law. Far enough back to be near the tribal elders but not quite at the top of the tree just yet. They laughed and joked with the rest of the gang and as they neared Harriet's stop they both got up to exit.

This was met with the usual jeers that arose when a couple left the bus together. Harriet hung her head, an embarrassed smile on her face as she climbed down the curved staircase one third of the way down the length of the bus. The staircase placement seemed as if the designers had wanted the pair, and others like them, to be visible to as many people as possible as they departed together.

After dropping their bags inside the door of the

house and racing upstairs, the couple emerged, relieved, from Harriet's bedroom. The pair had then grabbed the two Labradors waiting impatiently and headed towards the endless miles of coastline that make up the edges of the Wirral Peninsula.

In one spot sits a small car park, entered from a long straight road that starts in the village of Lower Heswall and slowly descends towards the shore. Here Harriet and Max sat, perched on the edge of a large, wooden picnic table admiring the view and chatting. Max was excitedly telling Harriet about the progress he was making in finding other members to join him on his quest. Harriet listened attentively, a smile painted on her face as she witnessed the passion flowing from his mouth.

'Alistair told me he left and thought about nothing else all day,' Max said. 'He called his dad and reached his assistant, but his dad was in a meeting so had called back a bit later. Alistair asked him what he thought of the idea and his dad had said to him, "It'll be tricky, he's a very busy man, let me see what we can do." And it had been that simple.'

As she listened to him, Harriet couldn't quite believe it herself. She'd humoured him when he'd told her about the idea the night they'd both come home drunk, thinking it was the ramblings of a drunken boy. Now it seemed that this was something more to Max. Cautiously, she began to let her scepticism subside slowly.

'Okay, so what happened at the interview?' she probed.

'I don't know, they're still there. It's probably happening right now. I can't wait to hear about it.' His eyes were wide.

She could see the excitement in his face as he talked.

'It's like a story. One day you have an idea to interview the Prime Minister and weeks later it actually happens.' The whole thing seemed like a bit of an exaggeration.

He wouldn't go this far to impress me, would he?

'I know, I can't really believe it either,' he exclaimed. 'I would have loved to go and do it. Imagine being in Number 10 and meeting David Cameron.'

'You should have, that's a once in a lifetime chance.' She thought back to his speech about how much he distrusted politicians. It was, however, a once in a lifetime chance. One she envied hugely. She wondered why he had not asked her to be part of the group. Surely, she had more to offer than some of the boys he was asking to join? She loved the idea of being part of something big. And getting to spend more time with him would be an added bonus.

'Have you not had just a glimpse of what we might be capable of?' he pushed on. 'We managed to do this in just weeks. Give us ten years and you'll see what we can do. Anyway, Sebastian will live there at some point, so I'll have the chance to go then. May even get to stay the night!'

'I won't lie, I am impressed,' she said. 'But you can't rely on Alistair's father to help you all the way through this.'

'I know that, and we won't. We've got each other to rely on. That's the whole point of this. We'll combine our heads and ideas and that's how we'll be successful. Anyway, I recruited one more yesterday, so we have another brilliant mind to add to the pile.'

Suppressing her jealousy, she tried to sound as excited as possible for him.

'Ooooh, who's this one?' she leaned in and tickled him around the waist, raising her voice. She knew he was ticklish and loved to tease him mercilessly, watching as he immediately recoiled and shifted away from her, scrambling to keep her fingers from making contact with his skin through his shirt.

She finally desisted, allowing him to wrap her up in his arms as she smiled into his blue eyes, kissing him on the nose, wondering what he thought as he looked back into hers, still breathless from her badgering. She hoped he felt exactly as she did about him.

After a minute gazing at each other and softly rubbing their noses against one another's, still holding her tightly, he spoke. 'It's Nicholas, do you know him? I play rugby with him. He's also a cadet with me at school.'

'I know of him, his sister's in my school, she's really nice. What part is he going to play?'

'I want him to go into the army. Well he wants to go into the army anyway, but I want him to be head of the army.'

'What's it called when you're head of the army? I think Sebastian has the best title so far as Prime Minister.'

'Well, Nick's won't be a bad one, Chief of the Defence Staff.'

'That has a certain ring to it,' she agreed.

'I still think mine is the best, Head of Intelligence.'

She could see his competitiveness every time he spoke. It was one of the things she loved about him but wondered where it really came from. Was it really just his desire to be the best? Or was it part of a deeper need to prove himself constantly? When they were together he was sure of himself, but she often thought back to the night they first met. She'd seen through his confident facade, sensing that there was a shy little boy beneath the bravado.

'Everyone will basically be calling me brilliant every time they say it!'

'Yeah, I like yours too.' She was quick to agree as she looked towards the shoreline where the dogs were frolicking in the advancing water.

'Well you know I like yours...'

'My what?' She turned back to see him staring down at her chest. 'Hey, cheeky, that's not for you.' She played coy with him, wondering whether it was just her body that he was interested in.

'It was earlier,' he joked back.

'That was earlier. You've had enough for today.'

'I'm not sure that's possible.'

'You're so easily distracted, keep telling me about the plan.' She liked hearing Max talk about the group, all the time thinking about how she could be part of it and what role she could play. 'How will Nicholas become head of the army?'

'Well it all starts with the cadets, he's doing that now, so he already knows all the basics and how the army is structured. You know ranks, regiments, all that stuff.'

'I don't but carry on.'

'After that he'll go to university. You can be sponsored by the army. So, he kind of joins before he goes to university and they'll pay for him to go and he'll join what they call the OTC.'

'OTC?' *How did he know so much about all this?*

'Sorry, Officer Training Corps.' He expanded the acronym. 'He'll just do normal university but with army stuff on some nights and weekends. He'll choose a regiment before he goes. And that's what we need to start planning and researching. We don't want him doing anything that will get him killed but it has to be infantry I think.'

'And infantry is?' she asked again.

'What do you think of if I say someone is in the army?'

'I'd think they run around and shoot guns and camp in forests, that kind of thing.'

'Bingo, that's exactly what the infantry is. The army is split into lots of different types of soldiers, but the infantry is the one everyone usually associates with the army. They're the ones who fight on foot and come into close combat with the enemy. They're on the front line whenever we go to war. From the research I've done, all the recent Chiefs of the Defence Staff that have come from the army all started in the infantry. The current one started in the Green Howards after Sandhurst.'

'You mentioned that before. What is Sandhurst?'

'Sandhurst is the Royal Military Academy. In the army you have officers and non-officers. The officers are the ones that give the orders basically, normally a bit more educated. They go to Sandhurst which trains them to be an officer but also tests them all the way through. If you manage to pass, you get what's called a "commission" and then you're an officer. So anyway, he started there, and most of the guys from the army before him started in the infantry.'

'Why do you say, "the guy from the army before him"? Aren't they all from the army?' Harriet was confused.

'I thought that at first. But they can actually come from all branches of the military, so the Royal Navy and the Royal Air Force as well.'

'You're so cute when you talk about this stuff,' she teased him. '"The Royal Navy", "The Royal Air Force", you don't have to be so formal.' She smiled and moved to tickle him once more but this time he dodged it and tickled her instead. 'And Nicholas is happy to go into the infantry?'

'Yeah, that's what he wanted to do originally really so it works out well. He actually wants to be a Marine, which is a specialist infantry unit which is really part of the Navy. That or the SAS.'

'I've heard of that, what is it?'

'The SAS is the best of the best. They're called the Special Air Service and they're the guys that we send in to the most difficult situations or when we need something doing secretly.'

'Like what?'

'That's a hard question to answer. They're called Special Forces and the government doesn't really talk about what they do. So, it's all a bit secretive. They've been on TV a couple of times, way before we were born though. There was a hostage siege in an embassy in London and the SAS was sent in to kill all the terrorists and save the hostages. You could see them abseiling down the building and blowing up the windows before going in. All you heard then was lots of guns firing and then it was finished. They're seriously good.'

'But isn't it really dangerous? What if he gets killed?'

'It's risky. But he's really keen that he wants to go into one of the elite infantry units, so I looked it up and one of the previous chief guys was in the SAS so it's definitely a potential route to get to the top. He would still need to go through the normal route of Sandhurst and then army. He'll have to make sure he keeps really fit and makes a name for himself in order to get noticed. There are a few good books which we're going to read between us to get some more information on the next bits. We may also try and set up an interview with someone who used to be in the SAS to get an idea of exactly how we can make sure he gets in.'

'You haven't told me how you plan to do yours yet.'

'Haven't I?' he asked, sounding surprised. 'There are a few options and ways in, from what I can tell.

There seems to be a strong connection between MI6 and Cambridge. Lots of the famous spies were recruited there. I have no idea how you go about getting recruited, I'm guessing they look out for certain traits and characters. That and a bit of luck. Anyway, I'm not banking on that. I'm going to join the army and then after a few years apply for a move into intelligence. What's up?' he asked suddenly.

She realised that her face must have given away her feelings. 'Nothing. It's stupid.' She faked a smile.

'Come on. Talk to me.' He leant in. 'Whatever it is, it's not stupid.'

'It's just hearing you talk about doing all these things. They just sound so... far away. And what does that mean for us?'

'Don't you worry about that. There's not a job in the world that is going to keep me from being with you. I can't ask you to base your life on mine, but please don't think that when I go off to university that will be the end.'

'You promise?' she pushed, eager.

He wrapped his arms around her as they looked out towards the sinking sun, kissing her on the cheek.

'I'll tell you what. I promise you that even when I go away to uni and you're still here for your final year, we'll come to this same spot every month, come rain or shine, and I'll tell you every time just how much I love you, and how much I need you.'

She pressed herself harder against him, wriggling herself closer and tighter into his embrace. 'I'm going to hold you to that, Max.'

12

Twelve hours ago, Sebastian had climbed on a train to London. Ten hours ago, Annabel had arrived and bowled him over. Eight hours ago, he was in a photo shoot in the Ritz. Six hours ago, he interviewed the Prime Minister. Four hours ago, he finally emerged into the daylight from the door of Number 10 and allowed himself to breathe.

Only over the last few hours had a huge wave of relief slowly spread through his body. His mind still reeled from what had taken place in just one day, but his focus was currently drawn by someone that had been there with him throughout all the improbable events.

He listened to her talk about her time with Alistair's father's company as she sat opposite him at the table in the Ritz suite that had been rented for them. She'd now changed out of the black work dress she had worn for the duration of the day into a pair of black three-quarter length trousers and a white woollen V-neck jumper. The remains of a cheeseboard was the only food left on the long mahogany table in front of them and the conversation had been growing more earnest as the last of the third bottle of wine dribbled into their glasses.

Annabel had asked Alistair about his father. She seemed interested to know how her boss had been so successful and how he liked to spend his money. Even when drunk, Alistair was being very careful about what he would reveal, and she teased, trying to get him to give her more and more information. Sebastian could see the discomfort in Alistair as the details were drawn out of him. He chose to divert the conversation elsewhere whenever possible, but she was very persistent. Once the penny finally dropped that he wouldn't give away any juicy details, she turned her attention to Sebastian.

'So, how about you then? What's your story? Why did you really want to interview the Prime Minister? Do you have designs on being a famous journalist?'

Sebastian took a moment to consider the question, and whether he was drunk. He was definitely not used to drinking this amount of wine and port, but he felt bold.

He leaned in closer to her and tilted his head. 'A famous journalist? Oh no,' he looked from Annabel to Alistair and back to her beautiful face, 'I'm going to be the Prime Minister.'

Annabel laughed and playfully hit him on the arm.

Sebastian joined in, laughing, returning the blow. Only when she had come to rest and got her breath back did he fix her gaze and change his tone. 'I'm not joking. Just you wait.'

As he leant back she examined his face, looking down from his eyes to his lips, those calm and still lips. His eyes didn't move, no smile crept across his face, he stayed motionless and let it hang in the air.

Alistair, observing the staring contest through the wine glass he was drinking from, softly rose from his seat. 'Right, you two. I don't know about you, but I could do with some air. Excuse me.'

It was clear that he was exiting solely for the purpose of giving them some space and neither moved an inch. They sat, on the edge of their seats, leaning in towards each other, only turning their heads to watch him leave and close the door behind him. Slowly, their heads returned to face each other once more. Staring into Annabel's eyes, he felt her hand gently touch his knee, just her fore and middle fingers, almost imperceptible. He slowly raised his hand to meet hers, gripping her fingers, running them through his.

'You're not what I expected,' she muttered softly, looking down at their hands.

'What do you mean?'

'I was expecting to meet two young school boys

off the train this morning. I'd pictured you both being about thirteen.'

'And what do you think now?' He lifted his other hand to her chin to softly raise her head to look at him.

'I don't know. You just strike me as much older than you are. If I didn't already know how old you were, I would have guessed that you were at university.'

'Does it bother you how old I am?' he inquired.

'Yes.'

It wasn't the answer he was expecting considering they were now rubbing each other's hands firmly.

'And no,' she continued. 'I'm glad we're alone. I was hoping I'd get the chance to be alone with you at some point, but now we are I'm not sure what to say.'

'You don't have to say anything at all. But I will. I shouldn't say this, but I might not get another chance. You're amazing. I thought it the moment I met you. I've had to fight the urge to tell you all day. When I should have been rehearsing what I was going to say, all I could think about was you.'

She looked down at his hand, twisting it round so the back faced her. She brought it to her lips and softly kissed it, her eyes never leaving his. He could feel her trembling nervously. His heart was beating out of his chest and he was sure she'd be able to feel his pulse through his intertwined fingers.

He stood up, still holding her hand and lifted Annabel to her feet. Silent, staring, he let her hand slip from his grasp and reached for her waist. She jolted, and he felt her move back slightly from the touch, now looking down, smiling before regaining her composure and re-joining his gaze. She reached for his hand and replaced it in the original spot that had caused the jolt. She rested her hands on his as he leant forward and rubbed his cheek against hers. Turning his head inward he placed the softest of kisses on her skin and allowed it to linger before she forced her cheek towards his lips, her lips eventually meeting his. The kiss started softly but within seconds the pair were passionately forgetting about the day's excitement.

Stumbling towards the table, hands running length of each other's backs, Sebastian picked Annabel up and sat her on the expanse of wood. He looked down at her, stopping briefly to admire her flawless complexion.

'Sebastian, I think we should move from here before Alistair comes back. I don't want my boss's son to see me kissing you. Which one is your room?'

As she asked the question, the screen on Sebastian's phone on the table behind her lit up and the vibration shifted it slightly across the surface. He read the message over her shoulder:

'It looks like they both are. Alistair got himself another room.' Sebastian smiled.

'That was awfully nice of him. In that case we can stay here then.' And with that they redoubled the kissing, passion melting them together.

Early the next morning, Alistair used his key to enter the room, knocking gingerly.

'Hello? Helloo-ooo?' He ventured further in. The door was ajar, room illuminated by the sun shining in through the open curtains. Emerging from the messy sheets was one hairy leg.

'Good morning, champ.'

There was no response from the sleeping Sebastian. Once again louder, 'Morning, champ!'

This time prompted the opening of eyes into direct sunlight, to which the response was a grasping of sheets and a covering of the pupils. It took Sebastian a minute to regain his senses before he sat bolt upright, looking at the empty bed stretching out next to him. 'Where's Annabel?'

'So, she did stay, you dirty dog. You're welcome by the way, I got the feeling you two were about to hit it off, so I thought I'd get out of your hair.'

Sebastian rubbed his eyes. 'Er, yeah thanks. Have you seen her?'

'No, sorry pal. When I came in it was just little old you. I can call reception and see whether they saw her leave. She probably had to go to work, remember it is Friday.'

'Oh yeah, of course.'

'So?' Alistair elongated the word and let it fade out until Sebastian responded to his question.

'Soooooo what?'

'You know what, don't be coy. What happened? I want details.'

'I'm afraid I'm even a bit fuzzy there. That was quite a lot of wine between three of us.'

'Did she stay all night?'

'I'm not sure, I remember kissing and drifting off together. Then I woke about two and she was still here, so she must have left at some point between then and now.'

'Maybe she couldn't wait to get out of here after seeing your, well you know,'

'Good one, very original, Alistair. I hope she's okay. I don't even have her number.'

'School boy mistake. Always, always get the number. That's it, you've lost her for good now.'

'You really think so?' Genuine concern crossed Sebastian's face.

'No, you numpty. We've at least got her email

anyway, I'm sure we'll get her number and you two will be reunited once again. Meeting the PM and pulling an older lady, quite the trip this has turned into for you, hey? I bet you're glad Max approached me now, aren't you?'

'Damn right I am. But I'm still taking credit for the PM, and for Annabel actually. She's amazing.'

'Yeah, I'll give you that. So, details, now.'

'What time is it? How are we getting back up north?'

'We've got loads of time. Jump in the shower and we'll go for some breakfast. We're being picked up at 12:30 and taken to Euston.'

'Okay, give me ten minutes.'

Sebastian lazily rolled his legs off the bed, sat upright and drank half of the glass of water sitting on the bedside cabinet. He didn't remember getting the water but to his dehydrated lips and mouth it tasted like it flowed straight from a mountain spring. He rose and walked into the bathroom, turned on the shower and started to piece the events of the previous day back together.

It had been a whirlwind, but very much his favourite memories of the day, seeing Annabel arrive for dinner and having the opportunity to spend the entire evening with her. He wanted to go back and live it all over again. He remembered lots of bashing into things, the table especially. Reaching down he could feel a bruise starting to appear. They had fallen onto the table, sending a wine glass and a plate to the wooden floor before moving towards one of the bedrooms. He'd never had a night like it.

He climbed out of the shower and thought of the interview with the Prime Minister. It was a proud moment as he stood and looked at himself in the mirror, still dripping from the shower. He smiled, slowly at first and then his face erupted into the widest of grins and he started to jump and dance around the bathroom. The Queen song 'We are the champions' had been in his head since leaving Number 10 and now it found a voice that filled not only the bathroom but the entire suite.

He was interrupted mid squeal at the climax of the song by a bemused looking Alistair. Sebastian's energy was contagious and within a minute they were dancing around the living room, jumping on sofas and chairs singing the anthem at the top of their lungs. As they ended the song they laughed and hugged, breathless, Alistair's shirt now spattered with droplets from Sebastian's undried skin.

'What are you so excited about, buddy?' Alistair asked.

'We did it, I can't believe we actually did it.

We interviewed the PM... of fucking England.'

'Well, it's technically the whole UK but I know what you mean.'

His sarcasm seemed to take a different tone today. Either that or Sebastian's perception of it had changed. He no longer felt like it was derision coming his way, more dry banter and he quite liked it. Whether it was the sense of accomplishment from the day before or the evening that followed, the world seemed a different place today. All these things they'd experienced in the space of twenty-four hours made him want to do more, to achieve more, to keep on going and not stop. For the first time, he felt the passion and drive that Max radiated every time they talked about the possibilities.

Out of the bay window of the bedroom, it was just possible to see the back of Buckingham Palace through the trees in Green Park. As he dressed looking at the iconic site, he thought about what his next challenge would be. One day, if all went to plan, he would drive through those gates in a government car with black windows, flanked by police motorbikes, and submit a request to form a government to the ruling monarch, whoever that would be. He had seen footage of Cameron's own drive out of the Downing Street gates, down Whitehall and onto the Mall, the road cleared of cars by the police bikes, helicopters hovering overhead filming and watching. During the interview, Sebastian had asked about that very day and the feelings he experienced when making the trip that so few people ever have the opportunity to enjoy. Mr Cameron's response had been sincere and heart felt. Sebastian thought it was a turning point in the interview where suddenly a politician, so used to being guarded and towing the line, was truly able to demonstrate what it feels like when years of sweat and toil cumulate in one moment that justifies it all.

Buttoning the collar on his shirt as he looked in the mirror, he no longer saw his former self, the shy, young school boy. He saw Sebastian, the tall, confident future Prime Minister ready for that one moment. And he believed it.

13

Max waited nervously in the studio above his parents' garage. Breathing deeply to calm himself, he wondered who would be the first to arrive for the group's inaugural meeting. One of the two new boys he'd recruited in just the last forty-eight hours? Or one of the two returning from London? A lot had happened in just the last couple of days and tonight was the first chance for Max to bring them all together and see how they interacted.

The sound of movement on the gravel outside summoned him to the door. He opened it to see Nicholas expertly gliding over the gravel on the crutches he'd been handed at the hospital only the previous evening. The injury that Nicholas had initially tried to walk off on the Army field trip had been confirmed as a fracture of the lower fibula. Over the hours that followed the incident, between Max recruiting Nicholas and the end of the field trip, the ankle had swelled dramatically and the pain had become intense. The decision was taken to drop him straight at the hospital on the way home. Max went too.

'How's it feeling?' He stood aside allowing him to shuffle through sideways on his crutches.

'Not too bad, mate. Got to have this on for a few weeks...' he nodded down towards the blue cast on his foot, 'but they said it will be fine soon enough.'

'How are you with stairs?' Max smiled at the three-sided staircase leading up to the first floor of the garage.

'I think I can manage.' Without hesitation, he scaled the stairs two at a time, reaching the top in seconds.

'I'd just about say so. You don't do things by halves, do you?' Max remarked as he climbed the stairs behind him, 'I like that. We're going to need that.'

As Nicholas was taking a seat and resting his crutches on the floor, more sound of movement outside entered through one of the open windows. Turning to descend the staircase Max paused. 'Remember, everyone here tonight knows everything so feel free to talk about it openly.'

Alistair was the new arrival climbing out of the passenger door of his mother's Porsche 911, followed shortly after by his mother from the driver's side. Alistair rounded the car, giving his mum a hug and a kiss on the cheek. 'Thanks, Mum, you're going to have to let me get some driving practice in some time.'

'Not in my Porsche, I don't!' She saw Max exiting the door. 'Have fun boys, how's your mum, Max?'

'She's fine thanks.'

'I won't pop in, I'm off to boxercise. Say hello from me.'

'Will do, Mrs Lovell. Enjoy.'

The two boys turned and headed for the door, Max holding out a hand for a handshake, Alistair obliging.

'How's the article coming?' Max asked.

'Really good. I think you'll be pleased with the results. We worked on it most of the day on the trip back. I'm meeting Sebastian over the weekend to finish it off and then it will be in the school newspaper when it comes out in two weeks.'

'Over the weekend? I'm impressed.'

He was pleasantly surprised at how quickly Alistair and Sebastian had bonded. More specifically how quickly Sebastian had changed his opinion of Alistair. He stopped just short of the door.

'I haven't seen you alone since you got back. How do you think it went? I mean, how was Sebastian?' Max was keen to see whether Alistair shared his confidence in their candidate.

Alistair paused, which Max took as a bad sign and readied himself for bad news.

'He was amazing. It was incredible to watch. He just turned something on, I didn't think he had it in him. He was really confident, and charming. He looked right at home opposite the PM in that room.'

'Ah phew. That's our boy, I knew he could do it. And I hear some fun was had last night.'

'I think you'd better ask Sebastian about that.'

'I have, and he's being very coy about the whole thing. Who is she?'

'Annabel? She works at my father's company and was our, well… chaperone I suppose, for the day. The two of them hit it off and that's all I know.'

'You're as bad as he is.' Max laughed as they reached the door. 'Nicholas, Alistair's here,' he shouted up the stairs.

As the pair reaching the landing Max's eyes rolled at the sight of Nicholas sitting down at the drum kit.

'You get thirty seconds and then you're done,' he ordered, half joking.

Nicholas knew the drill, he had been here before and witnessed Max's frustration as every person who crossed the threshold gravitated towards the drum kit. He took the opportunity to bash each and every component as hard as he could and as many times as he could before Max gave the signal that his time was up. Nicholas threw the sticks into the air and hollered, the cymbals still ringing from the assault.

The noise had masked the appearance of the next arrival and he joined the party just as Nicholas was grabbing his crutches to move over to the couch.

'You're getting much better, Max,' Sebastian joked as he entered the room.

Max raised a solitary finger in response.

'Right, we're just awaiting our newest member and then we'll get going,' Max announced.

'You've already spoken with Rohan?' Sebastian sounded surprised.

'Done and dusted. I think we've found our legal mind to take care of that element. I only spoke with him today, so he won't have done much research just yet, but I wanted him to be here for the first full meeting.'

Max had known Rohan for many years having started school together at the age of seven. When thinking about who a good fit would be to take charge of the legal side, Max remembered hearing about a competition Rohan had been part of at the Crown Courts in Liverpool for aspiring young lawyers and barristers. He'd not only won it but had been asked to be on the judging panel for the following year. It seemed like a match made in heaven.

'Does anyone need a drink? Or the toilet? Or anything before we get started?'

Hands went up for drinks. Nicholas enquired about beer but was poo-pooed by Max. 'Only after we've discussed everything.'

As he descended the stairs to collect refreshments, Max heard faint footsteps on the path outside. Once again, he opened the varnished oak door to be greeted by Rohan slowly advancing up the driveway, his eyes fixated on the sandstone detail of the house he was circumnavigating. Although they had known each other a long time, this would have been the first time that Rohan had been here. Max observed him, unseen, from the doorway.

'Rohan, over here.'

His head spun towards the source of the sound and he smiled. His grin was contagious, and mischievous. Max watched him approaching. There was something about the way Rohan moved that amused him. It was as if his body was always a second ahead of his feet, which seemed unwilling to fully leave the ground as he walked, giving the impression of a shuffle and slight lack of coordination. One shouldn't be fooled, however. The boy had serious talent with both a cricket bat and ball. Known for his pace, his bowling was feared throughout the school and the county.

'Thanks for coming, buddy. You're right on time. I'm just sorting some drinks. Can I get you anything?'

'A beer?' There was the mischief beaming out.

'I knew you'd say that. Later. We have things to discuss first. Head up, I'll be there in a minute.'

'Okay, just a water then, thanks.'

Returning with the drinks, Max remained standing and started to speak while passing out the glasses.

'Thanks for coming, boys. I think you all have some idea of why we're sitting in this room now. I've spoken with you each individually about what I believe we're capable of doing.

'Before we go any further, I need you to be one hundred percent honest with me, and with yourself, that this is something you want to be a part of. If it's not, that's not a problem and we'll of course still be friends, but you can't come any further with us. It's not something that we can change half way through. You need to be confident that you can do your part and be happy to do it. We're not planning for the next year, or even the next five. What we're talking about is our lives. Lives that we'll devote to one another, lives that we'll devote to this, to helping people, to making the right decisions and to influencing the world in the best way that we can.

'Every single part and person will be integral and as important as the others. We'll all have huge responsibilities, different responsibilities, and our lives will charter various courses. We need to make sure that whatever we're doing, or wherever we're doing it, this group has your absolute loyalty.'

The boys, split between the sofas that made up three sides of a square surrounding a rectangular coffee table in the centre of the room, watched as he spoke and moved around the room. He collected a brown, leather ottoman from against the wall and positioned it to face the group.

'Take these pieces of paper and a pen,' he said, pointing to the table. Sebastian leant forward and passed around a square, off-white piece of paper and a pen to each of the boys.

'If you're in, draw a pentagon with your initials in and fold the paper in half. If you're out, draw a square and write your initials in the middle, and again, fold the paper.' He paused for a beat, wondering how to phrase the next part. 'Again, it's not a problem if you don't want to be here. But now is the time to say. After this, it becomes a little more complicated.'

He passed a transparent Pyrex bowl to Sebastian sitting directly to his left. Without hesitation, Sebastian wrote on the paper, guarding his scribble with his other hand, folded it and placed it in the bowl before sliding the dish across to Alistair on his left.

Alistair looked to Max, then Sebastian, Nicholas

and finally Rohan, pausing on each face.

'Let's do this.' Alistair inscribed his name and his shape and folder the paper.

Next up was Nicholas. The pen touched the paper and started to write, before stopping.

'Do you think we can really achieve this?' He looked around the room.

All eyes were now on Max as they waited for his response. It was a question he knew would be coming in one form or another. He did his best to pretend that he was saying these words for the first time.

'I really do. We're in the best position possible to be able to achieve what we're talking about. We're young, we have time to make the choices required, and you've all been chosen because I know you're capable of doing what you need to. We'll get to the 'how' shortly, but for now, I just need to know that you are in.'

'If you really think we can do it, then I'm in. One hundred percent.'

Nicholas flipped his paper into the bowl.

Rohan was next and there was no hint of hesitation as he dropped the folded piece into the bowl, softly nodding as he looked from face to face.

Max, his nerves now starting to calm, signed his piece and added it to the others. Picking up the bowl, he picked up the stack of paper, and opened each one onto the middle of the table, aligning them neatly in a circle.

'Now we are all witness to each other's commitment to this. I want you to burn this memory into your mind.'

He refolded the pieces of paper and lay them in the bowl in a messy heap. Producing a long fire-lighter, he clicked it into life and placed it to the corner of one of the pieces of paper.

'No evidence shall ever exist of this, of us.'

The flames, quickly engulfing every piece, rose above the rim of the bowl briefly before all the fuel was consumed and only ash left.

'Do you all know which one your stronger eye is? Nicholas, Alistair, you should from shooting.'

'Sure, I know it's my right,' Nicholas confirmed.

Alistair nodded to indicate the same.

'I'm not sure. How do I know?' Rohan asked sheepishly.

Max moved his hands to demonstrate. 'Hold your index fingers out, now place both hands in front of you but one about a foot in front of the other and line them up in front of your eyes. Now, close each eye one at a time. When you close one your hands should still be in line, when you close the other they won't.'

'Ah, okay,' observed Rohan, 'when I close my left they're out of line.'

'Cool. That means your left is your strong eye, or dominant eye,' Max confirmed.

'Mine's right then,' added Sebastian.

Max reached into the bowl and rubbed his index finger in the ash of the charred papers, checking as it came out that it was sufficiently coated with black and silver ash. Raising hand to head, he drew the ash across his forehead above his right eye. A single, solid line, the exact width of his eye.

'Now do the same, just above the eyebrow of your dominant eye, draw a line with the ash,' he instructed.

The boys now looked at each other, confused.

'What does it mean?'

'It signifies the sacrifice that you are willing to make for the group and for each other. I'll go into more detail next time we meet and show you why it's significant but for now just know that this is the symbol of the wisdom that you'll need and the sacrifice you are willing to make.'

The group all followed his lead and marked their brows.

'This is something that we will do at the start of every meeting.'

One of the group repeated the question about its meaning but he didn't give any more detail.

'As I've said, I'll explain all next time we meet. But

this is a sign of commitment to the group. No one else can know about it. It's easy to wipe off so no one will ever see it, we just have to wipe our faces once we have finished meeting.'

'Will we have any other rituals? You know, like the masons and their handshakes, or the initiations of the Skull and Bones?' Nicholas asked. He seemed excited by the prospect of having a way for the group to identify each other.

'Glad to see you've been doing your research. But that's not how we'll operate. This is another area I need to talk to you all about. We will have no name.

'I know it's appealing to emulate our influences or other groups, but there's a problem with groups and secret societies like these. People know about them. There is information readily available on the internet, which is where I'm assuming you got yours from. We're different. No one can ever know about us. That means that we won't have signet rings, or badges, or symbols. We aren't going to recruit. Only we will ever know about this group and for that reason we will not need a name. We'll also never speak about any of this in public. If you need to refer to this group, then simply refer to it as "Us".

'I can't emphasise this strongly enough. You never discuss this in front of others, never discuss it on the phone, not on WhatsApp, not in text messages or emails. If you need to talk to one of us, or all of us, it has to be done in person, or in code. If we want this to work, we must be incredibly careful. When you come here to meet, we'll say we're playing poker or playing computer games, or doing school work. But the truth can never be known, and I mean to anyone. No parents, no girlfriends, no other friends. Does that make sense?'

He felt a pang of guilt as he thought back to his conversations with Harriet. Here he was asking them not to tell a soul, when he'd told her everything. Everything.

The only way he could justify it was to tell himself that she was more of a confidant who'd been there since the group's inception. As she already knew everything, she was part of it, like it or not.

'Does it really have to be like that? What if we get married one day? Can our wives know?' asked Rohan, slightly facetiously.

Max shook his head slowly as he held his friend's gaze, his expression apologetic. 'No, this is one thing I need to you understand. Total and utter secrecy is the only way this can ever work. Let's use an example a few years in the future. Sebastian is running for Prime Minister and some journalist gets a whiff that he was involved with a secret society in school, or in university, and still is. The media would investigate every element of his life, starting with school, then university. Let's say you get married, Rohan, and your wife knows about the group. One day you wake up and you don't love her anymore and want to leave. How would you deal with the fact that she knows about us?'

'I'd have to talk to her I guess. I'm sure someone you're married to would be okay and wouldn't tell.'

'I think you have a very rosy view of divorce. Listen, the reality is that this rule has to be in place from the start. It's one of the foundations of what we're going to achieve that no one outside of us can know. It's just too risky. Please tell me you understand.'

It felt like the gravity of what he was asking of them was finally sinking in. The boys looked pensive, almost deflated. The idea of keeping secrets from everyone around you could appeal to some, but not most.

'I promise you, you will not need to confide in anyone else, you'll have your brothers here for anything you need. And I mean, *anything* you need. The ash you have on your foreheads is a sign of that. You will make sacrifices to help the people sitting next to you today, they'll sacrifice for you too, and you'll be asked to prove that every time we meet. The ash above your eyes will be a constant reminder every time we're together that the group comes before everything. Does anyone have any questions or doubts?'

They all looked at each other. If anyone had doubts, they didn't raise any.

Questions however, there were plenty, and understandably. Max and Sebastian answered them one by one. At this stage, only the individual members themselves knew what role they had been asked to perform and their path in the plan. This was now about to change as the big picture was laid bare for all to see. If there was to be any disagreement or jealousy over others' future identities, this would be the time.

However, Max was confident that each of the roles carried enough importance and significance that each should be proud to have been assigned any of them. The only member who had so far shown doubts about their chosen life was Alistair. For now, those doubts seemed to have evaporated but it still worried Max.

Max stood and talked to the group about his vision, what he thought they could achieve and how it would benefit each individual, and each other. This had been a part of his life for months now, plaguing every waking minute. He found himself daydreaming in class, not only about his future, but of those seated around him now. It was critical to him that they understood that this was not a plan for him, but for them all.

It didn't work without the people staring at him now and only as a group would it be possible at all.

His passion was infectious. He strode around the room, standing behind the person whose life he was describing. Careful not to dictate what the future would be, but rather provide a picture of all the possibilities, both near and far, that were available as part of the group. He knew that he could not be responsible for making every decision that was required for success, and in these moments, he transferred ownership to the individual. By opening their eyes to what was ahead but not constricting, he suggested that each member took time to plan their goals over the coming years.

There were some key milestones that were prescriptive, however. University choice was key, and this would be each individual's first challenge. Academia. Success relied upon each of the group achieving good enough A-Levels to get into a top-tier university, all apart from Alistair, but Max knew that he would be one of the highest performers in the group anyway. Time was now of the essence. Universities accept students not only on their academic merit but also on their extra-curricular activities. Luckily, the group Max had chosen were already strong performers both inside and outside of the classroom. Most of the boys had been progressing towards a career in the same area that they were being asked to excel in, so they had already started the hard work themselves. Now it was time to refine those goals and add in as much as needed to guarantee their casting in the next act.

Each was asked to look at the universities that their predecessors attended and the courses they studied, the clubs they were part of and the jobs they did straight after university. Each was to know what the next two, five, eight and ten years held in store. And that was just the start. University applications would start later that calendar year and with only a few months left of the academic year, it was crucial to fill any gaps now ahead of AS-Levels that were starting in a few weeks. It was a tall order, but nothing about this was going to be simple. Max was confident he had chosen the right group who would make it happen.

The next part was one that he personally was very excited about.

'So, I'm sorry to have set you all homework but I hope what I'm about to say next will make it all worthwhile. We have just eleven weeks until we finish our AS exams and as a little treat, Alistair has kindly arranged with his dad that we can use his boat for a little blowout party.'

They all spun to look at Alistair, who bobbed his head in agreement, looking slightly embarrassed.

'I won't tell you too much just now, but you need to clear it with your parents as soon as possible and make sure it's all okay. I have something very fun in mind.'

'Where's the boat?' asked Nicholas.

'It's wherever we want it to be,' came Alistair's reply. 'It's moored in Saint Tropez, at the moment, but we can take it wherever we want. My dad said he may join us for a day or two, but we'll have it to ourselves for the rest.'

'What kind of boat is it?' shouted Nicholas excitedly.

'A big one,' Max emphasised. 'That's all you need to know for now, but I promise, you will not want to miss out.'

14

Max recounted the group's first meeting to Harriet as they sat alone in the school library. 'It went well. It was hard, but I think they're slowly starting to understand exactly what we're trying to do and what it will take to get there.'

He paused as he reached a certain topic, knowing he may have to defend himself.

'The one part they struggled with initially was the secrecy,' he continued. 'And, of course, I understand that, but that's why we'll have each other. I may have to keep reiterating it. All that keeps going through my mind is whether I can trust them all to keep it secret.'

'Do they know that I know?' Harriet asked.

'No.' He shook his head as he looked at her, studying her, waiting for her to say it.

'Isn't it a bit hypocritical you telling them they can't, but here we are planning and discussing it?'

'Yes. Totally. And I'm struggling with that part too. But this is different. You knew about it before it was even a real thing. And I trust you explicitly. I can, can't I?'

She leant closer over the corner of desk and held her nose only an inch from his, looking deep into his eyes.

'Of course, you can. I'd do anything for you, absolutely anything,' she answered softly and sincerely. 'I hope you know that. I've never met anyone in my life that I trust as much as I do you. And I want you to know that you can trust me. With anything.'

They bowed their foreheads to rest on each other's as she placed a hand on his knee which he met with his own. He raised hers to his mouth and kissed the back of it softly.

'Good. I feel exactly the same about you.'

'Now, tell me about the rest of the meeting.' She smiled.

Max described the events of the evening to her, revealing the blackened foreheads and their commitment to the group, to each other. He reeled off each of the questions and objections that had been raised how he'd overcome them.

She hung on his every word, once more the passion flowing out of him, hardly able to control the speed of his speech. Every so often, she would subtly point out another approach he could take when tackling a question or make him think about his argument in a different way. Although his enthusiasm was infectious, and maybe one of the reasons the boys had agreed to be part of the group, it could get away from him.

'Sometimes I think you just need to focus on the facts and logic,' she said. 'That's how you convinced me.'

When he'd finished filling her in with the details, she once again leaned in. 'Hearing you talk about it makes you sound so powerful. When can we go home?'

'I can't go until after this careers fair this evening. You can stick around and we'll go back together?' He was dying to leave with her right now, but duty called.

'I could, or we could…you know.' She winked.

'I'm not sure that's completely sensible here.' Max glanced around the empty desks.

'Why not? There's no one here.'

Being a sixteen-year-old and full of testosterone, he normally found it hard to be around her without wanting to touch her. When she goaded him, he found it nigh impossible. Leaning forward, he started to kiss her ear gently, his right hand finding her left hip.

'Huh-hummmm.'

There was a loud, purposeful cough from around the corner of the library stacks and they jolted apart. Max shot to his feet to see who was approaching as a familiar face appeared.

'Sir,' he exclaimed with unescapable guilt in his voice. 'I hadn't realised anyone else was in here.'

'Clearly, Mr Mercer. And who might this be?'

Harriet stood and approached the Head Teacher, confidently holding out her hand. Max made the introduction, 'Mr Howarth, meet Harriet. Harriet, this is Mr Howarth. Sir, Harriet is my girlfriend, we were just killing some time before the careers event this evening.'

'Very well. Harriet, would you mind leaving me and Mr Mercer alone for a few minutes. I shan't keep him too long.'

'Er, yes. Of course, sir.'

She turned and picked up the bags from the seat next to hers.

'I'll meet you at the usual place?' she asked of Max, to which he nodded. With that, she made her way down the stairs and out of the front library exit. Max watched her leave, admiring how confident she had been even after nearly getting caught doing what would be seriously frowned upon had Howarth only appeared minutes later.

Once the teacher was sure they were now alone, he turned back to Max, a wry smile on his face and proceeded to speak, 'I think we should have a little talk, don't you? Take a seat.'

They sat at the same table Max and Harriet had occupied only moments ago, Max expecting to be reprimanded for what had just taken place. To his surprise, Harriet was not to be the subject of conversation.

'I'm not sure if you realised, Max, but I have been reading only just around the corner for the last twenty minutes. Now, one hates to eavesdrop but it's hard not to overhear a conversation in an otherwise silent library. Your discussion seemed very lively and interesting.'

Max's face drew pale as he realised that the Head must have heard the majority, if not all, of his narration of the group's first meeting.

'Max,'—the look on his teacher's face was stern— 'I need to know what you're up to.'

15

Hi Sebastian,

So lovely to hear from you. I'm glad you got in touch. I'm sorry for leaving without saying goodbye but I was really embarrassed. I don't know what got into me. I promise you, I would never normally kiss someone I'd only just met. We'd had too much wine and I just couldn't stop myself.

But I don't regret it at all.

That was a really fun day. I haven't stopped thinking about you. I have to visit one of our offices in Manchester next Friday, I'm staying at the Hilton. I thought you could come to Manchester and we could have dinner?

Annabel

x

Hey Annabel,

I haven't stopped thinking about you either. I was worried you thought it was a big mistake. I had a lot of fun. I was hoping to see you in the morning to kiss you before you left.

Manchester would be great, I have a couple of free periods on Friday afternoons so I can leave early and come and meet you.

Sebastian x

16

'I can't believe they're finally done and out of the way!' Alistair's face now took on a form different from the one the boys had become used to over the last two months.

Max had been surprised by the change in his behaviour during the stressful exam period. Whilst it was normal for all teenagers to experience some degree of tension during the summer exam periods of the last few years of school, it was clear that Alistair's stress was a level above.

Max had tried to talk with him during the lead up to the exam period about planning the holiday but, aside from being told that it was all definitely happening and the date, he was repeatedly brushed off. He'd decided to let everyone do what they needed to do, and they would use the trip as a way of reigniting the flames.

It was clear from their very brief conversations that Alistair, being an intellectual and driven individual, had set himself the toughest of targets. Having originally set his mind on studying medicine at university, he'd accepted that failure was not an option, and anything less than his best would be a disaster. When the behaviour had first become apparent, Max had assumed that it was Alistair's parents setting the expectations. It was only now becoming clear that all Alistair's parents had ever said to him about academics and career was that as long as he was happy, that was all that mattered to them.

Now aboard the seventy-foot Challenger 601-3R business jet as it sat on the tarmac at Manchester Airport, Max watched the boys' disbelief at what was unfolding before them. He looked towards Alistair who had already taken his seat in one of the wide, swivelling executive armchairs situated towards the front of the fuselage. The pair exchanged a nod.

The supple, white leather was a stark contrast to the rich mahogany panelling at each end of the main cabin.

Max turned and joined Rohan in the cockpit where he was talking to the pilot and co-pilot, asking endless questions about what the panels and controls did. Nicholas and Sebastian were nosily walking up and down the length of the plane behind him, exploring cupboards and commenting on the opulence that was on display.

Two hostesses, elegantly dressed in navy uniforms with cream and red polka dot silk scarves, were preparing the plane for take-off. Standing by the front door, Elena, the head stewardess, tapped away at a control panel, commanding the door that also contained the stairs to raise slowly, perfectly sealing the cabin from the outside world.

'Gentleman, welcome aboard your personal flight to Toulon-Hyeres airport today.' The pilot's accent sounded distinctly British, but his pronunciation of their destination was in perfect French.

'Our flight time will be around two and a half hours. We're due for sunny skies all the way into the south of France, where we'll be arriving at approximately 12:15 local time. Please make yourselves comfortable, strap in, and enjoy the ride. Our fabulous cabin crew, Elena and Sarah, will ensure that all your needs are taken care of. To celebrate Alistair's upcoming birthday, Mr Lovell has kindly provided you with an assortment of drinks and as we'll be cruising at 37,000 feet I don't suspect the authorities will mind that you're not quite of age just yet. We'll begin taxiing to the runway in a few minutes ahead of take-off scheduled in just over ten.'

As promised, shortly after take-off, Sarah appeared with a bottle of champagne from the bar at the rear of the cabin and placed a glass in front of each of the boys. Nicholas took the opportunity to ask for a photo, Sarah kindly obliging. Not content with one, the boys proceeded to strike a variety of poses around the aircraft, even convincing Elena and Sarah to pose with them. The champagne kept coming and by the time they touched down, the group was merry, to say the least. After one final group shot with the captain and co-pilot, they departed the plane like rock stars touching down ahead of a sold-out concert, ready to greet their screaming fans.

A large black mini-bus waited fifteen feet from the bottom of the steps and the driver hopped out of the left-hand door as he saw the plane's steps begin to lower. He opened the rear doors of the bus ready for their luggage and within minutes they were fully-loaded and had set off along the coastal route towards the waiting Mufasa.

'You saw her again? Why didn't you tell me?' Max was questioning Sebastian.

'We've actually met up a few times. I haven't really seen you outside of school since we started our exams, so we haven't had a chance to speak about it.' Sebastian defended the lack of communication.

'You dog! So, tell me all,' Max said.

The pair had taken position in the first of the three passenger rows of the vehicle and the commotion drew attention from the others who now craned to find out what the discussion was about.

'What's all this about? Seb's got himself a girl-friend?' Nicholas was the first to ask, poking his head through the gap in the headrests. 'Have you been going down to the blind school again?'

The group laughed, including Sebastian. It was an old joke but sometimes those were the best.

'Come on, come on, come on!' Nicholas chanted in quick succession. 'We want to hear all about it.'

'I'm sure you do,' Sebastian said. 'She's a girl Alistair and I met when we were down in London interviewing the Prime Minister. She's amazing, and gorgeous. And she's totally into me, but, you know, how could she not be?' He laughed, initiating a chain reaction from the boys.

An empty bottle of water appeared from over the seat, thrown by Rohan who obviously thought Sebastian could do with being taken down a peg or two. He flinched out of the way, allowing the bottle to hit the back of the front passenger seat and land at his feet.

'Now, now, Rohan. Don't be jealous. Anyway, we ended up staying together in London that night. I didn't hear from her for a while so thought it was dead in the water, but what do you know? She got in touch and we've had a few trips to see each other since. I had to be a bit creative on my part. Oh—Max, if my mum ever asks, I've stayed at yours the last two weekends. Normally it wouldn't be an issue, but I was meant to be on lock-down during the exams, so I just said we were studying all weekend.'

'Don't bring me into this!' Max chuckled.

'Anyway, it's going great.'

'So, when do I get to meet her?' Max asked.

'Erm, I'm not sure really, we'll have to see. I'm sure she'll come and see me over the summer. We can all hang out. That reminds me, Alistair. Aren't we going to have the opportunity to meet your belle this week?'

Alistair had been listening to the conversation but stayed very quiet. He was admiring the view out into the Mediterranean, only turning to the group when he heard mention of his name.

'You will, indeed. She's actually already out here with her family. I thought while my dad is here she could join us and then we can have the rest of the week to ourselves.'

Rohan took the opportunity to find out a bit more about the mystery girl that they all knew very little about. 'So,' he probed, 'Who is she? What's she like?'

Alistair, as usual, was aloof with his answer. 'She's nice, you'll get to see for yourselves shortly. I think she'll be on the boat when we arrive.'

Sensing that the group's excitement was high and there may be some loose tongues, Max made sure to remind the group what they had discussed the last time they met, just in case the stress of exams had taken its toll on their memories. 'Boys, I just want to say, let's remember that we aren't to talk about "Us" around anyone else.'

He raised his right hand and ran it across his forehead above his right eye, nodding and looking each of them in the eye, waiting for their response. He glanced quickly over his shoulder at the driver, confident that this would all be meaningless to him anyway.

'Anyway, back to the fun and games.'

As they neared the town of Saint Tropez, villas and restaurants lined the narrow streets and the traffic increased, bringing the mini-bus to a stand-still. The sound of the French mopeds and taxis beeping their horns was audible even above the sound of the French radio station playing from the van's speakers.

The majority of the group took in the sights and sounds, pointing out the Ferraris and Lamborghinis crawling at the same pace as the rest of the traffic.

Finally, the road swept to the left and the lines of yachts came into view. Another five hundred meters along L'Avenue Gén De Gaulle, past hundreds of parked cars, and they pulled off the main road towards a private, gated car park. The tanned guard, dressed in olive trousers and a white shirt, recognised the driver and, within a few seconds, the white, steel barred gate began slowly rolling aside.

Ahead were small boats, some for fishing, some for leisure. Among the people standing or walking along the dock, Alistair saw a familiar face beaming back towards him. The young man jogged over to the van and pulled open the sliding side-door before stepping back and opening his arms wide. 'Welcome to paradise, guys.'

'Tom, how are you?' Alistair exclaimed. It was like the reunion of two long-lost brothers, Max thought. Alistair was blocked in the second row of the mini-bus so made his introductions from his seat.

'Guys, this is Tom, he's the First Mate aboard my dad's boat.'

As the boys climbed out one by one, he shook each of their hands enthusiastically, the wide smile never leaving his face.

'Nice to meet you, nice to meet, nice to meet you, nice to meet you.'

Alistair was the last one off and they hugged and slapped each other's backs.

'Good to see you, Alistair, we've got everything all set up for your trip and there's a special someone already waiting for you on board.'

'Good to hear it, thanks. How've you been?'

The two caught up for a few minutes while the others admired the view across the bay and the view of the hills in the distance.

'I guess we should get going then.' Tom moved around to the back of the van. With the help of the driver, they unloaded the bags and carried them towards the large, grey capping stones that marked the edge of dry land. The boys reached for their bags, but Tom insisted he would take care of them. Effortlessly manoeuvring the small stairs down to water, he deposited the bags one-by-one into the back of the thirty-foot limousine tender that would be their next mode of transport.

The shape and colour of the transport boat was mesmerising. Sleek, with a low profile at the back, the dark wooden hull extended out in front of them to a crisp vertical bow. The open teak deck housed two rows of white seats facing each other, enough for ten passengers to ride comfortably, and in style. The boys simply looked at each other, unable to overcome the urge to smile and shake their heads in disbelief. Usually, they only saw boats like this in films and on TV.

As Alistair took up position at the helm, Tom tossed him the keys from the quay. Picking up a captain's hat off the pilot's seat and positioning it square on his head, he turned to his passengers and saluted as he engaged the motor.

Because of the size of Alistair's father's ship, the Mufasa was moored two hundred meters into the Gulf of Saint Tropez. At 160 metres, it dwarfed all the surrounding ships, standing out like a majestic swan amongst a flock of seagulls. The boys, still unsure which of the yachts they would be calling home for the next week, pointed out various boats around the bay. Alistair toyed with them, keeping them guessing by setting course for one of the smaller boats before making a slight alteration, rounding each and setting course for another.

Max reclined in his seat, enjoying the heat and the soft spray from the water below as the boys excitedly flapped around him. He knew exactly where they were heading. The minute Alistair had mentioned the idea of the holiday, he'd found the ship online. It had been hard to miss as they entered the harbour, but he didn't want to ruin the fun for the others so kept it to himself.

They headed for a 68-foot Sunseeker Manhattan on which Nicholas spotted a group of eight or nine girls sunbathing and drinking on the deck. 'Tom, you said there was only one special someone waiting aboard, you didn't mention the other eight that you got for us.'

'You should be so lucky!' Tom laughed.

Nicholas demanded that Alistair take them in closer and rose to his feet starting to wave at the group. By this time, the blue and white striped shirt he was wearing, now fully unbuttoned and flowing like a cape in the wind, revealed the torso of the young rugby player and army hopeful. He was in no rush to hide his defined stomach and as they came within twenty feet of the girls' boat, he lifted his right foot onto the boat's side rail resting his right elbow on his knee, stroking his chin with his right hand in an attempt to look pensive and sophisticated. The females had spotted the approaching unusual craft heading towards them and now mustered to investigate.

'Afternoon ladies, if anyone needs a hand applying their sun cream, I'd be more than happy to oblige.' Nicholas flashed a cheeky look to his companions before returning his gaze to the bikini-clad group ten feet above them. It was clear from the chatter amongst the girls that not all of them spoke English, and as they conferred amongst themselves, a slender blonde at the front of the group translated his offer into French, at which point they all started to giggle.

'Come back when you have a bigger boat,' the translator dismissed him.

'I'll be sure to take you up on the invitation,

mademoiselle.' Now, turning to Alistair he whispered, 'Please tell me your boat is bigger than theirs?'

Alistair moved to respond but it was Tom who was first to speak, 'I don't think that will be an issue, just tell them to watch where we go.'

Now returning his attention to the ladies, 'In fact, we're just about to rendezvous with our other boat, keep an eye out, maybe you can join us later.'

He looked to Alistair for reassurance and received only a roll of the eyes and a chuckle from under the captain's hat.

Clearly not convinced by Nicholas's claims, the leader gave a condescending nod of her head, lowering her sunglasses from her forehead to cover her eyes, once again turning to the group to fill them in.

Max observed the boys, all laughing and joking together. He hoped this was a sign of good things to come. As he watched Nicholas, he admired his ability to make people smile just being himself, his energy. It made everyone around him lively and playful.

Nicholas blew a kiss to the girls as Alistair engaged the throttle and their tender disappeared from the girls' view as it circled their boat. He did not look back but raised his hat in the air as he remained standing on his seat.

'Is she looking?' he shouted down to Max, seated opposite.

Max laughed at Nicholas's vanity before turning to see whether they were indeed being followed by a group of eyes from the boat they had just left.

'They're looking, mate,' he shouted back up above the noise of the boat and the waves. He kept his eyes on the girls as they now crossed to starboard, watching to see where the craft would end up after it emerged from around the bow and set a course further out into the bay, this time pointing straight towards the Mufasa.

The boys now saw for the first time what Tom had meant. To Max's left, Sebastian leant forward in his seat and, mouth wide open, slowly pulled his sunglasses from his eyes. Max turned to see the others, all in similar states.

'Alistair, are you fucking kidding me?! Oh my god. That's the biggest yacht I've ever seen!' Rohan was shaking his head.

His sentiment was echoed by the entire crew who began slapping each other on the back and laughing with incredulity.

'It's most likely the biggest you will ever see. There's only a few that eclipse her in the world.' Tom was proud of the ship which he called home.

The beast continued to grow as they got nearer, casting a shadow across their transport, giving them an unhindered view of the blue hull and white decks. Along the port side, balconies and port holes ran the length of the ship, the glass reflecting the calm waters below.

Rounding the stern of the behemoth, into sight came a group of waiting people, ready to receive them, cheering welcomes. Amongst them the ship's owner, James Lovell, and Alistair's girlfriend, Rosa, her long dark hair flowing in the sea breeze.

17

As the crew served a starter of yellowtail and spider crab marinated in lemon zest, the host and guests chatted about the boys' journey that morning. Rohan complimented Mr Lovell on the ship, or what he had seen so far, marvelling at the sheer size and opulence of his surroundings. Mr Lovell gave a brief history of the boat and where he and Alistair had visited since taking delivery of it. His excitement whilst talking them through the process of designing the vessel was akin to that of a boy talking about his first trip to Disney World.

The others chatted among themselves, describing the rooms they had been given and the labyrinth of stairwells and corridors. With only seven currently dining at one end of the grand rosewood table which could accommodate twenty guests, there was plenty of spare room. The open sides of the owner's deck gave the party uninterrupted views across the entire bay and out into the Mediterranean.

'So, Alistair, how did you two meet?' Sebastian inquired, looking at the pair.

Alistair and Rosa, positioned immediately to the left of Mr Lovell, who occupied the seat at the head of the table, looked at each other, smiling, deciding who would tell the story. Alistair nodded for Rosa to take the lead.

'I was visiting China with my family last year. Have you ever been there, Sebastian?' she asked.

'No, but I'd love to go. I've heard it's amazing.'

'It is, you must,' she replied in her soft Italian accent, 'and if you do, you have to go to Xi'an, I think that was my favourite place of all.'

Her English was perfect, unsurprisingly, having spent much of her schooling in the South of England at Marlborough College.

'I may be slightly biased, of course, as that's where I met Alistair, but still, it's a beautiful city. They have an amazing water fountain show at the Big Wild Goose Pagoda.' She looked at Alistair and they both chuckled. During their time in China, they had taken much amusement from the name but could not articulate why.

'The fountain is huge, and I mean huge, like the size of a football pitch, and you can walk through and play in the jets of water which dance in time to music coming from speakers all around the edge. It lights up and there are people playing and jumping and getting soaking wet. It's magical. My little sister and I were having fun dancing and I shimmied right into the back of Alistair by accident. I fell over and my face landed right on top of one of the jets of water.'

Alistair chuckled and squeezed her hand. 'I'm sorry. I shouldn't laugh, but it was funny.'

'Maybe for you! I was nearly blinded. The jets were so strong! Anyway, Alistair being the gentleman that he is, picked me up and carried me to the side, out of the jets, and helped me catch my breath.'

Nicholas scrunched up his face and teased the pair, 'Aww, how cute, Alistair to the rescue.'

Alistair bowed his head, embarrassed, as he watched Rosa talk about how they met.

'It was very sweet of him, actually.' She jumped to his defence, smiling as she enjoyed seeing him being teased by the group. 'I don't really believe in fate but "coincidence" just doesn't seem to do it justice.'

'I didn't believe in fate either,' Alistair agreed, 'but that wasn't actually the first time I saw you.' He turned to Rosa. 'I nearly met you earlier that day at the Terracotta Warriors.'

The Terracotta Warriors are one of China's recently discovered wonders of the world. Found accidentally by farmers in 1974, they had been created over 2,200 years earlier to guard China's first Emperor, Qin Shi Huang di, and to serve as his army in the afterlife. The magnificent collection of nearly 8,000 life-sized, individually modelled soldiers of varying ranks, armed with weapons and chariots, formed just part of the colossal mausoleum which took almost forty years to build.

'I'd been looking at the endless rows of figures,' Alistair continued, 'when I spotted you across one of the walkways. You looked so cute lifting your sister up so she could get a better view into the pits. I stopped dead in my tracks and when mum asked me what was wrong, I just simply pointed at you. I told her I needed to go and talk to you and set off after you but because of the crowd of people, by the time I reached the spot where I saw you, you had already moved on and were nowhere to be seen.

'I didn't for one second imagine that I'd bump into you again.'

'Why have you never told me that before?' Rosa now had tears in her eyes as she stared at him.

'Well, to find each other twice in a nation of one billion is no mean feat.' Sebastian filled the silence.

'Hear, hear, Sebastian. If that's not a cause for champagne, I'm not sure I know a better one!' Mr Lovell saluted.

Without hesitation, Ernesto, the head waiter sprang into action, recovering two bottles of Dom Pérignon from the bar. He filled Rosa's glass first before attending to the rest of the group. James Lovell stood, glass in hand.

'I don't often get to spend as much time as I'd like with my only son, but it's moments like these that really make you thankful for everything one has in life. To my son,' he turned and bowed his head, 'may your life be filled with many more moments of serendipitous joy. To the rest of you young men, may you all find a catch like this Italian princess we have in our midst.' He raised his glass to the sky. 'Santé!'

The group rose and repeated the cheer like a battle cry. 'Santé!'

The following courses echoed the elegance of the starter. The presentation was like nothing the boys had ever experienced, aside from Alistair, even if it wasn't to all their tastes. The on-board Executive Chef, Emmanuel Durand, was nothing short of a master, highly regarded in culinary circles. Having won his third Michelin star six years earlier, James Lovell had the pleasure of making his acquaintance in Durand's Tokyo restaurant nine months before this trip. Durand had expressed that he was tiring of life in the East and was looking to sell his restaurant and move back to familiar shores. A recent family loss had taken its toll and he no longer took joy in running the establishment, longing for a more relaxed style of life back in Europe. When Mr Lovell called him personally upon returning to England, Durand welcomed the opportunity to spend an initial year aboard the Mufasa, creating masterpieces without any of the commercial stresses of owning a world-famous restaurant and had joined the crew two months earlier.

He personally accompanied the dessert, a symphony of strawberries with Tahitian vanilla, to the table. At Mr Lovell's invitation, he joined the diners for a glass of champagne.

'Emmanuel, meet my son, Alistair, and his friends. They'll be enjoying your delights over the next week. Seems a bit of a shame to waste such good food on these rapscallions but there we go.'

'It's my pleasure to meet you all. I am at your service.' His thick French accent had not been diluted by his years spent abroad.

After an hour of chatting and drinking, James excused himself from the table, at which point Durand also took his leave. The youths were left to finish the rest of the champagne before descending to the lower decks to their rooms. The plan was to meet in the tender garage thirty minutes later and take jet skis to go sightseeing around the bay.

Alistair and Rosa seized the opportunity for some time alone and the instant they reached their room Rosa let her azure sun dress drop from her shoulders, revealing her tanned skin, now only covered by her matching bikini. Alistair took a moment to look at her, admiring her beauty and her body before moving in close, wrapping his arms around her tightly, pulling her towards him. They kissed passionately, having not seen each other for three months. It wasn't long before they were fully undressed and writhing in passion.

Alistair was in no rush to leave the room after they had finished making love. Having spent the entire day with the group, he wanted nothing more than to enjoy time with the one person he really felt he could be himself with. The boys were fun, but after a long few months with the pressure of exams, he just wanted some time to decompress and relax. He was still getting to know most of them.

'If you're leaving tomorrow, that means we only have one night together. And most of it will be spent with all of them as well.' Rosa seemed upset.

'I know, baby. But it was your idea to bring them out.' Alistair smiled as he attempted to avoid the approaching spat. However much he loved her Italian fire, he had learnt to change the mood quickly when he noticed an air of tension. This avoided any lengthy contemplation about the time they had to spend apart.

'And anyway, why don't you stay out here after they go home and then we can go somewhere together, just the two of us?' Alistair suggested.

'I like that idea. I'll speak to mum and make sure she's okay with it, but I can't see any reason she won't be. My parents are going to be in Monaco next week, so we could meet there and spend some time with them,' she offered.

'That sounds great. As long as I get you all to myself for at least a few days.'

'I'm sure we can make that happen,' she smiled. 'We still have ten minutes before we need to be downstairs, why don't you tell me that story again of when you first saw me.'

⬠

Nicholas knew exactly where he wanted to go on the jet skis and was now chomping at the bit in the hope that his friends from earlier were still there. Most of the group had now assembled, watching as Tom lowered the machines into the water, one by one.

Rohan was the first into the water, diving headlong into the blue below, his bright yellow shorts visible under the waterline even before he resurfaced. As he came up for air, he beckoned the others.

'It's nice and warm, guys,' he lied as he caught his breath.

He climbed onto the back of one of the black and blue Sea-Doo GTR jet skis, wrapped the safety lanyard around his wrist and pressed the start button.

Manoeuvring to point away from the ship, he sped off in a loop around the Mufasa. As a contrast to the welcoming soft, plush interior of the ship, from water level he got a completely different view. Here, everything was hard and angular, shiny and durable. As the beast towered above him, it was easy to feel microscopic in comparison. Even the anchors nestled into the hull on both the port and starboard sides at the front of the boat dwarfed him. He wondered whether one day being part of the group would bring him riches that enable him to buy something like this.

Rounding the 160-metre vessel took him longer than he expected. By the time he returned to the open tender garage deck, Nicholas was aboard his jet ski circling in donuts creating as much spray as was physically possible. He saw Rohan approaching and calmed his steed, shouting up to the stragglers slowly putting on the life jackets, 'Come on, slow coaches, what are you waiting for?'

'Sorry, Nicholas, we were just waiting for the happy couple,' Max replied. 'And speak of the devils.'

Rosa and Alistair emerged through the entrance to the hangar ready for sightseeing.

'Alistair,' Nicholas shouted up, 'I'm going to pay our friends from earlier a little visit. What's our plan for dinner? Will we be going ashore?'

Rohan knew exactly what Nicholas was really asking. As he saw Alistair's face appear at the edge of the hangar, it was clear that he had also seen through Nicholas's crudely veiled question.

'If you can convince them to, they're welcome to come and have drinks over here. Just one thing, though, that jet ski is even smaller than the tender. I don't think that's what she really imagined.'

'Oh, I think we both know which boat I'll be saying is mine! Come on, Rohan, let's go.'

Without even waiting for a response Nicholas revved the throttle and the jet ski lurched forward at pace.

Rohan looked up at the gang on the ship, smiled, rolled his eyes and set off in pursuit of the Lothario. As he tried to catch up, he wondered what to say when they reached the girls' boat. He'd always struggled speaking with people he didn't know, especially girls. This was definitely not something he would normally do but here he was, in the south of France, staying on a yacht with a group of people who were all about to embark on a new adventure. Stepping outside his comfort zone might not be such a bad thing.

The remaining four watched them race off towards the familiar Sunseeker before taking it in turn to drop into the sea and onto their own jet skis. Alistair led the group towards a set of hidden caves in the north side of the bay.

Shouting over the noise of the machines, Max and Sebastian made a bet whether Nicholas would come back with a catch or tail between his legs. Max was confident that the lure of a superyacht would seal the deal whereas Sebastian held less optimism for Nicholas's tactics. Whatever happened, they agreed he would come back with an entertaining story.

What they would have witnessed had they been a fly on the wall was Nicholas's charm in full swing. Tipsy from the champagne at lunch and with a sure-fire plan, his confidence was through the roof.

As he and Rohan approached the Sunseeker, they could see a few of the girls dozing on the deck. Not one to make a quiet entrance, Nicholas turned to his companion and winked before proceeding to circle the boat at full speed, ensuring that all on board were alerted to his presence. Rohan, being a subtler soul, backed off and let his comrade do his thing. As before, the girls ventured to the side of the boat to investigate the commotion before moving to the stern where Nicholas had come to rest.

'We meet again. Funny how this keeps happening.' He directed his words towards the translator.

'I don't think this is accident.' Her English wasn't perfect, but it was far better than his French.

'Mind if we come aboard? I wanted to extend an offer.'

Rohan smiled from behind his sunglasses as he watched Nicholas become a character he'd never seen before. It was as if he was making a conscious attempt to resemble James Bond.

'I think this is okay.' She shrugged, aloof.

The pair brought their jet skis closer to the platform at the back of the boat. Nicholas was first off and helped Rohan from his.

'Play it cool, brother. I think we're in here,' Nicholas whispered as they locked arms and he heaved Rohan off the Sea-Doo. 'How old do you think they are?'

'Older than us, definitely. Maybe eighteen?' Rohan guessed, subtly looking over Nicholas's shoulder with only his eyes rather than his head.

'Okay, we're eighteen too then.'

They climbed the three steps up to the lower deck and Nicholas held out his hand to his conversational partner. She ignored the hand and moved towards him, kissing him once on each cheek.

'You English are so funny. In France we do not hold hand, we kiss hello! I'm Céleste.'

She greeted Rohan in the same fashion before turning to introduce the rest of her group. Now there only seemed to be five girls on the boat, at least visible anyway.

'Were there not more of you earlier?' Nicholas inquired.

'Ah yes, but the others, they... they are feeling "pissed", is this how you say?'

It was clear she had a fairly good grasp of colloquial English, even if she wasn't fully confident of it.

'That's exactly how you say it. Too much wine with lunch?' Nicholas responded.

'Yes, too much wine.'

'Do you all speak English, or just you?'

'We mostly speak English, but please, if you can speak more slow, maybe they understand then.'

'Ah, of course, not a problem.' His cadence now more leisurely. 'Well, it's lovely to meet you, Céleste, I'm Nicholas, and this is Rohan. We're here to extend an invitation for a party later on our boat if you have no other plans.'

At this point, another of the group, a striking tall, lean girl with dark brown hair in a red bikini stepped forward to greet Rohan. She smiled, and more nervously than Céleste had, leaned in and kissed him on both cheeks. This was the first time he'd noticed the young lady who had been towards the back of the group, but her beauty struck him immediately. He stumbled over his words, 'I'm, er, I'm Rohan, nice to meet you.'

She pointed towards herself, 'Gisèle. Nice to meet you.' Much less confident with English than Céleste, her speech was slow, purposeful.

Nicholas repeated the offer of a party, not having received an answer the first time.

'That is your boat, the blue one?' one of the other girls asked.

'Yes, that's the one,' Nicholas blurted. 'I mean, it's not mine...'

'Noooooo!' she exclaimed sarcastically, her phoney surprise turning into a laugh and she poked him in the belly, sending a jolt through his body and he stumbled backwards. The girls laughed. Even if they had not understood the conversation, his reaction to being poked in the stomach had amused them.

'I'm sorry, I did not want to cause pain,' she apologised, suppressing a laugh.

'Ha, no you didn't, it just caught me off guard,' he countered, regaining his balance and laughing it off. 'Anyway, that's where we're staying for the week, I thought you might like to come and see it.'

'Of course! Every persons in Saint Tropez wants to see it. We have dinner here and then we come?' She turned to her friends and retrospectively asked for their agreement, to which she received a collection of approving nods.

'How do we come to the boat?' was her next question, looking towards their jet skis.

'Well, er, how about I bring the boat from earlier and collect you all?'

'Oui, ca marche. Okay, this is good. Our friends may not come if they are still not well, but we come.' Céleste clarified pointing to the girls on the deck.

Rohan, who had remained quiet during the negotiations, mainly because he was unable to take his eyes off the girl who introduced herself as Gisèle, now realised he had been staring from under his sunglasses. He snapped back to life as the conversation ended and put one hand on Nicholas's back and confirmed his consent. 'That's great, we'll see you later. What time will you be ready?' He aimed his question directly at Gisèle and she looked to the others.

'A huit heure?' another suggested.

'D'accord,' Rohan replied. 'Eight o'clock it is.'

'I think you must leave now,' Céleste prompted.

Rohan was confused by her tone which seemed

abrupt considering the how their interaction had been going so far. The confusion on his face must have been obvious as she quickly corrected, 'No, no, I mean, you must catch your skis,' raising her arm to point past them out to sea.

Turning, he now understood her concern. Their jet skis, having not been tethered to the boat, had drifted in different directions at least twenty feet from the Sunseeker.

'Ah.' Relief spread across his face, now knowing that she was not banishing them.

'Oh shit.' Nicholas sprang to life. 'Well time to go. Au revoir, mademoiselles.' He saluted as the pair jumped the steps to the platform and dived into the water, each initially heading for the same jet ski, prompting more laughter from the ship behind. Nicholas quickly realised and changed course for his. Once the pair were reunited with the machines, they regrouped.

'How do you do it, Nicholas? How are you just so comfortable talking to them?'

'Comfortable? Ha, I'm glad you thought so. My palms were sweating! Still are, bud.'

'But you just make it look easy. I never know what to say.' He hoped he didn't appear completely useless.

'I just try to act a bit of a fool. If you can make them smile, then it's easy from there. It's the serious stuff I'm no good at. Just imagine you're talking to one of us. You don't have a problem talking to lads, do you?'

'No, of course not.' He mused.

'They're no different really, I think we just build it up in our heads and get nervous. Practice makes perfect. You'll get there, Rohan!' Nicholas shouted before setting off across the calm azure in search of the cave explorers.

18

Back on the boat after an afternoon of fun in the water, Max's phone buzzed in his pocket and he stepped away from the group.

'Hey, how's it going?' he heard from the other end.

'Good, everyone's having fun. You should see the boat, it's unbelievable. I've never seen anything like it.'

'Well, just keep going with the plan and maybe one day you'll be in a position to have one yourself.'

'You know that's not why I'm doing it,' Max emphasised.

'Is everyone getting along?'

'They're starting to. Well, apart from Rosa and Alistair.'

'What do you mean?'

'Well, it's funny. They're so loved up but then I heard them having a huge row earlier.'

'About what?'

'I'm not sure really, I could only just hear it, but

she was shouting at him about something, she was getting really upset.'

'You don't think it's about… you know?'

'No, I'm sure he wouldn't have told her.'

'You told me, didn't you?'

'Yes, but that's different, how could I have kept it from you?'

'You sound drunk, have you been drinking?'

'I'll say. It's hard not to. Everywhere you look there's a bar or a waiter handing you whatever you want.'

'Just be careful. Don't let anything slip. You haven't mentioned to anyone that we've talked about it?'

'No, of course not, I'm not that drunk.'

'Good, I'm not sure how they'd take it. I've had some more thoughts about how you can make it work. We'll talk about it when you get back.'

'Okay, I'll speak to you soon.'

'You too. Night.'

19

Pushing himself back away from the table, Max complimented the chef for the second time that day. 'I can't eat another bite, I'm absolutely stuffed. That was even better than lunch, Emmanuel, and that's saying something.'

Once again, Emmanuel Durand had accompanied the final dish to the table and enjoyed a drink with the guests. This time, however, the poison was not champagne, rather a favourite cocktail of his, to which he had introduced Mr Lovell at their first meeting at the American Bar in London's Savoy.

Little did Lovell know on that occasion that the cocktail contained 1858 Sazerac de Forage, 1950s Pernod Absinthe and Peychaud's Bitters from 1900. The price tag was £5,000, and as he was the one that called the meeting, he was picking up the tab.

Luckily for Mr Lovell, the youngsters' tastes were not quite so mature, and they made do with the champagne from the bar. As the sun lowered in the evening sky, Rohan recounted the tale of his and Nicholas's afternoon. Lovell relished in hearing of their bold landing and was nearly hysterical by the time Rohan got to the part about the boys' bungling departure.

'I'll have to meet these lovely ladies and ask them why on earth they would possibly accept your offer to collect them after they'd seen your competence with a jet ski!'

Alistair laughed alongside his father and not-so-subtly suggested that maybe it was best if Tom took the helm of the tender rather than risk it being lost at sea. Nicholas, seemingly oblivious to the fact that he was being teased, pleaded with them to let him captain the boat, bringing more laughter to the table.

'There's only one rule this evening gentleman... oh and lady,' Lovell corrected himself, nodding towards Rosa. 'Safety first. We don't want any more of you little blighters running around any time soon, and we all know what those French girls are like, so please, safety first. I will be leaving you this evening. Tom will take me ashore shortly as I have a flight to catch. He'll bring the boat back and then it's over to you, Ace.'

Nicholas smiled at his new nickname, even though he knew it was ironic.

Lovell rose, first moving to Rosa and Alistair. 'Rosa, it's been a pleasure to see you. Send my regards to your parents and wish them a pleasant holiday.'

She leaned in and kissed him twice before accepting his warm embrace.

'Alistair, keep this gem safe, and whatever you do, don't let her near Ace.' He winked towards Nicholas.

The rest of the boys stood to bid farewell to their generous host, circling him and each accepting his firm handshake and hugs.

'Enjoy the rest of your stay. Any problems, you know how to reach me.'

As he left the table and neared the staircase to climb to his room, he spun quickly to leave his last remark, 'Durand, there had better be some of that bloody Sazerac left next time I get here!'

Durand's response was silent but effective, with a smile on his face he simply raised his middle finger to his boss and received a smile and a shake of the head in return.

'I think I'll leave you, too. I have some business to attend to,' Durand said to the group and left with the remnants of his cocktail in his hand. 'Bonne soirée.' He waved as he departed the Owner's Deck.

The group took up position around the bar, Rosa finding the media centre located in the cabinet built into the bar's support. She connected her phone and volunteered to be the DJ for the evening, starting with a relaxed mix to accompany the cool sea breeze drifting across the deck. Eventually, Tom returned with the launch and Nicholas's wish had been granted. Tom threw him the keys.

'Don't lose it.' He smiled. 'If there's any trouble just grab the radio and talk, it'll come straight through to me.'

'Thanks, Tom.' He turned to the guys. 'How do I look?'

'Like a million dollars, Ace.' Sebastian winked. 'Go get them, what are you waiting for? Which one are you hoping to get to know better?'

'You'll meet her soon, hopefully. Céleste, like her name suggests, is heaven-sent. I have Rosa to thank for that very useful piece of information.'

'Sorry, I missed that,' Max interrupted, 'like the name suggests?'

'Céleste, as in "celestial", meaning from the sky,' Rosa clarified.

'Ah, of course. I've never made the connection. Well what are you waiting for guys? Your chariot awaits.' Max encouraged the boys to venture off and collect their dates.

Rohan and Nicholas jumped down the numerous levels of stairs to the tender garage where two of the crew were cleaning, out onto the lowered jetty and into the limousine tender they'd used earlier in the day. Rohan watched as Nicholas climbed into the pilot's seat and engaged the engines. He could feel his own nervousness building as they prepared to sail. The excitement on Nicholas's face made it hard for Rohan to tell whether he was feeling it too.

As they pulled away from the Mufasa, Rohan focused on trying to stay cool and collected. Nicholas must have been aware of the silence, prompting him to tease his friend about their earlier meeting. 'You couldn't have made it much more obvious if you tried! I thought you had turned into a statue and I'd have to drag you back here.'

'Well you saw her, didn't you? She's unreal. There are no girls like that back home. I think the language might be an issue, though. I definitely can't try to pull her in French. It didn't feel like she had a clue what I was saying.'

'You'll be fine. Just keep talking slow, like the dunce you are.' As they arrived at the Sunseeker, Nicholas jabbed him with his elbow to show affection rather than malice.

'Cheers, mate,' Rohan suppressed through gritted teeth, reeling from the pain in his ribs, just as they positioned the boat behind the Sunseeker.

This time, hoping to avoid any repeat mishaps, the

boys made sure to stay with the boat and let the girls come to them.

Céleste apologised for the absentees as just her and two of the girls descended into the waiting vessel, insisting it was only due to sun and alcohol. The group all exchanged greetings once more, Rohan showing them where to sit before taking his own place next to Nicholas for moral support.

Even before Nicholas had a chance to start the engines, the girls were keen to know the story as to why the boys were staying on such a big ship.

Rohan looked to Nicholas, expecting him to take the lead. The nod and wink that he received back were clear signs that Rohan should take the opportunity to speak to them.

He obliged, slowly at first before gaining a bit of momentum, just managing to finish telling them about their trip so far by the time they reached the Mufasa.

Tom helped the party from the tender and took the helm from Nicholas, patting him on the back as they switched positions.

Once introductions had been made with the rest of the Mufasa's natives, the volume of the music increased, and the partyers made the most of the beautiful setting sun and the warmth of the summer evening. Rosa immediately bonded with the girls, conversing with them in perfect French, leading them up to the sun deck at the top of the ship. The boys followed, taking up position in the seating area surrounding the giant hot tub on the top deck. Rohan found himself next to Alistair who was by now as pissed as a fart.

'How's it going, Rohan?' Alistair slurred.

'Good. Well, very good, clearly. Look where we are.' Rohan took in the surroundings.

'Not a bad place, hey?' Alistair's head lulled back. 'Not bad company, either. Rosa!' he shouted across to the girls as he raised his bottle to the sky. 'Cheers, gorgeous.'

She smiled and giggled with the others at her inebriated lover before raising her glass in return, blowing a kiss across the deck to him.

'I'm in love with her,' he confessed to Rohan, now much quieter than his last outburst. 'Have you ever had that, where you just can't wait to see someone?' Alistair's eyes were now nearly closed as he mumbled.

Rohan laughed to himself at Alistair's transformation from stoical and reserved earlier in the day to gushing and loved up after the day's fun.

'That's not hard to see, pal. You two are made for each other.' Rohan gave his endorsement.

'What about you?' Alistair enquired, eyes now open at least. 'I heard Nicholas tormenting you earlier about one of the French girls.'

'Ha, yeah. I had a bit of a moment when I met Gisèle earlier. Bit of stage fright. I'm hoping she didn't notice.'

'So, are you going to make your move?'

Rohan looked across to the girls sitting across from him, wondering whether he would actually be able to get the nerve to tell her that he liked her. 'I will. I'm just playing it cool, you know me.'

Alistair paused, a realisation crossing his face. 'No. Actually, I don't. Or at least I didn't. But I'm glad I do now. You're a good guy, Rohan. It's been fun having you here. I think my dad really likes you. You remind me of him a bit.'

'Thanks, man. You're not so bad yourself, I guess.' The pair smiled and clinked their bottles of Corona together.

Lifting himself from the pristine white leather sofa they had been reclining on, Rohan turned, holding out his hand to help Alistair to his feet. Alistair headed over to his girlfriend, leaving Rohan to attempt more conversation with Gisèle and her two friends.

As the night wore on, the gang explored the ship, playing hide and seek using the seemingly endless rooms and cabins to escape the nominated hunters. Rohan seized the opportunity to pair up with Gisèle. Her increased intoxication had also increased her confidence with English and the duo, now able to communicate more freely, were starting to flirt. On the last round of the game, she pulled him into a dark beauty salon room, closing the door behind them just as they heard footsteps coming down the nearby stairs. Still laughing and breathless from having descended those same stairs in a hurry, she raised her finger to his lips, staring into his eyes. 'Shhhhh, they hear us.'

The only light was the shimmering reflection of the moon on the moving water outside the long, narrow window that ran the length of the room. They stood, motionless for what felt like minutes, her finger never leaving his lips. When the noise outside had disappeared, she lowered her hand, but not her eyes.

Suddenly she jolted forward, her lips meeting his and she kissed him intensely, sucking his bottom lip. It lasted only a moment and just as he realised what was happening, she pulled away and span towards the door, pulling it open a few inches to peek into the corridor outside. Fearing it was over, or a mistake, Rohan stood, rooted to the floor but when she turned, grin just visible in the low light, she motioned with her head for him to follow, an extended hand gesturing for him to take hold.

The pair climbed the stairs, passing the bar on their way back up to the sun deck to collect more drinks, landing back on the same curved leather sofa he and Alistair had bonded on earlier. This time he was even happier with his choice of companion and they lay alone taking in the night sky whilst the others finished the game. A wisp of cloud briefly obscured the moon as they drifted off to sleep.

20

The next morning, Nicholas shielded his eyes with his hands as he emerged from the stairwell onto the top deck, or sun deck, where the rest of the group had gathered.

'Apple juice. Just plenty of apple juice please, Ernesto,' he pleaded. 'In fact, can you leave the jug, please?'

This wasn't the first time Ernesto had comforted a weary head after a night of festivity, though his usual patron typically had a few years on the assembly gathered around the table this morning.

'I trust you enjoyed the evening, sir?' he asked.

'It was incredible, fucking incredible. I'm not going back. Can you phone my mum and tell her that I live here now please?' Nicholas was only half joking.

'Certainly, sir. Although, it would sound better coming from the captain.'

'Well let's get him to do it as well then. Is Tom back yet with Rohan?'

'Not yet, but I'm sure they'll come for breakfast when they return.'

'Actually, I think I'll take you up on the offer of some food after all. Can I just have scrambled eggs on toast, please?'

'Wise choice, breakfast is the most important meal of the day. My mother always told me that.'

'She sounds just like mine.'

'I'll take the same, thanks Ernesto.' Sebastian was fresh this morning after heading to his room much earlier than the rest of the group. He'd called Annabel from the cabin's phone and had told her all about the previous day, the jet, the harbour and the enormous ship he found himself aboard. Annabel was back in London, seething with jealousy that Sebastian was having the opportunity to spend time on her boss's boat.

As he confirmed his order with Ernesto, his attention was caught by the sound of arguing originating from the opposite end of the sun deck. Rosa was shouting at Alistair, tears streaming down her cheeks. Alistair was trying to calm her down, but it was no use. She stood from her seat and stormed down the stairs. Rather than chasing her, Alistair joined Max, Sebastian and Nicholas at the table, sighing as he sat.

'Everything okay?' Max checked.

'Yeah, it will be. I told her that I may change my

degree from Medicine and she's upset. She liked the idea of me being a doctor. She'll be fine. I think she's also just sad that she's leaving today as well.'

'What time is she heading off?'

'Right now.'

Max found it strange that she hadn't said a word to the rest of the group on her way off. 'Oh right. I didn't realise. I would have said goodbye…'

The conversation was cut short by the return of Rohan, who had never looked happier.

'That's the face of a man who had fun last night!' Max took the opportunity to change the subject. 'I saw you two lovebirds cuddled up on the top deck under the moonlight. How very romantic.'

'What can I say? I'd like to take all the credit, but I think some of it must go to the monks.'

'The monks?' Sebastian inquired.

'The monk who discovered champagne, Mr Pérignon.'

'Ah, you could have just said "the champagne", Rohan.'

'Well, I could have but I thought the future PM would probably get the reference. You'll get there.'

The instant Rohan said the words, Max turned and glared at him before scouring the deck to see if anyone else was in earshot. Rohan got the message and immediately held up his hands.

'Sorry, Max. Slip of the tongue.'

'It's okay, there's no one else here. But please, just be careful what you say.'

Rohan nodded in agreement, sheepishly, before taking his place beside Max at the table, repeating his apology.

It was now Alistair's turn to change the subject. 'Right, guys. We have a decision to make. And here is just the man now.'

He angled his attention towards the figure climbing the last step to the deck. The broad gentleman wore a perfectly fitting shirt, tapered at the waist, the shoulders bearing two epaulets displaying four gold bars, the uppermost curled into a ring in the centre of the cloth.

'Boys, meet "The Commodore". This is one of my father's oldest friends and a highly decorated navy officer.' Alistair jogged over to the gentle giant and they hugged briefly. 'Good to see you, Commodore.'

Alistair knew the man disliked the title, but it was a name he and his father insisted on using to greet him.

'Thanks for your kind introduction, Alistair. But it's no longer Commodore, I'm just Captain these days.' Now speaking directly to the young men, 'or you can call me David if you prefer. I know I certainly would.' He flashed a smile towards Alistair before being welcomed with cheery handshakes all round.

'I apologise I missed your arrival, but I had a few matters to attend to on the mainland last night. I trust you're all now familiar with the ship?' He didn't wait for their response. 'Mr Lovell tells me that you would like to see more of the Mediterranean, so I've taken the liberty of suggesting a few locations. As we have no need to berth, we're pretty much free to go wherever you choose. Might I suggest the Amalfi Coast in Italy maybe, or some island hopping off the coast of Croatia? Both will be beautiful this time of year. I'll leave you to decide.'

He left a laminated map of the Mediterranean, complete with underwater topology, on the table for them to peruse. Picking it up, Max studied the complex page. 'I like the sound of the Amalfi Coast, isn't Capri not far from there?'

Alistair spoke up, 'Yes, not far. We could go to the mainland and see Pompeii and the ruins.'

'Really?' Nicholas challenged him. 'We've got this amazing ship and the ability to go anywhere we want, and you want to go and see a museum? Guys, come on. I'm sure we can be a little more imaginative than that.'

'Trust me, you'll be impressed,' Alistair pushed. 'Don't you remember seeing the pictures in history? The whole city was wiped out when the volcano erupted, the ash buried people where they were. You can still see the mummies.'

The sound Alistair received from Nicholas was the quintessential response a mother would expect from her teenage son after asking him to do chores. A groan followed by a relaxing of the neck muscles, allowing the head to roll back in exasperation, 'Okay, we'll go and see your mummies. But I get to choose the next place.'

'Deal,' Max interjected. 'Where first though? I've heard Corsica's nice, and it's on the way.'

'Okay, that's the plan then. Corsica, Pompeii, Capri and then to Croatia. I'll go and tell the commodore.' Map still in hand, Alistair descended the stairs to the bridge and found the captain and some of the crew sitting amongst the multitude of screens and panoramic windows, laughing and joking.

'Mr Commodore,' Alistair continued the joke. The crew found it equally amusing, not so much the name but the reaction of the recipient each time it was used. 'I mean, Mr Captain, I think we have our route.'

'Good to hear it, Junior.' David gave the usual shake of the head with a smile in response to the teasing. 'Let's prepare to sail.'

21

Blue Montblanc ballpoint pens, complete with their trademark six-pointed white star emblazoned on the end cap, lay in front of each of the recruits on top of Mufasa-headed stationery. The thick, ivory coloured paper drew a stark contrast to the rich, red interlocking grain of the spectacular four-metre cocobolo wood table in the centre of the stateroom the boys had locked themselves inside. Matchbooks, complete with the insignia of the boat, had been placed inches in front of the blank pieces before them, not by the crew but by Max as he had prepared the room for the meeting.

During his first tour of the boat, he'd identified this as the location where they would gather and whilst the rest of the boys were relaxing after lunch, he made his way down to the main deck to put everything in place.

At a speed of thirty knots, owing to the ship's innovative water-jet propulsion system, it had taken just over two hours to cover the distance from their point of origin, Saint Tropez, out into the Mediterranean and half way to Corsica. Even at this cruising speed, the ship swept effortlessly through the water, giving little indication to those on board that they were now bound for their next destination.

'Last time we all met secretly, I told you that I would explain the ritual.' Max had remained standing as the others had taken their seats.

When he'd run through this meeting in his head over the last few weeks, he'd thought carefully about how to set the mood, what he was going to say, and what he'd need in the room.

Now, as he stood behind his chair, his mind flashed back to the day when this all started. Standing, sweating, in front of his History classmates, dying for the words he wanted to say to be released from his throat. Max had spent the twenty minutes before the rest of the group arrived in the room pacing up and down, hoping that the same paralysis wouldn't appear again.

You can do this. They're all here because of you, there's no reason to be nervous. Thank God for air conditioning.

As the boys looked up at him, waiting for him to speak, he felt a pang of nervousness rising from his stomach, but he refused to let it overwhelm him.

'In Norse mythology lives a god by the name of Odin.' His prose was measured. 'He was known to take on countless different forms, some very different, and is portrayed varyingly throughout different cultures. His name means Master of Ecstasy, or Fury, or Inspiration.

'He was driven, challenging, competitive, wise, and most importantly, relentless. He would use any means necessary to overcome any challenge or limitation, often making great sacrifices in the pursuit of wisdom. Our ritual is symbolic of one of his biggest sacrifices.

'He travelled to a well whose waters were known to give those who drank it cosmic knowledge. Mimir, the guardian of the well, was an exceptionally wise being and some say a counsellor to the gods. In return for water from the well and therefore wisdom, he asked that Odin make a great sacrifice — his eye. As I say, Odin was relentless and would use any means necessary, so he gauged out his eye without hesitation and dropped it into the well.

'Symbolically, the eye is used as a metaphor for perception and understanding. In this case, it can be taken to mean that by sacrificing his eye, he exchanged his everyday perception for another higher, even sacred perception. An aptitude that I find very relevant to our journey. Seeing the world in a different way, a way that we'll need to in order to accomplish all our goals. To understand people and how they work, how they make decisions, how they view us.

'Odin was also known to have helped outlaws, people who had committed crimes. He didn't judge them by those crimes, but by the characteristics and strengths that enabled them to commit them. The ones he helped were known for being intelligent and creative and competent in achieving what they wanted to, qualities I see in every one of you. I found a quote which read, "whether such people become kings or criminals is mostly a matter of luck."

'We will not be leaving anything to luck, gentlemen. We will be the masters of our future. We are in control. We decide what happens. When I first spoke with each of you, I offered you the chance to change the world, for good. To do what other people cannot, whether through incompetence or being subject to a system that does not allow radical change to happen at the pace it needs to, or how it needs to. I need you to imagine how a god like Odin would view the world that we live in. What would he have done? What would he have sacrificed to make it a better place? Less corruption. Less greed. Less self-interest.

'Everything we've talked about accomplishing demands each one of us to excel in our personal achievements, but not for the purpose of personal achievement. Now, I want you to understand, really understand, why it's so important for every person in this room to fight to the bitter end to become the person you are supposed to become, to fulfil your role. Without the power of the positions we'll be in, we have no ability to create that change. You'll hopefully have realised that the roles we've chosen each have a distinct influence on a particular problem in the country and this strange world. Politics, law, the media, security, and the military. Some of the most powerful concepts and forces in the world. By infiltrating all these areas, our influence will be unassailable. The ability to give people what they need, whether that's education, information, aid, fairness, or a better standard of life. To protect them from wars or attack, other governments, or even our own. I can't think of any better way to contribute to the world, to leave our mark and make history.

'The line above the eye embodies all of this. Not only what you are willing to sacrifice for Us, but for the people who we'll be helping. I asked you to choose your strong eye to indicate just how far you'd be willing to follow Odin, how far you're willing to go. I'd lose my eye for any of you. Would you do the same for me, for Us, for them?'

He let the sentiment hang in the air, not expecting an answer and none was given. He looked at the group who sat silently in front of him, hoping that his impassioned speech had started a train of thought amongst them. After a minute of complete silence, aside from the faint hum of the air conditioning system, he spoke again.

'You know what the paper is for. Take the pens and show your commitment to each other. Though, this time, I don't want you to put the paper in the bowl. I want you to pass it to the person to your left. This is where we continue to build trust in each other. You trust that the person to your left will accept whatever decision you make, not just about Us, but about everything. If you ever have any issues, or questions, or doubts, you must be able to turn to anyone in this room and talk about it. I will happily talk about anything that's on your mind, any time, day or night. Exams, school, parents, girls, anything. Every one of you, I want to know about it. If you're stressed, in trouble, down, upset, or exactly the opposite. Every time you succeed, get the grade you needed, get into the uni you applied to. Everything.

'I need you to understand what we're doing. This will be your life. We will be your life. Already in the past days and weeks I feel we all have a better understanding of each other. Think about the conversations you've had with each other that you would have never had if we hadn't started down this road. Fuck, I feel like I know you all better already. And that has to continue. Take your oath and pass it on.'

He sat down and picked up the pen in front of him, the rest followed, each putting implement to parchment, folding the sheet and passing it to the left. The recipients opened the offering, looked to the man on their right and then to Max.

He studied the piece in front of him and turned to Rohan, sat to his right, 'Good man.' Max's palm extended, welcoming Rohan's in return. The others followed, shaking hands with the members flanking them.

That was all Max needed to see.

'Good, light them up and put them in the bowl,' he urged.

In unison, five books of matches were raised, one blue-tipped match snapped out of each and five bright orange flames increased the light and the temperature in the room ever so slightly. Five sheets of burning card fell into the deep, hollow-sided crystal bowl in the centre of the table. Each individual flame combined to create one significantly larger flare, the intense tip rising above the rim of the bowl, reaching its peak strength before subsiding and peacefully fading out.

All watched, hypnotised by the flame, silently waiting for the last embers to turn to ash. Four sets of eyes then lifted to look at their leader. No words were spoken, just a look and a movement in his right arm. Five hands met, index fingers thrust into the centre of the bowl, reappearing coated in white and grey ash, slowly turning to point towards their owners. Confident in his movement, Max touched his forehead, purposefully applying the mark. Four more followed suit.

An overwhelming sense of pride filled Max. He closed his eyes in a moment of pure calm and elation, his chest rising as he inhaled deeply, holding the air inside his lungs briefly before allowing it to calmly escape through his nose.

'Okay. Next I want everyone to write down your biggest fear and pass it to the person next to you.'

'Our biggest fear? Why?' Rohan asked.

'It's just a little trust exercise, part of getting to know each other better. Don't tell me, just write it down and pass it to your right this time.'

Once again pen went to paper and this time to the recipient on the right, or across the table in that direction. Max had already thought about his whilst creating this scene in his head, but he also knew it would have to be something at least one of the group knew about so that he couldn't cheat the system.

'Do you not have to do this bit?' Rohan looked confused as he looked to Max for his piece of paper.

'I will, but it's my idea so I can't tell you what mine is or I could just say something I'm not really afraid of. Sebastian knows it, so he'll have to tell you. Sebastian, what am I afraid of?'

'Mrs Stark?'

The boys laughed.

'Isn't everybody?' Max joked. 'But seriously. Come on, you know this.'

'Public speaking?'

Sebastian was right, however embarrassed Max felt that it had been noticed. He'd already resolved that he was going to overcome those fears. Being the leader of this group was the first step. He also planned to put himself in as many uncomfortable public-speaking situations as possible over the next few years to develop his confidence.

'Well, yeah. But there's not many places to give a speech around here. Something else. Whenever we've been in your garden, what always happens?'

'You get chased by a bee and run a mile.'

'There you go. I hate bees and wasps, the fuckers. Now that you've all written them down, the person on your right knows what your fear is. We're all going to help each other conquer those fears. This will show you exactly what kind of people we all are in times of pressure and fear. Knowing each other inside out is what will keep this group together. The trust that we form here will be the backbone to the solidarity of the group. We'll return to England a different group from the one we came here as.'

'How are we going to do that?' Nicholas was the first to ask.

'Well, mine's simple. We're going to go and find a beekeeper or a bee hive and I'm going to have to deal with it. Get some on me or something. But it's not just the person who's fear it is that has to do it. All of us have to do all of the challenges. Who knows, we might even end up conquering a fear we didn't know we had.'

He continued round the table clockwise. Nicholas, sat opposite Rohan, opened up the folded piece of paper.

'It says "heights". How can you be afraid of heights? We flew over here. Surely you must be afraid of flying as well then?' Nicholas asked, facetiously.

'It's not really like that. It's fine when I'm in an enclosed space like a plane, it's just when I'm near to a drop or an edge,' Rohan explained.

'I think that's more of a fear of falling then, really. How do we do that one, Max?' Nicholas looked again to their leader.

Max felt a sense of pride that he was the one they turned to for guidance.

'Well,' Max thought for a few seconds, 'we're on board a massive boat. We could jump off one of the decks. Or we could go and find some cliffs. I'm sure we'll see lots along the journey. Okay, let's keep going. Sebastian, what does Nicholas's say?'

He opened the paper. 'Spiders, really? You're scared of spiders?' Sebastian was surprised.

'Yeah, they're disgusting! Especially the big hairy ones.'

Max smiled at the thought of an army cadet and potential future recruit into one of the most elite fighting forces in the world being afraid of spiders. Maybe this was going to be more useful than he would have ever imagined.

'At least that's another easy one to deal with,' he confirmed. 'We'll find somewhere that either sells spiders, or we'll just have to go looking for some. Can't be that hard. Next, Alistair, what does Sebastian's say?'

'Needles.'

Rohan laughed. 'Needles? You must have had lots of injections. How can you be afraid of needles?'

'I don't know. I just hate them. I always feel like they're going to hit an artery or something and I'll bleed to death.'

Max interrupted, 'We can't laugh at these guys, and we all have to do them, remember. Rohan can go first when we do needles then.' Max winked across the table.

'No problem. How are we going to do that though?' Rohan asked.

'There must be someone on board who's medically trained. We'll just get them to give us all placebos.

Easy peasy. Lastly, Alistair, I've got yours.' Max paused, looked down at the card in front of him and read it out loud, 'Snakes. Hmmm. That's one's going to be harder. We can't really guarantee that we'll be able to find any snakes.'

'What about sea snakes? Are you scared of them?' Sebastian probed.

'They're even worse! They don't just travel in one direction, they can go up and down as well. And they're really fast.'

'Bingo, good thinking, Sebastian,' Nicholas chimed in. 'Tom's a Dive Master. We'll all go scuba diving and find some big ol' sea snakes.'

Alistair visibly shuddered. 'Okay, but if I freak out and die down there, you have to explain it to my mum.'

'Anything for a chance to see your mum, Alistair! I've got dibs.' Nicholas's response was met with a subtle shake of the head.

Max appeared to try and calm the situation. 'Come on now, Nicholas. Don't be like that. I think it would be best if we all went and paid Alistair's mum a visit if that happens.' A cheeky grin spread across his face.

With the challenges set, the group started to plan where each one could be completed. They decided that jumping off the boat wouldn't be as challenging as jumping off a cliff, so they'd keep their eyes open along the journey looking for ideal spots to jump from. They'd find somewhere that people were already taking the leap. That way they'd know it was safe and there were no submerged rocks to injure them.

They had a week to go diving and they would ask Tom for some advice as to where they could find sea snakes.

After some searching on Google, they found that Corsica was known for its honey and honey fairs. This gave them a clear indication that they would not struggle to find bees and, after approaching Durand, quickly learned that he had friends on the island who may be willing to help. Having attended many of the honey fairs on the island, he had regular producers that he would source from, often buying cases to take back to the mainland for use in his kitchens. The wide variety of flowers on the island produced six seasonal varieties of the nectar and he was keen to impart his knowledge to the boys. Once they explained that it was not the honey itself they were after, rather the hive creature that manufactured it, his enthusiasm for his lesson on the intricacies of honey waned instantly.

Sebastian told Max that he was keen to face his fear quickly and have it out of the way. 'I don't relish the thought of having this hanging over me for the duration of the trip, Max.'

The pair approached the captain and inquired who on board was medically trained. It turned out that the majority of the crew would be able to administer some sort of first aid, as it was a pre-requisite to obtaining the job in the first place. His advice was that the chief officer, an Australian called Brendan was the best choice due to his extensive medical knowledge gained in his years as an officer in the Royal Australian Army Medical Corps.

Brendan was initially hesitant about unnecessarily administering injections to the young men but once Alistair explained that they were doing it in order to cure their friend of his fear, he agreed to inject each with a small amount of saline solution. The ship had no facility exclusively for medical treatment so, making use of one of the spa rooms, the group gathered ready to participate.

'You can choose which order you want to do it in, Sebastian, as this is your challenge,' Max offered. He wanted to remove as much trauma from the experience as possible. The aim was to cure the fear, or at least help Sebastian deal with it, rather than to make it hard for him.

'I'll go first. Let's get it out of the way.' Sebastian sat down in the comfy white, leather treatment chair that on any other day would be used for a range of hair and beauty treatments and pulled up the right-hand sleeve of his t-shirt. Eyes closed and looking away from the medic, he scrunched his face into a ball, waiting for the impending prick of the needle.

'It's alright buddy, it will be over in a second,' Rohan's now calming words were a complete contrast from his earlier, mocking outburst, 'hold my hand if you need to.'

Sebastian opened his eyes, suspicion on his face. When he saw that the offer was one of true compassion, his scowl turned into a smirk. 'I think I'll be okay, thanks.'

As the antiseptic wipe touched the right arm, Sebastian flinched.

'It's okay, I'm just cleaning the area. I'll let you know when I'm about to put the needle in. Okay, ready. Take a deep breath, I'll count and when I get to three, you cough.'

'Okay.'

His head was back in its position facing away from the danger and as the count started his teeth clenched.

'One, two, three.'

Exactly on cue, he coughed and in went the needle. A slight pressure on the syringe plunger and two seconds later the exercise was complete.

'All done. Wasn't too bad, was it?' Brendan checked.

'That was it? I didn't even feel it go in. Why has no one ever told me to cough before?'

Brendan turned to the tray of needles to prepare the next. 'When I was in the forces, we used to get lots of guys scared of needles. I find this little trick works the best.' His Australian accent was soft but unmistakeable. 'It doesn't matter how big or tough you are, some fears are just there. It's how you deal with them that counts. I've seen guys who had to be restrained just to have a simple flu vaccination. You've done well there, mate.'

The rest of the shots followed in much the same manner, and although none of the others had listed needles as their biggest fear, it was clear that they weren't all totally undisturbed by the experience. Poker faces emerged.

Alistair, showing some obvious discomfort sat and closed his eyes serenely, head back and allowed the process to happen.

'I think this is what I miss most about the army.' Brendan was placing the used equipment into the sanitary waste container in the corner of the room. 'You guys have shown balls there. You didn't leave your man to do it all by himself. Not everyone would have done it. I respect that. I think you've earned a beer.'

As they arrived on the main deck, Ernesto stood

behind the bar, tidying his workspace and wiping down the varnished rosewood surface. His lively demeanour welcomed the brothers. 'Ah, gentlemen, where have you been? I thought you would be making the most of our approach into Corsica. Look at the island, she's beautiful, no?' His soft southern Italian accent and constant smile had made him a hit with the group who greeted him with high fives all round.

'What do you desire?'

'Five beers please, Ernesto.' Rohan took the lead.

'Actually, I'm in the mood for something different. I've never tried a vodka martini,' Max confessed.

'Neither have I, to be honest,' Alistair agreed, curious.

'Sounds good to me, shaken not stirred.' Nicholas clearly couldn't resist the urge to channel his idol.

'Certainly, Mr Bond.' Ernesto's supervillain impression was right on the mark, even down to the squint in his eye. Turning to the remaining two, his raised eyebrows asked whether they wanted to follow the consensus or stick to their original order.

'Why not? When in Rome, hey.' Sebastian agreed.

'Perhaps you would prefer comfortable seats? I will bring the drinks to you when ready.'

The rear of the main deck housed a rectangle of cosy low sofas, cornered with white posts that supported a canopy for cooler evenings. Filing in, Rohan took the side furthest away from the ship's side rail. Within five minutes, their drinks arrived, and one found its way to the front of each member.

'Will you not join us for a drink, Ernesto?' Alistair invited.

'That's a very kind offer, sir, but I have some duties to attend to. I shall be back very shortly, in time for your second.' He bowed flamboyantly as he left the table, the skip in his step portraying a happy character, full of the joy of life. He returned his gaze to the Corsican coastline and smiled.

Max was the first to speak, 'One down. Only four to go. Well done, Sebastian. Well done, all. To Us!'

22

Sebastian's head appeared energetically from the steps to the sun deck. 'Guys, it's time to go. Everyone's ready.'

Nicholas and Max had been discussing Céleste and the previous evening whilst watching the Corsican outline grow before they were disturbed.

'I think I might just stay here, I've just realised I need a haircut.' Max ran his fingers over his shaven head, freshly cut the day before they headed out to France. It had surprised the group when they saw him for the first time with the new look. Having allowed it to grow long and curly over the exam period and knowing that he would be disappearing to Army Camp a week after they returned from France, he'd decided to change his style and go for a number 1 crop all over.

'Oh no, you're not getting out of this, Max. This was all your idea, remember? And with a buzz cut like that, you can't be a chicken!'

Sympathy was not on Sebastian's agenda, especially

as his test was now out of the way. He descended the steps calling out further prompts for urgency.

Smiling and laughing, knowing that he would have to bite the bullet, Max slapped his hands down on the table, looked across at Nicholas and said, 'Let's do this.'

Alistair, Sebastian and Rohan had already climbed into the tender and were bobbing up and down in the small waves that lapped at the side of both vessels. Nicholas climbed aboard and took a seat at the rear whilst Max weaved his way through the legs of the others to take position next to the pilot. Before he'd fully had a chance to settle into his seat, Alistair moved the throttle lever forward and Max fell the last few inches into his place. Within minutes they were out into open water and Max span in his seat to address the group.

'Okay Rohan, let's see what you have.'

'It's funny, lots of this was part of my plan already really so it's been pretty easy. I'll give you the headlines. Cambridge for university, Christs College to do Law. I've already been down to see the university, it's amazing. For those of you who don't know, the exact job that I'll be aiming for is Lord Chief Justice.'

'I wonder why in the world you chose that one in particular,' Nicholas chimed in, sarcastically.

Rohan paused but didn't respond to his cynicism, 'Before that, I think there's really only one option and that's to become a barrister after university. I need to take a separate exam at the start of the next school year for Cambridge, but my grades are there. I think cricket will be a huge help, school and county captain, England schools, you know.

'Other extra-curricular: I've got Duke of Edinburgh, it will be gold level by then. I've already done work experience with a barristers' chamber in Liverpool for two summers. I think I'm looking good at the moment.'

'Have you picked a particular predecessor to emulate?' Max was interested to know.

'Not yet, I've looked at a few and the path seems pretty standard. Oxford or Cambridge, study and take the Bar exam and then apply for a pupillage at a barristers' chambers. From there, it's a case of performing well, making the right decisions about chambers and cases. It's something I already wanted to do well at, so I'll just stay on the usual course.'

'Sounds like you know your stuff. Well done. Next is to look at the longer term, I guess, and what jobs will lead you to the top.'

Rohan nodded a 'thanks' for Max's encouragement.

'Who's next?' Max's eyes made contact with the next to be tested. 'Nicholas, how's your research gone?'

'Same as Rohan, really. I'd been looking into the

army for a while but hadn't quite looked at jobs on this level. The role I'm aiming for is Chief of the Defence Staff. It's the most senior member of the armed forces in the country and directly advises the Secretary of State for Defence and the Prime Minister.' He recalled the information that he had clearly learned verbatim for this very purpose.

'I know you said to target one role, Max,' he continued, 'but whilst I've been doing some research, there's been one other that has jumped out. After my comment about Rohan's, he's going to laugh. But the thinking behind it isn't for the title, it's that the job seems to have more power and not just within the UK.'

'Let's hear it,' Rohan goaded, eager to see what the suggested upgrade was.

'Supreme Allied Commander.'

'Are you joking? And you made fun of mine! The cheek. Yours sounds more like a god than a job.' Rohan chuckled.

'I like that you're thinking bigger than we discussed.' Max mused. 'I guess really what we're doing here is setting the level that we want to achieve. It doesn't necessarily have to restrict us to a certain job title, or even the UK. Alistair's certainly won't. And, in fact, that international influence will be a huge strength. Good job, Nicholas. Rohan, I'm sorry, but your title loses in terms of swagger for now. What else did you find out?'

'I started with Chief of the Defence Staff and, so far, I've chosen one to base my career on. It's the current Chief. His name is Nick Houghton, actually Sir Nick Houghton. It tends to come with a knighthood from what I can tell.' He grinned. 'The path for me will be pretty standard for the first few years: university first, I'll join the University Officer Training Corps whilst there to get some extra training and field experience which will set me up well for Sandhurst straight after university. It's a year-long course there and then you're commissioned as an officer. That's where the next bit will kick in. Houghton and loads of others started in the infantry so that's what I'll join. He was in the Green Howards, but I don't have to make a decision about the specific regiment for a while, so I'll keep doing some research and find out if any in particular would suit me better. As for universities, I'm applying to Leeds, Edinburgh and Sheffield. They all have good reputations as well as strong Officer Training Corps so figure they're the best bets.'

'Good, well that's the next few years all covered then. Have you got the extracurricular activities you need as well?' Max probed.

'I'm on the Duke of Edinburgh scheme, same as

Rohan. I can also apply for an Army University Scholarship and then all my cadet time will help me with that. Obviously, I've got rugby: school, club and county as well.'

'Awesome. For next time, take a look at the potential jobs that you will do in the middle and how you'll climb the ladder to get where you need to be. One thing we should think about is that even though we're aiming for the top positions in the country, we still want to be able to influence things before we get to those positions.'

Looking ahead out of the vessel they were using as transport to the small island, Max estimated they had another ten to fifteen minutes before they arrived into the port of L'Île-Rousse on the northern coast of Corsica.

It had been chosen not only because of its beauty and ease of access, but also for its proximity to Nessa. Here lived one of Durand's honey contacts in the hills above the Corsican coastline but only about a thirty-minute drive from the shore. Their plan was to hire a taxi from the port and drive the short distance to the small town. Tom led the way on a jet ski up ahead whilst Alistair maintained a steady speed.

'We haven't got long until we'll be with Tom again, so let's crack on. Sebastian, you're next. Prime Minister's question time.'

'Mine is a bit more open than the last ones.' Sebastian looked to Max as he spoke. 'There's no clear, right path here. I've been doing my research and it looks like there are loads of ways to become PM, but this is what I've decided so far. The majority were Oxbridge educated, so that's definitely on there. Looking back, I can't find a single one who attended Cambridge in the last forty years, so I'll follow that logic and apply for Oxford. I think involvement as early as possible within one of the major parties will be the main thing, and also deciding which party to choose. You have to think what the country will be like when we're actually getting to these positions but it's too early to make that call just yet. Course-wise, I think it will have to be Philosophy, Politics and Economics, or PPE as they call it. It seems the most relevant and one that will set the right track. Either that or Law as that's what I would probably have done anyway, and I think it would still give me a good background to move forward. Although, looking at what the previous ones have done, I don't think the course will matter too much.

'My challenge is going to be mainly once I've joined a party. That's where the real game playing and backstabbing starts by the sounds of it.'

'Did any of your conversation with Cameron help at all?' Max asked.

'Some of it, although I didn't get the chance to ask about specific clubs and stuff to do at university. The rest of his answers were more along the 'work hard' route. I'll keep digging and having more conversations with anyone I can find in politics. I think some work experience over the summers during university will also help.'

'That and keeping your nose clean,' Rohan keenly point out.

'What's that supposed to mean?' Sebastian responded, sharply.

'I just mean that the PM has got to be as clean as a whistle. You can't be the Prime Minister if you've got a load of skeletons in the closet.'

'Rohan's right, Sebastian,' Max agreed. 'But that actually goes for all of us. Any of these jobs that we want to do are going to mean that we can't have any major blemishes against our names. That's also where the rest of us come in. We'll need to help and protect each other, stop us from getting into any trouble, help us out of it if it does happen. Problem solving times five.'

Glad that they were having these conversations, Max felt the need to constantly emphasise how much they would rely on each other throughout their lives. It would be very easy for each of the young men to disappear away to universities in different towns and cities and lose sight of the group and what they need to achieve. Whilst away from each other, it would be key that they stay in regular contact. A thought entered his mind.

'I've got an idea actually,' he started. 'I think we need to set up a regular meeting when we do all go off to university. We can work out the details closer to the time, but I think we need to be able to meet to stay in touch and keep up to date with what's going on. We can chat and email about general life, but we'll have to meet up at least once a month to discuss things we can't over the phone or emails. Sorry, that's just one thing that sprang to mind as we were talking. Sebastian, anything else for yours at the moment?'

'No, I think that's it for now. I'll keep researching and finding out exactly how to climb the ladder politically.'

'Okay. Alistair, you go and then I'll go last. We haven't got much time though so keep it short if you can.'

'I think mine seems to be the one with most options available. My dad has always hinted that he'd love me to take over the company when he retires so I know he'll be happy for that to happen. What I need to do in the meantime is make sure that I'm qualified to run the business. I think the best way would be to do a degree in Business Management, then go and do some journalism, but not working for him just yet. I'd like to go and write pieces about conflict, famine and developing nations.

'I'll use it for some research into the areas that I want to change and influence. At the moment, they seem to be the areas that really interest me about journalism and definitely the parts that need more attention and coverage. I'm going to apply for St Andrews. Rosa and I have been discussing it and she's going to go and do Medicine there, as I would have.'

Max paused for a second as his thoughts carried him away over the waves, though he didn't realise it himself. The simple mention of a name had triggered a recurring worry thought that would stay with him for the rest of the trip. Rosa.

'Max, we're nearly there. You'll have to do yours later.' Alistair's voice was faint in Max's distracted ears.

23

aving approached from the north, they shared their route into the small harbour with outbound and inbound ferries from mainland France. Tom threaded his jet ski through a stream of boats entering the port, keeping constant watch for other vessels that may be using the same shipping lanes. He'd given strict instructions to Alistair to stay close behind him and, having pointed out the size of some of the commercial ferries in this part of the sea, his instructions were followed closely.

Tom swung his jet ski to starboard and guided the crew towards the concrete, man-made wharf that formed part of the structure connecting the ferry port on the Isula La Pietra to the main island of Corsica. Making his way past the lines of boats on either side, Tom aimed for the far end of the port, finding just enough space for the tender and his jet ski. He leapt onto dry land and immediately began conversing with a short, hairy local in an open short sleeved shirt and sun-faded navy trilby. The exchange lasted only minutes, Tom maintaining his grasp on the mooring line for his jet ski before an agreement was reached and he turned to attach it to one of the curved, rusted rings sunken into the concrete surface below his feet.

As he completed the bowline knot, the second craft approached. It was usual for eyes to follow the distinctive tender wherever it went, and today was no different. Tourists and local fishermen alike observed the entrance of the long sleek craft, made even more conspicuous by the young travellers on board. The late afternoon sun, still high in the sky, reflecting off the highly polished craft caused some to avert their eyes briefly before returning to admire its colours and lines.

Picking up taxis near the harbour was an almost effortless task. Whether targeted by those eager drivers who had seen their boat enter the port, or by sheer luck that a ferry had only ten minutes since departed, no sooner had they stepped onto land than Tom was beckoning them over to the road. Here he had secured a silver Volkswagen van whose driver claimed he knew the village of Nessa well. The price Tom had negotiated in French seemed to please the driver, even for both directions and some waiting time. Tom confirmed his plan with the boys, 'Who knows if we'll be able to pick up another cab up there? Safer to just ask this one to stay with us for the afternoon.'

'Are you going to do the challenge with us, Tom?' Alistair goaded.

'I would love to,' he replied, unconvincingly, 'but I'm allergic to bees. And trust me, it does not look pretty. I'll be keeping a very safe distance. I even brought my epinephrine pen just in case I get really unlucky.' He brandished the medical pen and held it over his shoulder. Proof in case any of them suspected it was an excuse.

'I suppose that's just about good enough reason not to.' Sebastian smiled.

Expanses of dry, arid scrubland lined their route up into the hills, interspersed with lush fields which were constantly irrigated to maintain the moisture in the soil. The dusty road wound through the hills that rose up beside them, occasionally narrowing to the width of only one car, causing the driver to reverse to let an oncoming car pass more than once.

Having called from the ship, Durand had been unable to speak with the farmer himself but his wife had assured him that there would be someone at the farm to show them the bees. Tom had kindly agreed to come along as the translator as the French vocabulary amongst the rest of the group certainly didn't extend to "no, we're not looking for honey, we just need to cover ourselves in your bees."

The road now ventured into greener pastures, simple farmhouses emerging out of the dry-stone walls clinging to the side of the tarmac. Before too long, they arrived at an intersection where the driver's knowledge ceased and from the back seat it was easy to tell that both he and Tom weren't sure which direction to take. After uncertain shakes of heads and hands, they decided left was the best option before soon realising their mistake. After a six-point turn in a tight driveway, the Volkswagen was back on course. A small sign, fifty yards past the intersection at which they had chosen poorly, directed them off the main road and onto an even dicier path.

"Le Jardin de Miel", or "the Garden of Honey", awaited the party and after ten minutes of navigating the somewhat treacherous stone path, the farmer and his wife both came into view, standing at the door of the charming farmhouse and waving them to a stop.

'Bonjour, bonjour!' The farmer's wife hobbled over to the van, a walking stick at her side for support.

'Bonjour!' the group replied in unison.

'Ca-va?' The farmer was affectionate, smiling as he patted one of the two hesitantly approaching black and white collies. "*Ils sont gentiles, t'inquiète,*" he reassured

Tom, who was visibly not a big fan of dogs.

'Well I think we've found Tom's challenge for the trip, everyone!' Nicholas made his way energetically to stroke the aged pair who had seen better days. Whether it was the volume of his excitement or the speed at which he bounded over, the dogs cowered behind the farmer's legs, unsure what to make of this new creature on their land. One managed a small growl before the farmer sent them inside, away from the guests.

Apologising, Tom initiated his attempt to explain the situation. He was stopped after only a few words as the farmer's wife started to laugh and speak in an accent Tom was unable to distinguish, sounding more Italian than French. His blank expression prompted the farmer to enlighten him about the joke and explained that they already knew about what was required of them. It seemed the man's fondness for Durand had acquired the group time with the bees with little additional explanation needed from Tom.

Waving for them to follow, the woman made her way to the left side of the house, around an old rusting tractor that looked like it had last seen action many years before. The group followed, Max travelling at a noticeably slower pace than the rest.

'Are you okay, mate?' Rohan, once again, was a voice of comfort.

'I'll be fine, I just want to get it over and done with. I think I'll be okay if I can see them. It's when they fly around and you can hear but not see them that I hate. They're too fast, and stupid.'

'You'll be fine. Have you ever been stung before?' Rohan asked.

'I wasn't intending on being stung now, thanks! But yeah, once outside of school. I sat on a bollard and there was obviously a bee or wasp on there. Luckily, I put my hand down first or it would have stung me right on the arse. Not what you need before an exam.'

'Ha, lucky for the bee you mean. No one wants to go near your arse. I don't think that will be an issue today.'

'Let's hope not.'

The trees covering the front part of the land had all but obscured the stunning vista that awaited them as they rounded the last corner of the house. To their right was a collection of yellow and white stone chalets built into the hillside, topped off with distinctive red tiles. The house was half a kilometre short of the heart of Nessa and this was the only view they would have of the sleepy town. To the left, the valley dropped away dramatically, giving them endless views over the lower rolling hills, all the way back out to the Mediterranean Sea.

'Well, at least if you do die here, Tom, that's not a bad last sight,' murmured Sebastian as they looked out to the horizon.

From behind them came a question in French, 'Who first?'

This is it, Max thought. *Fix up, look sharp. This was my fucking idea, idiot. Time to lead.*

He forced himself to speak. 'I am.' He wasn't sure whether the group was buying his attempt to mask his fear. Maybe it wasn't them he was hiding it from.

He took a confident stride forward to the farmer, taking from him the protective veil comprised of a worn, brimmed sun hat with an even more tatty circle of mesh cloth sowed to the brim to protect the face. Placing it over his head, he noticed the shakes had returned once more. He clenched his fists.

The farmer led him slowly towards the row of six hives, aiming for the nearest, all the time speaking in French. Max had no idea what he was saying but there was something about the tone that was soothing.

An old, but well maintained tin bee smoker hung from the farmer's arthritic left hand in case the hive became too energetic. Wisps of the pine straw smoke entered Max's nose, reminding him of some scent from his past but he couldn't quite place the memory.

As they reached the hive and the hum of the swarm

grew in volume, the farmer touched Max on the shoulder, sending an involuntary jolt through him and he recoiled.

'Come on. You can do this,' he mumbled to himself as he steadied his breathing, wondering whether the group had noticed.

The farmer bent down, pushing softly on the smoker's bellow as he positioned it under the hive. Max had seen this on TV before and knew that it had something to do with calming the bees. He was sceptical, to say the least.

Next, the farmer lifted the flat outer cover of the wooden box, placing it on top of the next hive in the row. The inner cover followed thereafter and more smoke was blown onto the top of the hive.

Max braced himself, expecting a gang of the critters to erupt from the opening. He was pleasantly surprised to see only a few bees crawling around the top of the frames that made up the internal structure of the hive. The farmer motioned to him to come and take a closer inspection. Once more, he gritted his teeth and forced his feet forward a pace, bending at the waist to look into the hive.

He suddenly froze. Daring to look down at his arms, he realised that five or six of the pests had landing on his hands and wrists. He instantly stood bolt upright, hands stretched out in front of him, eyes squeezed, trying to find words, any words to instruct the farmer to get them off. His message was not lost.

'Tranquile, mon fils. C'est bon.'

Max understood enough French to translate in his head. 'Calm, my boy. Everything's fine.' It certainly didn't feel fine as the panic shot through him.

The farmer softly blew smoke over Max's hands as he forced himself to control his breathing again. Realising that he was not being stung, he finally dared to open his eyes.

Face this. He focused on the remaining two creatures exploring the veins on his hands. He raised one slowly towards his face, hand shaking more forcefully than ever before, inspecting the disgusting hairy body and legs.

Turning to the group gathered twenty feet behind him, he raised his convulsing right arm into the air, rotating his hand so that the back directly faced them and the evidence could be seen. He held it there.

'Well done, Max.' Sebastian was the first to call out. The others followed, some clapping.

Turning back to the farmer, he held both hands out and allowed him to brush the drones away. A huge sigh of relief left his lungs as he paced back towards the group, a toothy grin on his face. As much as he'd like to show his poker face, he couldn't contain himself.

'Fuck me. That was intense,' he exclaimed as he handed the veil to the next to face the hives.

One by one, the rest of the boys approached the living, pulsating colony, all having bees land on them only to fly off again without incident. Having completed his turn with the bees, Sebastian returned to the group of onlookers before spotting a Harvestman in the brush alongside the house. The Harvestman was not technically a spider, but Sebastian was unaware of this fact due to the striking resemblance. Having eight legs and a small, round body, the Harvestman was actually a member of the Opiliones order, the same as the daddy longlegs.

However, as it turned out, Nicholas was also unable to tell the difference, not that it would have mattered. Having slowly approached the area in which the Harvestman was resting, Sebastian scooped it into a cocoon he made with his hands.

As Nicholas removed the head mask after returning from the hive, Sebastian approached, hands in a ball. He blurted out, 'Hey Nicholas, I found a spider for you,' lightly touching his friend on the back with his still closed hands.

'You dick!' Nicholas jolted, throwing the mask to the ground, backing into the hive in a blind panic, swatting at his shoulders wildly as if he could feel something on him. That feeling was not that of a spider but one of the farmer's prized bees, a glancing blow transferring the creature onto his palm.

In fear for its life, the bee did what was natural to defend the hive, stinging Nicholas directly on the palm. He reacted instantly, swatting the bee away but it was too late. Two barbed lancets penetrated his skin, the barbs holding the sting firmly in place. When the bee was swiped from his palm it left behind not only the stinger but also part of its digestive tract: a death sentence for a honey bee.

Seeing the immediate panic from Nicholas, Sebastian retreated away from the area, trying his hardest not to laugh but the commotion was too much. It was not the sting that amused him, more the sheer alarm his friend displayed. Upon realising that one of his bees had been hurt in the melee, disappointment was clearly visible on the farmer's face.

The murderer apologised profusely, trying his best to explain his crippling fear of spiders and the farmer's dismay had soon evaporated leaving all well amongst the group once more. Acting quickly, the farmer's wife started to talk to the boys, motioning to the ground making a clenching movement with her first. Eventually Alistair picked up a handful of the dry dirt before she motioned towards the dogs' bowl.

With a little translation help from the farmer, he'd realised they were instructing him to soak the dirt with the water to make a home-made remedy for Nicholas's hand: mud. It took a few more handfuls of dirt and lots more water before anything resembling mud was achieved, the result then being slathered across the injured party's palm.

'How does it feel?' Max asked, concerned and sympathetic to his friend's reaction.

'It really helps, actually. Who'd have thought, hey? I'm going to kill that boy.'

'I'm sure he didn't mean to scare you.' Rohan jumped to Sebastian's defence trying his best to keep the peace.

Once the initial shock had worn off, the group persuaded Nicholas to take his chance to get his challenge out of the way.

'Well, if I don't do it with this, I'm sure you'll find something way worse for me,' he conceded.

With eyes clenched shut he held out his palms, ready to receive the package. Alistair softly dropped the imperceptibly light beast into the awaiting nest. Once in and realising that instant death had not befallen him, Nicholas plucked up the courage to open a gap between his two thumbs just wide enough to see inside. It was a small step towards conquering his life-long fear and putting that demon to rest. It would be foolish to say that this had completely cured his phobia but that wasn't really the point.

Max was well aware that it would take more than one good experience to fix each of the boys' deep-seated anxieties. This was about showing willingness and courage. Willingness to be part of something bigger, courage to do something that scares you. Both would prove crucial in the pursuit of power and change.

As every year wore on, each would be faced with new challenges, hard work, and the need to make tough decisions, but always the right ones. Facing a fear of this size would be dwarfed by the tasks they would undertake in the wider world, sometimes feeling alone, when the group wasn't immediately at hand to give support.

Looking at the group now laughing and joking again, he was proud. In one day, they had successfully tackled three out of the five challenges. At this rate, they would have them all complete within one more.

That evening they ate and drank, just the five of them, discussing the day and laughing about the events that had transpired. Sebastian repeated his apologies to his comrade, eventually convincing Nicholas that no harm had been intended. The conversation then turned to the previous night's party with the French girls, Rohan and Nicholas being questioned thoroughly about the evening.

Up until now, Nicholas had been surprisingly mute on the subject all day, a disappointment to Max and Sebastian who were keen to settle their bet.

'A gentleman never kisses and tells.' Nicholas avoided the question.

'Come on. This isn't like you, you're normally the first to brag about your accolades,' Sebastian pushed.

'Not this time.'

'So, nothing happened then.' Sebastian's attempt at using reverse psychology to coax an answer were not the subtlest.

'Say what you want, I'm not saying anything. It wouldn't be right.' Nicholas held his ground.

Max looked to Sebastian, with a small shrug of the shoulders. 'I think he's in love, what other possible explanation could there be? How about you, Rohan? How was your evening with Gisèle?'

'We kissed during hide and seek. Nothing major, I thought she wasn't into me and then at one point we ended up running to hide in one of the spa rooms.'

'Go on,' Sebastian prodded.

'She kissed me and then darted for the hallway. That's when we headed up to the deck and pretty much fell asleep.'

'In each other's arms though, that has to count for something?'

'Well, I don't know about that, but it was a great night.' Rohan continued, 'I think they had fun. She relaxed a lot after we'd had a few drinks but then this morning she was back to being super shy which made the boat ride back a bit awkward. Thankfully Céleste was there to do most of the talking.' He now switched topic. 'Alistair, what's our plan on the way back? Will we be in Saint Tropez for a night at all?'

'We can be, I think. I'd have to check with the commodore, but I don't see why not. I'm guessing you want to see her again?'

'Only if we have time. I'm sure Nicholas wouldn't mind seeing Céleste, I know she'd like to see him again. You've obviously made an impression on her.' Rohan turned to Nicholas.

Looking up far too quickly from the wine glass that he was rolling between his fingers, it was clear to anyone watching him that in that moment excitement had overcome him. It was almost like he was unable to control the smile that had taken over his face before coming to his senses and replacing it with a smug and aloof sense of calm. Max wasn't fooled.

'Well, I suppose if we had to see them again, I wouldn't complain.' Now playing up to his indifference, he diverted the conversation away and onto the next steps of their journey, keen to know what the next days had in store.

Alistair and Max took turns in describing the next stops. They were already en route to the southern coast of Italy, having navigated around Cap Corse which jutted out eighteen miles north from the island, adding a bit of extra distance to their route. At a distance just shy of three hundred miles, the ship would take roughly ten hours to travel from their current location to the Amalfi Coast.

'I do have some bad news, though,' Alistair gave forewarning. 'I don't think we'll have time to get all the way to Croatia and back. It would have been a stretch anyway and the captain said that it would be a bit of a wasted trip really as we won't have that much time when we get there.'

None of the group seemed overly fussed by the news, Nicholas and Rohan selfishly admitting that it would give them time to have one more night in Saint Tropez. The rest were just happy to be aboard this amazing ship and free in the wide-open Mediterranean.

'Okay, why don't we just spend a bit more time around Italy before heading back to France? Everyone happy with that?' Max checked.

'We can always do Croatia another time.' Sebastian

was also happy to go with the flow. He had no one waiting back in Saint Tropez and was relishing his time without the stress of exams and school.

He did, however, have someone he wanted to talk to, so excusing himself from the table, he descended the stairs to his room and picked up the phone.

24

The next morning, the group awoke in balmier seas off the west coast of Italy. The boys ate breakfast on the deck, as they had the previous day, and discussed their itinerary. Now that Croatia had been cut from the trip, they had more time to play with and were keen to make the most of it. With only two challenges left, they asked Tom's advice on both. He'd done more scuba diving than any of the group and had seen more of the Mediterranean than most people ever would, cliffs and all. It was news to the group to hear that sea snakes are generally found in the subtropical waters of the Indian and Pacific oceans. He advised the group to rethink that challenge.

However, the cliff diving would be much simpler and once they arrived in Italy it didn't take long before an enlarged group of guests and crew had found the perfect opportunity to test their mettle. Having observed a group of kiwi travellers diving from some jagged rocks outside the town of Atrani, Tom rounded up anyone that was willing to take the leap of faith and guided them to the perfectly situated rocks, forty feet above the sea.

A treacherous path was the first obstacle to overcome but the lead group all managed successfully, now just leaving the main event. Rohan, like the others, chose to go first to conquer his fear. Following another group of thrill-seekers, he picked his way over the rocks and moss lining the route to the makeshift jumping platform. Even this had been a major accomplishment, and one that he would have never have contemplated had it not been for the group of onlookers.

By this point in the holiday, it was clear to Max that the bond between the boys was growing stronger every day. Time, especially that spent at sea, does that to a group, confining them in a space and forcing them to spend time together. Each gets a chance to see what the others are like, not only in the moments they see them in school, or at a party, but every minute of the day.

Max's mum had often commented about him going away on school holidays or sports tours. A group of boys, often of different ages would board a bus on a wet Saturday morning outside the school, clear divisions visible between years and even friendship groups. Upon returning, it was always a surprise to see a completely different dynamic between the groups as they disembarked. Boys who wouldn't even talk at the start of the trip had suddenly become best friends. Or a group that was solid before the holiday would now have a new member. It all came down to time.

Max watched from a bobbing jet ski, looking out for the distinctive yellow shorts the gang had teased Rohan for wearing. He could see the climb had gone without a hitch, even if it had been slower than the rest of the people making the ascent, but he'd then lost sight behind some thick shrubbery. As he started to worry that something was wrong, and that Rohan may have turned back, it wasn't long before the yellow shorts reappeared.

Sebastian and Alistair had made the trip with Rohan, which was a comfort to Max knowing they would be on hand to offer any support needed. As the shorts reached the platform, Max could see that Rohan had retreated from the cliff and sat down on a patch of green about five feet from the edge. His two friends and some other supporters crowded around him and the noise began to build.

Confused as to what was happening and just too far away to be able to shout up to the divers, Max feared that it had been too much for his friend and the challenge was over. That, however, was not the case. The noise from the clifftop grew as the crowd now cheered their encouragement for someone. The yellow shorts came closer to the edge.

Expecting there to be a few failed attempts before finally seeing him leap, Max turned to the group of the Mufasa's crew still aboard the tender to ask them to make sure to get a photo of the jump. It was too late though and as he returned his eyes to the cliff face, he just caught a yellow blur plummeting towards the water. A huge cheer rang out from above and onlookers peered over the edge to check the jumper was still in one piece.

To Max on the jet ski, it felt like Rohan had been under the water for a lifetime. In reality, it could only have been four or five seconds before a head appeared and a fist pumped the air. Upon seeing the diver reappear, the noise from above grew in intensity, the crew, Nicholas and Max all joining in the congratulations. As Rohan climbed onto the back of the jet ski, it was clear that it had been an emotional ride as the adrenaline still surged through his body making him tremble and shiver.

'How was that, mate? It looked epic!' Max congratulated him.

Rohan was still panting. 'Well, I'm not cured, if that's what you mean. Just don't ask me to do it again.'

'You sure? You don't want to do it just one more time?'

Max started to manoeuvre himself to jump from the jet-ski and head for the path up the cliff. He was surprised when Rohan agreed, 'Fuck it. We're only here once, let's do it.'

'Yes! Go Rohan! Let's head up there before you change your mind.'

The pair jumped into the water and made their way towards the craggy shoreline to climb the rock face once more. As Max swam, he called out to the crew for them to join but it seemed that they had either lost their nerve or had no intention of jumping in the first place. Either way, he was sure they wouldn't admit to backing out.

After persuading the rest of the group to jump one more time, the day went by without incident. The only lasting effect was a blue bruise that appeared over the next few hours on Rohan's left thigh and buttock. His angle of entry into the water was just off centre, meaning that one side of his body took the brunt of impact. Luckily there was no lasting damage, just a tender wince each time he attempted to sit down.

Over the next few days, the boys travelled around the south coast of Italy. They visited Pompeii, where Nicholas was forced to concede that it was far more interesting than he'd imagined. He admitted that he'd not paid much attention in school when they had covered the disaster but being there, in the spot where it happened, seeing the ruins up close with the misshapen Mount Vesuvius as a backdrop brought it all to life.

Looking at the mountain, it was easy to imagine the shape it would have been before its cap had been ejected and vaulted skywards. Billions of tonnes of rock and debris had been thrown thirty kilometres into the stratosphere, the wind guiding the column of heat and ash towards the nearby towns of Pompeii and Herculaneum, resulting in the deaths of over 2,000 people from the surrounding areas.

Having been lost under twenty feet of ash and rock for 1,500 years, the site of Pompeii was then rediscovered in 1599. The 'mummies' Alistair had been referring to were created by pouring plaster into voids in the layers of ash, allowing the excavators to discover the exact positions in which people died in the tragedy.

Guides told harrowing stories as they wandered through the ruins, giving the gang some insight into the scale of the eruption and the devastation that followed. Seeing these low ruins of houses, the Temple of Apollo and public baths, the mind is easily transported back to 79 AD and the terror that must have taken hold of the residents once they realised that their homes were being demolished by the hand of nature. The macabre mood of the group was only mildly lifted upon hearing a near-by tour guide telling his troop of the penis shaped markers around the town, supposedly indicating the routes to brothels in the ancient city.

From Pompeii, they travelled to the beautiful island of Capri. Upon arriving on the small island, the group decided that they would stay here for a couple of days before returning to France. They would take the chance to explore some of the wonders like the Grotto Azzurra, or Blue Grotto, a fabulous underwater hidden cave entered through a hole just big enough for a small rowing boat. Once inside the cave, the light entering through the opening bathes the visitor in a sapphire radiance from below. For a place that seems so shut off from the outside world, it was buzzing with tourists.

They spent the next two days discovering spectacular villas offering views over the seemingly endless miles of coastline, dining under the lemon trees at Da Paolino and exploring the small, pebble beaches scattered around the coast. The relaxed atmosphere was a welcome break from the intensity and alcohol levels of the first few days, giving the boys time to talk and plan the next few months and the coming years.

Each day, Max asked the boys to go off on the scooters they'd hired and spend an hour or two with someone different to give them time alone to learn about each other and what the plan had in store for them. He was amazed at the difference even after only two days spending just a few hours alone with someone. Private jokes, catchphrases, and new banter appeared at every meal, fuelling the laughter around the tables. Even the crew had relaxed over the past few days, becoming more involved with the group, sharing the odd drink with them as the sun set behind Sardinia, directly to the west.

25

Da Luigi ai Faraglioni was precariously perched in a beautiful location on the south side of Capri. The boys had spotted the beach club from the tender on one of their sightseeing trips around the island and agreed that it would be a good location to spend their last night in Italy. Only accessible by boat, Tom dropped them on the private jetty at 6:30 pm, just as the temperature started to cool.

Not sure exactly what to expect, the boys had dressed up to look the part. As usual, the tender drew the attention of those still relaxing by the water's edge, as well as those starting to dine on the veranda of the restaurant.

Stepping off the boat, Rohan felt like a rock star. Never in his life had he had so much attention simply for just being. He hung at the back of the group as they strode up the stone stairs towards the elevated deck offering views of an incredible natural stone obelisk that rises from the water to form its own rocky island. This week, he'd experienced more glamour and luxury than he knew existed. If the group was a way for him to continue to live like this, then he definitely wanted in.

Having originally thought that the whole idea was crazy, he'd gone to Max's house for the first meeting only out of interest to see what crazy scheme he was cooking up. It had initially confused him when Max made the approach, considering Rohan didn't think of the pair as being friends. He'd always seen Max as an arrogant boy with a carefree life who thought he owned the school. If he was honest with himself, he wanted Max to fail, at least at first. Not just at this, but everything.

Even until they stepped onto the private plane at Manchester airport, he still had his doubts about the leader and a few of the boys. However, what he'd experienced over the past week was something he never had before. He felt part of a group. Accepted and welcomed. And by Max most of all. He saw the passion in Max's speeches, the sincerity of what he wanted to achieve. Striding up those stone steps now, he felt proud to be surrounded by these characters.

The group was welcomed by a stressed waiter who demanded to know how many they were.

'Cinque,' Alistair confirmed.

Of all the boys on the trip, Rohan had grown to

like Alistair the most. He had a sense of calm about him that was settling, and a sense of humility that was unexpected, considering who his father was. Even though he envied the life that was afforded by having such a wealthy family, he admired Alistair's attitude towards it.

The waiter led the group to an empty table in the far corner of the veranda, next to the railings overlooking the jetty and the obelisk. Rohan couldn't help but feel like they were being kept as far away from the rest of the guests as possible, maybe due to the expectation that they would be a loud party. It wouldn't matter though. Within twenty minutes of taking their seats, the rest of the tables were occupied with diners.

The boys chatted, admiring the view, commenting on the other guests arriving in tenders and small dinghies. As Rohan looked up from his menu to place his order, a family approaching the area in which they were seated caught his eye. Led by the father who was short but with the stature of a body builder, the family comprised of him, the mother, and two children. A teenage boy of maybe twelve or thirteen was followed by a beautiful girl who must have been roughly Rohan's age.

As the family took their seats at the table next to theirs, Rohan overheard their Scottish accents as they admired the venue. He didn't dare to look at the girl, scared that he would end up catching the eye of the stocky father.

The meal wore on and it became clear that the family were celebrating an event as they toasted their daughter with champagne. She'd been accepted to study Law at King's College in London, starting in September. The parents beamed with pride as they noisily celebrated her accomplishment.

Nicholas, now slightly tipsy, was the first to make contact with the family, joking with the father about Scottish rowdiness. The banter was taken in good humour and the father insisted they join him in congratulating his daughter, asking the waiter to bring more champagne for both tables. Glasses were raised in the air, names were exchanged and eventually the two tables were moved closer together just as the sun began to disappear.

'I'm Melissa. Lovely to meet you.' She leaned in and kissed Rohan on the cheek as she took her newly rearranged seat next to him.

Whether it was the alcohol or his newly acquired confidence as part of the group, he found chatting to her effortless. They talked all night about the island and their holidays so far, her soon to be new life in London and the career that she was hoping to have in international law.

At about 10 o'clock, Max ordered a bottle of Limoncello for the table, requesting glasses for all present and insisted that all partook. Melissa's father was clearly a fan of the liqueur, sinking at least four or five shots from the bottle. Her mother was slightly less gung-ho and declined any more after the first two. Marcus, her little brother, was allowed half of a normal-sized shot before he was cut off.

The first bottle disappeared and another was ordered, this time by her father, Sean, contrary to the advice of her mother, Gill.

He protested, 'Come on, we're just having a wee celebration for our girl. It's not like we have to drive anywhere, hen.'

She relented, even joining in for another round.

Live music emerging from a three-piece band invited those dining in the restaurant to dance in an area of the veranda that had been cleared of tables, splitting the group. Melissa and Rohan stayed put, still sharing stories and jokes, laughing and smiling.

'Would you like to dance?' Rohan asked, plucking up the courage.

Melissa turned to see her father romancing her mother with some classic 'dad' moves. 'I don't think so. I don't want to be seen anywhere near those two.' She laughed, shaking her head. 'Why don't we go down to the water instead?'

'Sure, I could go for a walk.' Rohan stood, wine glass in hand as he cleared a path for the two of them through chairs that had been left haphazardly by excited people making their way to dance. They found their way to the top of the stone stairs and descended, their path illuminated by the orange lights of the veranda.

To their right, a natural rock pathway connected the obelisk to the island. To their left was a stone terrace covered with sun loungers. Beyond that, was the dark, lapping water of the Mediterranean. She led him towards the edge and they picked their way along the rocks, her sandals making a clipping sound every time she took a step.

'Just be careful here,' he warned. 'It looks pretty slippery.'

'It's fine,' she slurred. 'Look, take my hand if you're worried.' She smiled as she reached out behind her, moving her body to the rhythm of the music from above them.

The further they wandered around the rocks, the more the light faded, and the more anxious Rohan became that she was going to trip.

'Why don't we just take a seat here?' he suggested, tugging slightly on her hand, willing her to stop.

'Just a little further,' she protested. 'I can see a wee flat patch up ahead. Are you scared?' She turned, smiling, goading him along the rocks.

He followed as she picked her way another thirty feet along the uneven rocks before coming to a stop.

'See. Much clearer view of the stars without the light.' She gazed upwards to the sky, tipping her head to take another sip of wine.

Well, she is right. He gazed at the intricate web of diamonds hanging above them.

'Sit with me,' she requested as she lowered herself onto the rocks using his hand to steady herself.

'Yeah, that's probably wise,' he agreed, just as the effects of the shots started to hit him.

They chatted for what felt like an eternity. Melissa confessed that she was nervous about moving away from home. The only time she'd been to London was to tour the university. It would be a very different life from the idyllic village of Aboyne, tucked away on the edge of the Scottish Highlands.

Although the boys had talked about going away to university, it still felt like a lifetime away to Rohan. He wondered what he would feel when it came to his turn to fly the nest.

'Come paddle with me. I'm hot,' she suggested, reaching down to take off her sandals. Without waiting for him to respond, she lowered herself off the rocks and into the water, finding her feet and turning to him.

Against his better judgement, he joined her in removing his shoes and slipped into the water. What neither of them realised in the dark was that the ledge that they were now standing on was no more than a foot wide.

Her grip on his hand tightened as she turned towards him, eyes meeting his. He dared to squeeze back just as she stepped forward with her left foot to bring herself closer. He closed his eyes, anticipating the kiss as she leaned forward.

Before their lips could touch, his hand was pulled downwards and away from him as she fell, full force, into the water. At the sound of the splash, he opened his eyes to see her disappear below the surface just as he was pulled off balance and the momentum carried him with her. He spread his arms and legs to try and stop himself from going under, but it was no use. His body fully submerged, the cold water taking him by surprise as it enveloped his head.

As he resurfaced, his legs scrambled for the bottom, for anything to get some purchase on. Kicking out to get some purchase, his shin caught on a rock, breaking the skin. Finally, grabbing hold of the rocks beneath the water, he turned to see Melissa floating face down, motionless, five yards from the shore.

'Melissa.' There was panic in his voice as he shouted to her. 'Melissa!'

She didn't respond. He jumped off the rocks, reaching for her legs, pulling her back towards him and solid ground. Managing to get his feet back onto the ledge, he pulled her head out of the water only to see a trail of thick, dark plasma in the water where she had been.

'Holy shit! Melissa!'

Still no response.

He turned her over so that her face was now out of the water as he dragged her towards the rocks. Grabbing the first thing that his hand came into contact with, he pulled at her dress, but the thin material of the shoulder strap snapped, releasing her back into the water. Once more, he jumped from the ledge. This time, he grabbed her firmly under the arms as he backed towards the rocks. He managed to get his feet onto the ledge and heave her from the water, resting her bum on the submerged rocks.

'Help!' he screamed, his voice cracking with the effort. 'Help me!'

Resting her floating body between his legs, he turned her onto her side to let the water drain from her mouth and airways.

'Somebody help me!' he called out again.

It was no use. The music from the band drowned out his pleas. He reached down, checking below her ear for a pulse. She had one. It was strong.

'Melissa.' He grabbed her face. 'Melissa. Come on, please.'

He looked back towards the restaurant. There was no way he could carry her over the rocks. He wondered whether he could swim with her back around the shore and try calling for help again.

Just as he manoeuvred himself to push off and back into the water, she let out a long moan followed by a sharp cough.

'Melissa!' He rolled her onto her side once more to allow her to cough up any water she may have inhaled before heaving her further out of the water. It was not easy. The combination of alcohol and being knocked out had made her unable to help him.

It was at least twenty minutes before she was able to speak again. Even then, her words were slurred and near incomprehensible.

'Can you move?' he asked.

'Yeah, I'm 'kay,' she mumbled, her head lolling around.

'We need to get you back. You're bleeding.'

'K.' She closed her eyes.

'I need you to stay awake, Melissa. Can you do that for me?'

'K.' She didn't open her eyes.

'Melissa,' this time louder and more forcefully. 'I need you to help me. Can you get up?'

She nodded, eyes still closed, mouth open and making sounds but not sense.

Struggling, he managed to get her fully out of the water and seated upright. Over the next ten minutes, her movement returned to the point where he could lift her up and support most of her weight. Walking on the side closest to the water, he battled to keep her upright as they painfully picked their way across the rocks.

Where their shoes were, he had no idea. He hadn't realised that after the initial fall they'd been pushed ten feet closer to the restaurant by the water, disorientating him. Every step hurt on the jagged surface below. Every five or so steps, she stumbled forcing him to use all his strength to catch her. It wasn't always possible though and she landed on her knees, more often than not, leaving gashes on her lower legs.

After what felt like an hour of slow progress, they rounded some rocks and the corner of the restaurant came into view. He breathed a sigh of relief as the floor levelled out and he was able to scoop her up and carry her in both arms.

As he got within one hundred feet of the restaurant, he spotted a group of people arguing at the bottom of the stairs down from the veranda. He couldn't hear about what.

'Help me!' he shouted out again.

The group stopped shouting at each other, turning to see where the sound came from. They started to run towards him just as he reached the man-made, flat concrete slab that made up the start of the jetty. He didn't recognise the first two men coming to his aid, but they were followed by Max, Sebastian and Nicholas. Not far behind them were Sean and Gill, along with two waiters from the restaurant.

'What the fuck have you done to her, you cunt?' The first to reach him was a man in his early thirties, English, and very pissed off.

Before Rohan could speak, the man grabbed the dishevelled girl out of his arms. Her torn, white sundress was soaked pink with bright red swathes of crimson running down its length. The second to arrive was even more aggressive. He grabbed Rohan by the collar before punching him hard in the side of the face.

The first man disappeared with Melissa, carrying her back towards her parents. Her mother stopped as the man lay her down on the ground, but her father continued towards him.

'Did you fucking rape my daughter?' Sean shouted as he approached.

Luckily, Max and Sebastian managed to intercept the flurry of punches that he attempted to heap on Rohan.

'Hey!' Max shouted, 'Just calm down. Let him explain.'

'She fell,' Rohan shouted, still panting from the effort of carrying her and the shock of being assaulted. Looking down, he now saw his shirt covered in blood, both his and hers.

'I didn't touch her, I swear.' he pleaded. 'She fell.'

'I'm going to fucking kill you,' her father screamed, now being held back by Sebastian and Nicholas.

'Just go and see if she's alright,' Nicholas instructed her father as he struggled against them. Eventually, he stopped resisting and turned to run over to his daughter and wife.

'Rohan, we need to get out of here now. They want to kill us. What did you do?' Sebastian asked.

'What have you done, Rohan?' Nicholas shouted aggressively.

'Nothing, I swear. We were just… we walked round the…' He couldn't get his words out.

'Get the fuck out of here. If you ever come back, we'll kill you.' The man who'd punched him shouted from over Sebastian's shoulder.

'Come on, mate. We need to go. They're going to call the police.' Sebastian started pulling Rohan towards the jetty where Tom and two of crew were just arriving in the tender. The crew jumped out while Tom tied the boat up.

'The police? Why?' Rohan was confused.

'They think you raped her, you fucking idiot,' Nicholas barked back at him.

'I didn't touch her. I need to go and talk to them.' He tried to make his way towards Melissa, but he was stopped by the first attacker.

'Leave, now!' he screamed, inches from Rohan's face.

'No!' Rohan pushed his head into his aggressor's. 'I didn't touch her!' He was now screaming himself.

The crew arrived just as more punches were about to be thrown, one restraining the older English man, the other grabbing Rohan, pulling him down towards the jetty.

'I didn't do anything!' Rohan shouted over his shoulder towards Melissa and her parents. As far as he could tell, she hadn't moved.

Max reappeared having been hovering around the parents as they took care of her, trying to find out what happened but had given up after being shouted at by her mother. 'Fuck, they're really upset. We need to go or they're not going to let us out of here alive.'

Rohan continued to protest as he was hauled onto the boat, soon to be joined by the rest of the group, crew and Tom.

A crowd had now gathered at the bottom of the steps, watching the commotion unfold as waiters rushed out with water and first aid supplies. They jeered and shouted towards the tender as it pulled away from the concrete jetty.

Rohan stood at the back of the boat, trying to see whether Melissa was okay, whether she was responding, but she was too far away to tell.

'You've fucked up royally, Rohan.' This time Nicholas was the aggressor. 'What did you think you were doing?' He grabbed Rohan by his shirt, ripping the buttons as he spun him round to confront him.

Max jumped to his defence, pulling Nicholas away and shoving him towards the front of the boat.

'What the fuck is wrong with you, Nicholas? As if I would do something like that.' Rohan's emotions were a mix of fury at being accused of something terrible and worry whether she was okay.

'Come on, man. Why was she half naked then? Just admit it,' Nicholas shouted from his new position at the bow.

The others were now joining in, either in agreement with Nicholas or in Rohan's defence.

'Everybody shut up!' The ferocity of Max's cry silenced all on board.

26

Alone in his room on the Mufasa, Max paced up and down the length of it as he waited for his call to be answered.

'Hi. I think there might be a problem. Well, more than one, actually.' There was stress in his voice.

'Well it's nice to talk to you too, Max.'

'I'm serious. It's all falling apart. Something happened tonight and I'm not sure what's next. We might be in serious trouble.'

'You're drunk?'

'No,' he protested. 'Well, maybe a bit. But this isn't about me. It's Rohan. We're not sure but he might have done something to a girl. She was in a pretty bad state. I think they called the police. I'm not sure what to do.'

'Bad state? What does that mean?' The voice on the other end of the line was concerned and confused.

'She was unconscious and covered in blood.' He sat at the room's desk, head in his hands.

'Jesus. She's definitely alive? Did they arrest him?'

'No. We tried to see if she was okay, but they wouldn't let us.'

'Max, what are you talking about? Who is they? And why didn't you wait for the police?'

'It's a long story but we couldn't stay. Rohan swears he didn't do anything and I want to believe him but not everyone does.'

There was a long pause. 'So, what are you going to do?'

'We're leaving Italy. Tonight.' Max wondered what response he would get.

He felt guilty, but they didn't have a choice. The captain had spoken with James Lovell who insisted that they bring his son back to France as soon as possible.

Max felt like they should stay to clear things up, but James had made a valid point. What if Rohan was telling the truth but the girl was too drunk to remember anything, and he was wrongfully accused of raping her? Rohan would sit in an Italian jail for months just waiting for a trial. And there was no guarantee that he would be cleared.

On the other hand, what if he did do it and they helped him to run away without any justice? Was the group more important than that? Could he really justify letting Rohan off no matter the cost?

'What's the other thing, Max? You said two problems.'

'I can't get this thought out of my head.' Max switched topics. 'It's Alistair. The fight he and Rosa had. She's trying to convince him to change his mind and stray from the plan. I just know it.'

'What did they say exactly?'

'I'm not totally sure but she left clearly upset and angry. When he came over to us he was talking about them both going to St Andrews. He said that he'd told her that he wasn't going to do Medicine.'

'Do you think she'll try to convince him otherwise? And do you think he'll listen?' The voice on the other end of the phone was calm, thinking, analysing.

'I don't know. He seems so resilient sometimes, but not when it comes to her. She seems to have a power over him. He's besotted with her.'

'Okay. Let's think about this. Alistair's not absolutely essential to the plan, but it would be a lot easier with him on board. Do you think she knows about the group?'

'Not at the moment. Not from the conversation I heard anyway, but it's only a matter of time. They're seeing each other again next week once the group leaves the boat. I'm scared that if she keeps pushing, he'll either just change his mind completely, or he'll tell her about the group in an attempt to persuade her to go along with it. And in any case, he knows about everything now. All the roles, the paths.'

'Well that can't happen. If you're really serious about this, then she can't be allowed to get in the way.'

'But how can we stop it?'

'I'm sure you'll think of something. Look at what you've been able to accomplish so far. You can do this, Max. The whole group is relying on you.'

'I know, I know. It can't stop here. This can't be what ruins everything, we're only at the beginning.'

'There's a long way to go, and you always knew this was going to be filled with bumps along the road. Trust in yourself, we will find a solution to this.'

'Thanks. I needed to hear...'

The sound of knocking on Max's door made him jump and the phone clattered onto the desk. Scrambling to pick it up, he ended the conversation in a hurry. 'I'll call you tomorrow. Bye.'

He pulled the door ajar to find Alistair outside.

'Max, can I come in?'

Max opened the door fully and moved aside. 'Of course.'

'Who were you speaking to?' Alistair asked, looking down at the phone in Max's hand.

'Oh,' he hesitated, wondering how much of the

conversation Alistair had heard. 'Just Harriet checking in. You know how nosy she is about your dad's boat.' He switched topics, 'Eventful night, hey?'

27

Of all the conversations Max thought he would be having on the trip, this was not one of them. Locked once again in the cavernous stateroom where the young men had taken their pledges earlier in the week, he and Sebastian had a choice to make.

'I don't see a way he can be part of it anymore.' Max was subdued as he admitted it aloud. 'Nicholas won't be if Rohan is. Neither will Alistair. What about you? Do you think he did it?'

'No. I believe him. And I think you should give him the benefit of the doubt too.'

'Well, it didn't exactly look good, did it, Seb?'

'Max, what you said earlier this week, in this very room, about standing up for each other, protecting each other, did you really even believe that?' Sebastian wasn't looking for a response. 'Here we are at the first obstacle and we're having to make a choice whether to kick him out.'

'Of course I did, and I still do. But it's no use protecting one of us if it means that we lose two. It doesn't make sense.'

'We can talk Alistair and Nicholas round.'

'They won't be in the group with a rapist, Sebastian,' Max snapped, angry at the situation.

'We don't know that he is one, Max,' Sebastian shouted back. 'It only happened last night, and we have no idea what really happened. You have to at least hear him out now that everyone has calmed down.'

'I've heard his side and it seems pretty unlikely. Why would he have taken her so far away in the pitch black? Why did no one hear him calling for help?'

'I don't know but at least let's get the answers first before we cut him loose. He knows everything about the group. If we kick him out, he'll find a way to destroy it. He'd just tell everyone about it and it would be over.'

'Okay, okay.' Max stood from his chair, rubbing his hands over his hair as he thought. 'I don't want to fight with you about this. We've done nothing wrong here. Why don't we get the others in here and see what they think?'

'No, Max. They don't decide everything. This isn't a committee. You're the leader here. So lead. Make the decision and then we'll convince them that it's the right thing.'

'You mean your decision?' Max challenged him.

'No, I mean the right decision. The best decision for the group. Do you think nothing like this is ever going to happen again? Can you really promise that you're never going to make a stupid mistake and won't need us to help you out?'

Max considered the question as he stared into space. 'No. I guess not. I'd hope not but I can't say for certainty. And, you are right. I was the one who said we'd stand up for each other no matter what.'

He moved towards the door at the end of the room with purpose.

'Where are you going?' asked Sebastian.

'Stay here. I'm going to get Alistair and Nicholas.'

He returned five minutes later with Alistair in tow. In Max's hands were pieces of paper, pens and matches. 'Nicholas is on his way, he's just in the loo.'

As Alistair took his place, Max slid a piece of paper across to the two boys who knew exactly what it was for.

Nicholas entered the room, clearly agitated. He spoke as soon as he saw Max place the bowl in the centre of the table. 'Max, you don't need the paper. I'm out. It's as simple as that. If Rohan is allowed to stay, I'm not going to.'

Max jumped up to close the door.

'I don't care if he hears me, Max,' Nicholas barked. 'He needs to know.'

'I'm not closing it for him. I'm closing it for anyone else who might hear, Nicholas. Even if you leave, the group still goes on so keep your voice down and respect that it's not all about you.'

'So, you're letting him stay?' Nicholas was getting angrier.

'I didn't say that. Just hear me ...'

'No, Max. I'm not letting him fuck this up for everyone. You need to kick him out. We'll replace him with someone better. The police are going to come looking for him. They don't just let you get away with this kind of stuff.'

'What's your problem with him, Nicholas?' Sebastian jumped in. 'Why won't you even hear him out?'

'What if that had been your sister. Or mine.' Nicholas pointed at Sebastian as he spoke.

'That's not what I'm asking you. I want you to hear his side of the story.' Sebastian now turned to Alistair. 'What's your take on it?'

Alistair looked around the faces in the room. 'If he did it, I'm with Nicholas. But I do want to see what he has to say for himself.'

'What? So he can tell us the same lies all over again?' Nicholas paced as he argued with them.

'Nicholas, you need to calm down,' Max shouted, not helping the situation.

'Fuck off, Max. Don't tell me to calm down. My sister was raped by a fucking scumbag. Do you know what it does to people? It ruins their lives. I've seen it.'

There was silence in the room as he made the revelation.

Max was the first to speak. 'Nicholas, I didn't know that. I'm sorry, that's terrible. What I'm saying is that we don't know that he did it. I know what it looks like, but we need to know for sure first.' He paused and looked towards Sebastian as he considered his words carefully. 'And even if he did do something, we all promised to stand by one another.'

'Not for this, we didn't,' Nicholas reacted.

'Yes. We did. For anything. You can walk away if you want, Nicholas. And I'd respect you for that. But I'd rather we worked together to fix this.'

'How can we fix this, Max? The damage is done.'

'Stop being so fucking stubborn,' Max shouted at him. 'The minute it happened, you made up your mind and you won't hear anything else. You're meant to be his brother, not the fucking prosecution.'

The door flung open just as Max was finishing his sentence. Rohan marched into the room holding an iPad in his hand. Stopping at the narrow end of the table, he placed it down and slid it down the middle to where the group was positioned.

'Fuck you, Nicholas,' was all he said before storming back out the room, slamming the heavy door behind him.

Max leant over and picked up the device. The screen was open on the familiar blue and white colours of Facebook. It showed a message from a girl called Melissa, presumably the same girl from the night before.

'What is it?' Nicholas demanded as he rounded the table to see the screen.

The message read:

"Rohan, I'm so glad I managed to find you on here. My parents told me everything that happened last night. I couldn't believe what they said. Thank you so much for saving me. All I can remember is falling into the water and then you carrying me back.

My mum said people attacked you and your friends because they thought you'd done something terrible to me. I told them that you were a perfect gentleman and that I wouldn't be alive if it wasn't for you. They're really sorry but they just assumed the worst when they saw me covered in blood with my dress torn.

My dad feels really guilty. He said that he can't really remember but he thinks he might have hit you. I'm really sorry, I hope you weren't hurt. I explained everything this morning when I came around. They're just glad that I'm okay. I do have twelve stitches and a very sore head to show for my clumsiness. I shouldn't have insisted we went round there. It was a fun night up until that point though :).

I hope the rest of your holiday is less eventful!

Melissa x"

'You need to fix this, Nicholas,' Sebastian instructed as he finished reading the message over Max's shoulder. 'You should have trusted him.'

Nicholas didn't respond at first but just nodded his head as he bit his lip. After a minute of silence as the boys looked at him, he finally spoke. 'Yeah. I fucked up. I just couldn't stop thinking about her mum. Mine was a total mess when it happened to us. I pictured her in the same state that mine was in. I'll go find him.'

'Bring him back here when you're done.' Max patted him on the back, much calmer now. 'There's something we need to do.' He nodded towards the paper and matches in the middle of the table.

After being gone for over an hour, Nicholas sheepishly entered the room followed by Rohan. The pair exchanged a look before nodding towards Max and the glass bowl on the table.

No one spoke as they performed the ritual. All wondering what had been said and what was about to happen.

Max breathed a small sigh of relief each time he opened a folded piece of paper to see another pentagon staring back at him. He flipped them over for all to see. By process of elimination, Max knew that the last to be opened was Nicholas's. He really had no idea what to expect and was unable to stop himself from jumping up to hug the pair who had been at war only an hour earlier.

After burning the paper and making the recognisable mark on their faces, Max was the first to speak.

'Rohan, I'm sorry. I should have trusted everything you said. It was just... well you could see how it looked. We all owe you an apology.'

'It's alright, Max. I know how it must have looked. But you also need to know that I would never do something like that.'

'I do. I think we all do really but with everything that was going on it was hard not to get caught up in it. I've got your back next time, mate.'

The pair embraced and Max whispered 'Sorry' in Rohan's ear. As they released, Max turned to the group. 'Well, I don't know about you guys, but I think I'm ready to go home. I've had just about enough excitement for one holiday.'

28

A suspicious feeling weighed on the mind of one of the boys after returning from their trip. It was unshakeable, burrowing deeper into his thoughts as the days passed.

What had really happened between Rosa and Alistair during their fight on the boat that day and why had she left without saying anything to the boys? Had he already told her about the group and the plan? Or was she just reacting to the news that he was no longer going to study Medicine with her?

He resolved to find out what was going on and had a pretty good idea of how he was going to do it. Even though he knew it would only take one call to get the answers he was looking for, he'd have to pay a price.

He reached for his phone and scrolled to the name he needed: Richard Ward. Hitting the green button, he waited for the rings as his mind thought about the potential trouble Alistair was already causing.

'Wardy, how you doing, pal?'

Ward answered. 'Alright man! How you doing? Long time, no speak. How was the hol?'

He sounded stoned already and it was only 11:30 in the morning. It was hardly a surprise. They had been neighbours for ten years and there was hardly a day in the last three or four that the smell of marijuana hadn't crept over the boundary line between their parents' houses.

'Wake and bake, Ward? I take it your folks are away?'

'You know what summers are for, man. Yeah, they're, err, well they're somewhere. I can hardly keep track of them since dad retired. Always exploring some random island in the South Pacific. What's up?'

'I wondered if I could come round?' the caller asked, not revealing the reason over the phone. 'I need a favour from someone with your skills with a computer.'

'What's it worth to you?' Ward asked, repeating the catchphrase he used whenever someone asked anything of him.

'Well, how about I don't tell everyone we know that you've been hacking all their social media accounts for years now?'

'Sounds fair enough, I suppose,' Ward agreed. 'Come round whenever.'

Less than thirty minutes later the group member knocked on the half-open door to the Wards' house, a familiar smell immediately hitting his nostrils. A response from somewhere deep at the back of the house beckoned him into the building. He pushed open the door before returning it to its original state, assuming it had been left open on purpose to create a draft to clear the smoke from Ward's bong, pipe, or whatever other implement he was using on this particular morning.

His assumption was correct, and as he entered the expansive living room that faced out in to the lush garden, he could feel the breeze coming in through the wide open French windows and hear the rock music coming from the large TV and sound system that accompanied it. He saw a large cloud of smoke rise from behind the couch, immediately giving away the location of the culprit.

The visitor approached and rounded the huge, brown leather sofa to see the stoner hanging over the end, lighter in one hand and a long green bong in the other. It was clear that this was not his first hit of the day.

Over the past few years, Ward had become more and more reclusive, from the physical world, at least. When these two talked, the visitor got the feeling that his childhood friend's life was transferring more and more into the virtual world, one which seemed to be taking him to some dark places with some strange people. Talk of 'resetting the playing field' and 'digital

Robin Hoods' wasn't all that far from the mantra of Us really when he thought about it, but it all existed in a world he couldn't quite wrap his head around. He did, however, know at least one use for the skills of his hacker friend.

Bloodshot eyes and a lazy smile stared back up at him as the resident started to cackle.

'Hey dude, how's it going?' Ward raised the bong to the newcomer, enquiring whether he wanted to share in the fun.

'Not for me, thanks. It's a bit early. Mind if I turn the music down a bit?'

'Why do you never get high with me anymore? It seems like you only did it that one time!' Ward seemed genuinely perplexed.

'It was only that one time!' The visitor struggled to shout over the volume of the TV as he searched for the remote, his host clearly in no rush to reduce the level of noise.

'Oh wait, wait, wait,' Ward, reached for the remote from the hand of his guest, 'I love this song, just leave it loud a minute.' He rolled over onto his back and closed his eyes to the sound of Everlong by the Foo Fighters, mouthing along to the words, 'And I wonder, when I sing along with you…'

'I'll just turn it down a bit, it's too loud. Your neighbours will complain,' the visitor insisted, hoping that the rest of what he needed to do wouldn't be as much like pulling teeth as simply turning down the volume.

'You are my neighbours, bro. And yeah, you are complaining so I guess you're right.' Ward giggled at his own joke. 'How was your holiday? What was King Alistair's boat like?'

'I can't even begin to explain it. It was amazing from the second we left. Private jet, super yacht, jet skis, booze. We basically saw the whole of the Mediterranean.'

'No way, man! A private jet? I knew they were rich but fuck me. I hate that guy even more now.'

'He's not so bad, you know.' An instinct made him defend his brother, even if he was struggling with his own feelings about Alistair. He hesitated before asking his next question, knowing that once he did, there may be no going back. 'That's actually the reason why I'm here. Can you hack someone for me?'

'Yeah dude, it's easy. Who do you need to hack? Alistair?' Ward joked.

'Bingo. I don't really need to but I sent him something by accident and I need you to get me into his account so I can delete it.'

'What did you send him?' the hacker enquired.

'Well, it's a bit embarrassing, it wasn't meant for him, but I clicked on the wrong person and didn't realise until it was too late. I know Alistair will take the piss out of me if he sees it. That's if he hasn't already but I think he's still away, so he probably hasn't.' He wondered whether his lie was convincing.

'I suppose I can help you, but I also need something from you in return, man.' It seemed Ward was unable to end a sentence with anything other than stereotypical stoner pronouns.

'I already told you. My silence is my payment.'

'Yeah, but that was before you became an accomplice to illegal activity. The price has increased.'

'Let me guess,' the visitor started, 'you want me to get high with you?' He predicted the same request that Ward made every time they saw each other. 'I told you, it's way too early for that.'

'Well okay.' Ward picked up his bong and prepped it for another hit. 'You obviously can't be that embarrassed about what you sent, dude. If you ain't willing to toke, I'm not sure I can help you. You know it's illegal to hack, how do I know you're not a narc if you won't have some of the cheese?'

It was clear from his mischievous smile that he wouldn't relent and when his guest rolled his eyes, Ward smiled. 'That's what I'm talking about!' he shouted as he leapt from his reclined position on the couch, glad to have a partner in crime. 'Okay, I'll pack the bong, you go and get my laptop from the table over there.' Ward pointed to a semi-circular, dark wooden side-table against the back wall of the room.

The guest made his way to the table. 'I can't see the computer, you sure it's in here?' He now realised this was not going to be the short encounter he'd hoped for.

As he searched, he thought about what he might actually find in Alistair's messages and what he would do next if his suspicions were true. What if Alistair had told Rosa? What if she knew everything about the group, about him? A pulse of anger shot through him.

'Yeah man, I was just on it earlier,' Ward replied dismissively, before correcting himself. 'Whoops, here it is. Sorry man, it was under this table. You should really let me teach you how to hack.'

'I know. You always say that, but I don't really need to know how. That's what I've got you for.' He winked at Ward.

'Well, all I'm saying is it could come in handy. Right, you take this and light it up. I want to see every last bit of it go and then we can get hacking.'

The reluctant smoker took a seat next to his push-er on the couch and raised the wide mouthpiece to his lips, fumbling with the lighter, unable to create a flame. This was not really what he had in mind for today, but what the hell? After three attempts to spin the metal wheel, create a spark, and catch the gas lever in synchronicity, an eager hand snatched the blue plastic lighter from his, expertly snapping it into life. The flame neared the bowl and the crystal covered, green plant started to curl as smoke rose from the leaves. Breathing in softly at first, not much of the smoke entered the chamber.

'You have to suck it harder than that, man. Come on,' a shake of the head from Ward accompanied disappointment in his voice, 'you're really not trying, are you?'

With the encouragement, the visitor began to inhale more deeply, filling the tube, then his mouth and finally his lungs with the light grey smoke. The vapour had been inside his body for only a couple of seconds before he suddenly pulled the green tube away from his face, expelling the contents of his lungs explosively, accompanied by saliva. The coughing fit lasted about a minute, his knees wide open and his head in between them, coughing towards the floor. His head instantly felt fuzzier, although he couldn't tell whether that was real or just his anticipation of what was to come.

His companion was now laughing, taking great pleasure in the misfortune of his friend. 'That's it, that's how you inhale. When you're ready, go again.'

'Do I have to?' the group member asked, still catching his breath.

'I said it all had to go, didn't I?' Ward confirmed.

'Okay, okay, you fucking stoner slave driver. I thought weed was meant to make you more chilled out!'

He returned the bong to his lips, his friend once again taking care of the ignition, ensuring that the whole of the supply was engulfed in the flame. The second inhale was smoother than the first, this time managing to only cough twice before completely blowing out the smoke from his lungs. Ward took the bong from his hand, once more putting the lighter to the bowl, finishing off what was left of its contents.

The novice breathed deeply, in and out, in and out, settling himself before finally raising his head to confront his torturer.

'Right, you've got me fucked now. Can we do this?'

A satisfied grin awaited him. 'You've passed the test, bud. Let's do it. What did you send the message on?'

'Facebook,' the visitor responded.

Ward reached for the computer, lifted the lid and opened up a set of windows on the machine, expertly navigating through them with deft clicks on the keys, faster than his accomplice could follow. As the THC started to interact with the CB1 receptors in the hippocampus, Ward's words lost all meaning to his sidekick, now struggling to keep up.

'Lucky for you, I know some pretty dodgy Russians

who developed some tools for this exact purpose. I suspect they may want me to pay them back someday but that's future Wardy's problem. A few years ago, this would have taken days but thanks to the cloud, I've got access to all the computing power I need.'

He opened a black window on the screen filled with lines of green code. After a few more clicks the screen went into a frenzy as it ran the program.

'If I'm as good as I think I am, that should be it.' Ward sat back, smug at his handiwork waiting for the screen to stabilise.

The initial hit now started to mellow and the visitor started to regain some composure, his mind thinking through what he was asking Ward to do. What if the group found out? Would they ever trust him again? He knew Alistair certainly wouldn't. This was more important than Alistair's trust, though. This was about Alistair's commitment, or lack of it.

This isn't just for me, it's for all of Us, he thought to himself, feeling like he owed it to the group.

'That stuff is fucking strong, is that what you smoke all the time?'

'Yeah. I've got a guy, he only smokes this, I only smoke this.' Ward sounded proud of his supply.

'Well, it's too much for me. How are you getting on?'

'Just one more second and we'll be in, my man.

I've done this tonnes of times before.'

The screen stopped. A few more keystrokes and he suddenly raised his hands from the machine, pinching his fingers and conducting an imaginary orchestra in front of him. 'Et voila. You're in. Where's your message?'

'Pass it here, let me have a look. I'm starting to feel hungry, mate. You have any food in the house or have you already eaten it all?'

'Hungry already?! That stuff really has hit you quick, normally takes half an hour before my munchies really kick in. What do you want?'

'I don't know, anything. Have you got any pizzas?'

'Sure do, the rents stocked me up before they went away. I'll throw some in the magic box, dude. Sit tight.'

He rose from the couch and skipped out of the open doors into the garden, stopping as he reached the edge of the flagstones and the three-foot drop down onto the lawn, throwing his head back and his arms out and back to the sides, basking in the summer sun.

Time was now of the essence and the real work of the visitor could begin. He wasn't sure how much time the food request would buy him alone with the computer, but he'd known that Ward would happily oblige in providing sustenance for a fellow stoner.

He didn't have to look very hard. Alistair's message inbox was not as active as his own, which was at any one time full of messages from friends. Below a family group message was Alistair's ongoing conversation with Rosa.

He hovered the pointer over her name and with a tap on the mouse pad the chain opened up. It was three days old, sent on the evening the rest of boys had returned from France, leaving Alistair on the boat back in Saint Tropez. Scrolling up to Rosa's last message, he scanned the text:

"Alistair, promise me you'll think about it, please. I don't understand why you've had such a sudden change of heart. I thought this was something we both wanted. To help people. To be doctors. We could go and work in so many wonderful places and help children who need us. I don't want to fight about it when I see you in a few days so please let's just agree not to.

I love you so much. I can't wait for you to spend more time with my parents. They love you too. My dad thinks you're the best boyfriend I've ever had!

Ciao. Rx"

He started to worry as he read the words, wondering about Alistair's response. He quickly scrolled down.

"Rosa, baby,

I do want to help people. It's always been my dream to be a doctor but I think I can help people in another way. I can't tell you here but when we see each other I will. To be honest, I'm having doubts too. I don't know what to do but my heart is telling me to travel the world with you and make a difference. I'll definitely still be at university with you, whatever I decide, it would just be on another course. Let's not fight, but I'll tell you everything and you'll understand."

The viewer froze. Was he correctly understanding what his friend, his teammate had written? Was Alistair really having second thoughts? Not knowing what to do and still fuzzy from the hit, he decided to forward the message to himself so he could reassess it with a clear mind. Not wanting to get caught in the act spending time reading the whole chain, he copied the text from their entire conversation, opened another browser window and emailed the content to himself. It was clear that this was not the first conversation Rosa and Alistair had had on the subject and it was essential that he know just how much had been said.

As he clicked send on the email, the familiar voice from the hallway, humming away to the music coming from the TV, told him he was out of time.

'All good, my friend,' Ward confirmed. 'In ten minutes' time, you'll have a whole Hawaiian to yourself. Did you get what you were looking for?' He reached for the remote from the coffee table, turning the volume back up to near its original level.

'Yes, bud. All sorted.' He had to shout once more, 'doesn't look like he'd read it yet so at least I'll be spared the embarrassment. He mustn't be checking his messages while he's away.'

Just as he was about to make an excuse to have to leave, a sudden wave of hunger hit him, and the prospect of a Hawaiian pizza became very appealing. 'Ward, are you going to fill that thing up again?'

'What?' Ward spun around from the TV in disbelief, elated that his friend may have been converted. 'Seriously? You like the good stuff, huh? Hell yeah I'll fill it again.' Once again, he chose skipping as his method of transport, now towards the couch and the bong.

'Yeah, what the hell. In for a penny, in for a pound and all that.' The visitor shrugged.

'I have no idea what that means bro, but I'm not gonna argue with you.'

'Can we take it outside though? It's too nice to be indoors.'

'Anything you say, boss. Just don't let me forget about the pizzas!'

The pair moved towards the door, Ward with a small, ornate wooden box in one hand, the green tube in the other, ready to repeat the cycle.

'Wardy, what's the most you've ever smoked in one go?'

'Oh man, I don't even know. So much I couldn't move a few times, people had to pick me up like a rag-doll.'

'I don't believe you, you can't smoke that much!' He baited his teacher.

'That sounds like a challenge to me. I'm game if you are.'

'Well I definitely won't be able to keep up with you, but I'll try.' It seemed the best option he had in the hope that Ward would forget about what he'd helped him to do. The risk was low that he would ever connect the dots but there was nothing to stop Ward going back into Alistair's account and seeing Rosa and Alistair's conversation or, when the time did eventually come, maybe years from now, making some link between an event of one random summer morning and some extremely powerful people.

The bong was packed and drained from green to grey. And again, thick smoke billowing from the dragons' mouths. The host was more than willing to show his prowess and, after devouring a whole pizza each, Ward was encouraged to smoke more and more. Once he was starting to show signs of struggling to keep up any normal conversation, his apprentice made his move.

'Ward, is it possible for you get me the password to

that account? You know, just in case I send any other stupid messages?'

'Huh?' He was flagging now, laid flat on the grass, legs stretched out in front of him but still eager to impress. 'Yeah man. I can do anything with that thing. Get me the laptop.'

The last act either was capable of was a few more keystrokes and a combination of numbers and letters being saved as a note in the visitor's phone.

29

Over the weeks that followed the trip, the four of the group that were now back in England saw each other every few days. Max made sure to keep in regular contact with each of them. Getting hold of Alistair, however, was proving much trickier.

Max hosted the usual Friday night meetings with the boys at his house, keen to stress that even though they were on holiday from school, there was much planning to be done if the next year was going to be fruitful.

Rohan had managed to arrange a month shadowing at a barristers' chambers in Liverpool, meaning that his days were spent watching cases in the city's Crown Courts. These ranged from assault and burglary, all the way up to murder. He regaled the boys with stories of theatrics and drama.

His favourite involved a cockney fraudster who had been caught laundering money for one of Liverpool's well-known drug gangs. A posh and measured barrister was questioning the man.

"Mr Davies...", Rohan stressed the delay between each piece of speech, adding the barrister's posh accent, "your account..."

Rohan explained that before the barrister was allowed to continue, the cockney had exploded with rage, interrupting him. "I'm a cunt?! You're the fucking cunt in a wig and gown, mate!"

It took the judge to intervene and clear up the misunderstanding. "Mr Davies, I believe the gentleman was trying to ask you about your *account* of the events on the night in question."

Rohan laughed as he told how the people in the court had to try and suppress their laughter at the delightful turn of events. All in all, he seemed to be enjoying his first stint as part of the legal system.

Nicholas and Max told of their travels back across the Mediterranean with the school cadets, this time aboard a Lockheed C-130J Hercules RAF transport plane bound for RAF Akrotiri, a Sovereign Base Area on the island of Cyprus. Here they'd spent a week in the scorching heat, learning how to shoot sniper rifles and pistols, and how to survive in the desert. A lucky few had been taken up in a Lynx helicopter to experience a flight with an Army Display Flight instructor.

Max just missed out, but Nicholas had the chance to experience being thrown around in the air by a veteran pilot who was determined to show the cadets what the aircraft was capable of.

He found Max when their troops were reunited at dinner.

'I've changed my mind,' he told Max excitedly.

'What do you mean?' Max had asked, sensing it had to do with Us.

Nicholas had barked at him excitedly, 'I mean, I don't want to do the infantry anymore. I want to fly, it's got to be flying. I'll do some research when I get back but I'm sure I'll still be able to...' he paused, 'you know, get there through the Army Air Corps or the RAF. I'm gutted you didn't get the chance to be on one of the flights. It was amazing to see what they can do with those things, I thought they'd be really slow and lurching, but he nearly flew the thing upside down. And then did you see those two Apache helicopters taking off?'

Max had found it hard not to feel energised simply through osmosis. It was one of those eureka moments, one out of which clarity and direction give new simplicity to the future. He knew this would only be good for Nicholas and for Us. It was this energy and motivation that would be needed all the way through.

Once back in England, Nicholas had arranged to visit an RAF Tornado squadron at RAF Marham to see the planes and speak with an old boy from the school, a pilot stationed at the base. They let him sit in the cockpit of a new F-35 fighter jet that was being prepared for a sortie, explaining what each of the controls was responsible for. That day had solidified the direction he would take and having become addicted, two days later he visited an Army Air Corps base not far away in Suffolk.

On his return, he'd presented Max with research assuring him that it was still possible to take the path they'd decided using this route, citing Peter Harding, David Craig and Neil Cameron, who all started as RAF pilots and successfully became Chiefs of the Defence Staff.

Max had showed nothing but support for his friend, even if he was secretly jealous of Nicholas's new-found zest for flying. It made him reassess his own options, but realistically it would not be the optimal career track for him to take due to the typical length of commitment of a pilot being three times that of an army officer. The army would give him the chance to join MI6 relatively quickly after university, but with enough experience in the field to make a good Intelligence Officer. He'd spoken with an army recruiter at the local armed forces office to discuss the process of applying and arranged to visit two regiments, the Scots Guards and the Grenadier guards, both on the recommendation of officers he spoke to whilst on the Sovereign Base in Cyprus.

Sebastian's approach had been to try and make inroads to meet with more Members of Parliament, or anyone involved with politics. He'd persuaded Annabel to get him the details for her paper's contact at Number 10 so that he could contact them directly. It was a move they would not thank her for. Over the space of a few weeks he had sent ten emails requesting to meet with various ministers. The responses were always very polite but kindly asked him to address any requests to the ministers directly. So he did, with varying degrees of luck.

Additionally, he'd decided that he would take on a bigger role in the debate club over the next year to ensure he had as much practice as possible when it came to public speaking. He'd written emails to the school master in charge of the club, a timid Latin teacher, Mr Rogan, but had yet to hear anything back. He suspected the old master barely used his school emails during term time, never mind over the summer holidays.

As the plans started to come together, motivation amongst the group surged. Still cautious not to discuss the group outside of private surroundings, it was not uncommon for one or more of them to call at Max's house, unannounced, having been researching something about one of their roles or another secret group or society. Having conversations with each of the group now felt like a strategy session for a battle plan, talking about jobs and promotions, places to live, places to work. It was the first time he'd ever heard the individuals so focused on any one thing. Previously, conversations at school consisted of school work, sports, gossip, girls. Now, conversations revolved around careers and extra-curricular activities, achieving the best grades possible, and how to do it.

Max was reminded of one of his earlier conversations with Harriet: "How many people are working with like-minded people to make sure that nothing stops each and every one of them getting to where they need to be?"

Obviously, he couldn't be certain that in some other school or country there wasn't another group of boys or girls planning the same type of meteoric climbs, but he was content that they couldn't be working any harder than Us to make sure they were as successful as possible.

30

The four of the group not lucky enough to be on a boat somewhere on the south coast of France sat and chatted in the Jug and Bottle pub beer garden. Thanks to the fake IDs now available online, anyone observing would have assumed they were just an average group of teenagers, maybe a little younger than most of the other patrons, as they admired the views out across the River Dee from their elevated position.

Being seventeen, three of the four had by now successfully passed their driving tests and were taking full advantage of their new-found freedom to roam, often spending the warm evenings by the beach or in the beer garden of one of the local pubs, no longer dependent on buses, taxis, and parents.

On this particular Friday, the group had decided to skip their weekly meeting and head into Heswall to have some fun. The conversation was an exchange of stories about their weeks.

Sebastian told of his trip to Bath to see Annabel and meet her parents. A few days in her parents' house in Hinton Charterhouse were a welcome break from the city weekends they usually had when they managed to see each other.

At the mention of Sebastian's happy new relationship, Nicholas became subdued. Max wondered what was wrong.

'Nothing, mate.' Nicholas brushed him off when he asked. He was starting to slur his words after having been in the pub two hours earlier than everyone else.

'Come on, just tell us,' a tipsy Sebastian pushed.

'Just leave it, it's nothing.' Nicholas wasn't convincing. 'It's just shit. You've got Annabel. Max's got Harriet. Alistair's got Rosa. Even Rohan's got someone.'

Rohan laughed. 'Oh cheers, mate. "Even Rohan", what's that supposed to mean?'

'I didn't mean it like that. Who would have thought after how you and Melissa met that you'd still be talking?'

'Fair point. You still owe me for that,' Rohan chirped back.

Max had made sure the pair spent as much time together after returning from France. He couldn't risk Rohan holding a grudge against Nicholas for the way he treated him after the incident on Capri. Over the past couple of weeks, the tension had subsided, and the pair seemed at last to be back on good terms.

Nicholas continued, 'She lives in France anyway so nothing's ever going to come of it, which is shit.' He turned to Max. 'Let's get back out there now. I'm sure we can just jump on the jet and go and see them. Let's do it.'

'It doesn't quite work like that, mate. I wish we could, sorry.' Max would give anything to be back on the boat.

'Oh well, that's just fucking great.' Nicholas clumsily swung a hand to reach for his drink, sending the glass cascading along the uneven table, end-over-end, smashing at least four or five other glasses along its journey. The group jumped to their feet to avoid the ensuing tide of nectar that now dripped between the gaps in the wooden table, Rohan visibly annoyed at having beer on his suit and shoes.

'Nick, don't be an arse. You'll get us kicked out,' Rohan said.

'Fuck it, who cares, it's just the fucking Jug and Bottle,' his voice grew to a shout before Max intervened.

'Nicholas. Come here, buddy.' He put an arm around his shoulder and escorted the drunken boy away from the table towards the lower level of the pub's garden. 'What's going on, mate? I've never seen you this upset before.' He had to steady his companion as they walked down the path.

'First girl I meet who's sexy, smart, French. And guess where she lives?'

Max was unsure whether or not to answer what sounded like a rhetorical question but the long pause from Nicholas made him offer a response to fill the silence. 'Fra...' He got only as far as the first syllable before relinquishing speaker's rights.

'Fucking France. Exactly. What am I supposed to do with that?'

'I know, mate, it's crap. You really like her, hey?'

'Yeah.' He looked at his friend. 'I really do. We've stayed in touch, but you know we'll never end up seeing each other again. It's like every other summer, you meet some girl on holiday and then come back and they disappear out of your life. I don't normally mind but this one was different. She's really cool.' Tears were starting to form in the corners of his moist eyes.

'Come on, bud. It's just the booze talking. There'll be others. Trust me. And anyway, you never know, stay in touch and you might see her again. You could do French with your degree and go and spend a year over there.'

His friend's eyes lit up at the idea of being back in France.

Sebastian's calm, sensible voice appeared over Nicholas's shoulder. 'Bad news, I'm afraid, guys. We've been asked to leave.'

'Okay, give us a minute, Seb. We'll be up in a sec.'

Sebastian left the pair to finish their conversation.

'Let's go, Nicholas, we'll get you home.' Max offered his hand to his friend perched on the wall at the bottom of the garden. It took him two attempts to stand up.

'What? It's still early. There's loads of the night left yet,' Nicholas protested.

'Well we don't have to go home but we've got to get out of here at least.'

'Fuckers. Alright, I just need to get my jacket out of my car.' Nicholas started to wander towards the car park around the back of the pub.

'Cool, I just need to settle the tab. I'll meet you by the path,' Max shouted as he climbed the small steps into the building. He was only inside for a few minutes but returned to see Sebastian and Rohan shouting and running towards the car park.

Instinct immediately told him what was going on and he gave chase. Arriving at the gates to the car park where the other two had stopped, he panted as he asked them what happened.

'The dickhead drove off!' Sebastian sounded furious.

'Why didn't you stop him?' Max shouted.

'We were still at the table waiting for you. We didn't even know he'd gone to his car. We just heard screeching of tyres and came around to see what was going on. We only saw the back of his car as he nearly hit the gatepost,' Rohan explained.

Three phones appeared, and the group began trying to call the drunk driver. The call rang out the first five times after they had agreed that one person should try to call to avoid blocking the line.

On the sixth attempt, Nicholas answered the phone. 'Sebastian, where are you? Come and have a drink.'

'Where the fuck are you, Nicholas? You need to get out of the car, right now.' Sebastian tried to persuade him.

'It's fine, I'm fine. I drive better when I've had a beer anyway, I've got my drink-drive license with me. I've just got to the Glegg Arms, come and have another.'

Sebastian shielded the mouthpiece. 'He's driven down to the Glegg, wants another drink.'

He looked to the group for reactions. He raised the phone back to his ear. 'Nicholas, listen to me. Get out of the car, go and get a drink and wait for us there, we'll be there in ten minutes. Don't get back in the car.'

'Okay, okay, I'll be here. Hurry though, I'm only doing one pint per pub now.'

'Nicholas, stay there. Whatever you do, stay there...' The line went dead but not before Sebastian heard the sound of a car door closing from the other end. 'Right, he's either just got out of the car to go into the pub or he's just got back in the car to go somewhere else. We've got to get down there fast. If he does something stupid and gets caught drink-driving after only having his license a month then we're fucked. Imagine what our parents will say.'

'Who cares what our parents will say. What if he hits someone?' Max said.

'If he hits someone, that's it for him. For Us.' Rohan sounded cold.

'Jesus, Rohan. This isn't about Us. What if he hits a little kid or something?'

'Sorry.' He lowered his head to avoid Max's fierce gaze.

'We need to get down there now.' Max switched his focus. 'Is anyone else alright to drive?' He looked around at shaking heads. 'Shit, we're going to have to run. Someone try and call him, keep him on the phone.'

The three of them set off down the road out of the pub at a sprint, rounding the library at the bottom of the hill and onto the main road. On a rugby pitch in sports kit, the group would normally be able to cover the mile in between the pubs in just over six minutes. Tonight would be a little longer due to less appropriate footwear and alcohol in the system.

As they approached the main roundabout outside the next pub, the street lights buzzed into life above their heads. Sebastian's phone had been pressed to his ear for the duration of the run, accompanied by cursing every time he got Nicholas's answerphone. The phone reception on this part of the Wirral was notoriously bad, making it impossible to tell whether he had turned the phone off or just had no service. On his last attempt as they crossed the main road into the car park, the sound on the other end was that of ringing rather than Nicholas's polite voice requesting a message be left.

'It's ringing. Can you see his car?' Sebastian tried to catch his breath.

'Not yet.' Max scanned the space in what was left of the low light, struggling to find any that matched Nicholas's. 'Fuck, this is all my fault. Why didn't I just take the keys off him?'

'Don't beat yourself up, mate. Who knew he'd drive off?' Sebastian's words were of little comfort. 'Nicholas! Can you hear me? Max listen, he's got his phone, you can hear him moving around.'

Max snatched the phone from his friend's hand, trying to remain calm. 'Nicholas, can you hear me? Nicholas!'

There was only muffled noise down the phone.

Eventually Max hard the sound of the phone being picked up, its owner realising that a call was connected.

'Sebastian,' Nicholas mumbled. 'Where are you? I told you I was only having one. Those buggers wouldn't serve me anyway so I'm going to the Black Horse. Come for a drink...' His speech was noticeably more slurred than it had been when he left the Jug and Bottle.

'Stay there. Nicholas, please, stop the car.'

'Max, you're not Sebastian. Why does it say Sebastian on my phone but you're not Sebastian?'

'I know, it's very confusing.' His patience started to wane, and his two fellow hunters saw the exasperation on his face. 'Look, we'll be there soon. Don't move.'

Handing the phone back to Sebastian, he once again set off at pace, this time down towards the coast and Lower Heswall where their friend was heading. Annoyingly, they were further away from him than they had been on the first run but that didn't slow them down. The trio sprinted down the quiet lanes, the quickest route possible, through the park and down the steep slope of School Hill, the last leg of the journey. As they emerged out onto the lower village road, Max saw what he had feared most.

A blue Volkswagen fifty yards down the road to the right, hazard lights flashing, had crashed into the back of three inwardly parked cars, coming to rest abutting the third. One car alarm sounded from the three and two's hazard lights had joined Nicholas's in casting an orange intermittent light over the village. Having barely slowed down by the time they saw the damaged vehicles, Max arrived at the driver's door first. The airbag had deployed and from behind the deflating sack of air he saw his friend, unscathed trying to make a phone call. As Max knocked on the window, Nicholas mouthed, 'It's okay, I'm calling the police,' through the window.

'Put the phone down. Hang up the call!' Max frantically tried to open the door. 'Put the fucking phone down!'

The door popped open allowing him to seize the phone from Nicholas's hand, quickly hitting the red button to end the call.

'You idiot, if you call the police you'll be arrested. Shit, what happened?' He grabbed his friend under the arm to help him out, 'are you alright?'

'I'm fine.' Nicholas seemed unaware of the drama he had caused. A crowd had now started to gather outside the pub behind them.

Max turned to Sebastian who was examining the damage across the cars. 'Help him out of here. Shit, what are we going to do?'

'We need to make it look like an accident of some kind.' Sebastian was quick to offer a potential solution.

'How the hell are we going to do that? He's hit three cars and totalled his own.' Max was feeling a sense of dread.

'Look.' Sebastian pointed back towards the pub. 'Look at the line the car has come down and crashed. It almost looks like it just rolled down the hill, as if the handbrake has snapped.'

'We'll never get away with that. Look at the damage, it's way too fast.'

'Not if we say the car started up there on the hill. It could have built up enough speed.' Sebastian's confidence felt misplaced. Max was sure this was going to end badly but he was willing to consider anything.

'Okay, stay here with him. I'll go and see if anyone saw anything. If they saw him crash then that's it, finito.'

Max wandered over to the group of bystanders now smoking and keeping an eye on what was going on down the road from the pub.

'Evening guys, did anyone see what happened?' He tried to sound like a casual bystander.

The first group had been inside when the smash had taken place. The pub quiz had been in full flow, only stopping for a break to allow time for the scores to be added up. After speaking with two or three more groups, he allowed himself to breathe in the knowledge that no one had actually seen the crash take place. As they asked what had happened, he used the moment to sow the seed that it looked like the car's handbrake had disengaged, causing the car to roll down the hill and onto the village road, building up enough speed to damage three cars but miraculously not injure anyone. There were few protests from the onlookers who seemed to lose interest quickly once they thought nothing major had happened.

As he walked back towards the crash site, breathing a sigh of relief, he caught a pair of eyes watching him from the fire escape in an alley that ran alongside the nearby off-license. Something about the way they watched him forced him to venture over. He drew closer, just able to make out the black hoodie covering the hair that accompanied the red eyes.

'Max, always causing some sort of trouble, aren't you?'

'Ward. What are you doing here? And what do you mean, "trouble"?'

'I could ask you the same thing. I'm just dropping something off for a friend who works in the off-license. Well firstly, he shows up at my house, asking about hacking,' Ward pointed towards the three boys now standing next to the car, 'then I see you all as thick as thieves, clearly trying to hide something.'

'Hold on, what are you talking about? Who showed up at your—'

He didn't have time to finish his question as Sebastian shouted over to him. 'Max, come on. Let's go.'

'Ward, I know what you're dropping off. I'm sure you don't want to see the police either. You were never here. We were never here. Got it?' Max hoped his knowing look at Ward's backpack was enough to scare him into silence.

He didn't have time to worry about that right now as he ran to re-join his brothers.

31

The first day back at school after the nine-week summer holiday felt like being wrenched out of bed at an unreasonably early time with absolutely no benefit whatsoever. The only consolation was that it was still warm enough to make the most of being outside before the ever-accelerating descent into winter began.

As the young men sat in a secluded corner of the square field at the centre of the school campus, they recanted the events of the summer to Alistair who had returned to England a few days earlier.

'Stop laughing, Rohan,' Nicholas protested.

'I can't, it's too funny. I don't understand how you can be such an idiot!'

'I made a mistake, have you never got pissed and done something stupid?' Nicholas reasoned.

'Yeah, but not like this. This could have been really serious.' Rohan's tone changed. 'What if you'd hit someone and killed them?' Rohan quickly looked towards Max, and back. 'You'd never forgive yourself, it would be impossible to.'

Alistair sensed some remaining tension among the pair. He was secretly glad to have missed the last couple of months. The last time he had seen the boys was as they stepped off the ship in France. At the time, he'd wondered, maybe even hoped, that the group had come to a predictably early conclusion at the first major complication. He stayed quiet, trying to gauge their current attitude towards one another, conscious that he'd been on Nicholas's side during the events on Capri.

'I get it. Don't you think I know all this?' Nicholas sounded exasperated at Rohan's tormenting.

'Did any of us even come into your mind for a second?' Rohan leaned towards his friend to convey the gravity of what he was discussing. 'You can't be Chief of the Defence staff if you've killed someone.'

'Er, I think it's pretty much a prerequisite,' Sebastian joked. 'You know, the military and all.'

Rohan didn't appear in the mood for the interruption. 'I think you know the point I'm trying to make. A conviction for death by dangerous driving isn't exactly the extra-curricular activity that universities are looking for, is it?'

'I admit it would probably be the first time they'd seen it on the UCAS form. Or maybe not, you never know what some people whack on their CV.' Sebastian chuckled to himself again.

'Rohan. It's done. We can't change it now, so we just need to make sure it doesn't happen again. Nicholas knows he fucked up.' Max was the voice of reason trying to deescalate the argument. He turned his attention to Alistair. 'I thought you were planning to be back here after your second week in France?'

'That was the plan, originally. But we spent a week with Rosa's parents and then decided to go out and join mum in Barbados. She was already out there with my sister, so we thought, "why not"? Mum invited Rosa's parents to stay in the villa, but they didn't want to crowd so they rented another down on the beach.'

The truth was that he'd wanted some time away from the boys and the pressure of the group. He found it a bit relentless at times with everyone so caught up in it. It no longer felt like he had a choice.

'Jesus, not only meeting the parents, but parents meeting parents. This is getting serious!' Nicholas had all but recovered from his earlier dressing down from Rohan.

'I know, I know. I thought that at first, but it's actually all been really chilled. I get on with her parents well and mum just loves Rosa to bits. Anyway, enough about me, I want to hear what this lush got up to.'

'Thanks mate, I thought we were done with that.'

Nicholas was unimpressed by being made the centre of attention once more.

'I'm serious, how did you pull it off? Surely the police were called?'

'Yeah. Well, someone called 999.' Max answered the question. 'I'm not sure who but we didn't have long before an ambulance arrived.' He was matter of fact about the events but looked grave as he recounted the story. 'We only just had time to get Nicholas out of there. Sebastian and Rohan took him off through the park. I stayed around outside the pub to try and keep an eye on what was happening. When the ambulance arrived, I think they were expecting to find someone inside but when no one was there, they just waited for the police and then left.'

'Surely the police could see that it wasn't an accident?' Alistair pushed Max.

'I don't know. I left the handbrake off and managed to get the door shut properly and lock it before I ran off through the park myself. The alarm was still coming on and off which made it look like it hadn't been opened. I watched from there for a while and then walked down after the police had arrived and were talking to some people outside the pub. Hopefully, it looked like I was just walking past on my way somewhere. They didn't even seem to notice me.'

'That was a ballsy move, or a stupid one.' Alistair wondered what had been going through Max's mind. Were things starting to spiral out of control? The Melissa incident on Capri, his dad ordering them back in case the police came after them, now this.

'I know. I'd already spoken to the people at the Black Horse, no one saw anything, thankfully. They'd all been inside doing the pub quiz. We're just lucky it was down there and not up in Heswall or he'd definitely have been seen. When I drove through the village a few days later, I looked around for CCTV but it's a tiny, sleepy village. Couldn't see any cameras covering that area.'

Nicholas hung his head throughout the story telling, clearly ashamed of his actions.

'Surely the police knew it was his car though?'

'It's registered in Nicholas's dad's name, so they contacted him. When he called Nicholas, I answered the phone. I just said he was staying at mine and was already asleep.'

'And that was it?' Alistair was in disbelief that their plan had worked.

'Well not quite, Nicholas still got an almighty bollocking from his parents for leaving the handbrake off.' Max held up his hands and captured the last four words inside quotation marks.

'Tell me about it, they were not happy,' the guilty boy eventually chimed in.

'Just imagine if you'd been caught for what you actually did. You got off lightly, very lightly.' Rohan reiterated his earlier displeasure.

'What's your problem, mate? I've said I'm sorry. I made a mistake.'

'What's my problem? You could have messed it up for everyone with your little joyriding stunt. What's the point of all this if you're just going to go and do something stupid every time you get bent out of shape over some girl?'

Alistair watched Nicholas get up, assuming he was about to walk off and leave the confrontation. To his surprise, the boy got up from where he sat and walked around the outside of the circle to Rohan's side. Crouching down, he put one hand on the shoulder of his friend who would barely make eye contact with him.

'Look. I'm sorry,' Nicholas started. 'I know it was stupid, and it won't happen again. I promise. Trust me. I'll remember this every time I ever go near a pub for the rest of my life. It was bad enough, and I owe you guys for having the clear heads to think of a way to fix it.' He paused, taking a deep breath. 'I'm sorry for what happened in Italy. I should have trusted you. I don't blame you for trying to punish me for this, but it won't take back what happened over there.

'What can I do to make it up to you, to you all?' He looked around the circle at his friends, his head dropping once more. 'I'm really sorry, guys.' He held his hand to his face to hide small beads of salt water gathering in the corners of his eyes. 'I didn't mean to balls up. I was just really upset. Please don't think less of me.'

Alistair felt humbled. Normally, he would expect Nicholas to make a joke out of the situation or laugh it off, but not this time. He watched as Rohan, unsure what to do, climbed to his feet and grabbed Nicholas by both shoulders, trying to force him to raise his head.

'Come on, mate. Don't be upset. It was stupid, and careless, and criminal. Just promise me you won't ever do anything like that again. If not for yourself, then for Us. I don't want to see you kill yourself in a stupid car crash. And I definitely don't want to see anyone else get hurt. Remember, we're all here to help each other. I'd prefer it if we help you by talking rather than by chasing you around the Wirral on foot as you're driving round like a mad man.'

Nicholas was silently nodding, regaining his composure. He wiped his face once with the black sleeve of his school blazer. He coughed loudly, inhaled deeply and straightened up, blinking his eyes to dry them out.

'You're right,' his voice was now firm. 'It won't happen again. I promise.'

⬠

As the group set off back towards the sixth-form block, Max felt glad to have Alistair back and part of the group again. Away from Rosa. The summer had felt strange after seeing him continuously for a week and then not at all for another six.

He allowed three of the group to wander ahead, catching Sebastian's eye and motioning with his head for him to hang back. 'Let's go this way, I need to talk to you.'

Sebastian looked confused but went along. Max shouted after the others, 'We'll catch up, I'm just going to get a drink from the dining hall.' The pair set off in the opposite direction from the lead group.

'What's going on, Max?'

'A couple of things. How does Alistair seem to you?' he asked Sebastian.

'Normal, I suppose. Why?'

'No reason, I just thought he seemed a bit quieter than when we were away.'

'Well, maybe. But he's always been quiet really, especially when we're in school.'

'Yeah, that's fair,' Max agreed. 'I'm just having a bit of a gut feeling that something's not quite right, like he's not as 'in' as he was when we were in France.'

'Remember though, we've spent the whole summer together, the four of us, he probably just feels a bit out of the loop.'

'Yeah, okay. I'm probably just looking into it too much. I'll forget it.'

'What's the other thing, Max?'

'I need to confess something. Someone did see what happened with the car. I haven't told the others. I didn't want to worry them.'

'What? Who saw?'

'It was Ward.'

'Ward? What was he doing there?'

'He was in the alley smoking when it happened. None of the others saw him but as I came back from asking the people in the pub he was there, just watching me from the alley.'

'Will he say anything?' Sebastian sounded worried.

'No. I hope not, anyway.'

'How did you manage that?'

'I think he was selling weed to someone around there. He's not the kind of guy that wants to talk to the police, I just reminded him of that. I'm not worried for now. It's just if his memory suddenly comes back in ten or twenty years when Nicholas is about to be made a general or you're in the middle of an election. Anyway, we can't stress too much for now, but I just wanted you to know. None of the others know anything about it but I thought you'd probably appreciate a heads-up.'

'Yeah, thanks. Wow. Shit's getting real.'

Max watched as Sebastian thought through the implications.

'Max, we need him on side. If you do see him again, it has to be on good terms. He won't have liked being threatened.'

'I didn't threaten him.' Max defended himself.

'Say what you want, Max, but it sounds like you did. Have you ever heard the saying, "keep your friends close but your enemies closer"?'

'Of course. I have a horrible feeling about what you're going to say next.'

'Exactly. You're going to have to stay close to him. At least for now, anyway.'

They ambled along the path that led from the cricket pavilion past the sports hall and up to the sixth form centre as the school bell started to ring.

32

After checking in for afternoon registration, one of the group headed to one of the computer programming labs on campus to while away some time during his free period after lunch break. The one in the sixth-form centre was normally quiet outside of break times so he was optimistic not to be disturbed.

Walking into the empty large square room, rows of desks with computers on either side ran parallel to the windows that spanned the length of the far wall. He chose a position facing the door but as far away from it as possible. Rather than risk using the school network, he pulled his own laptop and wireless mouse from his bag, placing them on the desk. He connected to a personal hotspot and opened his TOR browser.

After he'd left Ward's house that day, he'd decided to do some research and learn a bit more about how to cover his tracks. The Onion Router, or TOR as it is known, allowed a user to access information online anonymously, masking their location and browsing habits. It was perfect for what he needed.

He opened Facebook, entered Alistair's password which he had now memorised, and navigated straight to his messages.

After the initial exchange between Alistair and Rosa that had worried the hacker just after they returned from France, communications between the lovers had stopped via the account. He'd assumed this was down to them being together on holiday. Now that Alistair had returned, he hoped that there may be some more indications of what he and Rosa had discussed or decided about their future. It didn't take him long to find.

The top row was his ongoing thread with Rosa. It seemed that they had been messaging constantly since they were separated at Grantly Adams Airport on the southern tip of Barbados before Alistair returned to the UK. He scrolled down to the last of the messages he'd read at Ward's house, eager to make sure he didn't miss any of the conversation.

The older messages, sent just after the end of their trip, were full of nostalgic reminiscing, recounting different parts of the summer they had spent together, remote waterfalls they had explored and made love under, mountains they had climbed, water-skiing and scuba diving, romantic dinners, and lazy days.

Rosa was keen to start planning their next summer together already and it was clear that she wanted Alistair to herself. She wanted to tour South East Asia, ski in Queenstown, New Zealand, and then spend time with her parents on their friends' ranch in Plettenburg Bay in South Africa. It didn't sound like there would be much time for anything, or anyone else.

As he continued through the trail to a message sent only a few days ago, his heart skipped a beat. Buried amongst normal bit of conversation was a sentence that read strangely.

'I'm glad you told me about us.'

He pondered it. Was this a typo? No, it was too strange a grammatical construct to be a mistake. 'Us' on this occasion did not refer to the correspondents. It was a reference to the group, an unmistakable one. Would he really have told her? What would he have told her? An endless number of questions started to mount in his mind. He read on:

'Since we talked it through, I now understand why you've been acting differently for the last few months. You were obviously torn between doing what you've always wanted to, and what the group and your dad want

for you. And worrying about what I would say. I'm glad you've made up your mind and I'm so happy you've made the right choice. I can't wait to spend the next 5 years together with you at university! ☺ *When are you going to tell Max that you don't want to be part of it anymore?'*

The hacker was unaware of it, but the mouse groaned and cracked with the pressure of the clenched fist around it, a surge of rage coursing through him.

'Fuck!' He slammed the mouse onto the desk and the casing exploded, sending pieces of black and red plastic and electrical components into the air. He stood and turned to look out of the window, hands raising to his head in that instinctive way, urging his brain to work harder and comprehend the situation. What did he know?

Firstly, it was now absolutely clear that Rosa knew about the group. Secondly, the messages strongly suggested that Alistair was no longer going to follow the route he had described to the group. The rest was filled with unknowns. Who else had they told? Her parents, his parents?

'Okay, calm down,' he said to himself, 'breathe.'

He took three deep breaths, but it didn't help. Re-taking his seat, a piece of plastic that had landed in his lap and rolled onto the chair, prodded his backside as he sat down, causing him to jump and locate the nuisance.

Becoming aware of the noise the mouse must have made when contacting the wooden desk, he grabbed the loose pieces and scooped them into his bag. Then his focus returned to the computer. He instinctively reached for his mouse before realising that it was destroyed so had to the use the trackpad instead.

Hitting the 'Ctrl' and 'A' keys at the same time highlighted all the text in the Facebook message which he copied into a notepad file. Ensuring that he'd captured the whole exchange, he encrypted the file and stored it on his local drive.

As he closed the browser window, a familiar face appeared through the door. It was Mr Howarth.

'Everything alright in here?' he asked. 'I thought I heard a bang.'

The hacker was still reeling from what he'd just discovered, his mind clouded by questions and worry.

He tried to look composed, but his brain was struggling to think of an explanation.

'Er, yes, sir. Every… everything's fine,' he stuttered. 'I was just… er…'

Howarth fully entered the room and closed the door behind him, advancing to the row of desks where the boy sat.

Looking into the boy's eyes, he spoke in his usual soft and compassionate tone. 'You seem a bit manic. It's okay, I can tell what's going on. You can talk to me about this.'

33

The first few months of the school year passed quietly. The group would meet most Fridays in the usual place, normally for a couple of hours and then head out, sometimes together, sometimes apart. A couple would go to a party, some would go to the pub. There was no strict structure, but they were aware that they didn't want to be seen together constantly. Not that anyone would ever contemplate what they were doing but they were careful not to isolate themselves as a group. It was important to maintain all the existing friendships and activities that people were used to them doing.

Now was the time when the research they had done over the summer would shape their final school year ahead. Max made a point of dropping in regularly on each of the group to have some time alone to talk details. Not only was it good for them to talk and brainstorm about how to get to where they wanted to be, it also gave Max the opportunity to keep track of each of them.

They all submitted applications to their universities of choice, making sure to include every last item that would increase their chances of acceptance. Max sat with each to offer a hand and help proof-read in the hope of catching any silly mistakes that could hinder. For Rohan, Sebastian and Max, they would soon be required to visit their chosen colleges at Oxford and Cambridge to either sit entrance exams or attend interviews, depending on the requirements of the college.

Whenever they weren't playing sport, performing charity work for the Duke of Edinburgh scheme, running the school newspaper, or mentoring junior cadets, they were studying. Whether it was a feeling of competition between the boys or the pressure of having four others relying on you, it affected each of them differently.

Sebastian rose to the challenge. He and Rohan had taken the debate club to a new level, entering every competition they could find. This, however, meant travelling up and down the country sometimes two or three times a week. Having initially struggled to cope with all the demands, Sebastian sat down with his father to get some advice.

'Delegation, son. It's the most important skill you'll learn in life. Find people you trust and then empower them to deliver. Respect them, and they will respect you. But always let them know that you're the boss.'

On the back of his dad's advice, he'd taken on some keen lower-sixth formers to help with the organisation. Luckily, the type of boy wanting to join the debate club was typically not unlike himself. He knew they were eager to perform well and possibly have the opportunity to be part of the main team of four in competitions, should a space become available.

Annabel had started her degree at Leeds University, meaning that it was easier to see her when he had time as the city was only an hour's drive from The Wirral. She understood what he needed to do to get into Oxford, supporting him and not becoming upset or angry if he had to cancel plans because of a match or debate. She had even travelled to watch him win one of his debates in the Great Hall at Durham University.

Max loved having direction and purpose. Before starting the group, he only had vague ideas about what he wanted to do or what he wanted to achieve. With the end goal identified, he found it easier to work backwards, mapping out his future life.

That hadn't stopped him obsessing about which options to take. Universities, colleges, courses, regiments. Hours were spent researching over the summer, reading everything he could about the army, SIS, and famous spies. Now it was all clear in his mind.

This year, he had been made the most senior cadet in the school, a bone of contention with Nicholas. When it was awarded to Max, Nicholas was clearly disappointed. Max had decided that in reality he would not have enough time to perform all the responsibilities and had spoken with the CO to request that Nicholas be made Senior Staff Sergeant with Max as his second. Nicholas had revolted at the thought of pity, but Max had assured him that it had nothing to do with pity and was a strategic move that would help them both in the long run. Nicholas having a record as the most senior cadet in the school would benefit him more than it would Max. It also allowed Max additional time to commit to his other extra-curricular activities, of which he had more.

Harriet had now moved into lower-sixth and, having made the decision to study Medicine, was now completely focused on school work. Over the past few months, she'd started to envy what the group had. Seeing what Max and the boys were doing gave her a new drive to achieve and she became determined to be as successful as each and every one of them. Although Max had not asked her to be part of the group officially, she knew she was as much a member as every other one of them. She helped Max with almost every decision he made and was the first person he spoke to when he, or the group, achieved something, or messed something up. She also managed to calm him down and understand that he had to remove his ego from certain situations in order to get the outcomes he needed.

Only having a few hours spread throughout the week to see each other, the pair found it focused them even more, requiring them to use their time more efficiently. They studied hard when they needed to but always made sure they had the chance to stay together at weekends, alternating between the studio above the garage at his house, and her house when her mother was away.

Alistair had carried on as usual, quietly tucked away in the school library running the school newspaper. Max made extra effort to spend time with him and talk about life. Always obeying the rules of not talking about Us in public, he tried to connect with Alistair by discussing other things. They talked about his dad's business a lot.

Max wanted to see enthusiasm from Alistair about taking over the company and thinking about what the future could hold for the organisation. So far, he was unsure. Alistair's cool nature constantly made it hard to tell what he was thinking. Max's own feelings about Rosa wouldn't escape his mind. He figured that the best tactic was to be the one person Alistair would go to about anything, and that's what he set out to do. Every time they put matches to the paper on a Friday night, he half-expected to see a square containing the initials AL. It was a relief each time when four other pentagons appeared.

As with the others, Max had spent time with Alistair going over his UCAS submission, keenly taking note of the course that he had listed: Management. He would have liked to have been present when the form was submitted via the online portal but felt he may be overstepping the mark by insisting on it.

When they talked about Rosa, Alistair's behaviour became unpredictable. Often, he would retreat into himself, avoiding the topic and quickly finding a way to divert the conversation. Other times, he would wax lyrical about the last time they saw each other or the trip they had planned for the next summer.

Max had asked if Alistair would have any time to spend with the group after A-Levels, to which Alistair always enthusiastically replied that of course he would. He told Max that he'd already asked his father if they could use the boat again to celebrate finishing school and starting the next chapter in his life. His father had immediately agreed, filling Max with hope that he was still very much part of the gang and on track to take over his father's empire.

Nicholas, however, had been having a much harder time. After the incident with the crash, he'd made considerable effort not to be in the same position again. If he drove somewhere, he wouldn't allow himself to be persuaded to have one beer or even to leave the car there and drink for the evening. There was also a marked change when he did drink, making sure to restrict himself only to beer, and only ever a few.

Even with that under control, he still struggled with his school work. Having chosen to read Mechanical Engineering, his first choice of university was Leeds. The bar was set high. He knew that he would have to get all 'A's in his exams to be in with a chance of a place and the pressure was starting to overwhelm him.

In their private chats, he would open up to Max about his performance in Maths. Even with a tutor, he was still finding the material at this level challenging. The feedback from all his other teachers was outstanding but he felt he was failing in this one area, even though his school report gave him credit for outstanding effort. As the months went on, Max hoped that he would adapt and become comfortable with the material in the Advanced Mathematics lessons, but Nicholas's anxiety did not subside. Christmas passed, bringing with it the new year and the mock exams intended to indicate how a student was doing. Regardless of the amount of time he allocated to this particular subject, Nicholas's confidence was so low in that area that it affected all his work. The results from the practice exams only fuelled the worry. It was now so great that he talked about it openly with the group when they met, having previously kept it between him and Max. The 'B' grade he'd been predicted after the mocks was not good enough and, being at the bottom end of the bracket, it was possible that he'd only achieve a C grade.

At one Friday evening meeting, a suggestion was floated as the group discussed how they could help.

'I've been doing some investigation,' Sebastian confessed, 'very quietly, obviously, and I've heard people talking about getting copies of stolen exam papers before the exam. I wouldn't ever normally suggest anything like this but...'

'You're asking me to cheat? On my A-Levels. Are you insane?' Nicholas protested.

'I'm just saying that there are options.' Sebastian attempted to calm him down.

'I won't cheat, Max. I won't do it.' Even though it had not been Max who suggested the idea, Nicholas directed his objection to the leader. 'How will I ever feel that I deserve to be in the position I get to if I know I cheated? Not only that, but what if I got caught?'

Max looked around the room, scanning their faces

for a consensus. It wasn't an easy conversation to have. Not only was it tough to see Nicholas so upset and stressed, the others all knew that there was a chance that Nicholas's journey may go no further. At least on the planned trajectory. That would potentially have implications for them all.

'What about if you chose a different course?' Rohan offered a suggestion.

'It's too late now. I've already applied. They've given me the offer and I have to get those grades, or I won't get a place.' Nicholas now stood and started to pace the room, searching for ideas. 'It's too much, I just don't have enough time to learn it all. I'm trying my hardest but it's just not good enough.'

'Okay, well what if you get lots more practice exam papers? Would that help?' Max explored any available option.

'I'm doing that already. My tutor has loads of old papers, but I just can't seem to get it.'

'Okay.' Max was at a loss for what to suggest, the others sat quietly, a feeling of helplessness amongst the group.

'Right,' Max jumped to his feet, 'I know we don't normally do this but let's just go out, the five of us and have some drinks. We'll stay local to here and we'll just have some fun, no talk of Us. Let's just go out and relax. I think the last few months have been tough on everyone. We're seeing less of each other and less of the people who we want to see.

'I know that I've asked all this of you and I hope you all still feel as strongly as when we started this. For me, as we get further into it I get more and more excited by it all, but I know that there's a sense of pressure here, and I'm sorry for that. The group was meant to support each other, not lay burdens on anyone. Nicholas,' he looked at his friend now, 'we're going to find a solution to this. I promise you. Not tonight, but we will. Tonight, we forget all about school.'

Alistair was the first to agree. 'I think that's a great idea. We haven't all been out together for months. I know there's a reason for that but once won't hurt. Come on, let's go.'

Nicholas was coming around but was clearly worried about his mental state and the temptation of alcohol. 'Okay, but don't let me have too much, we don't want another episode.'

'I'll take care of you, buddy.' Rohan threw his arm around him. 'It'll all be fine. Trust me. Everyone stresses about exams. It's a good thing that you're stressed, it shows you care. Some people can't do anything without there being some pressure to light the fire under them. At least you know what you need to improve and that's something you can work on.'

The group stood around their comrade, patting him on that back and offering words of encouragement.

'Thanks, guys. I'm sorry, I just don't want to let anyone down.'

As the group descended the staircase to head out of the door, Max caught Sebastian at the top of the stairs. Sure to allow the others to reach a safe distance out of earshot, he raised the subject once more, 'Sebastian, how much are the exam papers?'

'I don't know exactly, I'd have to ask my mate. I reckon a few hundred quid, maybe a bit more. Why?'

'Okay, get the paper,' Max instructed him. 'Don't talk to any of the others about it but get the paper. When you need the money let me know and I'll get it for you.'

'You're sure? He said he wouldn't do it.'

'I know, but it's just in case. I don't think we'll need it, but it can't hurt to have an ace up our sleeve should it get to that. When will you be able to find out how much and when we could get it?'

'I don't know. I've just heard rumours at the moment. I'll find out as soon as I can and I'll let you know.'

'Good. Like I said, no one else knows about this, okay?' What he asked for weighed heavily upon him and the gravity was evident in his expression, easy for his companion to read.

'Yeah, I understand.'

'Thanks, let's catch them up.' Max set off down the stairs.

The forerunners had instinctively set off in the rain for the nearest of the two pubs within walking distance. This old, country pub felt like a time warp on a Friday evening, the elderly local residents donning their best attire for the trip to the establishment. The décor, however, warranted no such effort. The old red wallpaper desperately needed updating, as did the worn leather armchairs that made up the majority of the low seating.

The last two joined the rest as they reached the bar, having jogged to minimise the drenching by the downpour. Alistair volunteered to get the first round at the bar, coolly acting as if he belonged, while Nicholas, Rohan and Sebastian located a long, unoccupied table towards the back of the pub.

'Alistair,' Max joined him at the bar and got his attention. 'Should we tell them tonight? I think it might help to give them something to look forward to. Nicholas especially.'

'Yeah, I'd been thinking the same.' Alistair agreed. 'I'll let you tell them.'

'Really, why?'

'Well, it was your idea.'

'Yeah, but it's your boat.'

'Not technically but I get your point. You tell them, honestly. You're the leader, it should come from you.'

Max faked some modesty even though he secretly took a great deal of pride whenever anyone referred to him as "the leader".

As they approached the table with the drinks, he gave them the news. 'Right, guys. Alistair and I have a little surprise for you. Alistair, go on.' Max urged him to tell them but once more was rebuffed. 'We were going to wait until a bit later in the year to tell you, but Alistair's dad has said that we can use the Mufasa again after we finish our exams.'

'Are you serious? That's amazing.' Sebastian high-fived Alistair and then Max. 'I can't wait to be back out there.'

Max now looked to Nicholas to gauge his reaction. It was hard to tell what was running through the boy's mind for the first few seconds. Eventually, his face broke into a wide grin and he seemed to transform into a different person they had comforted only ten minutes earlier at Max's house.

Max continued, 'Not only that, but we thought why not take the girls along? Harriet, Annabel, Rosa.' He looked to Rohan, not really sure what the status of his relationship was at that particular moment. 'Melissa too?'

He now focused on Nicholas. 'You can see if Céleste will be out there at the same time and she can join us too.'

The tactic had the exact result he'd hoped for. Nicholas seemed to have forgotten all his worries, immediately reaching for his phone to send a message. It didn't take a genius to guess the recipient.

'Sebastian, how about it? Think Annabel would be game?'

'I don't think you'd be able to stop her! She was so jealous last year that we got to go on Lovell's boat. She's going to be made up.' He was soon busy writing a message of his own.

'She's already text back.' Nicholas beamed. 'She's there all summer, she said she's definitely up for coming on the boat.' He was a new man. Maybe this was what he needed to distract himself from the single-mindedness of the last few months and what they would need to do over the next few. The light was now at the end of the tunnel. No matter what happened with exams, at least he would have the chance to see his precious Céleste.

34

After the boys' first group outing in what felt like an age, the coming weeks and months seemed to crawl out of the bleak winter months. The cold darkness brought with it the weekly routine of the same classes, clubs and activities, usually finishing with nightly revision.

It felt a far cry from the last school year and the summer of relative freedom that followed. They had all agreed that for the next few months they would prove that it was within each of them to focus on what they needed to achieve.

As the days started to lengthen and the winter sports season arrived at its climax, the monotony they'd each subscribed to was now finally entering its ultimate phase. The exams they'd been working towards for the last nine months quickly advanced, meaning the young men saw even less of each other as a group outside of the classroom. Constantly busy with duties to perform and responsibilities to fulfil, making time for any social life whatsoever became a challenge. Max made it absolutely clear that they must all make time to get together for one hour a week, but they could be flexible on the day and location. He'd observed how hard they had all been working and the results were clear to see, there was no point adding extra distractions now.

Each of them had glowing recommendations from every teacher they came into contact with. Class tutors predicted the highest of grades in each of the subjects they had chosen, and the boys were on course to get the results they needed and the opportunity to be part of the next chapter. All bar one, at least. One tiny grade, a letter on a piece of paper. Out of everything they were doing, how could it be that the only chink in their armour was Mathematics?

A month before the exam, Nicholas snapped in an after-school maths class, a bark of frustration aimed at the teacher. He was kept behind after everyone else left, expecting the sharp end from the educator. Instead, the short, stern Yorkshireman, known for his awkward manner, sat next to the young man and leant forward over the table, picking up a pair of compasses and adjusting the diameter. Without looking up, he breathed deeply, 'What's up, lad? You haven't been yourself lately and it's starting to show.'

'I know, I'm sorry, sir. I just need to get the hang

of this, and quickly. I'm nearly out of time.' Nicholas sounded downbeat.

'You're not doing so bad. You've gone from a C to a solid B on all of the tests lately.'

'I know, but it's still not good enough. I need an A.' Nicholas was insistent.

'Listen, son. I'm not sure whether you'll remember me telling you boys about a mathematician called Paul Halmos.'

Casting his eyes from the instrument he twirled in his hand, he continued despite the lack of response from Nicholas. 'He was a brilliant man, incredibly accomplished at a very young age. He broke it down very simply. His wise words were, "the only way to learn mathematics is to do mathematics." You need to just keep at it, lad. You'll get there, and I'll be here to help. Let's take a look at what you're struggling with.'

Max approached Nicholas a couple of days later in school, having heard about the incident, and made plans to talk that night. He was keen to see how Nicholas was coping so they agreed to meet after Nicholas's tutoring session at a golf driving range on the coast. It wasn't the most productive discussion. Max left Nicholas angrily swinging at ball after ball, riled by the conversation that had taken place and the news Max had given him. As he walked to his car, the piercing sound of the oversized driver club head sending ball after ball in rapid succession out towards the dipping sun was a clear sign that Nicholas was not keeping his stress levels in check.

Driving back along the coast, replaying the conversation with Nicholas in his mind, it was hard not to appreciate the surrounding views across the river, sailing boats and windsurfers making use of the high tide and warm breeze. This was how Max kept his stress in check. He stopped at the Marine Lake, an artificial coastal lake, to watch the sails dancing across the water in the sinking sun. His total journey to Harriet's house from the golf range had taken no more than twenty minutes. By the time he arrived, he was still filled with doubt over his handling of the conversation.

'Why's he upset with you?' Harriet asked as Max slumped onto the couch.

'You know I told you that he was struggling with one of his subjects?'

She nodded her agreement as she took her place next to him, bringing her legs up to rest them across his lap.

He paused before continuing, 'Well, we heard about someone who could get copies of the papers before the exam.'

'Are you serious?' she shouted. 'Sign me up! Why

have we been bothering to study for these things?'

'I thought you'd be shocked.' Max was confused. Harriet was no goody-goody but when it came to school, he'd always seen her to be scrupulous.

'It was only a matter of time. People say you can get anything these days, for the right price. I am joking, of course, but I'm not shocked. I think I can figure out what happened.' There was a hint of sarcasm in her voice now. 'You saw he was struggling and wanted to help, you offered him the papers and he said no but then you went and did it anyway and you've just tried to give them to him. And now he's mad at you.'

Max smiled as he turned to look at her. Not only did she continue to surprise him with her attitude to life, she also knew him inside out. He'd avoided telling her about the papers previously, thinking that she would judge him or convince him to find an alternative route.

'Very good, Sherlock,' he teased. 'At first he was really pissed off. Lucky, it was quiet down there, he started shouting at one point. I managed to calm him down and explained that it was only a last resort and that he could even just use it for the type of questions he knew would trip him up.'

'And what happened?' she asked as she stroked his arm.

'He took it. Reluctantly, but he took it. Only he'll know whether he needs it.'

'Well then, I'd say you did a good thing.' She corrected herself, 'Well, a bad thing, but for a good reason. Are you sure it's the real paper?'

'I trust the person who gave it to me, so I think it is. It looked legit. And it wasn't cheap, I had to call in a favour.'

Getting up from the couch, she pulled him by the hand, urging him to rise too. 'Well, I'm now calling in a favour. You promised me a massage last time I saw you and that feels like weeks ago.'

'That's fair, I did. I have been so very neglectful of you,' he mocked as he walked behind her up the stairs, pinching her waist and bum. It was fair to say that the times he spent with Harriet were the highlight of his weeks.

As they reached the landing, his phone started to vibrate in his pocket. He reluctantly retrieved it, wondering whether it was Nicholas needing a lengthy chat. Luckily, it was Sebastian meaning Max could get rid of him honestly if needed, so he picked up.

All Sebastian was calling to say was that Annabel had just confirmed that she'd be coming with them on the ship. When Sebastian had told her over the phone, she'd screamed with excitement down the line.

'That's great news, pal.' Max was impatient to get off the call. 'You've just reminded me about it, but listen, I need to go. I'm in the middle of something.' Hanging up, he looked up at Harriet who was staring curiously at him.

'Oh yeah.' He'd been planning to surprise her at a later date, but he figured getting her excited would only make what they were going upstairs for even more pleasurable. 'How would you like to come and stay on Alistair's dad's ship?'

'Oh my god, that's amazing, yes!' she shrieked. 'How come you're breaking your men-only policy?'

'We thought it would be nice to have all the girls there as well. People will be going away to university, so it may be the last time we spend some time together for a while.'

'Count me in, I can't wait to see it. You would not stop going on about it last year.' She rolled her eyes. 'It sounds immense. Maybe now I owe you a favour. We'll see. My massage first though.' She turned and led him down the hall to her room.

35

Depending on how lucky one gets at the hands of the exam schedulers, it's possible that one could have slots evenly spaced over the five or six-week exam period but with a relatively early last exam. This would mean the perfect balance of time in between each to revise for the next, but with the benefit of still finishing them all early so the summer could really begin.

On this particular year, Physics, Chemistry and English Language were being held over the first two weeks and most of the boys were taking one or two of those subjects. General Studies and languages were next, French and Spanish crossing a few more from the list. By the last two weeks of the period, the only exams any of the boys had left were a final Physics paper, taken by Max, Rohan and Nicholas, and finally Nicholas's two remaining mathematics papers. Even though it was annoying that they all had late finishing dates, it at least meant most of them finished at roughly the same time.

As the final week started, Alistair and Sebastian were lucky enough to have now finished all their modules. Cautious not to gloat or distract, the pair had celebrated together in local pubs and Liverpool bars with any lucky others from school. Each night, more and more revellers would join the brouhaha, the pubs now full of free and newly legal drinkers. For those left with exams, the end was at least in sight, with only a few remaining days left hearing tales of the nights passing them by.

On the morning of Nicholas's final paper, the last of them all to finish, Max woke early, leaving Harriet asleep in her bed, and drove to pick up Nicholas. He used the excuse that it meant Nicholas wouldn't have to leave his car at the pub after school, but it was more so he could see how he was feeling on the big day. He was keen to arrive early at Nicholas's house to ensure as little stress as possible. Unsure of what to expect whilst waiting on the drive outside, he was pleasantly surprised to see Nicholas stride calmly out of the front door, shouting a goodbye to those inside before jogging to the car.

'You're looking amped, mate,' Max commented.

'Yep. It's here. Whatever happens, in approximately'—Nicholas raised his left wrist and checked his watch— 'four hours, they will all be finished and it's in the hands of the gods. I feel good. Sun is shining. Have I ever told you my theory?'

Max turned the car towards the gates and set off. 'No, what's that?'

'I reckon everyone is about thirty percent happier when it's sunny.'

Max laughed. 'How can you measure it as thirty percent?'

'I don't know, it's just a feeling. Have you got a better number?'

'No.' Max shook his head. 'It's probably not a bad guess.' He took the chance to ask the question on his mind. 'Speaking of numbers, have you decided what to do?'

Nicholas hesitated, switching his gaze from Max to the world outside, and nodded. His response was a short, 'Yeah.'

Max had no idea what that meant but sensed he would not get anything further, so he changed the topic to lighter themes, talking about what they were going to do that night. Arriving at the school, he promised to return to pick up Nicholas, armed with the change of clothes now sitting in the boot of his car so they could head straight out once time had been called on the last test.

Having only been gone forty minutes, he returned

to a still sleeping Harriet. Unable to get a response from her phone or the doorbell, he'd resorted to climbing through the dog door into the utility room and was greeted by two large wet tongues and wagging tails. The pair jumped and barked, keen for their morning food. After setting out the bowls and diverting their attention, he poured two large glasses of water and headed upstairs, climbing back into bed and enjoying another hour with his love. The pair relaxed, cuddling and snoozing as the breeze drifted in from the open window, bringing with it the sounds of animals in the garden and surrounding woods.

After peeling himself from her arms, Max called in at his house to shower and change, before jumping back in the car and heading towards the school. He felt happy as he drove through the narrow lanes flanked by fields, windows down, summer music enhancing his mood.

His usual station, Radio 1, broadcast a news flash every hour with the headlines from the day. As was usual, much of the coverage at this time of year centred around exams to cater for the station's younger audience. That morning driving with Nicholas, there had been no radio. Max had turned it off so they could talk. This was the first news broadcast he'd heard of the day and it was deeply worrying.

A group of exam board staff had been caught after an ongoing undercover sting operation by the Guardian newspaper. Grainy pictures shot by secret cameras during meetings with the culprits were on the front page of the paper that morning. Although the meetings had taken place weeks and months earlier, the paper had been asked to hold off on publication in order not to alert any would-be cheaters that the fraud had been caught and the papers switched. Today, being the final day of all exams, was the date they had agreed to hold the story until. The Radio 1 report claimed that one of today's mathematics papers was among those found to have been copied.

Looking back now, it seemed like fate that he and Nicholas had not heard that report four hours earlier. Nevertheless, Max arrived at the school devoid of the elation he'd started the journey with only twenty minutes earlier.

Pulling into the gravel car park for the staff and sixth form pupils, Nicholas was already waiting outside the school hall, chatting on his phone excitedly, his smile and gestures confusing Max. He wasn't sure what to make of it. Nicholas jogged to the car, threw his bag in the back seat and jumped into the front passenger side.

'All done, yes!' He held up a palm to high five Max.

Max help up his hand in response. 'So, it went well? Have you not heard the news?' he asked, unconsciously looking towards the radio console in the dashboard.

'What news? I've been inside there, haven't I?'

'They switched the exam paper.' Max was matter of fact.

'What do you mean?'

'They found out that today's paper had been stolen and had switched it in time. It's been on the radio.'

Nicholas seemed unfazed. 'What did I tell you when you first said it to me?'

'I know. But we just wanted to be sure. I didn't want there to be a chance that you missed out on what you wanted to do. I'm sorry, it probably did more harm than good.'

'Max, listen to me. I told you I wouldn't cheat. I didn't look at the paper. I can't say I wasn't tempted but I couldn't do it. I know it must have cost you a lot, but I couldn't go through with it. I wanted to earn it.'

Max breathed a sigh of relief. A mix of emotions ran through his mind. He was impressed at the self-control it must have taken to resist the urge to take the easy way out but was also concerned that Nicholas would risk not getting the grade for the sake of his pride. He attempted to hide the latter. 'I think you've definitely earned it. How do you think it went?'

Nicholas couldn't stop smiling, 'Honestly, I think I've nailed it. I got a new tutor two weeks ago and something seems to have clicked. I think I've just about done it.'

'Ah buddy, that's awesome news. Well done. Let's go and have some fun. It's about time. We haven't seen you with a smile for months! The boys are waiting in the Caernarvon Castle around the corner. Get changed in the back and then we'll go.'

'Fuck that. It's my last day here, ever. I think I'll get changed outside.'

He ran to the back and pulled out his bag before stripping off his black blazer, throwing it into the boot. The black sixth-form tie came off next, then shirt and finally trousers. He stood, boxer shorts and socks only, cheering at the boys leaving the exam hall, deciding to run a lap of honour in front of the sixth form centre to make the most of his leaving experience. Students from other year groups would not finish summer term for another two weeks so were still present about the school, along with their teachers.

'Nicholas Archer!' It was one of the school's kind old art teachers, Mr Jarvis. 'I'd advise you to put some clothes on and leave the premises. You never know, you might fail and be back here next year!'

Nicholas recognised when it was his time to go,

raising an arm to apologise before climbing back into the car, half-naked, and being driven off.

The story went down well in the pub where the others were waiting. They cheered the arrival of their freshly finished accomplice, insisting that he drain the pint of beer already on the table as a starter. Within an hour, they'd travelled the five miles into Liverpool to enjoy the sunshine and festivities. In this weather, the bars in the iconic Albert Dock offered music, sun, food and drink outside along the water's edge. The group had no trouble securing a table overlooking the square dock surrounded by tourist shops and restaurants.

Here they ate and drank for hours. As the noise of the bar increased, Alistair treated the rest to some Hoyo de Monterrey Cuban cigars he'd been given by his father on his last visit to the UK. With some assistance from the bar staff, they managed to cut the end off each of the stogies with a knife before polluting the surrounding area with the thick silver smoke. Their fellow revellers were less than impressed, but the boys' spirits would not be dampened. This was their celebration and they had earned it.

36

Starting off like any other morning, the sound of the heavy front door closing sent two crows flapping from the front lawn of Max's house; the sound of feet on gravel had the same effect on a squirrel which raced up the nearest tree. His mother climbed into her silver Mercedes and left through the already open gates at the bottom of the drive, leaving thin dust from the gravel hanging in the air.

Awoken by the rumble of life outside, Max leant over to the cabinet on the left-hand side of his bed to check the time. It was still early. He rolled to his right and saw the dinner suit hanging from the pine cupboard. Tonight, was the last time he would share a room with everyone he'd spent the last ten years getting to know, or avoiding.

Leavers' Balls are the pinnacle of the final year. Stories circulated about parties of years gone by: teachers getting drunk with students, new couples getting together, after-parties getting out of hand. Each year, there was at least one new anecdote that would be passed down to the next year group. He'd been looking forward to this for a long time.

Subconsciously, his eyes flicked towards the phone charging next to his bed, hoping to see signs of life. It had been over twenty-four hours since he'd heard from Harriet, an unprecedented amount of time. Of the numerous calls and messages he'd left her, not a single response had been received.

He rolled out of bed and pulled up the blinds. The view from his window in the morning sun was one of his daily pleasures, the lush grass wet with dew, birds singing from the surrounding trees. In the fields to the west of the house, he could see cows grazing up against the wire fence separating the farmer's land and theirs.

Stretching as he padded across the carpet to the bathroom, he sat down on the toilet and read his last text to Harriet. As he did, the phone's screen flashed, and the handset began to vibrate.

He answered the call, 'Sebastian, how's it going?'

'Max, we need to talk.'

'Uh oh, that sounds ominous. Do I need to grab my boxing gloves?'

'No, nothing like that.' Sebastian's tone was direct. 'I'll get you and we'll go for a drive. I'll be there in twenty.'

'Can't you just—' The line went dead. It wasn't the first time Sebastian had hung up on him, but the circumstances were usually much more heated when it had happened before. Confused, he returned Sebastian's call, but the line rang out. He tried calling Harriet once more but with no luck before jumping into the shower.

There had only just been enough time to get ready when the gate buzzed, and Sebastian's car pulled into the driveway. The driver didn't get out. Max grabbed his phone, watch, wallet and keys and descended the stairs, calling out to see whether anyone was home. The lack of response meant it was safe to lock up. As he set the house alarm, the beeping followed him out of the door, finally stopping ten seconds later, just as he drew level with the passenger side door.

'Morning, buddy.' Max held out his fist as he climbed into the car. 'What was that about? Why did you hang up?'

'Sorry, mate. I was just in a rush to get out of the house. Are you excited for the do tonight?'

Max paused, confused. What was so urgent twenty minutes ago that was now less important than the Leavers' Ball? Something about Sebastian's demeanour was off. He stared straight into his eyes. 'Sebastian. What's going on? You're being weird.'

His friend's perfect smile wavered momentarily, just long enough for Max to notice.

'We'll get to that, pal. Let's just drive first.'

They followed a familiar route, through the fields and high-speed bends of the winding roads to Heswall, branching off right, down towards the coast. As they passed the spot of Nicholas's crash, Max guessed where they were headed. He knew the car park and picnic area that awaited them well. Realising that Sebastian wasn't going to discuss whatever it was he wanted to in the car, Max tried to relax as they chatted about the upcoming holiday and the boat.

Pulling into the wide gateway, with the River Dee to the left and fields to the right, they'd arrived at their destination. The car park was deserted except for one empty Volvo estate car, presumably a dog walker at this time in the morning. Exiting the car, Max regretted not picking up some sunglasses from home. The morning sun reflecting off the shallow water of the creeping tide forced him to shield his eyes as the pair walked to the picnic table the group usually occupied whenever they came here.

'Okay, we're here now. What is it?' Max demanded before Sebastian had a chance to take a seat. 'Why can't I get in touch with Harriet?'

Sebastian looked shocked. 'How did you know—'

'Come on, mate. I've called her at least twenty times with no answer and then you call being all mysterious. Tell me what's going on.' Max was starting to lose his temper as he feared some sort of unimaginable betrayal by his best friend.

Sebastian was still taking his place but paused as he settled, clearly contemplating what he was about to say. This only added fuel to Max's paranoia.

'Max,'—he paused, and took a breath— 'she's pregnant.' He let that hang for a moment. 'She was too afraid to tell you. Sorry.'

The words physically knocked him backwards.

'How does she know? I mean, is she okay? Whe... where is she now?'

More words spilled out, in no particular order. Sebastian gave him a minute to catch his breath.

'She's fine, she's at home. She took a test last night, well about five, actually, and they're all positive.'

'Positive? They've totally cocked up the labelling system there. How is this remotely positive? It's a disaster.'

'Not what you were expecting today, hey? You alright?' Sebastian looked concerned.

'Yeah. Yeah...' Max stared towards the ground as he tried to comprehend what this meant. He repeated himself, not entirely in control of what he was saying, 'Yeah.'

'She'll come down and meet us here shortly if you want to see her?' Sebastian reached for his phone as he asked the question.

'Of course! Why wouldn't I want to see her?'

'She thought you might be mad at her, you know, for getting pregnant.'

'That's ridiculous,' Max protested, 'it's no one's fault, I just want to make sure she's okay. Tell her to come.'

Sebastian pulled his phone from his pocket and sent a text. Less than thirty seconds later, he received a response.

'She's on her way.'

Max sat in silence, staring out at the water as he waited for her, a thousand questions racing through his head.

When she arrived, she ran to Max, throwing her arms around him and bursting into tears. Holding onto him like she never wanted to let go, she kissed his neck, apologising over and over.

'Don't be silly, why are you apologising to me?' Max asked her. 'This isn't your fault, it was an accident. We've always been so careful.'

He couldn't bear to see her upset. Every tear that dropped from her eye felt like a knife in his heart. 'It's going to be alright, we'll work through this.'

In truth, he had no idea what to say or do. He'd

barely had enough time to process the information he'd been given. All he cared about was seeing Harriet and making sure she was okay.

Once her crying subsided, Sebastian made his excuses, knowing the pair had a lot to discuss. Harriet loosened her grip around Max's neck, exchanging the solace of Max's embrace for the sympathy of Sebastian's, thanking him for his help. She found it difficult to hold back the tears and they started to flow once more.

'If you guys need anything, give me a call. Any time, day or night and I'll be here to help.' He patted each on the shoulder before making his way to the car.

The remaining pair walked back to the picnic table, Max straddling the bench so that he could look directly at Harriet who sat, head in hands, at the table.

She fought to speak through the tears, an involuntary reaction from her diaphragm interrupting every few words. 'I spoke with mum last night after I took the tests. She's angry, really angry, Max.'

'Why didn't you tell me? I would have been there in a heartbeat!'

'I thought you'd think it was my fault. I thought you'd hate me.'

'I could never hate you. No matter what happens, know that. I hate the thought of you even thinking it would be possible for me to hate you. And for something like this.'

'I'm sorry.' She wiped her eyes, regaining some composure.

'How did you know you were pregnant?'

'I missed my period three weeks ago, but I thought it might just be stress of exams causing the timing to be off. When I still hadn't got it yesterday, I asked Charlotte to come with me to get some tests and they all came out positive. I don't know why they call it positive, that's the complete opposite of how I feel!'

Max chuckled, a soft smile on his face. Harriet looked confused.

'What? Why are you smiling?'

'Nothing.' He looked intensely into her eyes, still smiling while raising his hands to hold her face. 'I love you so much.'

'Oh Max, I love you too.'

'How are you feeling? What did your mum say?'

Something stopped her from being able to answer his question, tears running down from her eyes as her face contorted around the words, 'She thinks it's best to have an abortion.'

A shaking cry came from her body that made him tighten his arms around her in comfort.

'Wow. Really, your mum? But she's so, so, so...' He

struggled to find the right word. 'Traditional. I would have thought that would be the last thing she'd suggest.'

'Yeah, I know.' Harriet seemed equally puzzled by her mum's attitude. 'She's also a realist, though. She knows that having a baby at seventeen would basically kill my chances to go and study Medicine. She also knows that you're about to go away to university. Would you really miss all that to have a baby now?'

Having just turned eighteen, this was not a conversation he'd imagined himself having for many years to come. It certainly didn't fit in with his master plan. But nor did a lot of things that had happened over the past year.

'I haven't really had much time to think about it all. My first thought was how you were feeling. What do you think? Would you want to get rid of it?'

'I don't know.' Tears started to run down her face once more. 'I never thought I'd have to make a choice like this. Especially not with you. If it had been with someone I didn't care about it would have been an easier decision. But with you? I love you. I want to spend the rest of my life with you. Let's face it, though, we all know what happens to childhood sweethearts. It never works out.'

'Harriet, don't say that. It may not work out for everyone, but it *can* work out, and we can make it work.'

'Max, listen to yourself. Just think for a second. How are you going to go away and join the army and do all the things that you need to do if you have a child.'

He didn't respond but did what she asked and thought, silently. His attitude towards abortion had always been one of choice. He believed that people should have the ability to make a decision that is right for them. Not one mandated by religion, law or societal pressure. In this case, logic told him that an abortion was the right decision. For both of them.

That was all fine in theory, but it felt different now somehow. Now the moment was upon him, he had to admit that there was a part of him that had instantly become protective of the embryo that he'd just learned of.

He reached out, placing a hand on Harriet's stomach. He knew that the life that was in there could only be weeks old. At this age, the foetus would be the size of a raisin, and look more like a seahorse than an infant human. Still, an overwhelming sense of pride filled him knowing that they had created life. Whether intentionally or not, it amazed him.

She covered his hand, struggling to control her emotions, leaning forward to be as close to him as she could be. 'I'd always thought that if something like this happened, it would be a simple decision to make.' She sobbed. 'But now that it's happening, I feel torn. Knowing that there is a little baby, however tiny or young it may be, it's hard to think about terminating it.'

He hated that word. It seemed so clinical and uncaring. He knew she didn't mean it to be—it was just her using medical terminology, as one studying medicine would have.

'What do you think? I know your mum thinks that's best but at the end of the day, it has to be your decision. We're the ones who have to live with it.'

'I know, I know. I think I need a bit longer to think about it all. Will you stay with me today?'

'Of course, I will. What do you want to do? We could go and get breakfast?'

'I'd like that. If I can keep anything down. I've felt pretty nauseous for the last couple of days.'

They walked hand in hand back to her car before making their way to a café in Heswall and spending the day together.

⬠

Cold water dripped down Max's face, pooling on his chin before gently dropping into the basin below. The two doors separating him from the main function room of the hotel did little to drown out the music coming from outside the bathroom. So far, it had been a surreal day, the events of which he was still trying to comprehend.

A change in the tempo of the music coming from the ballroom outside the bathroom he now found himself in snapped him back to the moment. He had no idea how long he'd been staring into the bathroom mirror. Wiping his face dry with a hand towel from the basket next to the sink, he felt bad for leaving Harriet alone this evening.

Two years earlier he'd made a deal with a friend from the girls' school that they would accompany each other to their Leavers' Balls. Not only did it ensure that they would both get to go to both the girls' and boys' schools Leavers' Balls, it also meant that they would have a confirmed date for each.

After realising he'd made the deal before meeting Harriet, he explained that he would speak with Sarah, his date for the events, and change the arrangement so that he could take his girlfriend. Harriet had protested at the idea, insisting that he had to honour the original agreement, however much she wanted to go with him. Harriet, being one year younger, had reasoned that she would get the chance to go to both events the next year. He'd finally succumbed and agreed to keep the arrangement. That was weeks ago.

After getting the news of the pregnancy this morning, it seemed like there could be no worse time to leave her alone, but it was now too late to find another date for Sarah. He felt obliged to go. Harriet had encouraged him to try and enjoy it as much as possible, complimenting his dinner suit as he left her and Charlotte on the sofa for the evening. He'd promised to return as soon as he could.

As he dried the rest of the water from his face, the only thought on his mind was how to explain his swift departure from the dining table minutes earlier. Elena, a sweet hockey player from the girls' school, had asked him how Harriet was. It was an innocent enough question, but one that brought back all the drama of the day. He'd risen from the table quickly as he felt a wave of emotion overcome him, weaving through the packed round tables to get to the toilet before anyone would notice his attempts to hold back his emotion.

Once he arrived at the bathroom, he used an old trick to rein himself back in. Pinching. He gripped the tender skin on the inside of his bicep and squeezed, hard. He found this helped him in a variety of situations. He used it to psyche himself up in the gym or on the rugby pitch. The pain triggers the adrenal gland to release adrenaline into the body. In some, this reaction actually creates fear, but Max found it brought him power and control. The pain would focus his mind, allowing all other, uncontrollable emotions to evaporate. Back in charge of his feelings, he removed his phone from his pocket and sent a simple text to Harriet.

'I love you, I wish you were here. x'

Replacing the phone, he checked his face and shirt for any signs of water before leaving the bathroom.

He stepped back into the wall of noise coming from the party, stopping dead upon seeing the familiar face waiting outside the bathroom for him.

'Everything okay, Max?' It was Howarth. 'You've been in there a while.'

Max didn't respond but turned his head towards the entrance to the ballroom, checking to see whether anyone could see them.

Had he been waiting for him the whole time?

'Yes, I'm fine, Anthony. Sorry,' Max corrected himself, 'Mr Howarth.' He looked around once more. 'Can we talk later? I need to get back to my table.'

'Certainly, Mr Mercer. Go and enjoy yourself. You've earned it.' He patted Max on the shoulder.

Max hurried away, making his apologies as he retook his seat, attributing his quick exit to a shot of Sambuca he'd been handed earlier by one of the rugby team. Finishing his conversation with the hockey girl, he scanned the room looking for Sebastian. It was Annabel he spotted first, looking radiant in a floor-length red gown. Sebastian, as expected, wasn't far away.

'Annabel, you look absolutely amazing.' Having missed their first meeting in London, Max only had the joy of meeting the young lady when she had been to visit over the previous summer. He'd instantly seen why Sebastian had fallen head over heels for the girl. It was clear that she felt the same for him.

'Thanks, Max. You look rather dapper yourself. How's your night going?'

'Good, thanks. I just wanted to have a quick chat with Sebastian, if possible?'

At the mention of his name, Sebastian span from the group he was engaged with and joined his girlfriend's side.

'Max, how are you, buddy?' He clumsily raised a glass. 'Cheers! What a night. And it's far from over yet.' The young reveller leaned in to meet Annabel's cheek with a sloppy kiss, mouth freshly wet from a sip of champagne. She recoiled as his cold, wet lips made contact with her skin, unimpressed about her now wet face. She dipped her index finger into his glass and flicked a few droplets in his face as payback before the pair smiled and laughed at each other.

'Sebastian, can I have a quick chat?' Max motioned to the door with his head.

'Sure, just Us?' Sebastian emphasised the 'Us' a little too obviously.

'If that's okay?' Max turned to Annabel. 'I won't keep him long, promise.'

'Yeah of course, I'll just hang out with these guys.' She pointed to the group of girls she'd bonded with over dinner.

The two gents left via a door towards the expansive illuminated gardens of the hotel, passing a group of smokers in black and white, heading towards the giant chess set accompanying other garden games at the far end of the lawn. Max guided them towards it looking for a reason to be milling around outside. As he moved his first white pawn, he explained what had happened after Sebastian had left him and Harriet that morning.

'Shit. That's deep. Her mum really suggested an abortion?' Sebastian mirrored Max's move on the board with his pawn. 'Although, I kind of agree with her. You can't have a baby. You still are a baby.'

'Thanks for the support!' Max laughed, but it felt empty. He kept talking as he made his next move. 'I know. It's big, right? We don't know what to do. Harriet's weighing the options.'

'What do you want? You're part of it as well, remember.' Sebastian slid his piece into position.

'I've been thinking about it all day. I think I just

want to try and enjoy tonight and look at it through fresh eyes in the morning.' He moved his queen forward. 'I just needed to talk to you about it. Obviously, this goes no further. You can't tell Annabel. You haven't already, have you?'

'Of course not, no way. We can talk about it whenever you like. And don't worry. I won't say a word, you can trust me. You're my best friend, my loyalty to you is tribal.'

'Thanks, that means a lot.' The pair hugged, Max slapping Sebastian on the back. 'I'd say you're about to lose this one.'

'What are you talking about? I've got you exactly where I want you.' Sebastian released the hug, looking down towards to the chess pieces to prove his position. His balance was far from perfect. At a loss for the piece or move that he had imagined, he now saw Max's impending move, queen to F7, shielding her with his knight on G5, pinning Sebastian's king and ending the game.

Traditionally, a player conceding knocks down their king softly, indicating resignation. Sebastian's king, however, could be seen flying across the garden after a sharp punt from his polished shoe. He departed back towards the entrance, mumbling about his defeat. Max caught up with him, laughing at his friend's reaction, 'You'll get me one day, mate. It takes a lot to be the master.'

As the pair stumbled back into the function room past a new group blowing smoke into the air, another figure in black and white emerged from a summer house next to the chess set they'd occupied a minute earlier. Ward expertly flicked his cigarette away as he watched the pair from the shadows.

37

'Have you thought any more about it?'

'I can't stop thinking about it. This is too big a decision to have to make. Can we really go through with it? We're talking about a life here.'

'Do we really have a choice?'

'There's always a choice. I just want to be sure we've looked at all the possible options.'

'What else is there? There aren't many options open to us, unfortunately. I don't want this to happen either but think about the consequences if we don't. I wish there was some other way, I just can't see one. And the longer we wait, the bigger the problem gets. The whole future could be ruined.'

'Well, it's definitely ruined for someone if we do go through with it.'

'I know this is hard, but sometimes doing the one thing you never thought you'd have to is the only way. It's the hardest thing to do, but in the end, you know it's the right decision.'

'What if people find out? What would they think of me?'

'I think we've just got to forget about that. No one will ever find out. How would they? The only people who will ever know will be us.'

'People always find out about this kind of stuff. And when they do that's it, it'll be news of the world.'

'Okay, well we haven't definitely made the decision yet. There are other risks to think about as well. We need to be sure that we want to go through with it.'

'I think "want" is a bit strong. We're never going to want to do something this drastic. We'll just have to learn to live with the choice. For ever.'

'Well whatever you decide to do, it's between us.'

38

Max jumped out of his mother's car as they arrived at Sebastian's house. She had kindly offered to drive the group to the airport to meet with the rest of the gang.

'Annabel, lovely to see you again.' Max hugged her. 'And so soon. How are you?'

'Good thanks. How about you?'

Annabel and Sebastian looked confused as they climbed into the back of the waiting car.

'Are you alone?' she asked.

'Afraid I am. Harriet's too ill to come.' He felt guilty lying to the sweet girl, but he had to respect Harriet's wish. 'Some kind of gastric flu, we think. It's pretty nasty, she's absolutely devastated she couldn't be here.'

'You're joking, she can't come at all?' Annabel was clearly upset. 'I was looking forward to spending some time with her. That and having one more female here to deal with all of you boys.'

'Well, Sebastian's practically female, isn't he? He

spends more time on his hair than any girl I know, anyway.' Max teased his friend.

'At least I have hair,' Sebastian taunted back, commenting on Max's buzzcut that he'd gone for again this summer. 'Hope she's okay, she didn't want you to stay with her?' He gave a look that was imperceptible to Annabel but not Max.

'No, they...' He stopped himself. 'She was worried that I'd catch it so there was no use for me there. Thought I might as well make the best of the situation and join you guys for some fun in the sun. I can't tell you how gutted she is to be missing out on all of the action.'

He hoped he was managing to hide his own feelings about having to leave Harriet. In truth, he had not had a choice in the matter. Her mother had refused to see or speak to him since the news of the pregnancy. He'd tried on multiple occasions to go to the house to discuss it with her without success. He'd sent pleading texts to her, explaining that he wanted to be there with Harriet when she went to the clinic to have the procedure, but she wouldn't allow it. The tension had reached a point where she had banned Harriet from seeing Max at all.

Annabel expressed her condolences again as they cruised along the motorway towards the airport. The boys were familiar with the private terminal at Manchester Airport, having had the pleasure of this exact start only one year earlier. Annabel, however, was in a new world.

Having had the dissatisfaction of hearing firsthand about last year's trip from Sebastian, she was determined to absorb and remember every single detail, now having the chance to experience the opulence for herself. The joy of bypassing the check-in desks and queues. Walking across the tarmac to the plane. Embracing the smell of wood and leather upon climbing through the door and the warm greetings from the crew onboard the private jet.

'What time do you call this?' Nicholas had already made himself at home, having arrived on the jet twenty minutes earlier with Alistair, Rohan and Melissa. 'Don't you know I have an appointment with someone who I haven't seen in far too long?'

He stood, welcoming the newcomers, kissing Annabel on each cheek and embracing the boys. It was Alistair who first noticed they were a number short, but rather than asking loudly, waited until his ear was next to Max's as they greeted.

'No Harriet? Everything okay?' he whispered.

'No, unfortunately not. She's really ill, some kind of flu thing. Came on a few days ago. Hoped she'd kick it by today but no joy. I was going to stay with her but there's nothing I could do so thought I'd come and join you.'

Alistair withdrew from the hug, a questioning look in his eye. 'Right, well that's crap. Guess it means we'll have to come again next year so she can see the ship once at least!'

Max was quick to speak up, turning to the group, 'You all heard that, Alistair's just promised we can do it again next year, it's confirmed!'

The group laughed but anyone who had been on the trip the previous year knew that the enthusiasm was not misplaced. The newcomers were in for a treat.

Max turned to Melissa, who he'd not seen since Capri. She stood to welcome him.

'Hi Max,' she looked sheepish as she spoke in her soft Scottish accent. 'Nice to see you again. I'm sorry about all the mess last time.'

'Don't be silly,' he bellowed. 'It all worked out in the end. We're just glad you recovered so quickly. How's the head?'

She leant forward as she raised a hand to the spot where her stitches had been. 'All better now, thanks.' She smiled towards Rohan.

Sebastian now greeted Melissa and introduced her to Annabel.

'So, where will we be meeting your two lovely ladies then, lads?' Sebastian was interested to know the plan as he questioned Alistair and Nicholas.

'Not until we get to Split in Croatia,' Alistair informed him. 'Rosa's flying out there at the moment and we'll meet her at the airport. What time is Céleste going to join us?' He posed the question to Nicholas.

'Same, she might be a little later than us, but she'll meet us in Split.' He was positively giddy at the excitement of seeing his French belle once again.

A familiar accent to most of the group now spoke to them from the door of the cockpit.

'Welcome, ladies. And welcome back, gentlemen. I trust you have everything you need and are ready to get moving?' The tanned pilot had climbed aboard after finishing his final checks of the exterior of the plane and was now in the process of ensuring the hostesses were ready for take-off. A few minutes later they'd be airborne and heading for Croatia.

Having failed to make it there during their summer tour of the Mediterranean the year before, they had decided this time to explore the former Socialist Republic's coastal region. Starting in Split, they would travel to the nearby island of Hvar, before sailing south towards the beautiful, old city of Dubrovnik. With only two destinations on the itinerary this year, they would have longer to spend in each of the locations and really explore their surroundings.

As they watched the beautiful country below out of the windows on their final approach, the gang had been having fun onboard for just over two hours and the mood was jolly. They descended the stairs from the plane into the blinding sunshine of the Balkan summer with only a light breeze from the Adriatic Sea to cool their faces.

Alistair left the group to collect their belongings as he raced towards the arrivals terminal to meet Rosa. Max prompted Nicholas to follow him if he didn't want to get lost. Ditching his bag, he leapt from the plane feeling a twinge in his left ankle as he landed on the tarmac. The adrenaline was enough to dull the ache as he followed his love-struck brother out of the heat and into the terminal building.

Rosa stood, patiently waiting for them at arrivals, having landed thirty minutes earlier. A wide smile covered her face as she spotted Alistair. Nicholas was unaware of it, but Céleste's connecting flight from Geneva had been directly ahead of their business jet on approach and landing. He would have to wait only a few minutes longer before seeing her once more.

Their meeting was cute, Céleste hugging him shyly at first before letting herself go and kissing him long and hard on the forehead and briefly on the mouth. He grabbed her bags and Alistair led them back out to the waiting transport.

In line with the previous experience, a black van with tinted windows collected them at the airport and drove them the short distance to Kaštela Bay. Leaving the airport, a keen observer would have spotted their colossal home for the next week moored in the centre of the bay, the high polish finish glistening in the sun as the clear blue water lapped at its base.

The Cesta Franje Tuđmana road follows the contour of the coast, every once in a while giving the traveller a view of the water beyond the collections of villas and shops that line the narrow road to the Marina Kaštela, where Tom awaited them.

'Good to see you again, Tom.' Rosa was the first to greet him, hugging him warmly. She then introduced the three new girls, ensuring them that Tom was more than capable, despite his years. Once the girls were finished, it was onto the boys for hugs all round.

'Welcome all,' Tom shouted, moving away from the group so they could all see and hear him. 'It might be a squeeze to get everyone on with the luggage, so we may have to make two trips as there's a few more of you than last time. Are we missing someone? We were told to expect ten of you.'

Max apologised on behalf of Harriet.

'Well, I reckon we can fit up to six or seven with luggage, who's going to stay behind?'

'We'll wait for the next one.' Max spotted an opportunity, glancing across at Sebastian with a nod.

'What are you two up to?' Annabel had clearly picked up on their non-verbal communication and quietly demanded an explanation as she gave Sebastian a hug.

Without hesitation, Max reprimanded her nosiness, 'Nothing for you to worry about. We wouldn't want to ruin the surprise now, would we?' He winked.

The group made their way through the narrow mesh gate and down the five steps down to the level of the dock, Sebastian carrying Annabel's bag for her.

'What do you think of the other girls?' Sebastian took the chance to ask Annabel now they were away from the others.

'Melissa and **Céleste seem** really nice. I haven't had much chance to speak to Rosa yet. She seems glued to Alistair so far. Is she going to be like that the whole time, do you think?'

'Put simply, yes.' Sebastian was matter of fact. 'Last time we were here it was pretty much the same. It's hard to get his attention when she's in sight, too. You'll be hard pressed to spend any time with her on her own,' Sebastian warned.

'Well, we'll see about that. I'm determined to get to know her. Starting now. I'm going to make sure I sit between them on the boat.'

She skipped down the stairs after the others. Sebastian watched as she ran straight to Rosa and linked arms, ready to board the boat together. Now that they were alone together, Sebastian turned to Max and raised an eyebrow. He waited for the boat to pull away from the dock and the pair waved at the departing group.

'I thought I should probably fill you in on what's going on.' Max spoke without taking his eyes off the tender.

'You could have done it more subtly that that! They're bound to wonder what we're talking about.' Sebastian jokingly chided his friend.

'I know, but we have actually got a little surprise for them on the boat, so we'll just use that as the excuse.'

'Really? What's the—'

'You're as bad as them, I knew you'd ask that. I'll tell you later, we don't have much time. Harriet's not here because she's having the abortion on Tuesday. We had a big fight because her mum wouldn't let me be there with her when she has it.'

'Why the hell not? It's your child as well.' Sebastian was outraged.

'I know. She doesn't see it that way, for some

reason. She says it's all my fault and I should have been more responsible. I don't think she likes the thought of her little flower being, well, deflowered.'

'Are you okay?'

'Yeah, I'll be fine.' He looked pensive as he answered his friend, running his hand over his hair, replacing his hat and sunglasses. 'Let's face it, having a baby now is in no one's best interest. Of course, I'd like to have been there with her to make sure she's okay but that's not allowed, apparently. I just feel terrible I'm not by her side.' He took a deep breath. 'But, it'll be fine. Let's just have a good time here and by the time we get back everything will be sorted.'

'You can talk to me at any time about it, mate.' Sebastian nodded empathetically as he made the offer.

'I know, and thanks for that. You've really been there for me. Looks like it's all going well with Annabel.' He wanted to change the subject before his emotions were no longer easily hidden behind his sunglasses.

'She's great, this is going to be a fun week. Could Harriet fly out after the, you know?'

Max looked out towards the bay, watching the incoming vessel heading directly towards them. His mouth curled in a pained expression. 'I don't think so. We'll be miles away by then. I don't know the toll it will take on her. Plus, I doubt her mum would allow it.

Anyway, let's go, it's time to start the journey.'

Aboard the Mufasa, it seemed that the group had already chosen rooms by the time the second landing party arrived. Alistair and Rosa had promptly disappeared, having said a cursory "hello" to the crew.

Annabel greeted the latecomers. 'I tried to make pals with her but she's like a magnet with him. The second we stepped on board it was like she was ripped from my grasp. Anyway, have you seen this bar? It's incredible!'

This was the very same bar that Max and Sebastian had sat at many times the previous year, looking out across a multitude of captivating sunset silhouettes, discussing the girls and the boys, and Us. Many times had the pair asked each other questions about the feasibility of what they were trying to achieve. Many times had they taken turns in assuring the other that it could be done, that they weren't crazy. Looking at it now brought back those conversations.

In light of what had happened over the past fifty-two weeks, those exchanges now seemed petty, considering the amount of dedication and commitment they had been able to inject into the group. The things they had gone through so far. Every single member had shown what they were capable of and it had paid off. Everything, bar a few small hiccups, seemed to be going to plan.

'You forget, my darling, that we were here last year.' Sebastian was smug. 'Remember when you were crying down the phone with jealousy?' He laughed and stuck out a bottom lip as a crying child might.

She turned and attempted to jab him in the stomach with an index finger from each hand.

'Oh, ha ha, you're a very funny one, aren't you? Well if you know it so well, why aren't you sorting any drinks out?'

He struggled to avoid her poking, moving backwards, laughing and returning with his own indexes. 'Okay, okay, I'll get the drinks.' He held his hands in the air and turned towards the fridges and sinks behind the long oval-shaped bar.

As if by magic, unable to let another touch the tools of the barman, Ernesto appeared from the stairwell onto the deck.

'Please, sirs, allow me.' He was neither angry nor upset, only courteous and polite. 'What can I get for you?'

He shooed Sebastian from behind the bar. 'Please take a seat, sir.' He whisked Sebastian to the bar stool and pulled it out for him, before returning to take charge of his workspace.

'Now, Madame, I'm Ernesto. I am in charge of the bar aboard the ship. If there's anything you need, please let me know.'

Annabel held out her hand. 'Nice to meet you, Ernesto. I'm Annabel. Here with this reprobate.' She swung her arm around Sebastian's neck and kissed him on the temple. 'Ernesto, can we please have some drinks?'

'Of course, Madame. What would you like?'

'I think we should probably try some cocktails. Do you have a favourite to make?'

'I have a few I think you like. Why don't you take soft seat and I bring over drinks? First some champagne, you are celebrating graduating high school, yes?'

'That is true, Ernesto, for most of us at least.' She pointed to the boys. She, of course, had left school two years earlier and had now finished her first year at university.

'But I think we should wait for the others for the champagne. Cocktails they can miss out on.' She smiled at the barman.

ownstairs on the owner's deck, Rosa paced across the sumptuous cream and gold swirling carpet of the master bedroom.

Alistair had protested when the others had insisted the he and Rosa have the best room, offering it to the other couples, only to be rebuffed. Rosa had given no resistance whatsoever, smugly walking to the residence she wanted.

'Alistair, I don't know how you can expect me to be around them. They know that I know about the group. I can tell. I feel like they're staring at me, like I know all their secrets.'

'Babe, I promise you, no one suspects that you know. Why would they? It's just that you feel guilty for knowing. Everything's fine, trust me.' Alistair perched aside the giant mattress.

'I do trust you.' She softened slightly, hugging him for comfort. 'What will they say when they find out that you switched your university application?'

'I'm not even going to think about that for now. All that matters is that we are going to be together doing Medicine. I'm sure all of this will just fizzle out eventually. Everyone will start new lives when they go off to university and it will fall apart. I bet it doesn't last another year.'

He was torn. After telling Rosa everything the previous summer, he'd immediately regretted it. Not only did he feel like he'd betrayed the group, but he'd now also given Rosa all the information she needed to try to convince him to do what she wanted. Yes, it was true that he wanted to study Medicine. And yes, he did love her. But more and more he felt like she wanted to isolate him from the group, for obvious reasons he supposed. Maybe last year that hadn't seemed like a problem to him.

However, a lot had happened since he first told her. He'd grown closer with all his brothers over the last twelve months, most of all Sebastian. Having not initially taken to each other, for reasons unbeknown even to Alistair, the pair had become true friends, Alistair very nearly revealing to Sebastian that he'd told Rosa about the group. He now wondered what would have happened if he had. What would Sebastian have done? Told Max? And the rest? Then what? Max would surely understand his side of it. Wouldn't he?

It was a question he was glad he did not have to answer right now. He would stay quiet and keep everybody happy for the time being. It would be easier to tell the group when they weren't stranded on a vessel for a fixed duration, also allowing him some more time to think.

'They seem pretty committed to me,' Rosa pushed. 'Look at all the stuff you've done in a year.'

'Well even if it doesn't fall apart, they can't have me. I'd rather be happy and do something I love than have power.' He said what he knew she wanted to hear.

'That's why I love you, Alistair. I'm so happy you've chosen to do the right thing. I knew you'd see that I was right eventually. You don't need them to be happy. We can be happy together, we don't need anybody else.'

'No, we don't.'

He paused. Was Rosa right to demand that he completely cut himself off from his friends? It worried him that he was being manipulated and blinded by his love for her. He couldn't risk alerting her to his feelings, so he resisted softly. 'But while we're here you should try to get to know the girls, they're great. Let's just forget all about this for now and have some fun. Come upstairs and relax. We've earned this trip, let's enjoy it.'

'Ten more minutes down here and then we'll go wherever you like. I just want a bit more of you to myself.'

Outside the door, a heart pounded harder and harder, faster and faster, as its host struggled to control his breathing, a realisation slowly cascading through his cells. The conversation he'd just overheard only confirmed what he already knew, but even now, he struggled to believe that she really knew, that he'd really told her everything.

How could he do this to Us? He silently demanded an answer.

He'd seen the messages between the pair but somehow hearing it directly from her mouth caused a bigger reaction than he had expected. It was the pulsing anger that surprised him the most. That Alistair could betray them and tell his whiney, snotty girlfriend.

A grave decision that had plagued his heart and mind for weeks suddenly no longer bore the same burden.

Turning once more to check that no one was watching him as he listened through the partially open door, he forced himself to breathe deeply. Regaining his composure, he moved quietly away from the master suite, put on his best happy face and climbed the stairs to join the rest of the holidaymakers on the Bridge Deck.

40

As the ship's captain made his way round the circumference of the group shaking each of their hands, the girls swooned over the tall, broad ex-Navy man.

'Chaps, good to see you again. Ladies, welcome to our version of paradise. Please make yourselves at home and enjoy everything the old girl has to offer. I'm David, the captain.'

After shaking his hand, Annabel turned and exchanged a look with Céleste, leaning in to whisper in her ear as the captain's attention moved on to her boyfriend. Céleste agreed with Annabel's sentiments as the pair now stifled their laughter and blushing admiration.

The captain's discussion with the party was mainly business; routes and plans, times of departure and arrival back into Split at the far end of the journey.

'What time will we be setting off for Hvar, Commodore?' Nicholas enquired, smiling smugly.

The party island of Hvar was set to be their first

port of call. Known for its beautiful coastlines and the night-time attractions of its main settlement, Hvar Town, it was a popular destination for travellers from all over the globe looking for sun, sea and long nights full of music and dancing.

'That's a good question. I need to check on that myself. We're currently awaiting delivery of a new part we were expecting yesterday.' He plucked the two-way radio from his belt, clicked a button on the side and spoke into it, 'Tom, it's David, can you come to the Bridge Deck please?'

The response was crackly, 'Right away, Chief.'

He can't have been far away as he was stood at the captain's side no more than thirty seconds later, looking fresh in a pristine white polo shirt complete with the ship's motive on the left breast. Max arrived only seconds behind Tom, following him to join the conversation around the bar.

'Yes, Captain. How can I help?' Tom asked.

'Tom, has there been any word on the pump we're waiting on?'

'I spoke with the courier an hour ago and they're expecting it to arrive at the airport at about eight o'clock this evening. After that, it should only take half an hour or so to have it unloaded and I'll bring it straight here from the airport.'

'Good, thanks, Tom. Sergei assures me it won't take long to replace and then we'll get moving.' He now addressed the group, 'I suggest we set sail for Hvar as soon as it's been fitted then you guys can wake up there in the morning ready for whatever you have planned. Where are young Lovell and Rosa? I assume they arrived with you?'

Max was the first to respond, 'I think they're just getting settled in their cabin. They shouldn't be long.' He quickly changed the subject, 'How long is the sail to Hvar, Captain?'

'Not long. Just over an hour.'

'Great, well let's wait for those two and when we sit down to eat we can all make a plan—'

Max was interrupted by the captain who saw the stragglers approaching. 'Rosa, Alistair, nice to see you. How are you both?'

'Good thanks, Commodore.' Alistair held out his hand and received the captain's.

'Hello, David.' Rosa leaned in and kissed him on each cheek before making her way around to the furthest end of the bar and ordering a drink from Ernesto.

'Alistair,' Max continued what he was saying before they arrived, 'we're just waiting for something to arrive and then we'll head to Hvar. I thought we could make a plan at dinner. Everyone happy with that?' Max extended the conversation to everyone at the bar, causing those who hadn't been paying attention to the conversation to look up from their own.

'What's happening?' Annabel asked. She had still been laughing and joking with Céleste, admiring the captain's physique.

Sebastian repeated the conversation to his partner.

'Sounds great.' Annabel smiled. 'What time are we eating? I think these cocktails are going to my head. I'll be blind drunk if I don't eat something soon.'

'Not long. I'll check with the kitchen now,' Tom replied. 'Feel free to head down to the owner's deck whenever you're ready and we can bring some bread and appetisers to soak up some of those mojitos.'

'Brilliant. Céleste, Melissa, care to join?' She held out her elbows to accompany the invitation. 'Rosa,'— she called across the bar— 'shall we head down?'

Rosa looked from Annabel to Alistair. He gave a nod in return, mouthing the word 'Go'.

She snatched her drink from the bar and sullenly followed the other three to the stairs, looking once more back to Alistair. He didn't reciprocate.

Max hadn't failed to notice the look that had been exchanged between the pair. It would have been a lie to say that he wasn't slightly pleased. Was the hold she had on him weakening? Maybe all his worry had been in vain.

As the girls disappeared out of sight down the stairs, he made eye contact with Alistair who flashed a pained smile. Conscious of the others, and not wanting to draw any attention to the matter, Max subtly raised the scuba diving sign for 'okay?' of index finger and thumb touching tips to create a circle and the remaining three fingers straight up in the air.

The response was easy for Max to read. Classic Alistair stoicism. Now was not the time or place to get into the subject so Max stood from the stool he had been perching on, halfway between Alistair and the group, patted him on the back and pulled him towards the others to join the conversation.

Rohan and Nicholas were trying to persuade the captain to allow them to take the helm at some point over the trip, each doing his best to present a reason why he would be a wiser choice than the other.

'Commodore,' Max was instantly met with a stern look, 'Captain, sorry, I mean Captain,' innocence beamed from his cheeky grin, 'you'd be a fool to let either one of these reprobates take control of this beauty. I'd keep the bridge locked at all times if I were you.'

'Very sage advice. Looks like he's got your number, lads. I think we'll play it safe and let the crew take care of her this time,' the captain agreed.

'Thanks, Max, I was close there.' Rohan shot Max

a joking scowl. 'Well if I'm not going to be driving anywhere, I suggest we have a toast!' He moved around the bar and reached behind it.

'Let's go down and have the champagne with the girls,' Alistair was quick to intervene.

'Oh no, this one is just for us. No champagne for us just yet.' Rohan produced a bottle of white Sambuca and six small shot glasses, setting them down on the table before cracking the seal on the bottle. Sambuca was clearly not the drink of choice for the usual patrons of the Mufasa.

The captain must have sensed that the extra shot glass was intended for him and took the opportunity to make an exit away from the excitable mob. Ernesto followed him down the stairs to attend to the ladies.

With the glasses measured out, Rohan started to speak only to be quickly cut off by Nicholas, 'Sorry Rohan. I just wanted to say something before all the partying begins.'

Rohan yielded, bowing his head to indicate that the floor was his.

'This has been a tough year, really tough,' Nicholas began, his speech slow as if carefully searching for the right words. Eyes down at the floor, it was clear that he felt emotional. 'There have been times when I nearly couldn't cope and just wanted to run away from all the stress of exams and the extra stuff.'

Looking up towards Max, he locked eyes. 'I have to be honest, Max. There have been times when I've blamed you for all of it. I wondered what the last year would have been like if we'd never had that conversation. Would I have enjoyed our last year at school more? Gone out more? Partied more? Relaxed more? I don't know.

'The pressure that you put on me, put on all of Us, I don't know if you fully understand how much it really got to me.'

His voice cracked, his eyes blinked, and he wiped the corner of one, his finger coming away wet. 'There have been times when I hated you for that. The thought of letting everyone down, letting you down, I couldn't stand it.' He wiped both eyes now as tears formed in both, cascading down his cheeks.

'I need you to understand how hard it's been. But then, at the same time, you've also been there, every step of the way, every day, trying to help. And I know you've done that for every single one of us. So, I tried to imagine how much you've had to put into this and what you've been through as well. I don't know how you've made time for it all.'

He looked around at all the faces now. 'You've all helped me, on more than one occasion, and I can't thank you enough for that. I made some stupid choices but thank Christ nothing bad came of them. That wouldn't have happened if you all hadn't been willing to put your necks on the line for me.

'Last year, when this all started, I didn't really think we'd go through with it. I thought it was a cool idea and we'd just talk about it. But the things we've done and the effort that we've put in, I wouldn't change it. I would have never pushed myself so hard, in school, outside of school, cadets. I wouldn't have met Céleste, wouldn't have set foot on board this ship. All of it.'

He shook his head as recounted the memories of the last twelve months. 'I guess what I'm trying to say is that, even though there have been times when I wanted out, I can see now why we're going to be so strong. Together. And I'll never want out again. I'm in, for good.'

He ran his finger across his right eyebrow. Rohan mirrored the action above his left eye and the rest followed suit. All apart from Max. He looked down at the floor, a hand raised to his face, thumb on one temple, middle finger on the other. Still.

They all looked at him, but Sebastian was the first to speak. Standing directly to his left, he placed a hand on his shoulder. 'Are you okay?'

Max nodded softly, keeping his face covered by his hand. He took a deep breath and straightened up, eyes and cheeks moist. He looked towards Nicholas.

'I'm sorry. I didn't realise how much pressure I'd put on you, on everyone. I don't want you to think for one second that you could ever let me down. This was never just about me. I wanted us all to be the best that we could, to achieve everything that we're capable of. I didn't realise how you felt. I knew you were stressed but I guess it's been so busy, trying to keep on top of my own stuff and trying to be involved with all of you that I missed something. I thought I'd really tried to know exactly what was happening with everyone's lives but I only scratched the surface.'

More tears ran down his face, but he spoke with conviction. 'I couldn't have done a lot of what I've done over the past year if it hadn't been for you guys. You talked about letting me and Us down. That's exactly how I felt. I was scared that I'd fail, that I'd start this all and then not be able to live up to the expectations that we set, that I set. And I'm so happy that you've all been there to share it.

'We've all got other friends, but when I look at the other guys from school, I don't see any of them being as tight as we are now. I don't see them having four close people who they can share absolutely anything with. Hopes, fears, problems, all of it. Even if this were to all end today...'

He paused and looked around their surroundings.

The ship, the sea and the Croatian coastline. 'I'd be able to look back and say that I've made some of the best friends anyone could hope for. And I hope it stays that way forever.'

He crossed the circle and approached Nicholas, arms out wide to embrace his friend.

'I'm sorry, man.'

As they hugged, he struggled to suppress more tears as the emotions and the stress of their last school year slowly erupted. Nicholas let go of his own emotions and the pair gripped each other hard, tears now streaming down both of their faces. Sebastian looked to Alistair and Rohan, his own eyes glassing over, before joining the embrace, wrapping his arms around the locked pair. Within moments, the remaining two joined the emotional scrum and they all stood, as one, in silence.

A large inhale through a snotty nose allowed Nicholas to break the quiet. 'If anyone sees us now, this is going to look so gay.'

The group, still hugging, laughed in unison and, one by one, peeled away, patting each other on the backs.

Rohan returned to the table and now passed around the shots. 'I was going to say something, but I think time for talking is over, and time for celebrating should start. To Us.'

He raised his glass in the air, the group following suit, clinking glass-to-glass-to-glass before emptying the contents into wide-open mouths.

Their reactions, although varied, all bore the same hallmarks. Contorted faces, hands to chests as if somehow, by magic, that would stop the burning as the alcohol coursed down their throats. Deep breaths followed to exhale the left-over vapour, and some bent at the waist as if expecting another rendezvous with the liquid.

A shout from the deck below drew their attention away from the discomfort and a familiar voice called out to them.

'Oh boys! There are four very hungry ladies down here! We're going to start without you if you're not down soon.' Annabel's hunger was at fever pitch.

'I guess that's our cue, guys. Everyone alright?' Sebastian asked.

He was greeted by nods and faces still waiting to return to normal.

'I might need just another minute,' Nicholas pleaded.

'That's probably wise. And actually, I don't think the girls should escape without punishment.' Sebastian scooped the clear bottle from the table. 'It's their turn now.'

The familiar rosewood dining table had been laid out immaculately, just as every other time they'd had the pleasure of eating at it. At the nearest end to the stern of the ship, the girls had taken up position and were already picking away at a selection of olives and bread. Ernesto greeted the boys, causing the girls to turn their attention.

'What's taken you so long?' Annabel stood to kiss Sebastian as he arrived at her side.

'You know, just guys' stuff.'

'Well, we've nearly finished all the appetisers so thank god you're finally here and we can have dinner.' She tutted at him whilst kissing his cheek.

'I'm sorry, honey. My fault. What have you girls been talking about?'

'Well I've just been learning a bit more about these three beautiful ladies. And maybe we've had some drinks. Some more than others.' She whispered the last part so that only he could hear.

As she made the comment, Rosa finished the gin and tonic in her hand and called over to Ernesto for another. Alistair added another G&T to the request, also asking that Ernesto open the champagne now that the group was all together.

On the far side of the table, a muted conversation was taking place between Céleste and Nicholas. She had stood to greet him and tactically moved him a few feet away from the group.

'She seems really upset.' Céleste subtly looked towards Rosa. 'I don't know why but she won't talk.'

'What do you mean?'

'She doesn't speak. We asking her questions but she sits and stares, just drinking.'

'Have they had a fight, do you think?' he whispered.

She shrugged. 'I don't know. She hasn't said about a fight. I think better to leave her alone.'

'I'm sure it will all be fine and she'll calm down. Stay over here with me.' Taking her by the hand he guided her towards the middle of the table to take position as far away from the troubled girl as possible, finding themselves next to Max on their left and directly opposite Sebastian and Annabel, who'd purposefully sat herself next to Rosa having sensed her agitation.

Alistair's position at the head of the table had been insisted upon by Rohan, saying it was only natural as it was his father's ship. Alistair had protested, as he had previously, but with Rosa already parked in the seat to the left of the head seat it was a logical space for him to occupy.

He leaned in and touched her on the leg and hand. 'Are you okay?' he asked quietly.

The response from behind her large sunglasses was a mere dry smile.

Positioned to Alistair's right, Rohan witnessed the

awkward moment, and in an attempt to feign disinterest, immediately turned to Max on his right and started a conversation about what they were going to do on the holiday.

As the sky changed from the crisp, clear blue of the afternoon to the warm orange and reds of the later hours, most the group laughed and chatted. The food had been showered with compliments from all at the table, the girls amazed by every dish that touched down in front of them. Three empty bottles of champagne now sat in the bin behind the bar and the gang had moved onto wine, vodka, and gin, deciding that the champagne was far too nice to be used in drinking games.

Endless rounds of 21s and the name game, interspersed with side games like thumb master and international drinking rules, had given every participant their fair share of drinking forfeits, one in particular leading the charge. Rosa's participation consisted of the minimum effort to appear involved, but it was clear that the game held less priority for her than the consumption of alcohol. Alistair's attempts to slow her rate were met with slurred objections, eventually causing him to focus his attention elsewhere.

By the time the sun finally disappeared behind the hills to the west, shortly before ten o'clock, Alistair told Ernesto that they would take care of their own drinks, leaving the barman to graciously retire from the deck. It had really been a tactic on Alistair's part to stem the flow of gin and tonics that the barman felt obliged to bring Rosa each time she inhaled the last, even though he was aware of her less-than-sober state. He'd welcomed the opportunity to remove himself from the awkwardness of the tussle between the two young lovers, quietly asking Alistair on his exit to make sure that she didn't have any more.

From far below, the familiar noise of the tender approached the vessel, bringing with it the part that had delayed their departure. Max moved to the ship's rail to watch the tender's approach, waving at the First Mate from high above the water.

'That looks like Tom with the thing. It shouldn't be long before we can get moving. Why don't we have a change of scenery? Let's move inside now that the wind is picking up and find some more comfy seats.'

'I think that's a good idea. If it gets any colder my nipples are going to tear through my shirt!' Nicholas erupted, standing bolt upright sending his chair crashing to the floor behind him. 'Whoops. Who left that there?' he rhetorically quizzed the group, getting a howl of laughter from his sloshed audience. 'Now, Madame,'—he held out his hand to beckon his belle to join him— 'where shall we continue the party?'

She rose, much more delicately than his attempt, allowing him to pull her towards him and wrap his arms around her and nuzzle into the hollow of her neck with his lips. She turned her head, struggling against her drunken admirer, rolling her eyes and smiling. 'Alistair, where is best?'

'Well, I suggest you guys head down to the lounge on the main deck or the cinema room and I'll join you shortly. I think Rosa may need some fresh air, hey hun?'

She appeared deeply offended by the suggestion, jumping to her feet, and before he could stop her, dragged Annabel with her towards the glass doors leading to a modern, minimalist sitting room and into the belly of the ship.

'I'm fine,' she shouted back. 'Why don't you stay with your precious group and get some fresh air? We're going to have more fun.'

41

The four giant engines of the Mufasa finally roared to life shortly after 2 am. A stripped thread on the replacement pump caused a challenge for the engineers, solved by some innovative thinking but delaying their departure nonetheless. Their course would take them between the islands of Brač to the port side, and Šolta to starboard, the same route used by the commercial passenger ferries in the daylight hours. By this time in the evening, those boats would be securely on their moorings, leaving a quiet shipping lane for the behemoth.

At a reduced speed of fifteen knots, and accounting for the time to manoeuvre the ship out of Kaštela Bay, they would be coming to a stop in the waters outside of Hvar just before 4 am. Thanks to the latest technology, including rubberised vibration-dampening mounts under the engines, from most parts of the ship it was hard to tell that they were even running at this speed.

In the cinema room, fifty yards away from the now

roaring powerplant, only one of the sleeping guests stirred at the slight movements of the ship. Squinting in the low glow emanating from concealed lights at the edges of the square room's walls, Rosa lifted her head from the soft red fabric covering the giant couch the group lay strewn across. She wiped her eyes as she scanned the room, looking at the unconscious partyers for signs of life.

A sudden jolt in her stomach forced her upright and she raised a hand to her mouth. After taking a few deep breaths, she used both arms to push herself towards the edge of the couch, knocking someone's leg as she swung her own onto the floor. She staggered towards the door, using the wall to guide her to the front of the large room.

Another pair of eyes was now open, watching as she struggled in the low light, hands to her mouth, trying not to leave a trail of vomit along the gold carpet. It was no use. Her mouth filled with the warm, thick sludge and it spilled from her lips as the pressure increased beyond bursting point.

She made her way to the elevator in the centre of the ship and hit the button for the Bridge Deck before slumping to the floor, barely managing to keep her eyes open and her head up as the doors closed behind her. Her head fell backwards against the polished mirrors as the lift began its climb and a small red blinking light in the top corner of the cube caught her attention momentarily before blurring out of focus.

As the wood-panelled doors began to part, she heaved herself to her feet, using the lift's railing for support. Having come up one too many floors, to her right was a corridor leading to the bridge, to her left an exit to the deck. The sound of two men and a woman laughing about a guest who'd stayed on the ship the previous year echoed down the hallway, forcing her to stumble in the opposite direction towards the exterior stairs down to her room where she could enter by the glass doors looking out onto the deck.

Just as Rosa was stepping out of the elevator, the same button she had used to summon it only one minute earlier, was pushed again. The lift arrived, announced with the same 'bing' that had betrayed Rosa's route to bed. The same doors opened, and he stepped in.

Assuming she was heading straight to her room, he chose the floor where the master suite with the panoramic view was located. As the silent doors of the lift slid open, he paused, listening for any signs of life. Nothing.

He wondered what he would say to her. Could he

make her change her mind? Would he be able to convince her that she couldn't tell anyone about the group and that what she knew already was too much and put too many people at risk? After her outburst earlier, he wondered how long it would be before she blurted out the truth to everyone on the ship.

Whether it was the drinks he'd had with dinner, or the adrenaline that was building in his bloodstream, he now started to feel woozy and unsteady. He stopped, trying to calm the beating of his heart, breathing slowly, deeply. Could he really confront her? Was he actually considering doing what he and Howarth had talked about? Surely there was another way.

Maybe she'll listen to me. Maybe she'll come around and help keep Alistair as part of the group. His mind was now racing. *I can't hurt someone, especially a girl, my friend's girlfriend, his idol.*

His feet wanted to push him forward to find her, to confront her, but his brain wouldn't let him. He was rooted to the spot, overcome with the decision he'd made upon hearing the conversation outside Alistair and Rosa's room. The pressure was too much, and he sank to the floor, his back sliding down the wall as he raised his hands to his temples in the hope that applying some pressure would slow the synapses, allowing one thought to conquer all others.

Tears started to build in his eyes. What had this group turned him into? Why was this burden left on him? None of the others even knew the mental struggle he had been going through over the past months, having to keep this secret to himself.

Then it all came back to him. The messages he'd read at Ward's house and in the computer lab at the school. The overheard conversation through their open bedroom door. How could Alistair have done this? It was all his fault. His lapse of judgement, his inability to keep their secret had all led to this.

And her. Why couldn't she have stayed out of it? Why couldn't she just let Alistair be his own man, make his own choice?

An anger rose up inside him, feeding on his own fears that now reared their ugly head again, having once found a place of peace when he became part of Us. This had been his chance to be part of something. He wasn't willing to let her risk that and take it away from him, from them. He owed it to the others.

I can't let her destroy what we've done, what we're going to do. It's bigger than her and me, and Us.

His cheeks still streamed with tears, but they were no longer contorted in an effort to restrain them. His eyes stared forward now, a mix of anger and betrayal giving them a hardened edge. His lips, however, portrayed the battle still raging inside. As his thoughts flicked between what he knew he must do next, and the image of the pain that he would cause, wincing, he suppressed the involuntary gag that accompanies a whimper and put his palms on the floor. He pressed downwards, bringing his feet underneath, slowly standing up straight.

Rosa had not been in a good state the last time he'd seen her. He'd half-expected to see her on the floor of the corridor as he'd steeped out of the lift, but she was nowhere to be seen.

She could barely walk, where the fuck could she have gone?

To the right was the hall of the Owner's Deck, lined with mirrors and artwork, leading to the master bedroom and the spot from which he'd eavesdropped on their concerning conversation. What would he say to her? Was she even capable of having a conversation?

Moving as quietly as possible towards her room, he hugged the wall in an attempt to see inside the room through the slightly open door. There was no light indicating presence within. A nudge with his shoulder swung the door inwards, casting light from the hallway into the otherwise darkened room.

What he saw as he moved inside were the approaching lights of islands on either side of the ship out of the curved windows in front of him. The realisation that they were moving only now hit him, having not seen a window since leaving the cinema room. He watched as the two islands approached, wondering if they were already at their destination. Their course, however, stayed true as the ship's bow pointed at the gap between the rocky pair who emerged from the black sheet below.

A fleeting moment of peace as the view distracted his mind was broken by movement to his left. Outside the window, a pink cushion flew across the deck, connecting with the thick glass window. He moved to investigate, immediately finding the source. Through the window, he watched Rosa unsuccessfully attempting to lift herself from a leather couch covered in an abundance of soft pillows. With one final push, she stood to throw her head over the ship's rail just as he joined her on deck.

'Rosa, are you alright? You don't sound great.'

'What do you care?' she slurred back at him.

'I wanted to make sure you're okay,' he lied.

'I'm fine.'

Just by looking at her, he could tell she was not. She struggled to stay upright even with the support of the ship's rail.

'Where are we?' She didn't wait for the answer. 'I bet you all hate me, don't you?'

He was slightly thrown off by the honesty of her question. 'Why would you think that?'

'Because I know about your group thing.'

He froze, just like every time any one of the group mentioned it outside of the usual environment. He tried to maintain the anger that he'd felt in the hallway, which was now hard seeing her in distress.

'Well, it does go against the rules. Alistair must have told you that, right?'

'Yes. I know the fucking rules.' She was becoming angry, shouting at him from her bent over position. She held the rail in both hands whilst her body wandered about behind them, head rolling in the middle facing directly at the floor.

'Why shouldn't I just tell someone, everyone? At least then Alistair wouldn't have to choose and blame me for making him. I can tell he does.' She let go of the railing and stumbled back a foot, head still down.

'That would be very damaging. To all of us, you included. I can't let you do that.' His voice cracked as he said the last words. He hoped she wouldn't turn and see the tears on his face or the look in his eyes. She would definitely sense he was an emotional wreck. He felt his nose start to run and inhaled deeply through it to try and stop it.

'Look'—he slowly moved forward—'you don't

want to throw up on the deck, let me help you, do it over the railing.'

The water below surged past the streamlined frame of the ship, the wind and waves increasing in size the further toward the Adriatic Sea they ventured. Having passed between the two islands, Brač and Šolta, the orange lights from shore no longer reached their position and only faint shadows remained.

She now made it to the rail once more with the help of her companion. It was a struggle to keep her head fully over the edge to avoid any accidents as her legs no longer wanted to cooperate with the rest of her body, forcing him to grab her by both shoulders to hold her up.

'When I said that I can't let you do that, I meant it.' He turned her so she could look at him. 'You're turning Alistair against Us, knowingly, purposefully, through manipulation. Do you love him?'

'Of course I love him. That's why I want him to come with me.'

'Then you should have respected his choice. This wouldn't have all happened if you had.'

'Don't you dare try to blame this on me!' She screamed at him now over the sound of the waves below and wind rushing past the ship. 'Blame it on you and your stupid fucking boys' club. You're delusional, you think that you're going to change the world. How the fuck are you going to change the world? You're just children! It's time to grow up.'

'Rosa, he could have had both.' He closed his eyes and shook his head. 'You, him, Us. There was no reason to make him choose. We've worked too hard to lose him to you.' His eyes now looked past her. 'Can you stand?'

'What?'

'I said, can you stand on your own?'

She was still angry. 'Of course I can stand.'

He relaxed his grip on her shoulders. She couldn't.

'Do you think you can swim?' he asked.

As her eyes rotated right to look towards the water, her mouth started moving to ask a question, but he had already started to lift. At five feet, four inches with a slender frame, she was no match for his strength.

She was a foot off the ground within an instant and tumbling over the railing before she realised what was happening. It took all his strength to push her as far away from the rail as possible. It would be no good if she survived. As she fell, he gripped the railing, eyes fixed on her.

He followed the shape of her body down towards the water, unsure whether the muted cry was real or in his mind. Whatever the case, it was instantly drowned out by the passing beast below.

Spinning side-over-side, she plummeted towards the wake of the ship, taking the impact directly on the top of her head. The last he saw of her was two tanned legs, feet covered in blue and white deck pumps, as she disappeared under the turbulent water. He instinctively followed the spot where she went in but with the speed they were travelling and the low light he had no way of knowing if she had resurfaced.

Unconsciously, his grip on the railings tightened until his hands could stand no more. A surge of adrenaline exploded from within, his body trembling with the effects of the shock. Eyes bulging, tears poured from their edges. He hadn't taken a breath in what felt like minutes. A bolt hit him, standing him upright, forcing him to turn away from the drop below. He raised his hands to his mouth and sucked in as much air as his lungs would hold.

That was not how he'd imagined it happening. But it had been quick. And it was done. Not a soul was around to see it. Time to think.

What have you touched? The bedroom door? No, you used your shoulder. The external door? Yes. Wipe it down. The railing. Wipe it down. Which is the quickest and safest way back to your room? Now go.

42

Not many teachers' offices could claim to have a view as glorious as this one. An expanse of freshly cut grass, now sprinkled with crimson and tangerine leaves no longer bound to their mothers, sparkled in the dew of the morning. The low sun rising in the east cast magnificent shadows across the spaces and buildings that created this secluded world.

These first few weeks of term had been anything but normal. Unbeknown to most of the staff and pupils at the school, that summer had been the setting for a terrible event. Even for those who had heard news of the tragedy, the information remained sketchy.

As he stood and gazed through the glass at the clock tower on the far boundary of the grounds, he took another deep draw on the cigarette resting in his left hand. He blew the smoke out of the partially open window before tapping the spent tobacco into the ashtray sitting on the window sill. On any other day at nine o'clock in the morning, the school would be teeming with life, laughter and energy. Saturday mornings were, however, quite the opposite. As it was too early in the year for even the worst students to be issued Saturday detention, these were rare moments of peace and calm. No screaming, no shouting, no balls visible in mid-air as the masses chased them around concrete playgrounds.

Tranquillity.

Or so he thought.

An unexpected figure from the grass below walked towards the building, shattering the bliss. His heart rate soared, and panic bound through every fibre in his body. He was sure that the advancing male had already seen him through his ground floor window. It was time. He'd known this moment would come and this had to be dealt with at some point. Now was as good a time as any. Watching the stern face of the approaching young man, he extinguished his cigarette with as much composure as he could muster before fully opening the small, high window further to allow the smell of the tobacco to escape. His office door was behind him to his left and as he lost sight of his quarry, he knew it would be only moments before the sound of flesh and bone knocking on his thick white door would fill the space. He waited, rooted to the spot, imagining the conversation that was about to take place, as one so often does before a confrontation.

The door shook with the force of the battering, summoning him to open. He took one last deep breath before straightening up and moving towards the source. As he clicked the lock, the door imploded towards him.

'What are you doing here?' Howarth demanded as he stepped aside to make room for the intruder. 'I thought it would be clear from the lack of contact that we shouldn't be seen together.' He checked the hallway outside to see if anyone else may have seen the boy arrive before closing and locking the door behind them.

The teacher strode round behind his desk, extending an arm indicating where his guest should sit as he lowered himself into his worn, leather chair. As much as his own fear weighed on his conscience, he could see that the emotions of the newcomer were of a different breed altogether. He couldn't help but feel guilty.

The boy hesitated. 'I needed to talk to you, to someone. Why have you stopped responding to me?'

'After what happened I didn't think it very wise to keep in touch.'

'I needed your help.' The boy was agitated.

'And what do you think I would have been able to do? I can't work miracles. What happened out there?

Tell me it was an accident. Please, just tell me you weren't involved.'

The request was met with a look of confusion. The boy's mind flashed back to the conversations they'd had over the phone and in the computer lab. *Had he misinterpreted what Howarth had said? Had he created this plan alone?* No, he was sure. He remembered clearly, '*sometimes doing the one thing you never thought you'd have to is the only way*'. He had not misunderstood what was to happen. His face turned to anger.

'What do you mean? We talked about this!'

'I didn't mean this. I mean, I didn't really ever think that you would go through with it.' Howarth sighed a defeated breath, denying the reality with his head but not his heart. A slow acceptance of culpability for Rosa's death grudgingly penetrated his conscience, causing his eyes to close and a pained expression to flash across his face. A small twist of the head, intended to hide his face from the young man seated before him, achieved no such success. *What had he done? What had they done?*

'Well I did it. And now I can't stop thinking about it. About her. I keep seeing her face. Every night I dream about it, waking up sweating and shaking. My parents are really worried about me.' His cadence grew faster as the emotions poured from his soul. Tears streamed down his face as he stood and paced around the room. 'And I'm sure you've heard about Alistair? Seeing what this has done to him. How can I ever forget that?'

'How is he doing? Where have they taken him?' Howarth had clearly not heard.

'He's up in some rehabilitation centre in Scotland, not far from Edinburgh. I think it's called Castle Craig. They're calling it Post-Traumatic Stress Disorder and alcoholism. When we got back, he just disappeared. No one could get in touch with him. His mum hadn't seen him for weeks, but he'd text her at least to say he was okay. She got a call a week ago from some friends of theirs in Cornwall saying he'd showed up and asked to stay for a few days. But then he just sat in the garden and drank all day, every day, staring at the sky or sleeping. They were worried, so they called his mum. Apparently, he hadn't told them anything about what happened.'

'I'm just surprised it's not all over the news.' Howarth sounded incredulous. 'A girl dies falling from James Lovell's yacht in the Mediterranean and not a single paper covered the story? How was it not leaked?'

'They were very efficient at that, weren't they? As soon as they discovered that she was missing in the morning, the first call was to James Lovell. He flew over to personally meet with all the right people to keep it quiet. He said it was for the sake of Rosa's family to give them time to grieve, alone rather than in the spotlight of the press. That's such bullshit. It was to protect him.'

'But just think. It's also protected you,' Howarth pressed. 'If the press had become involved, you all would have been household names. Every one of your faces would have been known and then the whole plan would have been dead in the—' he paused, realising what he was saying. 'Would have been finished.'

'The plan?' The young man now shouted at his former teacher. 'You think I care about the plan? I don't care about anything anymore. All I want is to feel normal again. I couldn't give a damn about the group!' He started to pace once more, rubbing his head in his hands as if to squeeze the memories from his skull. Howarth stopped him, seizing him by the elbows, just about managing to keep him in one spot.

'Look at me,' Howarth pleaded.

The boy's eyes didn't leave the floor.

'Look at me!' he repeated.

Howarth calmed himself and took a deep breath. 'Rohan, please look at me.'

Raw, red eyes found the kindly face of the teacher.

'If you let this break you, you stop being part of this. What was the point of doing it in the first place?

This was a means to an end, my boy. A horrible end. But an end, nonetheless. And now you need to move on. How many lives have already been hurt by this? Don't allow it to claim one more.'

Rohan's glassy eyes stared straight ahead, not focusing on any one thing. 'I'm meant to leave for university tomorrow. Look at me. How am I going to go there like this?'

'It will be good for you to get away. A change of scenery will help. You're probably suffering with some form of PTSD yourself. Removing yourself from memories that remind you of it will help you forget.'

'What if I can't forget? Or don't want to forget?' The energy left his body and he slumped into the chair in front of the teacher's desk. Once more, his eyes lacked focus as he stared at the nameplate perched on the wooden surface in front of him. 'I should be punished for what happened. After I did it, I went to bed thinking that it would be obvious that it was me. That someone would have seen me leave after her and connected the dots. But no one did. Everyone had been so drunk that they barely even remembered what had happened, never mind who went where and when.

'In the morning, I woke up early and went up to the main deck. I didn't want it to look like I was hiding when they found out. But no one was up yet. It was another thirty minutes before Alistair woke up in the cinema and went to his room to find Rosa. When she wasn't there, he assumed she had slept in one of the other rooms. Her body was found by a fishing boat before he'd even told the captain that we couldn't find her on board.'

Tears broke as his face contorted at the recounting of the aftermath. 'After the first call to Mr Lovell, it wasn't long before another came back confirming that she'd been found. I expected the police to come and ask questions. But the only person who spoke to the police was the lawyer. We were left on the boat, everyone crying, Alistair howling. It was unbearable. It sounded like his heart had been torn out. He blamed himself, he said that he should have taken her to bed when he had seen that she was too drunk. Everyone told him that it wouldn't have mattered. She wouldn't have let him when she was in that mood. But he wouldn't accept it.

'After it happened, the ship was turned around and we returned to the bay for another day while Lovell arrived and did the talking. He and Alistair barely spoke. Alistair just sat at the back of the boat, drinking more and more. We just sat around him most of the day making conversation and trying to distract each other. The next day he got really drunk on the flight back and that was the last time any of us saw him. He went off grid after that. All of that is my fault. All of it. I'll never forget that, I'll never be able to wipe that from my mind.'

'You have to. Not just for you. But for the group. What would this do to them, to Max, if he knew that she died to protect you all?'

'It would kill him. He'd never forgive himself either.' Rohan was matter of fact in his response.

'That's right. Think about what you've all been through in the past year. All of this ends right now if you can't try and move past it.'

Rohan was struggling to comprehend what he was hearing. Here he was, confessing to a murder. And this man, his teacher no less, was comforting him, telling him that it was all going to be okay. As if he'd dropped a mug, or dented the car, or failed a fucking exam. It was what he needed to hear but not what he'd expected.

Had the fog of emotion not dulled his senses, it would be clear to him that Howarth was concerned not only with the welfare of the young man sat before him, but terrified for his own skin as well. The pair were inextricably linked, not only by the school itself, but by phone calls and the hacking. Should there be any suspicion at all around any of these young men, it would not take long before these connections were unpicked and the whole mucky story became a headline.

Howarth changed the topic. 'Where are the others now? Have they all left for university?'

'Mostly. Leeds started two weeks ago so Nicholas is already up there enjoying himself. Max and Sebastian went down last week. Max is already doing a college debate this evening, I think Sebastian's gone down to watch him.'

'That's right.' Howarth sounded hopeful now. 'Max will be with you at Cambridge, so at least you'll have some support there. He's going to a different college, so it won't be the case that you're seeing each other all the time but it will be nice to have someone you can talk to.'

'Not about this. I can't ever talk to anybody about this.' Rohan sounded defeated.

'Look, I'll make you a deal.' Howarth took a seat in the chair next to Rohan, leaning in, speaking softly. 'Anytime you need to talk about this, you can call, and I'll answer. Obviously, we can't discuss details over the phone, but you can tell me how you're feeling and I can try to help. If there's an emergency, you just get in touch and we'll work something out. For now, we have to act as if nothing ever happened. You need to head down to Cambridge and get settled in. Dive into it head-first and I'm sure that you'll feel better soon. I'm not saying it will all just disappear, but a new life at university, new things to learn, new friends, girls—these will all help to dull the hurt that you're feeling. Can you do that?'

'I'm going to try. Let's just hope it never comes out.'

'Do you remember the day when I found you in the computer lab hacking Alistair's messages and you refused to tell me what it was about? You had strength then, and you've got strength now. You wouldn't believe that I was involved until I proved it to you. We came here to this very office and used that ashtray there.

'I don't know if Max has told you this, but he hadn't intended to involve me. It was only thanks to a careless slip on his part that I found out. From what I already knew there was not much he could do in terms of denying it. Although, he was as surprised as you when I told him that I would support your efforts. He asked me why and I told him, "this is not a new idea. It has been done before, very successfully, and it will be done again."

'I see five very intelligent young men in you all. Out of all the young men in this school, he couldn't have picked a more suitable group. If it had been anyone else, I think I would have laughed, safe in the knowledge that another crazy idea or scheme would never be more than just that. I felt it then, and I feel it now. Fear. I wasn't scared or worried that he, that you, would fail. It scared me that you would succeed. History is not very kind to those who have had the joy of power. Nearly all men can stand adversity, but if you want to test a man's character, give him power. I'm sure you know the adage.'

Rohan did. 'Abraham Lincoln.'

'He knew about power. And so must you. If you get it. When you get it, do you know what it will feel like?'

Rohan mulled over the question. He had no way to respond.

'That's what scares me, Rohan. How does power feel? Does it make you feel any more satisfied? Is that why people who want power never stop trying to get more? The one thing that they think they want more of is the only thing that never can satisfy them.

'Ambition is a great gift, but a poisoned chalice in more cases than not. It's a morphing creature, a mirage on the horizon. As you arrive, you realise it wasn't there at all, it was on the peak of the next mountain, or the one above that. The point is that the peaks don't matter. It's all about the climb. You don't stay at the peak forever. You look at it, take a photo, catch your breath and then it's onto the next one. People climb for days to spend ten minutes atop a mountain. It's the climb-

ing they love, not the photo, not the summit. Climb
with a group of people who offer support and you are
much more likely to succeed than without them.' He
stopped himself. 'God, why am I using so many climbing metaphors?'

Rohan looked up from his stare, a hint of a smile at
the corners of his mouth.

'Don't live a life that is simply about the pursuit of
something that isn't real,' Howarth continued. 'Make
sure you enjoy yourself along the way. Remember
what's real, the things and people who matter. I think
you boys are in for some exciting times, but it's not going to be easy. Everyone is capable of things you never
thought they were. Be careful every step of the way.'

Rohan nodded at his teacher's words. 'Look, I
need to go. Mr Howarth, thanks for talking with me.
But what's in this for—' he wasn't allowed to finish
his question.

'Rohan, before you go. We need to do something.'
Howarth looked towards the window, more specifically the ashtray perched on the window sill. A wide,
shallow, crystal object, rarely used now that the school
had outlawed smoking in the teachers' offices. Today,
however, it contained the twisted butt of a recently
smoked cigarette.

'I need to know that you're still fully committed

to the group.' Howarth scooped up the ashtray along with an A5 pad from the desk. Tearing the first page in two, he handed the sheet and a pen to the member sitting in front of him.

Rohan had never done the ritual with anyone outside the other four original members. It felt strange and alien that anyone outside of them knew about it. He paused for a moment, seemingly reluctant. Picking up the pen, the familiar shapes appeared on the page, he folded it, as usual, and handed it to the teacher. Howarth handed him his, taking Rohan's with the other hand, looking at the paper. 'Good, I'm glad to hear it.'

Rohan stared at Howarth's sheet and a smile broke out across his face. 'I'm glad to hear it too.'

Rohan picked up the matches, took his paper back from Mr Howarth and lit the two pieces so no trace would be left. Once the flames were out and the ash had cooled, each put a finger into the middle of the ashtray, spreading the residue above their strongest eye.

The pair stood, two feet apart, in silence for a minute.

Howarth moved first, ushering Rohan out of the room. 'Remember what I said, call any time. No details.'

Printed in Poland
by Amazon Fulfillment
Poland Sp. z o.o., Wrocław